BLOW - INS
By
JO FARRELLY

All rights reserved. This book or any portion thereof may not be reproduced or used in any manner whatsoever without the express written permission of the author.

Chapter One

-- Here, sit in there by the fire, Seamus instructed Bill. Trow a few tick ones on will ye, tis cold enough this morning.
Bill looked at Lynn questioningly. He still had a problem understanding what people were saying. She pointed at the logs packed neatly around the stove. Ah! He managed to squash an extra one in, trying to keep his face back from the fierce blaze.
--Ye'll have a cup o tay now?
Pleased with the welcome and the charm of Seamus's caravan, Bill and Lynn settled themselves on either side of the stove.

The caravan stood in a small quarry, along a bohreen that was surrounded by what Seamus called The Crag- mile upon mile of hazel thickets, impenetrable in places, but in others carpeted with emerald moss and shimmering with wind flowers and wood sorrel. The beginnings of the Burren were detectable and there were places where its ledges of silver limestone sprouted lush gardens of ferns. Through it all, adding to the feeling of hushed expectancy, ran little pathways, of what you couldn't be sure.

On every shelf and little table in the caravan were Seamus's Arrangements; pieces of bark with attractive lichen on them, displays of leaves and ferns, heaps of pretty stones and bones. There were skins on the floor and colourful blankets on the seats. It looked charming, but it was very difficult to move around without dislodging something. When you stood up it was worse. You'd swear that the bunches of herbs on the ceiling were deliberately grabbing you by the hair.

--I was just tidying the place up, remarked Seamus. Kids make an awful mess...
--I think you swept some things out by accident, said Lynn. Earlier, they had seen Seamus in the distance, busily shaking out bits of bright material, rugs and skins and hanging them on the bushes. As they arrived, a library book, pair of knickers and a baby's dummy came flying out of the door. Seamus was busy with a twig broom.
--Arrah, tis all old junk! I'm killed trying to keep the place tidy, said Seamus dismissively.
--Where's Nuala? asked Lynn.

--She's gone to the baby clinic in town. She went off early to be sure of getting on the bus. It goes on a Tuesday from Conlon's Cross.
--Well that's good to know., said Bill. We might be needing it. The van's broken down. It's at Joe Kennedy's .He's not sure what's wrong with it yet.
--Joe Kennedy? Seamus was aghast. You never left it in with him! You'll be a long time waiting, let me be telling ye.

The stove was beginning to roar. Lynn was beginning to sweat. She moved carefully to the seat by the window. Seamus moved in after her to straighten the skin on the vacated seat. Lynn was wondering about Nuala. You saw Seamus everywhere, but not Nuala . Lynn wondered why she had an Irish name and an English accent. And whether she minded her knickers and library book being swept out of the door.
--I was just making a bit of breakfast, Seamus explained, moving nimbly between the Arrangements to the gas stove in the corner where he had a pan sizzling, There was another on top of the wood stove which he had just relieved of a pile of fried bread . He began to load it with eggs. The smell was tormenting, even if they had eaten muesli earlier and were normally vegetarian.
--You'll have an old egg now, and some pudden?
--Yes please! cried Lynn.
--Er, Pudden? queried Bill.
--Tis the best, from Casey's, explained Seamus helpfully. And a rasher. You'd be needing a good breakfast these cold mornings.
--Well, if you're sure there's enough. But just egg and bread for me please, said Bill hastily. He tried not to look too shocked as Lynn stuck her fork into a fat sausage. The first she had eaten in years.
--There's plenty sure, plenty! Seamus assured him.

The breakfast was eaten, a lot of tea drunk and Seamus was rolling a joint. Lynn was feeling a bit queasy. She gave Bill a significant look.
--Er, Seamus,do you think we could borrow your donkey and car for a few hours? (Why was it called a Car, not a Cart?) We want to get some wood in while it's dry. We were hoping to get the van back and get a load of turf- we're nearly out- but from what everyone's saying about Kennedy's, it might be a long wait..There's a big tree that came down in the gale along the old track behind the house that I'd like to bring in.
--You could, said Seamus slowly, You could....only I haven't him at the

moment. I loaned him to a friend.
--Oh. When will you get him back do you think?
--I'll let you know. Jaysus, what's that? Seamus was up, thrusting the joint at Bill,and leaning out over the half door. He liked it to be open in all weathers, like the old cottage doors of his childhood.
The bit of air was needed too, thought Bill, mopping his face. The metal teapot was red hot and sizzling. He lifted it carefully off with a piece of cloth. Seamus came over at once and smoothed the cloth out, tucking it behind a pile of stones that looked as if they might explode in the heat. Strange noises were to be heard outside; there was distant banging and cursing. Lynn, sweat trickling down her back, got up as well,collecting a garland of dusty meadowsweet. Its cat pee smell seemed worse than usual and she felt desperate for some cool clean air.
--You can have that, said Seamus. Meadowsweet. Good for headaches. Jesus! That's Christy down below, he's after carving up his van again. Wait til you see the mess he's making in there. Twas a good enough little van til he got hold of it with his ideas of carpentry.
--Seamus,asked Lynn, Have you a toilet?
--You can use the bushes.
Lynn headed out along one of the little paths.
--Mind the dogs called Seamus. Come on Bill, wait til you see this,tis gas!
Contorted with suppressed laughter, he pulled the bemused Bill towards the farther end of the quarry.

Lynn made her way through the hazels. It was what was known as a Grand Hard Day- a frosty start and now bright sunshine. Lovely. Clean,sharp air and a sea of catkins dangling around her. The noise in the distance had stopped. Shit; this probably meant that Seamus and Bill had settled in Christy's place now for more tea, stories and the inevitable joint. Although she and Bill had come to Ireland for the laid back lifestyle, neither of them had ever been particularly fond of being stoned all round the clock. They made plans but their days seemed to get hijacked.
Ah well...In here, in the Crag, it was pure Fairyland. Except God,what WAS that, snuffling up behind her? With dawning horror she regarded the gang of dogs which had slunk out of the fusty darkness beneath the caravans (so many...seven, no, eight! Even that decrepit, stinking old terrier was wheezing up in the rear to join the rest) And all were watching her with the keenest anticipation. She realised they weren't

waiting to pounce on her, just on what she needed to deposit on the ground. Dogs didn't normally do that did they? Or was it just that they didn't get the chance? She tried to picture Aunty Pam's poodle at the same repast. Surely any self respecting dog would prefer a tin of Kennomeat? They must all have worms or something. A Depraved Appetite the books called it. And having witnessed it for herself she decided the title was most apt.

As Lynn hurried away, the silver silence was hideously shattered by a horrible yodel that was suddenly emitted by all the dogs at once. Up in the tall trees at the quarry's edge, crows and magpies flapped and screeched. A rabbit popped out in front of Lynn, its eyes bulging in terror. She shrank back, as ,oblivious to her presence ,the dogs crashed past. Up the bohreen they raced. At the front were two lurchers, (Seamus called them Hounds)
Next came a battered-looking beagle,and a skinny sheepdog, and not far behind,a snarling mass of terriers. Sometimes the leaders leapt over protruding branches or bowled over the faster of the terriers, who quickly righted themselves and continued to run, their little legs united in a common blur as they strove to reach the object of their entertainment
It was the highspot of the dogs' day: the Oldfella was coming along the bohreen.

--Oh,Jaysus, tis the Oldfella! Seamus informed Bill,after a quick peer out of Christy's window. Keep your head down while he passes. I don't want him to see me or he'll start giving out about the dogs.
Christy was grappling with a battle -scarred terrier. It was meant to be recuperating from a fight but it obviously didn't want to miss the fun. Christy was a shifty looking character, thought Bill. He was a lot younger than Seamus ,and darkly handsome. He had a snappy, nervous energy.
--I'm going to see if Lynn's all right! said Bill, trying to break free of Seamus's restraining arm.
--Keep your head down will you! She's only after going to the toilet, not the North Pole, said Seamus with his usual lack of logicality.
Reluctantly, Bill crouched down again. Outside, the racket was appalling. Yapping, growling, barking, cursing. That was a man's voice he could hear, so Lynn must be safely out of it....unless the dogs had already torn her up! Bill could stand it no longer. He shook off Seamus,and dived for the door. (Lord, what was that grey, globular stuff

in the bucket there?) He gave it as wide a berth as he could in the small space and leapt outside.

An amazing spectacle met his eyes. There stood Lynn, looking, to his huge relief, just as she had done twenty minutes earlier. But beyond her a violent battle was raging. It was hard to make out exactly what was happening, there was such a blur of teeth, fur and snapping jaws. Occasionally a dog came out of the scrum with a yelp, having sustained a welt of the stick that was being wielded - and heavily enough, but it was hopelessly inadequate against so many dogs with such varied lines of attack. And yes, there was a bicycle in there...some rubber those old tyres must be made of to withstand the gnashing they were getting!

It was that old boy who worked for the Corporation, Daly his name was. He wavered by with commendable punctuality every morning, greeting Maggie, who would be going for the school bus.
--Hello, Gerrel, Howye! Tis a Grand Day Now! And how is Mammy, God bless her ? Is she settling in all right now?
It was extraordinary. Even now, in the thick of the battle, he had caught sight of Lynn and was pausing in his exertions to call out greetings.
--Hello there, Missus, tis a grand -before being nipped on the backside by a particularly tenacious terrier that looked as if it was bouncing on an invisible trampoline.
--Come here,you blackguard, I'll pull the fecking tail off ye, so I will!
The lurchers and the beagle had hold of his coat tails and ankles.
-- Lucky he's wearing the big black wellies, thought Bill.
 The terriers weren't willing to take second best and were bouncing amazingly high in their efforts to get a grip somewhere. As they grew tired, they began to settle for the odd grind with the lunch tin strapped on the carrier, or gnawing at the wheels - or sometimes even at the bigger dogs' tails.
Only the sheepdog,, which was a recent arrival, seemed to retain some distant memories of domesticity. Alone among the rabble it seemed happy to run in circles round its comrades, pausing here and there to sniff and cock its leg.

Apart from his brief asides to Lynn, the Oldfella never let up in screaming obscenities, not forgetting to add, 'Scuse me,Missus' to Lynn - who was now endangering herself by trying to drag out one of the lurchers - which only ignited the dogs into further frenzy . Suddenly, he

caught sight of Bill.
--CALL THESE FECKIN DOGS UP, SONNY! he roared.
--Try and catch that one! shouted Lynn.
What one? Bill had never liked dogs . When he was a kid, the neighbour's farting Cairn would keep inexplicably grasping his leg with its forelimbs; then there was a Rotweiler lurking on his paper round ; and later a girlfriend's over- possessive dog had bitten him on the privates . He tried to gather his stoned wits and brave the fray, but the crazy cavalcade had reached the boundary of what Seamus and both sets of dogs knew to be Christy's patch. This marked the end of the fun (and was also the place where they usually got a beating.) They slunk away towards their underworld of sickly smelling straw, chewed boots and disappointingly dry bones. The sheepdog paused long enough to approach Bill in the hope of getting a pat, but he was unable to oblige.

Then, to Bill's huge astonishment, the Oldfella calmly mounted his bike and rode away. Bill watched,expecting him to keel over and die of a heart attack. But he rounded the corner steadily enough and disappeared from view.
Lynn came up and leant against him. She was shaking. As he put his arm round her, Seamus stuck his head out of Christy's window and called cheerfully ,'Is he gone ? Come on in here will you, there's no buses along this road!'
They exchanged looks of anger and perplexity. It was another of those Strange Days (they tended to happen around Seamus.) Weird situations that they didn't know how to deal with. Sometimes they were charmed but more often they were left feeling ineffectual and uneasy.
--Come and see the new bed Christy's after making! ordered Seamus, with no concern for the goings on which had left his visitors looking like bomb blast survivors. He's well out o' the draft now anyway!
It was obvious that no further reference was going to be made to the dogs' behaviour.

The caravan was a big one, and since Christy had removed all the original fittings and made no attempt to replace them, it now resembled a skittle alley. He had optimistically tried to mimic the handiwork of the talented Mike Hehir, who had completely refurbished his van with pine pinched from the forestry. It was panelled throughout, with bookshelves, cupboards and a lovely double bunk bed for him and his Missus with space for the kids underneath.

Bill looked around. There was a heap of broken ply in a corner, and a solitary chair, the one item to survive Christy's march of progress. The bed, made in hopeful imitation of Mike's charmingly rustic but also safe and solid one, was a botch on uneven stilts.
--You'll be all right when the river floods anyway! quipped Seamus.
--Don't lean on that post! snapped Christy. I didn't fix it to the wall yet.
--You'll have to shorten the legs a bit, observed Bill, or you won't be able to squeeze between the bed and the ceiling-
--I will o' course! returned Christy.
--You will in the fuck, muttered Seamus rather too loudly.

Lynn was looking at the terrier which lay panting in what had once been the kitchen. You could tell because Christy had sensibly left one shelf behind, on which sat a mangled packet of butter, a pot of jam, tobacco, and half a loaf with a huge knife embedded in it.
Also, there was a badger skin. It was weighted with two cans of baked beans and had obviously only been recently parted from its unfortunate owner because it was still covered in greasy grey fat.
--What are you putting on this cut? It looks infected.
Bill felt proud. Lynn had worked as a vet nurse before their move.
--Arrah, no, replied Christy with irritation, He's after fightin with a badger, that's all!
--Put a bit o comfrey on him and he'll be grand, advised Seamus, heading for the door in another of his lightning changes of subject and venue. Come on til I show you the river, Bill! There's grand fishing down here. I left an old rod set- maybe I've caught something.
Reluctantly, Bill followed him, trying not to look at the bucket of guts, and resolving to talk to Seamus about the badger baiting and uncontrolled dogs When The Time Felt Right.
 --Bill, said Lynn, noting with irritation the slightly bewildered way in which he was obediently following Seamus, I'm going home. I want to take some photos today.
--Okay. I won't be long, promised Bill unconvincingly.

Lynn hoped to sell photos and paintings of Burren flowers and old cottages. And possibly, local characters. She was fascinated by the strange old people you saw wandering around
but she wasn't sure if it was demeaning to leer at them like creatures in a zoo... she would have to get to know people a lot better first, she reflected.

Half way home was a beautiful old cottage with a thatched roof. This roof was uneven and sprouting weeds in places but that added to the charm. You would never find a thatched cottage in England that wasn't pruned and permed. as if had come straight from the hairdresser's . A few hens clucked about in the walled yard and a matted, mis-shapen old sheep dog lay in the porch. There were geraniums on the windowsill and the door and window frames, though they hadn't seen fresh paint in years, were still a bright yellow. They hadn't met the owner yet.

There was a smell of bacon in the air. It was shameful, but she was hungry again. She looked at her watch: only 11.45.

How beautiful it was here, there would be orchids out soon, and yesterday she'd seen a big hare bounding over the tussocks behind the house. It was one continuous SSSI really, even if people did dump used nappies along the roadsides and there were deviants like Christy living below....

It was odd how quickly the weather changed. Already Sliabh Caorigh, the mountain that rose in the distance was enveloped in mist and a ridge of cloud was building up beyond it. The Grand Hard Day looked as if it was already changing back to one of soft misty rain.

Chapter Two

Lynn reached the house with relief, wondering why she felt so tired, a sort of Bashed With a Telegraph Pole sensation behind her eyes. Perhaps it was the strain of dealing with Seamus, who could make you laugh, and told fantastic stories but was impossible to have a logical conversation with. She tried not to feel angry with Bill for not getting things done.
She reminded herself that they had come for the originality, the craic, the letting things happen in their own time.
Right now, she really needed a cup of tea. Normally, it would have been coffee, but for some reason today she just wanted more tea. And, as the stray cat that was trying to adopt them shot out of the empty goat shed, she remembered that they were out of milk. Also that, a fortnight ago, she had given Seamus money to buy them A Grand Pair O' Goats that he knew of. But for some reason they had not materialised yet. This was one of the things they had meant to ask him about this morning. She hoped Bill would remember....

There was a shop of sorts a couple of miles away at Conlon's Cross. You could knock on the house window at any time and some one would open up. The stock consisted of tobacco, briquettes,bread, butter, Calvita cheese, Flaherty's porridge oats, jam and milk Oh, and sometimes bacon and sausages. At Conlon's Cross there was also a Post office. Only you had to be introduced to it or you would never know that it wasn't a ruin in the middle of a field.
 She would bike over there and get milk and a few other things.
 Ah, no....
She had lent the bloody bike to their neighbours up the bog road, young Dermot and Jimmy Ryan. The cries of 'Mam, Mam , will ye look at this bike!' had been touching . So had their admiration of what at home was a pretty ordinary machine. So she had let them borrow it, assuring Mrs Ryan that of course it wasn't needed, they had the van. Mrs Ryan might have preferred that it had been needed, as a violent fight erupted over who was to have the first turn. Dermot dragged Jimmy off the bike and in retaliation Jimmy pushed him into a particularly black piece of bog.
She decided to hitch. It was safe enough around here. And it wasn't the

reserve of the young. You saw middle aged women with their shopping bags standing outside the town waiting for passers by to stop. There wasn't the expectation that you would automatically have a car if you were over twenty one, or that you would only be hitching if you had some sort of personality disorder.

Due to the lack of traffic, she had walked half the way before a car stopped. Her suspicions about the weather had proved correct and a soft drizzle was falling. The car was a beaten-up old Volkswagon with a chugging, watery sounding engine. Despite the safe reputation of hitching here, Lynn felt some trepidation as it drew up beside her, and was relieved to see an elderly couple inside. Rape now appeared unlikely, but she still feared one of the relentless grillings that people around here inflicted. They had a way of asking the most personal questions and fired them so quickly that, stunned, she often told all. Today, she resolved to stick to Seamus- style answers: changes of subject, making jokes, heading off at handy tangents.
She was near a tiny crossroads. Nearby was a ruined church where white lichen glistened on the subsiding gravestones half hidden in grass and weeds. The little road opposite, from where the car had come, led up to the remotest part of the mountain.
She looked inside
.--Howye, she ventured. Where are you going?
This was a stupid thing to say; they had to pass Conlon's Cross going this way. The old woman obviously thought so too.
--Climb in, Gerrel, climb in! she urged.
Lynn did as she was told. The interior of the car was dusty and strewn with bits of hay, string and old feed bags. Also it was plastered in holy medals, luminous plaques and little statues placed there to protect its occupants from the perils of travel.
When she was installed in the back seat, the old man shouted --What's her name?
The old woman repeated the question to Lynn, and for the rest of the journey the conversation was conducted in this manner.
--My name's Lynn Suningham. I live up at-
--She says it's Sullivan, John.
--It's not Sullivan, it's-
But John was keen to know more.
--Tell me now, Mary. Would she be a cousin to Barney Sullivan over at Clongrish?

Mary, skewed around in her seat ,was staring intently at Lynn. It was unnerving. And she had whiskers on her chin.
--No, I'm not a cousin of his, began Lynn rather despairingly, You see my name isn't Sullivan, it's -
--She would not, John! Interrupted Mary, with relish, Lynn felt, as if she was pleased that the old boy didn't know everything for a change.
--I never heard of any Sullivans living around here, mused John suspiciously. O' course, there's always been Sullivans in the village...
--But I'm not a Sullivan, I'm---And is she married? demanded John, having decided to leave the perplexing loophole in his local demography behind, and perking up again, Is she married,Mary?
Mary turned her unwavering gaze on Lynn again. Chug, chug, chug went the car. How could it be so slow, wondered Lynn desperately, when every other vehicle- those belonging to Blow-ins and tending to be bit short of documentation, the farmers' vehicles that felt more
like canvas wagons as they slopped and slewed around the bends, even the odd classy vehicle belonging to a stray business man – they all of them swerved happily along among the fallen rocks, stray cattle and corporation men leaning on their spades with never a touch of the brakes or lessening of acceleration. But not this one.
--Yes, I'm married, said Lynn. That was good, anyway. All legal and respectable. Although not in the Catholic church....
---Married to a Sullivan is it? mused John after Mary had relayed this information. He was sounding depressed again but perked up as another question entered his mind. How many children has she?
--How many children have ye Ma'am?
--I've a daughter, Maggie. She's nearly eight.
--And is it only the one she has! exclaimed John, breaking his conversational code of waiting for the information to come via Mary in his horror that Lynn had not been working harder to populate the world.
--Ah, sure, God is good, they'll be more yet, Ma'am, said Mary comfortingly.
Suddenly, both old people began to writhe energetically. Lynn realised they were crossing themselves fervently in the hope that God would soon rectify her shortage of children . Embarrassed, she tried to change the subject.
--Er, do you live near the cross back there yourselves?
They named a remote townland that she knew covered the wildest part of the mountain and bogland. In its midst, was a deep valley named Garran An Blathanna, which meant, she had been told, the Grove of

Flowers. Unfortunately, this beautiful spot was inhabited by two feuding lunatics. Fortunately, she had so far only heard about them.

At the head of the valley lived a German family who were a wonderful example of self-sufficient living. Seamus had taken herself and Bill to meet them. She couldn't help noticing that Seamus did not get much of a welcome. But the family were so impressive- horse and cart transport, growing all their own vegetables, a few pigs and goats, home made cheese, honey...and Anja made nearly all the family's clothes herself. There was only one word for the way the baby was fed though- Revolting.. Bill and Lynn had escaped the sight of it by needing to admire the garden again and hastened outside to where the valley stretched below and the smell of thyme and heather came on the wind, while the dedicated parents continued to regurgitate their masticated pulp of home made organic bread from their own mouths on to the baby's hand- carved wooden teaspoon.

Seamus was already out in the garden. He wasn't allowed to smoke in the house because he would pollute the Medicinal Herbs hanging up to dry, which people paid a lot for since this place was one of the cleanest in the world.

--Oh, yes, said Lynn, We visited some German people up there. They live just above, sorry I'm not very good at pronouncing it, something Blathanna, it's a beautiful spot isn't it, all those flowers -

Oh, Jesus, they were off again, crossing themselves even more ferociously than before. Two men conversing at the roadside were just turning to salute the car. They squashed themselves back against the wall as it swerved towards them; John had let go of the steering wheel in his haste to clutch his holy medal and seek protection from whatever horrors lurked in the Valley of the Flowers as fast as possible. Now Lynn felt grateful that the car was travelling so slowly.

--God help us, expostulated Mary when she had got her breath back after her own violent exertions, God help us, we wouldn't go near it, not if we were paid a thousand pound, we wouldn't go near it!

Lynn was lost for an answer. Anyway, they were at last pulling up at Conlon's Cross, and oh joy, it was time for her to get out.

--Will ye come in for a quick jar? asked John as she was thanking him for the ride. The Conlon's one room shop also doubled up as a very basic bar.

--She will not, John! snapped Mary quickly.

--I'm afraid I can't, said Lynn. I need to be home before my daughter gets back from school.

As she hurried away she heard Mary calling to Mrs Conlon, who was hanging out washing in the yard beside the house..
--Hello, Howye, Are Ye Well. And how is Bridie going on? Next week is it? Ah,the Cra'tur!
Com'ere, did ye ever here of Sullivans living up near the wee cross above?

Chapter Three

Bill was stumbling home from the river below Seamus's caravan where they had spent most of the day fishing; and smoking. He knew he'd had a list in his mind this morning of Important Things To Do, only now he couldn't remember them, there was only an uncomfortable awareness that they hadn't been done.
They'd caught several trout and Bill had a couple in his pocket, wrapped in newspaper. Seamus did not read newspapers but he collected supplies of unsold ones from the shop in the village to use for fire lighting.
Sitting by the river, Seamus had told him some things about his boyhood.
--My father was a great man for the fishin'. But it wasn't very often he'd take me with him. When he did it was magic. Riding along on the back of the ole bike, all along the little country roads, getting our tea in a house somewhere along the way....But mostly, he couldn't be bothered and he'd leave me at home. So one day when he was out- and he was out a lot, he had a great voice so he was always out around the bars singin', and my mother in a desperate way at home and no food in the house- Anyway, this day, I was left there at home and I spotted the fishin' rod, and didn't I get hold of it and bait it up with an ole worm.. Mrs Molloy, our neighbour, had hens in her garden, and I threw the worm over and pulled one up. Seamus laughed out loud. He came up flappin' and squakin', (Seamus called everything 'He', even Nanny goats with milk spurting from their udders) Well, Jesus, you should have heard the noise, Mrs Molloy and all the neighbours roarin'- they had some job to get him off the hook.....Mrs Molloy was roarin' at myself but the rest got great entertainment out of it altogether and one old fella gave me money! Seamus kicked his legs in glee. But my mother....I think that's what decided her to send me to The Aunts....
---The Aunts? queried Bill.
Seamus was suddenly sombre.
--Very strange things happened to me there. I can't explain it at all.
He pronounced Things as Tings. Bill wished he could speak so colourfully, and get rid of his Surrey accent. He was enjoying listening. Seamus's memories seemed genuine and were so entertaining. In other circumstances he could be really irritating, pretending to be some sort of Sage and coming out with all manner of half baked bullshit. It didn't

matter how much you disproved his arguments either, he somehow avoided answering you directly. But he had a real affection for his homeland and the Old Ways, and he was a wonderful story teller.
--My father was an awful boozer, my mother had a hard time of it and he not doing what he should for her, continued Seamus. She never thought a lot of me anyway, he added ruefully, Twas Morris my younger brother was her favourite....
These Aunts had been tryin' to get hold of me for a while. Maybe they thought a young fella round the place could chop their wood and things like that. They were sort of religious maniacs, dyin' to put the fear o' God into me, if I hadn't already had enough beatings off the Brothers....
It was after I fished up the hen that my mother decided to let the Aunts have me after all. Well, Jesus, if you saw them two old hags you'd wonder how I'm still here at all! Here, roll another joint there will ye.
--I don't think I want to smoke any more. I was meant to-
--Well, sure, roll it anyway, ye can decide after. These Aunts of mine, they were really Heavy. Always tellin' me how bad I was and how the devil would get me. We spent all day prayin', and when they weren't at that they'd be spoutin' the bible at me...I never went to the toilet so much in my life, twas the only place to get away from them. Oh, they thought I was very bad altogether.
--Did your Mum know what they were really like?
--She did, I suppose. Maybe she thought they'd do me good! But mostly, all she was thinkin' of was having less kids to feed. One day, though, they took me out walkin', and we came to a church, a ruined church it was. There was somebody standin' on the wall. In a long black thing. Like a monk.
It scared the shite out o' me, but they kept draggin' me towards it...the church was all dark and it was one of those days with the sky really purple and the grass too green. And I terrified. When we got there- and this is the honest truth, now-
(Bill was learning that Seamus's reminiscences, however subjective, were indeed a lot more truthful than most of the other stuff he came out with.) - when we got there, wasn't there a devil's face - with horns and all -lookin 'at me from under the hood.
Bill was both fascinated and appalled. His chest was constricted with the useless emotion of being an onlooker- for he was seeing not the swirling brown water that yielded up its trout so congenially, but a ragged, terrified kid at the mercy of two lunatics- many years too late to intervene.

---You poor bugger, was all he found to say.
--Well, Jesus, I screamed and I screamed, and they pullin' and draggin' me along. Later, we all had to pray....The next day I stole a bike and rode all the way home -twas miles. I screeched the place down when I got there until my eldest sister, Eileen, persuaded my mother to have me back..
You couldn't blame my mother for what she did   She was just a simple woman from the country, married to a bowsie. We were near starvin' for years. We weren't the only ones, there were a lot of families the same way. Myself and Morris went to the Christian Brothers' school with the arse out of our trousers – that was handy for them o 'course, with their feckin' beatings for this and that - and sometimes in our bare feet. We had these tin mugs tied to our belts and we got cocoa and a bun at dinner time. That wasn't much different to what we got at home a lot of the time; we spent years livin' on bread and jam.
My father was well -liked for his singin', so sometimes he'd come home with presents of food and we'd have a grand feed -bacon, cabbage, loads of butter on the spuds- and he'd have money... but twas rare my mother would see any of it.
--Are your parents still alive?
--My father's gone a long while. My mother isn't well. My sister lives in the house with her now. She's married to a builder and they're well enough off. All my mother has done for the last ten years is eat. She's huge now. It's like she can't believe there's so much food and she has to keep eating it to make sure. I've even been there and she'll scuttle over to her chair and shove a plateful of bacon and eggs underneath it, not lettin' on that she's eatin'.
--That's sad. It would be great if she could just relax and enjoy it.
--That's for sure. What do you think, though? What do you think that devil thing was?
--I think....well, I don't know who it could have been standing on the wall, but perhaps a monk or a priest? He was probably just looking over....why would he be standing on a wall? When you're a kid adults seem enormous sometimes, especially when you're scared. Maybe you just thought he was on the wall because he seemed so tall?
--Maybe.
--And those Aunts of yours had you so terrified and full of talk about the devil that you actually saw it. If you believe in things enough, you begin to see them....

--And I tinkin' I was mad all these years! quipped Seamus.
It was refreshing, thought Bill, the way he didn't bear grudges. Seamus would never start
psycho-analysing himself or blame his upbringing for his problems. In fact, he never seemed to have any problems.
Seamus cocked his head suddenly,instantly alert.
--Do you hear sometin'?
--Yea. Through the fug that Bill's brain had become, there were some discernable noises- shouts, horses hooves.
--Here, take this ordered Seamus, handing Bill the rod. He sprang up the bank on to a big rock, one of his look out posts. He liked to keep an eye on all the comings and goings in his vicinity and was always perched somewhere handy if he wasn't peering out of his half door..
--It's Tinkers! he cried excitedly. Horse drawn ones, travellin' the proper old way. Wait'll you see this. They're coming down here!

Lynn picked her way along the vague path that led to the Post Office, which stood on a little hillock in the middle of its field. She pushed open the door. There was a counter of sorts but otherwise no division between the post office department and the rest of Miko Flynn's domestic dwelling space. You could find strange and unexpected goings on not normally associated with a Post Office.
Today, the counter was littered with a bicycle chain and a plate of congealing bacon rinds. The place appeared to be empty. She could see through the open door to the back room: dark furniture, the edge of a big saggy old bed, holy pictures on the walls and sacks of turf piled along one side.
Suddenly she heard Miko's high, squeaky voice. Hello there, Missus, can I help ye?
She jumped. He was on the floor behind the counter, on his knees amongst other ancient bike parts.
Miko would have been highly placed in a competition to find the grimiest individual in the county. Not denying that there would be plentiful competition; Mary, for example had sported several fine blackheads amongst her whiskers, and the grease on John's collar was as thick as a tyre.
--Oh....Hello, Miko. Can I have four stamps please.
--Ye can to be sure. Would you like these pretty ones now? giggled

Miko, holding up a sheet of costly parcel stamps. Then, his blue eyes glowing out of his oily face, he drew out a blackened wallet from inside his jacket, thumbed through it with filthy fingers and triumphantly drew out the stamps. Lynn felt very honoured to receive them.

Outside, two postmen from the town, in proper uniforms, were struggling through the cow pats with a sack of mail.. They greeted Miko and dumped the sack resoundingly on the floor. Miko began to pour tea from the pot on the end of the counter.
--Is there a letter here for me? asked Lynn.
--Wait'll I see now, murmured Miko, peering into some cobwebby pigeon holes that ran along the wall. He shook his head. One minute, one minute, wait'll I see now- He seized the mail sack and upended it on the floor, making no effort to avoid the mechanical paraphernalia and dollops of oil. Passing comments all the while to his tea drinking companions,he got onto his knees again and sifted haphazardly through the letters and packages
--Here you are! he announced, handing her, with a flourish, an envelope covered in black fingerprints. As she left he was still sprawled there, in happy conversation about the local hurling team.

Seamus had been right. A crazy cavalcade was coming down the bohreen at a clattering gallop. The dogs went beserk, but luckily the tinker dogs limping along behind the wagons had no energy for a fight. One privileged canine, who was riding on a sidecar, began to growl and was instantly cuffed hard across the head by a little girl.
--Shut up out o' that, you!
--Jesus,the filth on her! remarked Seamus cheerfully, ye wouldn't know what colour her dress is supposed to be at all.
The horses were wild eyed and trembling. They were soaked in sweat and as they came by they flung off gobbets of foam. There were two sidecars, piled high with children, pots, bender poles, tarpaulins and bales of straw.
There were several big lads; crazy looking, thought Bill through his stoned haze. They were in charge of the horses and they had them unharnessed and chased off up the bohreen while they were still trying to drink from the pool that collected in a depression in the middle of the quarry.
The two barrel-topped wagons looked pretty all right, with beautiful

paintwork and big wooden wheels, not the car tyres he and Lynn had seen on the pictures of the ones you could hire for holidays.
But the people....it was what he had always wanted to see, traditional travelling tinkers...but right now it seemed too overwhelming, too far outside hos experience to cope with.
A teenage girl was striding carelessly into the pool to fill a kettle. She had big sloppy leather boots on her feet and as she came back you could hear the water sloshing inside them. She was dressed in a short skirt and fishnet tights and she had thick, yellow coloured hair that looked as if she had bleached it. She was good-looking, proud. But like them all, so – leathery. Even the younger children seemed to have that texture to them. Weather, Bill supposed,and the obvious washing difficulties. There were a lot of broken noses and scars to be seen too. The kids pushed and shoved to get at the bread and jam that was being handed out.
He felt relieved when a glance at his watch told him Maggie would soon be home from school. He called to Seamus, who was already deep in horse and dog talk, that he had to go. He wandered away,looking in perplexity at a piece of red material he vaguely recognised. That was it- the knickers that had been swept out this morning. Further on, he was presented with a sodden cardboard affair by the sheepdog, who was hoping to play Fetch. A sad sticker clinging to a corner claimed it to be the property of the County Library.

At the corner of the bohreen (Jesus,was it that late?) he met his daughter.
--Hello Daddy. Guess what, Majella Connolly's invited me to tea. And she gave me these-holy pictures, look.. I'm going to make a little shrine in the garden.
--Er – that's nice. So far, Maggie hadn't become Catholicised. They had decided on the local school because people had said that it was much harder to integrate with the locals if you chose the Steiner school, lovely as it was with its artistic, celebratory attitude to the religious calender and reverential attitude to children. It would have meant driving her a fair distance as well.

The school teachers seemed to accept that the Blow- ins were all heathens and not their problem. Maggie had never asked to go to Mass or anything. Although last year, when there had been mania for weeks before the Pope's visit, the Ryans had taken her to Limerick with them

when he spoke at a huge rally there. The shops were sold out of folding camp chairs, flasks, etc, and Maggie had a flag to wave and came home with a Pope mug.
--Dad, why are your eyes all funny?
--Funny? They're not, they're fine.
--Yes they are. Sort of like- Maggie cast around for a suitable comparison and found it- Dog Pee.
Luckily, while Bill in his turn was casting around for a suitable excuse for the state of his eyes, she had linked arms with him and was enthusing about something else.
--I met a dear old man down the road this morning. His name is Matty Keane. He's got a dog called Jimmy and he gave me a bar.
--A what?
--You know-a bar of chocolate! she informed him, slightly scornful of his ignorance.
--Where did you meet him? You didn't go into his house?
--Of course I did. He said there was no point waiting there, the bus broke down and they're using another one and it's really slow. There's a letter about it in my bag. He said I should come in and warm myself.
Alarm bells were shrilling in Bill's head.
--Was his wife there?
-- don't think he's got a wife. He talks to Jimmy -that's his dog - all the time. He says Ah Jimmy Boy, and then he talks about all the things he used to do years ago. He used to have a little black pony called Molly that pulled his cart. And he says there's a magic hare round here that he sees sometimes. And it wears trousers and everything, but he doesn't want me to tell anyone....oh dear.....
Bill looked down at her crestfallen face. Thick grey eyelashes, soft cheeks, rosy from her walk, strands of thick cornfield coloured hair that had escaped her pony tail and were curling in the damp air. He needed to find the right warning words that would not ruin what was probably an entirely innocent meeting. But Maggie was already on to another subject.
--Oh, and Dad, I found a donkey Tied up in the bushes down the road. He's really fluffy with funny bumpy knees. He looked all sad and he was eating a really prickly old bush. He looked at me and made a sad sort of Humph noise. He didn't have any water, Dad! Do you think we could take him some?
Bill decided to meet her from the bus from now on, before she came home with all the tinker's dogs and horses.

And, despite the assurance of other Blow-ins, whose kids cycled mile unsupervised to visit each other, and who enjoyed a freedom unheard of in England, he felt decidedly uneasy about the Dear Old Man.
--Can we take him some water, Daddy?
--He must belong to someone. I'm sure they'll give him water...
--But he didn't even have a bucket! objected Maggie.
--Well, we'll have a look tomorrow.
--That's a long time for him to wait without any water! Can't we go back now?
She was right, really. But he didn't like to interfere too much. He would ask Lynn what she thought.
--When are you going to Majella's?
--She said if I came on Friday I could stay the night. We can go to the dance class in the morning and her Dad will bring me back in the afternoon.
--That sounds good. As long as her parents don't mind.
--She says her Mam always says one more won't make any difference.

Lynn was riddling the range when they reached the house.
--Bloody thing went out, she remarked, after greeting Maggie. Did you ask Seamus about the goats?
--Oh, no....I forgot. Bill was saved from the Look he knew was due to him by Maggie clamouring to tell Lynn the news of her day. He retired to the far end of the table and poked half-heartedly at his chain-saw, which sat dismembered on some newspaper. He was incapable of cleaning it and quietly watched as Lynn sat down and Maggie snuggled against her. Lynn had dark hair, thick like Maggie's, which she usually had clipped up, with untidy tendrils making a charming escape. She had something exotic about her eyes, Bill couldn't say quite what but it made her stand out. He'd been smitten the minute he saw her.
 Maggie had been two years old when they actually got married. .
They had a sweet photo of her in her frilly bridesmaid dress at their wedding (which had only been in the local registry office). What a little darling she had been, and was. But even then, what a job to persuade her to wear the dress. She preferred her dungarees and she was very strong-willed. Perhaps she was a bit spoilt. One woman in a shop had called her Bold and said she needed Checking.

Lynn was so good with Maggie- so stable and matter of fact, warm but firm; and great with animals, her voice seemed to hypnotise and re-assure them. She was okay with people too - IF they came singly. But she clammed up in group situations, and avoided social situations where conversation was required as much as she could. |Her mother, who could never accept that Lynn just didn't like mixing with lots of people and never would, had confided to Bill that she was Most Concerned about Lynn becoming Too Isolated, and endeavoured to impress upon him the dangers of her becoming a Complete Recluse.

Later, Bill heard about the lift to Conlon's Cross.
--I got a letter from Cathy. It's taken ten days to get here. She's coming over this weekend! She thinks we can meet her with the van? What can we do?
--If we can't think of anyone else who might pick her up, we can always get a taxi from the town. Seamus's brother drives a taxi.
--Yea, but the money...
Too late, the Plan for Today was coming back into Bill's mind. They were running short of everything now. Paraffin for the lamps, briquettes...and they needed to do a proper, big grocery shop. He had better get up the track and cut up some of that wood. Bugger, why hadn't he at least got a wheelbarrow...the Ryans would lend him one but by the time he'd been up there, and exchanged the expected pleasantries, it would be dark. Besides, it was embarrassing always appearing so inept and ill prepared.

The Plan had been as follows:-
Ask for loan of donkey and car, drive into village, get some basic supplies, see about van's progress while there.(When Bill actually became acquainted with the donkey, he realised what a ridiculous idea this had been. Maggie would have starved to death by the time the creature ambled home.)
Next, having ascertained that Seamus was not getting them any goats after all, get their money back and go and buy some themselves. If they didn't manage to borrow the donkey and car, he was going to come straight back, walk up to the Ryan's place and ask for a lift the next time they were going anywhere near the village or town. Perhaps he should go up there now, but he was still chilled from sitting so long by the river. Outside the sky had cleared again, which was good, but the evening was going to be cold. The range was warming up and he felt like pulling up the baggy old armchair and lazing in the mellow evening light, cuddling Maggie.

She seemed to be doing well, he reflected. It had been their biggest worry, moving her from her friends, not only to a new school but to a completely different culture as well.

Right now, Maggie was rooting in the bag of shopping Lynn had brought back. She took out a bag of Flahavan's Progress Oatlets, milk which she stood it in the bucket in the corner, then -
--What's this, Mum?
--Nothing for you, said Lynn quickly, taking the curved thing wrapped in white plastic. She was blushing, Bill noticed, his interest aroused. What on earth could she have bought to make her blush like that? Conlon's were unlikely to have a stock of dildos...
--Stop pulling that stuff out, said Lynn rather sharply. Why don't you go and make a start on your shrine before it gets dark..

As soon as Bill had braced himself and gone out into the cold evening air to start work with the bow saw, and Maggie had gone outside with her holy pictures and some dried flowers, Lynn grabbed the black pudding and went to the door. After ascertaining that Bill was safely on his way , she hid it in the manger in the goat shed. Then she remembered the stray cat. And probably there were mice, rats even. They'd all be after it.
She went back inside and found a big old jar with a lid. Thank God Maggie hadn't seen that it was a meat item, and made mostly from blood. She, the staunch vegetarian, was desperate to eat it. Down at Conlon's, there'd been a row of pork pies on the counter; she'd had two on her way home.
She couldn't drink her tea. It was tainted with the sickly-sweet smell of turf smoke -like everything and everyone. It was the smell that, every year they had come to Ireland, she had rejoiced in encountering again. And when she had begun to smell of it herself, it was like being an initiate in some wonderful cult. But now, it made her feel sick.
She went out to the well at the top of the garden and got a mug of very cold water. That was better.

They were lucky with this house. The German man they had bought it from (with Seamus as a bizarre sort of estate agent) had more or less built it from scratch, on just the shell of an ancient cottage. They had more mod cons that many Blow Ins; water on tap (which under
 normal circumstances could not be distinguished from that in the well,

but for some reason tasted oddly stale today) and even a couple of radiators running off the range.

A bath and a toilet, bramble strewn, waited patiently in a corner of the yard as they had done for years. And it would cost a lot to get the ESB all the way up here, but the challenge of living without luxuries was what appealed to them.
--We should be used to living with limited electricity anyway, Bill had joked, After all the bloody power cuts at home last winter! And I can't believe you're cribbing about a bit of rubbish after the mountain we had outside the house for weeks.
--Yea, but that normally gets collected. And did when the strike ended. And it was in a city. It's sad when you see it in lovely countryside and know it'll be there for years.
--The tinkers don't have much option but to leave it behind them...But sometimes I wish disposable nappies hadn't been invented...

For a while it had been blissful not to be bothered by a ringing phone every time you settled down to do something. But it was hard to get on with the local pay phones. She couldn't get the hang of pressing buttons A and B at the right time. She thought she had got through to Cathy today, from the one at Conlon's :it sounded like her voice, but there was so much interference she couldn't be sure, and when she spoke, Cathy couldn't seem to hear her.
At the village post office, Mrs Kilbride would help you. But apparently she would pass on all your business- something Seamus was always warning about.
--Don't be tellin' this/that/the other one all my business now, if he'd just introduced you to someone, He/She's a nosy old fecker!

She had to cook dinner. Normally she loved cooking on the range, it was great for slow beany stews, and she usually baked bread, that was kind of compulsory amongst the
alternative community...but tonight, well she was having a good chunk of that sausage before the others came back.
Shit. The way she'd been feeling was pretty un-mistakeable but she'd been trying to ignore it. It was only after the questioning of John and Mary (and even more after the pork pies) that she'd admitted it to

herself. She was pregnant. She didn't need the doubting medical profession with their tests. Just as she had done with Maggie, she felt almost from the time of conception, not only sick, hungry and tired but completely and utterly Different. Which she wasn't at all pleased about. Much as she loved Maggie, she wasn't that keen on babies. They had never made her coo. She especially detested bald ones. And she Hated Being Pregnant.

It was a kind of joke amongst the Blow-Ins Couples who had tried for years to have a baby suddenly found themselves blessed when they set foot in Ireland. Something in the air. It was a fact that before the Famine, people living only on potatoes and a bit of buttermilk or fish were the most prolific in the world.

Bill would be pleased. He would see it as nature giving their coming here her blessing. After all those house-hunting trips they'd nearly given up. Places were amazingly cheap here - but still just out of their range, until they'd met Seamus at Carnsore Point anti – nuclear festival and he'd told them about a Grand Cottage he knew of. He'd made himself good money out of it of course, and now it was a bit awkward. He seemed to feel that he had a share in it, in their lives almost.

The weird lassitude and lack of energy were alarming. She could see her moneymaking plans with the photography and paintings going out of the window. How did those women cope in the past, feeling like this, or when they were huge, doing everything with no mod cons and a crowd of kids already?

Here, they had a generator, she comforted herself, which – sometimes - powered a washing machine, and a couple of electric lights. They were out of fuel at the moment though, and using paraffin lamps. There was already a pile of dirty washing waiting for her attention.

She tried to think about the nice bits- little clothes, a wicker basket, names; the hormones that took you over entirely, the little soft thing cradled against you when all the pain and months of discomfort were over. Bill bringing her breakfast in bed. The cards and presents.

But super imposed on all that were being sick, lugging yourself about, not being able to sleep, constantly looking for a place to pee, the indignity of people groping about inside you, the labour itself – that inexorable tidal wave of pain you couldn't stop and just had to endure- leaking milk, agonised nipples, sleepless nights and worry.

She didn't know how Maggie would take it. She had never shown much interest in dolls, or babies, being keener on animals. Her favourite toys were her farm and her family of cloth animals. Some of those had been left behind in Gran's loft. But Scatsy Bom Bom the teddy had made it, along with Ali Boo Boo, a little dog. And, against Lynn's better judgement, the awful Fred Nerch. Maggie had picked him up when they were looking around a second hand shop. He was in a box of house clearance stuff. She made such a fuss when asked to put him back that they had to bring him home. He was ancient. He had a wire frame and both his feet pointed the same way. He was stuffed with leaking straw. Lynn had given him new blue button eyes which were now very faded, like his dusty felt blazer. His expression was bizarre and she always tried to make sure he was parked where he wasn't looking directly at her.

Lynn hoped that the idea of a little brother or sister would be more acceptable to Maggie here, where lots of the kids came from large families with babies and siblings at home. In fact, not long ago she had watched, amused, as Maggie showed Bill how to fold a nappy. The girls at school were all adept at it so she felt obliged to be too.

Things were falling into place,. Maggie was happy, they were getting to know people..a baby would round it all off, she told herself bravely, producing a watery smile for Bill as he came back in.

Chapter Four

--It was great at Majella's! enthused Maggie.
It was Sunday and she was in the big old bath tub. There was finally enough hot water with them burning briquettes again. It was nice lounging back in it in front of the range, but emptying the thing was a nightmare. Like the bucket toilet. It was peaceful out there, looking at the birds or the moon and stars, but the bucket with its layers of ash or sawdust filled far too quickly. By the weight of it you'd think a couple of elephants had been using it on the sly. The speed at which the composting trench at the bottom of the garden filled up was depressing too. Anyway, there sat the bath and toilet behind the brambles, it all just needed plumbing in....
--What did you do?
--Watched telly! And then we went down to Flynn's and we got free burgers because Majella's sister works there. We minded the baby for a bit as well and we took him for a walk in his pram.
That sounded hopeful, thought Lynn. They hadn't told Maggie about their own baby yet.
--Majella's family think you're bonkers! continued Maggie gaily, Coming and living in damp cottages they've all moved out of!
--Actually, this one was newly built, said Lynn, Well, mostly...
Bill stumbled in and headed for the kettle, sort of checking her over on his way. That morning she had woken to find him studying her – breasts in particular. The outsize T shirt she slept in had given up the battle and was bunched in a less strained position around her neck.
--You're pregnant aren't you? he 'd exclaimed, with amused, admiring relief. He had been wondering if her mother was right with her thinly veiled hints about the loss of sanity that living in such a lonely place would be sure to produce.. Perhaps the strain of moving had been too much for Lynn. He'd discovered the stashes of meat and when she'd been sick one time he thought she might be developing Bulimia.
His joy increased as the thought occurred to him that there would be No More PMT. Lynn suffered badly from it – and so did he and Maggie. Lynn knew it, but you risked your life if you tried pointing it out to her when she was crying over something someone had innocently said to her, or yelling horribly at Maggie . As the full moon approached, all he could do was try and keep himself and Maggie out of her way.
--You're pregnant!
Lynn wasn't able to reply. Bill was smothering her with kisses and murmuring into her neck, I love you Lynn, I love you...

If it hadn't been for the untimely but predictable arrival of Maggie in the room he would have liked to go further in expressing his sentiments. He sighed.
--Maggie, you're meant to knock..
--You can't knock on a curtain! retorted Maggie, unabashed. You said I could help you in the garden today. When are you getting up? I've been awake for hours, and it's really cold downstairs...
--Where's Aunty Cathy?
--Still asleep. Shall I go and wake her?
--No!

Jim Ryan had come to their rescue. He'd picked Cathy up from Limerick, swearing that he had to go down that way anyway and it was No Trouble At All, None In The World to go to the station. The train was two hours late due to a rough ferry crossing holding up its departure from Rosslare, but Jim remained the soul of kindness and was drinking tea with them at midnight, seeming in no hurry to get home to bed.
--Is it goats you're after? he'd laughed, Surethere's a crowd of 'em running wild in the crag behind here! Why don't you go and catch a couple!
It had taken them a minute to realise he was joking.
--I think I know someone who'll sell you a goat or two, he'd continued, Nice and tame, and good milkers. I'll let you know in a couple of days.

The day before Cathy's arrival, they'd had a lift into town, done a big Quinnsworth shop, loaded supplies of briquettes and other stuff onto his trailer and then, while Jim went off to see someone about buying some calves, headed for the luxury of a drink in Devlin's
Hotel. The toilets in there were pure heaven.... The deep red interior of the lounge with a huge fire blazing was pretty good too. The hotel catered for rich German and American tourists here for the fishing and golf, but the lounge bar was a comfortable place for anyone to sit and all sorts of people went in there. It was hard to get up once you'd relaxed with a hot whiskey. It was also a safe choice today because Lynn had gone off alcohol and it was the one place where you could ask for a mineral water without feeling that you were offending anyone or putting on airs.

In the toilets, Lynn met Nuala. She looked very young, thought Lynn, less than twenty. Quite beautiful. A cloud of long dark wavy hair, greeny blue eyes,and a slightly wistful face.
She was wearing a long ethnic dress. The Punk revolution had

happened in Britain four years earlier and you sometimes saw odd mixes of fashion amongst the Blow ins – there was one frightening girl who still wore long skirts but had the sides of her head shaved and a Mohican crest. The Punk thing was a mystery to Lynn and it made her a bit sad. Hippies were going to change the world, stop wars, spread peace and love, get everyone back to nature. There wasn't meant to be anything else. Then suddenly it was All Change and there were angry young people covered in safety pins and dressed in bin bags whose views and behaviour made her feel oddly conservative. And Old. Even if some of the music (the Stranglers, the Buzzcocks, wow) was brilliant....but they weren't the heavy duty ones and anyway, the Stranglers were around before Punk happened...

Lynn was comforted that Nuala obviously wasn't influenced by Punk. She had the neck of her stonehenge dress pulled open and was trying to hold the large baby slobbering at her front so that she could get his mouth halfway discreetly onto her nipple.

All the toilet cubicles were full..

This is usually a great place to come and feed him, she explained, lowering her voice, but there's a big crowd of Yanks in....

Mikey had set up a frustrated moaning which gave way to furious bawling as he slid down his mother's chest. Nuala struggled to hold him nearer the object of his desire without exposing it altogether.

--Oh,Jesus, sorry- She looked down to see that she was spurting milk. At last she managed to get her nipple, along with a corner of material, into Mikey's mouth, but not before the jet had hit Lynn and filled Mikey's eyes. As he settled down to ferocious sucking, a woman came out of a cubicle. She looked shocked, and crossed herself.

--All those children, Lynn told Cathy later, but they still seem shocked by breast-feeding.

Meanwhile Bill was making Supportive Male Statements to Jim Ryan and a neighbour, Willy O'Rourke.

--Jesus,man, exclaimed Willy, ye don't really want to see women all over the place with babies hangin' off their tits, sure ye don't ! while Jim nodded in agreement.

--They should keep them at home! Anyway, they can use them feedin' bottles if they want to go out with 'em!

Bill didn't know which remark to challenge first...so he didn't begin.

--I've been up to see Seamus's sister. I was just going to hitch home but Mikey got hungry so I had to come in here. explained Nuala.

--Why don't you come and have a drink? invited Lynn, rather hoping that the answer would be No, because she and Bill had been enjoying sitting quietly together in the lounge.

Also, Nuala was covered in milk, despite her efforts with a toilet roll. Plus she would be obliged to ask Jim if Nuala could have a lift back with them. And it was obvious from remarks that he had made that he didn't think much of either her or Seamus. Especially not Seamus.

--Wife is it! was the first thing. That young wan isn't his wife! Nor the one he had before either! And the two o' them lookin' more like his daughters...Twouldn't be so bad if he stuck to them hippy ones, they're mostly as good as prostitutes anyway- (here, Bill and Lynn had not dared look at each other and they had thanked heaven again that they'd got married) – but that young gerrel now, sure she wasn't long out of school, over here workin' for her Aunt when he got hold o' her. And look at her now! Stuck there among the Knackers with a babba hangin' off her!

--Thanks, that would be great, said Nuala. I could do with sitting down. I stayed over at Maeve's last night -she's Seamus's sister- and as soon as I put my head down, Mikey was up and raging around...He's not used to the noises in the house and even the street lights seem to keep him awake.

Mikey was a sturdy chap, not fat but strong. He had that lusty yell and an incredible disinclination for keeping still. It would be fun when he started crawling, thought Lynn. Seamus's Arrangements didn't stand a chance.

--Haven't you got a pushchair? she asked as they went towards the lounge.

--It broke on me yesterday. And I had a bag of washing in it that I was bringing to the launderette. I had to leave it behind a wall up near Conlon's. I still had to come in, for the baby clinic-

(And the library, she thought privately. The only way she kept her sanity was her escape into the world of fiction. But they were being difficult, demanding the return of a long overdue book that seemed to have completely disappeared...)

-- Maeve borrowed a few things for me from her neighbour. I'd nothing left to put on Mikey. I'm killed trying to do all the washing by hand out there.

I knew the pushchair was on its last legs and I've been saving for a new one. I don't know how I managed it, but I forgot to bring the money! I got a bit upset about that yesterday. .Maeve was very kind and said I should have a rest and a bath and stay the night. I didn't really want to because Seamus-- she stopped and changed tack. I nearly walked out to the Poor Clares-

--The who?

--They're Nuns. They give stuff to the tinkers and people on the dole. But it's a couple of miles out the road, and I've got the money for a nice new one. Seamus can get it another time.
As they stood at the bar, Lynn was aware of Looks. People always clocked you anyway, but a man seated at the bar nudged his companion.
--The hippies are out in force today! He leaned in and said something else, and the other man turned and leered unpleasantly.

Bill spotted them. He got up gallantly and came and bought their drinks. As soon as they had sat down, Mikey was reaching out for things on the table.
Lynn gave him her keys, but the minute their attention wandered, he executed a particularly vigorous squirm and managed to grab an ashtray, stuffing some butts into his mouth before
Nuala could stop him. He soon spat them out again, leaving his mouth smeared with vile grey goo. Nuala got to work with her toilet roll again.
--Here, Mikey, have these. She reached for a couple of crusts left over from their lunch.
--Is he hungry? I'll get him a sandwich, suggested Bill, How about you?
--Thanks Bill. But no point really, he'd only manage a tiny bit. He prefers the crusts-something to chew. I'm okay, I'm not long after breakfast.

Bill wasn't saying much, Lynn noticed. He'd always been good at playing Jolly Uncle Bill with friend's children, but he was worrying, like her, about Jim Ryan. It was nearly time to meet him up near the Mart.
--Bill, I've still got to do some shopping, she said, hoping he would assume it was some mysterious Women's Stuff to do with the pregnancy and wouldn't quiz her. Why don't you go on with Jim and I'll get a taxi back with Nuala in a bit?
--I'm sorry, I've no money, said Nuala, But we'll get a lift easily enough.
--No, you get a taxi. Tommy is a relation of yours anyway isn't he, Nuala, expect he'll give you a bargain fare, said Bill. It's only the once, we'll have the van back soon. ...
Every time he said this it was with less conviction. And the money they had expected to tide them over for a good few months had dwindled alarmingly -he had decided that he had better sign on. But paying the taxi fare was worth it to avoid the discomfort of being caught between Jim Ryan and Nuala.
Mikey spat a streamful of ash-flecked, soggy bread across the table.
--We'll see you later then, said Lynn decisively, kissing Bill on the cheek. and picking up her bag.

Bill watched them leave, feeling both rueful and relieved. Suddenly he noticed the two at the bar making comments. Before he knew it, he was up and striding purposefully towards them. He wasn't very good at lunch time drinking. And his protective feelings about Lynn were heightened at the moment. He was going to throttle the snidy little weasel who had evidently just said something insulting.

Regarding Nuala, he was feeling guilty for not being very welcoming, for being both a coward and a hypocrite. But having connections with Seamus, and by association, Nuala, seemed to blight relations with a lot of other useful and decent people.... Seamus generally dismissed these people (behind their backs) as STRAIGHT, signifying that they were therefore lower than worms.

Still, Seamus had found the house for them. And although certain other things didn't quite add up, he hadn't done them any harm as yet. Bill's personal creed had always been to make his own judgements. He had certainly never felt like sneering at Nuala and he was intent on murdering the fellow that was doing it now.

Luckily, the snidy weasel one had suddenly noticed the laser eyeballs that were trained on him . He hastily re-arranged his horrible smirk and lowered his head to concentrate intensely on his pint. Seeing that his point was taken, Bill managed at the last second to alter the direction of his charge towards the door. The weasel flinched as the hot gust of Bill's rage passed harmlessly by, only grazing for a second the sleeve of his jacket. Outside, Bill was aware of the uncomfortable rush of unused adrenalin, and his heart pounding horribly all the way up to the car park by the Mart.

--Nuala, said Lynn. I've got my cheque book with me. Why don't we get the pushchair now and you can pay me back later?
--Are you sure? It can wait, honestly. Seamus'll think I've been giving you the poor mouth.
Sod Seamus, thought Lynn She could see what a struggle it was for Nuala lumping Mikey about. She remembered too how invaluable a pushchair was for rocking babies off to sleep when they were ill or teething; you could lie down in your exhaustion and just push it gently back and forth with your foot until they dropped off. And the caravan....it was so far away from anything. The walk Nuala had done to Conlon's to get the bus yesterday was a good three miles. She'd be completely marooned without a pushchair.
 --I think we should get it now. It might be a while before you can come

back into town again. And I'd like to see what they've got in the shop myself.
--Well,if you're sure. Thanks, Lynn, that's really good of you.

--Come in and have a cup of tea, invited Nuala, as the taxi driven by Tommy Lynch , Seamus's cousin, swerved into the bohreen. Lynn was feeling sick. It would be nice to get out here and walk home in the fresh air.
--All right, thanks I will.
Two little tinker kids playing with some pots stared as they passed the benders that were put up along the little bit of verge. The car halted outside the caravan ,sending a spray of gravel into the faces of the emerging dogs. There was no sign of Seamus. Lynn paid Tommy who said, Any time, any time!
--Thanks, but we should have our van back soon. She instantly regretted saying that, knowing what was coming.
--Where is it?
--It's at Joe Kennedy's being-
--Is it Joe Kennedy's! I wouldn't trust him with me son's tricycle! He drove off shaking his head and laughing to himself.

--Come inside quick, said Nuala as she unlocked the door, or the women over the way will be wanting us to go over and have tea in the bender. They're always hassling me, trying to get me to swop my bracelets and things.
 She put Mikey down on a rug. The caravan was very tidy and a good supply of logs was stacked neatly round the stove. Mikey stretched and grunted, trying with all his might to reach a display of ferns and lichen -covered twigs.
--Would you mind him for me there while I get the kettle on? Ah, feck it! The gas has run out. Do you mind waiting a bit...I'll have to light the stove. It's okay, Mikey can chew that...
I had an awful job to get Seamus to put the small stones away off that pile- he nearly choked on one before he agreed to move them. Honestly, he's like an old woman, he has to have it all perfect ...he has me driven mad with his fussing- Nuala stopped guiltily. She shook the box of firelighters and found it empty, These are good for firelighting, do you use them? She tore up a wax milk carton, and paper and soon had the beginnings of a small blaze going.
 --Sorry Lynn, it's going to be a bit of a wait. Shame there's no gas – I like to use the gas cooker and have the stove left out sometimes

because the heat in here gets too much altogether. Seamus goes mad throwing logs into this thing. The walls will melt one day.
--Is there anything I can do to help?
--You could bring up a bucket of water. I'll show you where to go. There's a spring.
She went to the door and directed Lynn down the little path that went towards the river.
--It's in on your right there. You'll see a tub with some clothes in it on the rocks and it's just after that. But have a look in the barrel at the back of the van first.. There might be enough rain water. It's funny, I stayed in town last night and I've no idea if it rained or not. Here you can't miss it with the noise of it drumming on the roof. She turned and grabbed Mikey by the heels, just stopping him from grabbing one of Seamus's collection of bones that adorned a low table. Mikey, who had been struggling for several minutes to reach his prize, howled with fury.
--Poor fella, Nuala told him, kissing his fair topknot that looked just like the one on his
father's head -the rest was definitely thinning -It's not fair on you is it. We'll get rid of these old things now.
She found a pot and with Mikey balanced on one hip and still flailing angrily, managed with difficulty to scoop up the bones. She went outside and threw them as far as she could. A couple of dogs appeared, had a disgusted sniff at the meatless relics and slunk away again. Then she noticed that her dress had a big wet patch on it and Mikey's dungarees were soaked..
--Jesus....not again...

Lynn arrived back with the water.
--Thanks Lynn. Could you put a couple more small bits in the stove? The kettle's nearly boiling. I need to change Mikey.
--Shall I make the tea? For Lynn, the day had been an unpleasant reminder of all the work a baby entailed. At least Mikey hadn't been sick-posseted as the books sweetly called the stinking stuff - he was probably past that stage now, but all that dribble and goo...and though he wasn't yet crawling he was such an adept squirmer that you needed to be constantly vigilant to stop him poisoning, drowning or decapitating himself. The way Seamus had this caravan organised, you'd think he'd designed it specially to aid the little fellow's suicide.

Nuala cleaned Mikey with baby lotion and cotton wool and dressed him in the last set of clothes Maeve had given her. At least there was a line of clean dry nappies hanging above the stove. She threw the wet one

out of the window into an enamel bucket that stood on a table outside.. When it was full, she would rinse the nappies in the river, bring them back to boil on the stove and then have to rinse them again. She usually managed to do this while Mikey was asleep . Otherwise, it was hell, trying to get down the uneven path, clambering about with a bucket of shitty nappies and a baby. If she put Mikey down, she worried he would roll into the water. And he tried to stuff his mouth with soil and dock leaves.
Carrying water up in a bucket wasn't much good, you needed so much to wash and rinse stuff, and usually she was encumbered with Mikey's pee soaked and milk be-slimed clothes as well as Seamus's things. Jesus,she wished Seamus would leave off wearing the wellingtons; his socks were rotting, the wool was like a solid fecking cheese...

The new pushchair was standing outside. Mikey had already christened it. While they were waiting by the monument for the taxi he'd unleashed a flood that the nylon seat was no match for. She had to wash it,along with her shoes, thrown off under the caravan, and get it inside before the new neighbours saw it and tried to haggle for it.

Nuala fed Mikey a couple of rusks. She had turned her back on Lynn while she massaged out some of her own milk to moisten them. Now she was sitting with him on her lap.
--You look after Mikey very well, said Lynn, drinking her tea and watching as he sucked happily at Nuala's breast.
--Do you think so? Nuala was pleased. It's hard living here. I have to think all the time of keeping enough clothes and nappies washed. Some of those English people, no offence Lynn, but that crowd in the forestry, they're awful. I was up there with Seamus not long ago and there were little kids with snot crusted on their faces and bare backsides blue with cold...they just leave them to wander around like that.
--That's terrible.
--That crowd are the worst. Most of the Blow -ins are very decent, like yourselves. You just have to keep away from the bad ones. Here, have another piece of brack. Could you pour me a bit more tea?
--Does anyone official keep an eye on those kids?
--I don't think so. The nurse calls out here to see Mikey sometimes because he was born in the hospital and he's registered at the clinic and all that. She says he's in great health and well cared for. But most of the ignorant shites round here wouldn't bother looking, they've got it in their heads that there's only one way to do things. Seamus tries to lecture them and that annoys them. And they think anyone living in a caravan is

no better than the tinkers. The tinkers are all different, from what I've seen. They're rough with their kids but they've usually got so many...The old woman out there lines the girls up every now and then and does their hair. And she tells them stories. That crowd in the forestry are just off their heads all the time. I think that's worse.

Mikey, after a -for him- fairly modest seize of Nual'as second nipple, was falling asleep. The whole room seemed to be sighing in relief.
--He'll probably be up half the night now, said Nuala in a tone of resigned exhaustion, it's a bit late in the day for him to have a nap.
Lynn had been savouring the peace but now felt a bit guilty.
--Ah well, it'll give me a chance to do a bit more washing. That's one good thing about Seamus's fires -I can always get stuff dried quickly. Oh, feck it! Didn't I forget to ask Tommy to stop and let me pick up that bag of clothes I left behind the wall up near Conlon's this morning...
--Oh dear.... I was like that after having Maggie. I forgot everything, I was blitzed for at least a year, Lynn remembered. How is Seamus's mother? I heard she was ill.
--She's back in hospital, that's how I could have a bed last night. Maeve doesn't think she'll
last that much longer. At least she's had a few good years living with her and Joe.
--Sorry to hear that....Are you Irish or English Nuala?I can't tell.
--Irish- my family name is Malone- but I grew up in England. My parents moved there when I was a baby. I always felt Irish . We used to come on holiday here and stay with my Granny near Cork and I loved it. I remember I went off for a bike ride one day and there was a beautiful girl sitting on a bridge with her little brother and she was singing. If you did that in England people would just think you were mad. And all the music here -magic. Every time I went home the people seemed more boring and robotic. She pushed her breast back into her dress. My Granny died but I used to have a holiday job over here with my Aunt. She has a big house and she lets some rooms. I helped there, and with the kids.
--Was that where you met Seamus?
--No......There was a silence. Nuala stood up. I'll get you the money for the pushchair.
--There's no hurry-
--Well I have it here, sure. I knew the old one was on its last legs so I've been putting a bit of money away whenever I could. Wait a minute.
While she was opening a drawer at the back of the caravan next to the basket where Mikey now slept angelically, a racket started up outside. Through the back window they saw two of the big tinker lads hurtling

down the bohreen, driving the big cob in the sidecar as if they were starring in Spartacus. They were drunk, whooping and yelling and whipping the horse, who, with sparks flying from his hooves, was in a frenzy. He had endured this treatment all the way from Moroney's Bar down near the Limerick road and he was no longer capable of thought or judgement. Somehow, no one got run down. The two smallest children, who seemed to stand around all day clutching grubby chunks of bread and jam, stared in silence, while their mothers ran out and screamed after the car, which had rattled on up the bohreen without slowing at all.

Suddenly, Seamus appeared in the doorway.
--Jesus, that lot are goin' to kill somebody In fact, Mary, that's the red haired wan, wasn't she tellin' me that they already ran over the old fella a couple o' years ago- that's why he has that arm all twisted and useless. He looked around and took in Lynn, turning back from her viewpoint at the window. Hello Lynn, Howye. Are ye all okay here?
--We are, replied Nuala, except- Seamus, I need a word with you.
--Let's have a cup o' tay first for the love o' God! Seamus looked suddenly work-worn and pathetic.
--I need a word with you NOW.
--Well, I must be going, said Lynn, sensing tension. My sister's coming over at the weekend and I need to sort out a bed and things.
-Well, bring her in to the session at Geigan's on Saturday, Seamus told her. Tis the best for miles around. We could all go in your van. Tell Bill I'll help him with sometin' in return.
---I don't know when we're getting the van back.. And someone will have to stay at home with Maggie. It sounds great though. We'll let you know.
--If you haven't it back, persisted Seamus, we'll all go in on the donkey and car. Twould be gas. Full moon and all.
--Seamus, Nuala interrupted from behind him. She sounded very angry. Lynn hoped she didn't think she was flirting with Seamus. It was so hard to know how much to talk to or look at other people's men . From what she'd noticed, Seamus was an awful letch. The other day, while they were in Christy's van, he had winked at her. Bill had spotted that but not the squeeze he suddenly and sneakily gave her as she passed by to avoid the bucket of guts....She didn't want to do anything to encourage him.
--Well, I must go. Bye Nuala. And we'll let you know about the session, Seamus.

Nuala's wrath couldn't wait. Before Lynn was out of earshot she heard a very loud yell, which she was stunned to realise came from someone so soft voiced and mild.
--SEAMUS! WHERE'S THAT FUCKING MONEY I HAD HIDDEN IN THE RED SOCK? Now she definitely sounded as if she came from Greater London. Funny how Feck always sounded so much nicer than Fuck thought Lynn.

Chapter Five

On the way up the bohreen, Lynn met three dirty little girls, dragging a bin bag between them. It was full of holes and clothes were spilling out of it.
--Er....Hello girls, she said warily.
--Hey, Missus! Look what we're after finding behind a wall. Grand clothes for our babba and all!
--Oh dear... I think those might belong to Nuala in the caravan there.
--They do not !answered the biggest one defiantly, they were above in a field! Mam! Look what we're after findin'!
The dark haired woman came out of her bender.
--Hello Missus, Howye, will ye come in for an old cup o' tay now? She ignored her daughter's clamouring. Come on in now, Missus. Bernie, will ye shut up out o' that,now!
Lynn didn't want any more tea. She wanted to go home. But she didn't feel able to say so.
--But,Mam, we're after finding some grand clothes and That One says-
---Will ye hold yer whisht for the love o' God - The mother aimed a clout at the girl's ear but she dodged it skilfully and retired sulkily to a corner of the bender.
---Tis a grand day now, Missus said the woman to Lynn, who had just perched herself on a milk crate.
The stove, made of a half barrel with a door cut in the front, was chugging away and the woman, who was called Mary, put the metal teapot on it and sat down on an old car seat. She sent the girls to fetch more water.
--And then go on away and don't be crowdin' in here! They drive me mad, she said to Lynn, hangin' around as if there was no space outside...
But they were soon back, staring at Lynn and sidling up to her.
--She has lovely hair doesn't she, Mam, said the middle one admiringly.
--Will ye lave the woman alone! I'll not tell ye again.
--t's all right, said Lynn. What are your names?
They all spoke at once.
--I'm Bernie!
--I'm Winnie and that's me sister Bernie
-- I'm Maria and these are-
And then a row broke out.
--Will ye shut up, you, I'm tellin' her- ---Well I was tellin' her first- ----I'M tellin' her, I'm the eldest- until their mother aimed another clout.

--Winnie is the eldest, she's going on thirteen. This is Bernie and this one's a first cousin belonging to me brother's missus over there in the other bender. They've a crowd o' kids. They have the wagon as well, some of 'em sleep in there.
--The wagon is really beautiful. Is it very old?
--It is Ma'am, it is. Me Mammy and Daddy are gettin' very ould as well but they've travelled all their lives and they won't leave the road.
--What about the big boys, are they yours as well?
--Two of 'em are. Paddy's me eldest, then I had Johnny but he died God rest his soul. The other fella you seen out there is Joseph. Then there's a son of me brother, and a lad who's stoppin' with us a while, belongin' to me sister's family on the big site down outside Limerick.. He's good with the hosses. Me sister and her husband left the road on account of him hurtin' his back bad. He hasn't the strength in him any more.
Mary was spooning condensed milk, tea and a pile of sugar into her pot. She handed Lynn a mug of the brew. The girls got theirs in jam jars. They had wisely decided not to bother Mary about the bag of clothes for the time being and were looking through the other spoils of the day. Someone had given Bernie a medal and she was quizzing little Maria.
--Who's this?
--Our Lady Queen o' Heaven, answered Maria dutifully.
The RE lesson over, Winnie opened a carrier bag and quietly brought over bread and a packet of tea. As her mother seemed to be keeping her fists to herself, she ventured to speak.
-- A woman in the big house gev them to us. She said Come back tomorrow and she'd give us a bit o' bacon.
--We got these in a barn, put in little Maria proudly as soon as there was a pause, opening a woolly hat. Lookit, nice eggs!
They looked suspiciously like the ones laid by Lynn's marrans.
--Give 'em here before you go breakin' the lot, said Mary.
 The sugary tea and the smell in the bender were making Lynn feel sick again ; the straw on the floor had a sickly reek of dog, even though the one that had dared to try and come in had gone back out of the door at a rate of knots with a boot up its behind. And she was worried about Maggie. What if Bill hadn't got home in time to meet her....what if that weird old man-
--Thanks for the tea, she managed to say firmly, I've got to go now. She pulled her wrist away from Winnie who was examining her watch closely.
--Can ye tell the time, Missis?
--Yes.
--Can ye teach me?
--Maybe another day.

Outside, she took a grateful gulp of air. Clattering hooves were coming down the bohreen.

--It's that feckin' Joseph again tryin' to kill us all! shrieked Mary from behind her, I'll have Johnny tan his arse tonight, so I will! Isn't he already after nearly killin' the ould fella-that's why he has that arm all crookit. Joseph ran right over him and broke it ! Me brother and his Missus over there have a young fella that's not the full shillin' – he has them worried to death, they nearly left him in to the nuns a couple of times – well, he wouldn't know to get out of the way, sure he wouldn't. It's a wonder he's not killed long since. Tis Joseph is the worst. Paddy was always quiet, but Joseph and that fella of me sister's, when them two get together they're pure mad!

Here she took a swipe at a toddler she had pushed into the bender for safety.

--Get back in there, you!

She erupted into full decibel screeching as Joseph hurtled by again. He was astride the horse bareback and it was wearing only a head collar. Lynn followed, keeping close to the wall and eyeing up places where she might scramble over. Winnie appeared at her side.

--Me cousin's gettin' married soon. You know, the one with the blonde hair.

--Oh, is she? Lynn had noticed her. The older women usually wore tight jumpers, cardigans, tartan skirts and little pointy wellingtons. Their hair was long and lank, tied back. The
younger women often had layered haircuts of the type favoured by skinhead girls in the early seventies. This girl had bleached hers a bright yellow colour as well. She had a selection of short skirts and holey fishnet tights. She wore an old suede coat and the floppy leather boots were always on her feet. She had an insolent sort of style.

--Who is she marrying?

--A second cousin on me Aunty's side. He's UGLY!

--Oh....I don't expect – what's your cousin's name?-I don't expect she thinks so, does she?

--Eileen. She can't stand him! But she'll have lots o' babbas soon, she added in a satisfied tone.

--Oh...Yes, I suppose she will, concluded Lynn. How old is Eileen?

--Sixteen I think...Mam knows when MY birthday is, she had me in the hospital and she got a certificate and all! Joseph and them were born on the road but that last babba in there -the one that was asleep in the wee box - he was born in the hospital too. Me Mam was in town to do a bit o' beggin' and the weather got bad, there was a big flood on the road and

she couldn't get back to where we were camped, so they brought her in to the hospital. She said it was lovely for a coupla days but then it had her driven mad, stuck inside, so she walked out of it.
God. Whilst expecting Maggie, Lynn had been influenced by a book called Spiritual Midwifery. It was full of pictures of hairy commune members busy populating the world, managing to grin exultantly as they did it, thereby propagating the unfortunate myth that labour wasn't painful. It said that contractions were better considered as Rushes of Energy. When her labour began in earnest, Lynn knew they could only be honestly described as Bloody Agony. She wouldn't want to got through it without gas and air...and what did Mary and her relations do about all that liquid that gushed out of you, and what about -
She could hardly ask young Winnie, though she suspected she might know a fair bit about it.
They were near the road now.
--Eileen doesn't want to get married, chattered Winnie. Me Da arranged it. Before she Gets Herself In Trouble, she added importantly. Your man Willie will keep her in order. When she's gone I'm sleepin' in her bed. She's a bed in the wagon with the ould wans to keep the boys aff her.
She suddenly took off into the bushes.
--There's an ould ass through here! she called back, Me sister's are after havin'a ride on him. Don't tell the fella below, will ye?
The fella below? That was Seamus. So he had the donkey back again. Yes, he'd mentioned going to the session with it hadn't he....Why was it hidden away down here? Perhaps there was a bit of a field through there....She called Goodbye to Winnie, feeling relieved that the brazen girl wasn't going to follow her any further. But also sorry. The poor kid would have been so happy if her mother had just once managed show some interest in her.

She headed out onto the road. Evening was coming on. Suddenly she heard a loud and echoing howl. She looked up to the ridge that ran behind the Ryan's place. For a second, she thought she saw a figure, tiny in the distance, stooped and running, before it disappeared over the skyline. She hurried on towards the comforting presence of Bill and Maggie.

Nuala was worn out with screaming at Seamus about how she couldn't keep anything safe from him.-
---Arrah, he smiled innocently, we needed shoppin'. I got bread and eggs-

--Eggs? We've loads of them ,in the press there!
--They got used. Seamus hurried on before she could ask how. And I got sausages. Ye like an old sausage for breakfast don't ye. And I was out o' tobacco.
--Now we have it! cried Nuala bitterly. Twas the tobacco you went for. And a few pints.
Seamus didn't deny this.
--Well, I met Patsy Holloran for the first time in ages. I got briquettes as well. He didn't seem to notice that Nuala was less and less impressed at each purchase as he hopefully listed it.
--Jesus! she exploded, What do we want briquettes for and it hotter than hell in here
already?
--I heard it's goin' cold again. If ye'll just let me tell ye – Patsy has a coupla fields he wants
stones picked off, and there's two or three days work for myself and Christy. Ye'll have the money back in a day or two. I got the briquettes on account of I won't be here to cut wood.
Defeated, Nuala subsided onto a cushion beside the stove. Seamus always turned out to owe every bit of money they got to some shop or other. If there was any change, it would go in his own pocket. It was probable that, for one reason or another, the stone- picking money would be gone before it ever got home. She suspected that he'd long since spent Lynn's goat money, but it wasn't worth probing, she'd never get a straight answer. She knew he'd given someone a fine breakfast with all those eggs and now he'd milk them for favours in return.

Seamus was good at looking Humble on these occasions, and Worried. And he always had some Offering to show that he cared that she was warm (God help her,cooked was a better word for it) and well fed. And a promise that Times Were Going To Change in the form of a day's work, or the sale of a dog.
She started wanting to kill him again when he began enthusing about the session. With Mikey, she didn't stand a chance of going to it. Seamus didn't know a jig from a reel , but he could sing passably. He'd be dealing blow, talking and laughing. She sighed loudly and glared at him. The sly, smug bastard. She'd so wanted to tell Lynn how she'd ended up here. But she was far too ashamed. She would go on living the lie. Seamus didn't notice. He was tending his blaze. Defeated, she went outside to grapple with more washing before it got completely dark..

The Grove of the Flowers, or the Heavenly Valley, as it was mockingly known in some Blow-in households, looked more beautiful than ever with the full moon just rising over it. But the thoughts of two of its habitants had remained untouched by either the balmy afternoon or its ethereal Spring beauty.

Chapter Six

Old Mattie Keane was shutting up his hens. There were only two left but that was plenty enough eggs for him and Jimmy. Jimmy liked an old egg, and he deserved it, wasn't he the best friend in the world.
--Arrah, Jimmy, shall we take a little walk so? Tis a lovely evenin'. He took his stick off the mesh where he had hung it and went slowly across the uneven yard, past a fallen gate and out into a little sloping haggard. Jimmy hobbled dutifully after him. The moon was already making the solitary ash tree on the slope cast a blue shadow on the long silvered grass.
Up there, in a cluster of rocks, was the remains of his poteen still.
--Ah, Jimmy, them were the days...Do ye remember all the people that used to come? Sure ye do! Or was it Norrie I had them times? Twas the best in the county and put through the worm twice...
They reached the big old ash and Mattie lowered himself down against it. His knees creaked.
--Ye'll have to pull me up out o' this in a while, Jimmy! Wait'll I see now...I have a wee drop in my pocket. He took out a hip flask and put it to his lips. I've me pipe here and all...which pocket did I put it in now....
Jimmy sat down, put this grizzled old muzzle on Matty's leg and gently moved his tail. It was a bit difficult because it was encrusted with ancient burrs.

A little evening breeze was stirring the grass. A ripple was running up the hillside. There they went . Rolling and bowling and capering with joy. Mattie gazed over towards a big flat stone just below the old still. A flash of a tantalising eye, an impression of quantities of hair and a billowing dress; the young ones were making merry in the tiny dell at the roots of the blackthorn. Music and laughter tickled at the edge of his conscience then ran gleefully away again. He gazed at the base of the tree and saw only bark, soil and moss.

There used to be so much music and laughter. Where did they all go, all the neighbours who told stories, sang and danced? Some came just to buy a drop o' poteen but most were good friends too.
A lot went off to America....He remembered an old song.

Oh come all you young people of Erin's green isle
Pray stand attention and listen awhile

Your sons and fair daughters are going away
In thousands they're sailing for Americay...

Oh their friends they all gather and the neighbours also
The trunks they are packed up and waiting to go
And it's there in the morning the tears fall like rain
As the horses are leaving going down to the train....

He hadn't heard it in a long while. He would sing it to Jimmy if he had enough breath. He remembered the people going off on the train from Limerick...
Then a voice said, Tis a grand clear night, now.
 Mattie made out a little lumpy old fella made out of bark..
--Ah tis,tis, agreed others sagely.
 They were sitting on the big stone.
--Twould be even better if we had our fort to go back to, said another voice. This one had a skin so like granite that you couldn't be sure it wasn't rock you were looking at until he spoke.
The voices came like little whispers on the wind. The faces came and went.
--Arrah, that's long done now, and aren't ye well enough livin' where ye are, said Mattie, but they didn't notice him. Maybe he hadn't actually said it out loud. He got muddled between his thoughts and talk. He took a draw of his pipe..
A green-veined shadow, like a slightly tired oak leaf towards the end of summer suddenly spoke.
-- There's different people there now. When that wan has her babba we should give her a changeling!
--Begod, no, said a warty one with toad coloured skin, We gev that up years ago.
--Why? asked a younger fella who had so much energy he couldn't sit but had to keep capering about like a cricket
--Stop makin' me dizzy and I'll tell ye! said Tree Bark grumpily.

Mattie remembered his aunt whispering to his mother about a family that had a changeling.
Him and the other garsoons had seen him sometimes, a little stick of a fella, all hunched up. They had fun spitting at him then, but he hardly came out. He never went to school, or Mass. Mattie wondered what had become of him. He probably died young like most changelings did.

The cricket one managed to fold his long spindly limbs into a sitting

position.
--Twas the women! said Tree Bark.
--Ah, twas, twas, agreed Granite sagely. Ah, the fun we had those times though..
--Twas a lot o' work for' em, lumping those big human babbas around, continued Tree Bark. Twas grand fun leavin' some old sthreel of a woman with a sickly fairy babba ye'd only put out for the crows, but o' course, our women got lumbered with one o' them big bawlin' helpless things in exchange! What would the women be wanting with that? It took a power o' magic movin' em about and they caterwaulin' blue murder all the time!

The Cricket was hopping about again.
I used to jump like that, thought Mattie. I was the best dancer in the county. Won prizes at the Fleadh. And me sisters....The brother played the fiddle, and we took the old door off its hinges so they could dance on it.
That little gerrel that was living above reminded him of his favourite sister with her big grey eyes, shining hair and glowing cheeks. Sometimes in the mornings, when his legs let him, he made his way down to the cross by the big road, just to see some people go by. Even a salute from a passing car was good. Now he looked out for Maggie. It was grand to have a wee chat with her before she got on the bus. He hoped she'd be able to stop long enough one day for him to tell her a story.
 There was another little gerrel he'd told stories to....that was it, she was his own little darlin', Maura....and her Mammy, his lovely wife, sittin' there in the bed in the cottage below on the day she was born with her eyes all big and shiny....

The grasshopper one capered.
--Will someone give that fella somethin' to do! complained Granite.
--Send him to search for Biddy Early's bottle! said the Toad meanly.
--Let him go over to Mattie's still and see if our cup is full yet, suggested Granite. Go with him, you, and see he doesn't spill it all on the way back..

The moon was high over the haggard now. The silver light was bright but the fairies seemed to be gone. That was the way of it. Mattie was cold. Jimmy looked up gratefully as he began to get up, bracing himself against the ash for support.
 Jimmy was thinking about his bed by the range. Maybe Mattie would forget again and feed him two dinners.

Chapter Seven

Willie Kildare, known locally as The Doc, was ferociously hurling boulders in all directions, as, soaked in sweat and cursing to the heavens, he finished demolishing his neighbour Con Henchy's attempt at a boundary wall. One of Con's sons had turned up to watch from a safe distance.
--Me Da has a map to show that our land ends there, he called tentatively.
--It does in the feck! yelled Willie, slinging a rock towards the lad, who turned and scarpered. Willie distinctly remembered the Witch Hegarty pointing with her stick THIS side of that big rock – and that made at least five feet of difference in his favour. Con's wife appeared below.
--Con'll have the guards on ye when he gets back! she shouted.
Willie paused. His thick black hair was plastered to his skull. He fixed her with his crazy, oversized blue eyes.
--Will ye look at the mad head o' that, muttered Con's son.
--Guards is it! Willy shook his head like a rabid dog, showering droplets of sweat around him. Mind yerself now, Missus! He heaved a mighty rock in her direction.
She stepped back a few paces but dammit if she wasn't opening her mouth to start yapping again. Willie let out an enraged howl, the kind that bemused and alarmed neighbours sometimes heard echoing round the townland below. The young fella, terror stricken, dragged his mother away. Willie threw a few rocks after them for good measure.

At the entrance to the bohreen, Seamus was loading people onto the donkey and car with the air of someone organising a charabanc outing to Blackpool in the 1920's.
Lynn was staying at home with Maggie. She was also, not without trepidation, babysitting Mikey. She wasn't getting sick in the mornings: for some reason got sicker and sicker as the afternoon progressed. It reached a peak around tea time when she got snotty as well as really nauseous. Cathy had been great, spending time with Maggie so she could lie down through the worst of it. But she felt far too tired and disgusting to go out..
Maggie was fussing over Meehaul, the donkey, who, in his harness cobbled together with string and old socks, looked decidedly unenthusiastic about the coming expedition and was

refusing her proffered carrot. Coming to see Meehaul set off was the bribe to aid Maggie's fairly civilised acceptance of not being able to go on this occasion.

Bill was looking intently at the donkey and trying to decide if it was the same beast he and Maggie had seen tied in the bushes last week.. He was nearly sure it was, but Seamus had told him he had lent the donkey to someone else and only now got it back. again. He couldn't make it out.

--Hold tight now, ordered Seamus. He goes a bit fast to begin with- Meehaul set off at a gallop. Bill and Cathy clutched the sides of the rattling car. Seamus sat up, swinging his legs over the side with an exaggerated air of casualness that Bill found irritating.

--Grand evenin' now, he called to two men behind a wall. They stared after the car.

--That's the quare fella of the Lynch's. Goin' into the taxi businesslike his cousin!

They both held their sides laughing.

It wasn't long before Meehaul's pace slowed to a wobbly trot. And then a dolly step that got slower, and slower.....and yet slower. His sad-looking nose was almost scraping the ground.

--Jesus, said Nuala, We'd be better off crawling! I'm getting down for a walk.

Cathy was still enjoying the novelty of it all and the pure, peaceful evening. It was her first time in Ireland.

Bill was beginning to feel a prat. Although Seamus seemed to think he was attracting the admiration of passers-by, several people in passing cars had laughed and were obviously making rude comments. Bill was glad there was hardly any traffic and they were turning now to go over the Old Road. Soon he was stiff and chilly and got down to walk beside Nuala, though he sensed that Seamus didn't like it.

--I haven't seen Christy lately. How's his carpentry going?

--It isn't. Actually, he's gone away for a bit. He's after getting the young one of the Quinlans pregnant and her family aren't very pleased about it. She's been sent off to stay with some relations across the water and the baby will probably be adopted. Christy needs to keep out of the way of her brothers for a while. But he's gone off and left a crowd of dogs and Meehaul behind him.

--Oh...so its Christy's donkey?

--It is of course. Oh, I see- Nuala looked behind her. Meehaul and his passengers were a long way back. Seamus was entertaining Cathy with

some story.
-- Seamus likes to pretend Meehaul is his,she confided. He couldn't let you have the loan of him while Christy was around or he would have had to let on who really owns him. And I don't think Christy finished paying for him. That's why he's been hiding him, in case the owner came back for him.
Seamus, sensing that he was being talked about, called out crossly.
--Will ye come up out o' that now
They both jumped guiltily. They waited until Meehaul drew alongside.
--Surely he'll walk faster if we stay off the cart? said Bill. Privately he thought that nothing but a snail could move more slowly than Meehaul. And he was harbouring savage fantasies about the creature, wherein a grenade exploded extremely close to its stupid woolly arse and taught it the meaning of movement.
--Arrah, come on up here will ye, insisted Seamus, tis miles yet to Geigan's and a good few hills in it. Ye can't walk all that way. Pick a big stick there, Nuala,and we'll see will he go a bit faster.
Nuala picked a big stick and Seamus laid into Meehaul with it. Meehaul sighed the sigh of the downtrodden and continued at his pointless, meandering pace. After another twenty minutes, during which there had been little progress made and no-one had dared say anything, Arrah, feck it! cried Seamus,suddenly relinquishing all ambition of being a representative of Real Ireland, We'll have to hitch.

The moon had risen. The night had grown extremely chilly. They all got down, Cathy nearly collapsing because her legs were so numb. Seamus tied Meehaul to a bush in an overgrown drive leading to a ruined cottage. He tilted up the sidecar a bit further on and they stuffed the harness underneath.
 --Let Cathy and myself go ahead,said Nuala, Four of us together will never get a lift. There's hardly a car along here anyway- maybe we should just-
--Ye will not! said Seamus quickly, I 'll get us all a lift, now will ye shut up out o' that.
A loud howl suddenly echoed from somewhere above them where the crag gave way to bare mountain.
--What the hell was that? asked Cathy nervously, moving closer to Bill.

--Don't mind that, now, Seamus told her, Tis only the Doc Kildare rampagin' around a bit. Let's keep walkin' til a car comes, we'll keep warmer that way-
--What do you mean? demanded Bill.

Seamus laughed. His good humour was restored now he had a chance to resume his role of Local Guide, imparting inside information, rather than being made an eejit of by that feckin' donkey. No wonder Christy had left him behind.
--Willie Kildare, he explained. From the valley above. He goes mad on the full moon.
--He's not exactly sane the rest of the time, remarked Nuala.
Cathy had a grip on Bill's arm. How do you mean – mad? she asked.
--Arrah...howlin' and the like, Seamus told her casually. They call him the Doc on account of his name being Kildare but also he's always makin' strange potions and eatin' weird tings. Jesus, the last time I saw him he was after eatin' a worm out of a can! He offered me one but I told him I was just after a big feed o' spuds.
--There's some dispute over the land up there- began Nuala but Seamus interrupted her.
--He and his neighbour, Con Henchy -he lives at the other end o' the valley, d'ye see – they hate each other. All they think about is getting' revenge for the last bad thing the other one did. Con has a wife and kids. She's driven mad by it all, she can't stand all the carry on. She's always threatening to leave.
--Is Con mad too? Cathy was feeling a bit braver. Bill felt big and solid beside her and it had been quiet for ten minutes.
--He has a desperate temper. If he ignored the Doc altogether, things would quieten down...but he always does somethin' in return. Tis a weird old place, that valley. If people weren't strange to begin with, twould make them that way.
Suddenly Seamus stopped. Here's a car! he announced. The others began to move to the side of the tiny road but Seamus held onto Nuala and boldly took up position in the centre .A red mini came into view, and, confronted by Seamus, was forced to halt. He opened the passenger door.
Hello, Howye, Grand Evenin'. Ah,Katie ,is it yourself, how are ye?
Hello, Seamus, are ye well. Are you living out here now? I heard you were out the country somewhere.
--I am, I am, smiled Seamus (like a wolf, thought Bill in disgust) Sure, it's Katie Whelan, he informed the others. Listen Katie,ye wouldn't do us a favour – could ye give us a lift to the session at Geigan's. These are my neighbours and ye know Nuala-
--Arrah, now Seamus, that's right out of my way and I'm late already- I don't think I've enough petrol to go all the way out there either.
Bill suddenly noticed that the lady in the car was crippled. There was a stick leaning on the passenger seat and she sat in an odd twisted

position. He knew he shouldn't assume that this affected her ability to deal with life's problems (Seamus being one of them) and here she was very capably driving her car. Nevertheless, he felt embarrassed in the face of Seamus's unrelenting harassment.
--Seamus, we can wait for another lift.
Seamus ignored him.
-- Where are ye going Katie? Hennessy's, oh is it Larry's birthday. Well sure, no one will be there this early! Geigan's is only a couple o' miles out the other way-
At this point, they heard frantic crashing in the dark crag behind them, the bushes parted and a dishevelled figure blundered out onto the road. Jesus! cried Seamus, Tis The Doc!

Civilities were forgotten in the rush to get inside the car. The unfortunate Katie suddenly found herself chauffering a chaotic heap of passengers. Nuala and Cathy were clinging together in fright and screaming at her to drive on. Bill managed to close the door as they took off to the accompaniment of one of the Doc's howls.
--Er, sorry about that, Katie, ventured Nuala after a safe distance had been put between themselves and The Doc, Only your man back there is dangerous. You could leave us off at the next cross.
--Will ye go away out o' that now, Nuala, said Se amus immediately. Katie, ye'll drive us up to Geigan's won't ye, tis only a little step out o' your way.
--But Seamus, I haven't enough petrol. And I don't want to be late. This is a formal sort of party.
--Sure, we'll buy ye some petrol on the way. It's left up here now, this way's a short cut, said Seamus, helpfully turning the wheel for her.
Bill had long ago lost interest in the idea of the session. He was wondering how he could get back to Lynn and Maggie. What if that nutter back there -

Katie Whelan left them off at Geigan's, telling Seamus she had no petrol and anyway she'd be so late now she'd be mortified to go in at all. Bill handed her a fiver. She was only slightly mollified because she didn't think there was anywhere she'd get petrol at this time of night and out here. It had been a fair old drive. Bill reckoned it would have taken about a week on the donkey and car.
--What will she do? worried Cathy.
--Someone will give her an old can of fuel, said Seamus carelessly.

Inside Geigan's, the session was raging. A fug of whiskey and cigarette fumes hit them as the door opened. The heat and noise were intense. Seamus and Bill began battling their way to the bar while Nuala and Cathy squeezed into a corner. The musicians were hidden by a crowd of laughing and shouting people. They didn't appear to be listening raptly, but when ever a set of tunes came to an end there were cries of, Good Man Yerself! Powerful, powerful playin'! Sure aren't you the great gerrel! Mighty lads, mighty altogether! And so on.
At last Bill managed to buy a round and he and Seamus struggled back with a bit of liquid still left in the glasses.
--I've to see someone, announced Seamus as soon as he'd handed Nuala her glass, and with no further explanation, made off into the crowd. Nuala looked uncomfortable. When there was a slight break in the noise, Bill managed to tell her that he was worried about Lynn and Maggie.
--They'll be okay, she began, but the rest of what she said was drowned in the cheers as the unaccompanied rendition of Shanna Golden came to an end. Cathy was trying not to cry. She'd never heard anyone sing like that before. The singer was an old man, small and wiry, and his voice was reedy. But so moving. Singing like that on your own was the bravest thing anyone could do, she thought, completely baring your heart....
The musicians launched off into more reels.
--THEY'LL BE OKAY! yelled Nuala at Bill. THE DOC IS ONLY BOTHERED WITH CON!
Bill was not convinced.
--WHY DID WE ALL JUMP INTO THE CAR THEN?
--WELL, YOU WOULDN'T WANT TO DANGLE YOURSELF UNDER HIS NOSE. BUT HE WOULDN'T GO ALL THE WAY TO YOUR PLACE - NOT UNLESS CON WAS THERE!

After a while, Nuala managed to convey to Bill and Cathy that there was another bar up the road where there were usually not only a few musicians but seats and enough space to get your drink near your mouth without getting your teeth knocked out by people squeezing past as well.

On the way up the road, an old fella passed them on a bike. In the basket on the front sat a little white terrier. The old fella was singing, and talking to the dog at the same time.
--How much is that doggy in the windy - Ah, ye're a good boy, so ye are, ye'd never catch me sellin' me little doggy, sure and ye wouldn't!

Inside Brady's, there weren't any seats after all, but there was enough space not to be spat or sweated on, or engulfed by bellies and breasts. Bill did slightly regret the last loss but wisely decided to keep the thought to himself.
They could get close to the musicians.
--The bodhran player is Vinney, said Nuala. He was in school with Seamus's brother Mossy. He's a good electrician but he hardly bothers to work. He goes to sessions all the time. He gets free drink and he says that's all he needs. The fella with the bazouki is Brendan O'Holloran. He's training to be a solicitor. Those two girls now, they're local, but studying in Dublin. Lovely players aren't they? I like the flute best of all. I prefer the music in here. That old accordion player is always up the road. I wouldn't be so keen on that.
Cathy watched Vinney and thought he was very fine. He had thick black curls and a transported expression. He was playing the bones now in a perfect snappy rhythm.
The dog man was at the bar, holding his little friend up on its hind feet and helping it to dance. He was talking and laughing animatedly to those around him. Next to him was a stout, florid-faced man, who was slumped on the counter, muttering and glowering.
--That's Finbar, said Nuala. He drinks too much.
Bill avoided Cathy's eye. That meant this man must drink trough fulls.
--He's always as cross as Norrie is happy. You'd wonder how the two of them could be friends...You're not still worrying about The Doc are you, Bill? You shouldn't. He does strange things but he's never harmed anyone but Con. He hardly notices other people.
--It's just that Lynn and Maggie are on their own, no phone....
--What did Seamus mean about the valley being a weird old place and all that? asked Cathy.
--What's that about me? asked Seamus, suddenly appearing.
--Nothing, Nuala sighed. Cathy was only asking about the valley. Will you get us some drinks?
Their glasses were empty but she didn't have any money.
--I've no money, Seamus informed her. Didn't I meet Tom O'Keefe, miserable ole fecker, and he givin' out about a tenner I had off him months ago. Jesus, wouldn't ye think the mean old shite would have forgotten about it by now, he concluded in disgust.
--Didn't you sell anything?
--No. Guard O'Rourke was in the bar.
--I don't want another drink anyway, said Cathy. I still feel as I'm on the boat. The ground keeps moving.
--Are ye sure it wasn't poteen you had in your glass there, Seamus

nudged her jovially, I've a bottle of the best back in the caravan. Matty Keane's. Come down for a drink sometime.
--Matty Keane...mused Bill. Is he the old man down near where the school bus stops?
--He is. In along the old avenue there.
--Is he- Bill didn't know how to explain his fears. He's quite safe is he?
--Well, he got caught there a few years back but now we have Guard Hennessy down in the village there's no trouble. Mattie used to give him an old bottle now and then to keep him happy. But he isn't makin the poteen any more. They say he still has a few bottles hidden away somewhere. Did ye not meet Guard Hennessy yet? Seamus seemed surprised. He's a gas man altogether! Here he suddenly left the table they had managed to move into and waylaid a passer by with affectionate greetings. He returned shortly, having procured himself a pint. Cathy got up quietly and fetched drinks for Nuala and Bill.
--Guard Hennessy has a drink problem ye see, Seamus was telling them. (Surprise, surprise thought Bill) So they put him out the country where he won't cause any trouble.
--But Mattie Keane, pursued Bill, The reason I was asking is because Maggie went into his house on her own. Is he- is he safe with little girls? Seamus threw back his head and roared with laughter.
--Arrah, he is o' course! He never hurt a fly. He reared a big family. He's just dotin' a bit since his wife died. And he does think there's a talkin' hare or somethin' about the place, but sure, what harm. A lot o' kids used to go in there one time. I had tea there with my father years ago, ye should have seen the grand spread he put out for the two of us. No, he never hurt a fly. Is it one o' them child molesters ye thought he was! That's gas! You should tell the
Ryans above- he's some relation of theirs you know.

There was a mighty crash as Finbarr suddenly crashed backwards off his stool, taking his pint with him. He lay prone, in a pool of beer. The glass rolled off his chest onto the floor, luckily unbroken.
--Will ye not stay in your seat like a christian, now, Finbarr! Don't be sleepin' down there in the draught now! cried Norrie gaily.
A tall, gaunt man with a roman nose, clad in the classic black coat and wellies, got down beside Finbarr and began to pour beer into his open mouth, to the horror of Cathy who was just returning from the toilet.
--Don't do that, he'll choke! We should put him on his side, she called anxiously to Bill. Nobody seemed a bit concerned.
--That'll wake ye up now, said Roman Nose comfortably to Finbarr, sloshing more beer at his mouth. Luckily he was too drunk to direct it

very well. The pool of porter around Finbarr grew. Spluttering and spitting beer, he sat up.

--Feck off! he growled at the onlookers, before flapping like a walrus towards the bar.

--It's too much for your old motor, Finbarr warned Brady from the other side of the bar. And amn't I always tellin' ye to sit over on the low seat by the window.

--Feck off, grunted Finbarr again to no one in particular.

--Don't mind that fella, said Seamus. He does that every week. Tis lucky he was born with no brains or they would have got knocked out of him long ago.

--It must be nearly closing time, said Bill. We should get on the road.

--I wouldn't mind, agreed Nuala. It's been great to get out but I'm beginning to feel all wrong without Mikey

--Will ye let me finish my pint for the love o' God! said Seamus. I'll tell ye why that valley is no good, he went on, leaning forward and settling himself so he had everyone's attention. That valley is cursed. The Witch Hegarty lived there and she was evil. She left a curse on it.

--I thought it was just a dispute about boundaries. Bill was irritated by Seamus's self-important manner, but intrigued despite himself.

A glass of wine arrived at their table.

--That's for Florence Nightingale over there! called Norrie.

--Arrah, no one fights about boundaries like that. Not when there's nothin' but rock there.

And they killin' each other over it. They've lost their reason because of the curse.

--Why did she curse it? Cathy wasn't sure if he was joking or not. The whole evening had been a puzzle.

--She was always cursin' people. When I was a youngfella, ye'd hear about the Witch Hegarty. Everyone was frightened of her. Ye'd have to give her what she wanted or she'd curse you. Make your animals ill or somethin'. Well, that's what the old people thought – that her curse did it-but she probably poisoned them. Anyway, bad things would happen to you. The only person who went near her was The Doc. It's years ago that she stopped travellin' around, but there was a time when she was always out the road. And no one daring to refuse her a ride to wherever she wanted to go. And she'd turn up inside houses, even when they were locked up! Can you imagine it, Jesus, coming home to find the likes of that sittin' at your table! Honest to God, now, I knew people it happened to!

Anyway,The Doc arrived from somewhere or other, and bein' a bit mad himself, he wasn't afraid of her like everyone else. He's meant to have given her twenty pound or somethin' for the bit o' land-she wouldn't know the value of money. No one knows where she went. Did The Doc murder her or did she go away out of it altogether. Or is she still wanderin' around in the night? There's been some Strange T'ings have happened....he concluded with ominous emphasis.

--But Con's just a bit hot tempered?

--Con came there after The Doc. From America. His family once lived in the valley and he had plans, from way back, to prove it. If he'd just left The Doc alone, instead of arguin' about a few feet o' land.....That's the Curse, ye see, makin' him do that.

--Ah well, Bill stood up. The worry about his family was really eating at him after this conversation and he desperately wanted to be moving homeward. They felt such a long way away and horribly vulnerable to roving lunatics and witches...he was even ready for a punch up with a soliloquising bunny. Ah well. At least the Germans at the top of the valley are fine aren't they.

---Ah God, no, said Seamus authoritatively, Let me tell ye-

But Bill was off out of the door, pulling Cathy with him.

Chapter Eight

--Twill be easy to get a lift back anyway, panted Seamus as they sprinted up the street. There were a few people getting into the cars jammed all the way along it, but it ended very shortly and suddenly there was only the flittering moon, dark crag, and the glimmering, empty road winding off to God knows where. However, Seamus seemed to have been right about getting lifts. He and Nuala soon climbed into a car full of whooping young fellas from town, and then a car slowed for Bill and Cathy. Gratefully, they climbed in.

God, it was nice to be enclosed in a warm man-made box of logical metal that would whizz them past the lurking deranged and evil spirits and see them safely at least some of the way home.

--Er-where are you going? asked Bill after a couple of silent minutes, during which it had dawned on them both that something wasn't right. He had been trying to open his window. The fumes of alcohol in the car were enough to cause spontaneous combustion. (Another of those inexplicable mysteries which were great to read about as long as there was no threat of it ever happening to yourself) He'd also noticed that their driver had some sort of postural problem which meant that he could not sit upright in his seat. There was no answer to his question.

Seamus had reminded them of the way home before they'd parted. Firstly, they had to take a left at the second cross; not many cars would go that way, they'd need to persuade the drivers to take a little step out o' their way. Bill tried again.

--We're heading for-
--Aishy, Sonny, aishy! slurred the driver.
--What? queried Cathy from the back.
--He means Easy, easy.
--Bill, Cathy leaned through the seats, whispering. He's very drunk isn't he?
--Yea, I know. Oh shit- Bill grabbed the wheel just before they hit the wall bordering the road.

The driver lurched awake and pushed Bill's hand angrily off the wheel.
--Who's dhrivin' dis car anyway, Shonny! He slurred.

They resumed their haphazard course, veering from one side to side of the road to the other. Several times more, their drink-sodden chauffeur lost consciousness and Bill had to grab the wheel.

--Will ya lave de feckin' wheel to me, whoosh dhrivin dis car anyway! he admonished again.

--You're not fit to drive it! So I'm helping. You stupid old sod! Bill replied after the third time.
--Aishy! Aishy!
--Anyway, Let us out. Here will do.
--Yes,let us out! clamoured Cathy.
--Dash not de way to Sliabh Caorigh! Ye's live around de front o' dere. Ye need de second crosh. I'm goin dat way, Shonny. As if to prove his point he accelerated. Cathy screamed.
--All right, all right, said Bill hastily. Just take it easy will you, you've had a bit too much to drink.
--Let me tell ye, Shonny...Oh shit, he was nodding off again.....I've been dhrivin' dis car....for fifty years......
That was a bloody lie, thought Bill. He was hardly likely to have had a car in 1930, and certainly not this one, even if it was a relic. He grabbed the wheel again,but this time the driver's anaesthetised foot had fallen off the accelerator. The car slowed and stalled.
--Quick, let's get out, shrieked Cathy, opening her door.
Bill looked out. He thought they must still be on the right road, but otherwise, he hadn't a clue where they were. He thought it was still a good couple of miles to the cross.
--Maybe he'll let me drive, he suggested. The driver had woken up with a jerk when the engine stalled and was now fumbling about, trying to turn the key in the ignition.
--Listen-
--Whasshat Sonny?
--Why don't you let me drive the car for you?
--Ah God no! No one ever drove dish car but meself! Will ye tell your wan to shut that feckin' door!
They were off again and now Cathy's nerves had gone entirely and she was yelling at Bill for being such a fool and not getting out alive while they had the chance, and bargaining with God about all the things she would do better if only she was allowed to survive.
They passed the cross and despite their clamourings their driver wouldn't stop. He drove on for another half mile and turned into a drive. There was a big tree down across it. Further on they could see the stumps of others that had once formed a grand avenue.
--LOOK OUT! They screamed in unison. THERE'S A TREE -
Their driver was roused from his coma enough to put some feeble pressure on the brakes and remark, Jayshus, who put dat dere, before his foot slid off the pedal. The car went forward and came to a halt with a horrible crunch.
Cathy leapt out, sobbing, We're free,we're free!

But Bill's door was dented and jammed shut. Hang on! he called. We can't just go off and leave him.
--I don't care! Cathy was uncharacteristically callous in her relief at being alive.
--Well, wait for me, whined Bill a bit desperately, I can't get out!
Reluctantly, Cathy came back. She went around to the driver's door and opened it.
--Wake up! Can you hear me! Wake up! Old pig! she added.
--He might be concussed, said Bill. He peered at the driver's face. There's no cuts or blood but he could have banged his head. I had my arms over my face but I hit the windscreen quite hard. He might have had more of a knock.
--Well he should get himself a seat belt. Come on now, WAKE UP!
Cathy renewed her efforts, pulling on his arm. Suddenly he slumped out of the car and onto the ground. Bill scrambled across behind him, alarmed. Then a familiar voice murmured, Whoosh drivin' dis car anyway....before loud snores took over.
--I don't think he's hurt. But I suppose we should tell someone, said Cathy reluctantly.
Bill got out his torch. They made their way up the drive. There was a big old house at the end, all in darkness.
--This must have been a really fine place once, Cathy peered around. Knock again, Bill, they're probably all asleep.
They were greeted by silence.
--He must live on his own. said Bill.
--There was a house back near the cross. We could call there. It's on our way.
--Okay, agreed Bill reluctantly. Immediate fears for his own life now over, his desperation to reach Lynn and Maggie had returned. He shone the torch beam on his watch.
---Jesus, its half past one. It's miles yet and there might not be any more cars ....

They stumbled back along the dark overgrown avenue. They passed the fallen tree and the crumpled car. There was a snoring body still on the ground . They reached the moonlit road and after ten minutes they cam to the house. It was in darkness but two vigilant dogs announced their presence. After a long wait, an old woman opened the door and peered out.
--Who is it? Is that yourself, Tommy? You're very late altogether!
--It's us, ventured Bill helpfully.
Cathy approached cautiously.

--Sorry to bother you. But there's been an accident. Your neighbour up the road has crashed his car into a tree.
The woman stared suspiciously but said nothing.
--Er- do you know the man we mean? tried Bill. He lives at a big house with a lot of trees on the drive.
To his frustration she continued to stare in silence. She had a nasty scrunched up face. Like an old cabbage, with the bits a round her mouth sunken in for lack of teeth. The gaze from her sluggy little eyes was a mixture of incomprehension, distrust and rude fascination. Someone appeared behind her, a young man, hoisting up his trousers.
--Who is it, Mammy? He looked out, bleary eyed from being woken but with an interested and friendly expression which his visitors registered with relief.
--Hello, said Bill. We're sorry to bother you but we had a lift with your neighbour and he's crashed his car-
--Come in, come in, invited the young man immediately, leading the way into a big kitchen.
Mammy, would ye put the kettle on there. Here, sit down there. Which neighbour would this be now?
The kitchen was warm. They sat at a huge table covered with an oilcloth on which sat the usual bread, jam and tea caddy, assorted tools, a box of castration rings for lambs and a yellowing pile of letters, bills and receipts.
--We don't know his name, explained Cathy, but he gave us a lift from Geigan's. He'd had a bit too much to drink- Here she faltered. She didn't want to sound as if she was passing judgement. However, the young man's gaze remained one of amused concern so she went on, He lives just up the road. There was a tree down on the drive that he didn't know about and he's crashed his car into it.
Their host threw back his head and laughed.
--Ah, Jaysus, that's a good one!
Bill smiled uncertainly. Cathy risked doing the same after a nervous glance at Mammy, who seemed to take no interest in the conversation but managed to exude disapproval as she stomped about. Her son went out to the bottom of the stairs and shouted.
-- Mickey! MICKEY! Will you come down out o' that! Wait'll you hear this! continuing to himself as he came back into the kitchen, Ah Jaysus, can you beat that!
Mammy put the teapot on the table, sat down and continued with her shameless staring.
Soon, another tousled son entered the kitchen.
--Evenin', he said, regarding them with preparatory mirth.

--Would you believe it, chortled his brother, These two are after getting' a lift with Bowsie Flynn! And didn't he turn up his drive and forget about that feckin' great tree he had felled this afternoon! He crashed his car into it!
While Mammy put cups of tea in front of them and sliced bread, the brothers wiped tears of mirth from their eyes.

--By Jaysus, said Mickey, when he could at last manage to speak, You're the brave people to go hitchin' lifts with your man!
Bill suddenly noticed Cathy's stricken face. She was confused and exhausted. The contrast between the handsome laughing sons who regarded everything as a huge joke, and the dour countenance of Mammy- who had sat down opposite her to add to her discomfort- only added to the loss of normality that had been building all day.
--I'm Bill Suningham. This is Cathy-
--That wan isn't your wife, said Mammy suddenly.
--No, she's my sister in law. My wife is at home-
--Is she now, Mammy nodded knowingly to herself.
--Mammy, will you stop! grinned Mickey. Here , have a slice of bread. There's the butter. There's jam there, or would you like some cheese?
 Bowsie had that tree cut down himself, explained Kevin, the first brother. He has the place above ruined, cutting down all the avenue and sellin' the wood for drink money. Well,there's not many bold enough to hitch a ride with him and that's for sure!
Mickey pushed more bread towards Cathy.
--Work away there, work away he encouraged hospitably. Pour us a drop more tay there, please Mammy.
Bill saw that he was about to roll himself another cigarette.
--We ought to be getting home now.. Perhaps he hadn't made Bowsie's condition clear enough. I don't think Bowsie - Mr Flynn, should be left lying on the ground, even if he's only drunk. Will you help us move him?
He was hoping fervently that they'd say, No need, of course they could manage by themselves.
--Arrah, no hurry! said Mickey, Aren't we always going up there and picking him up. Usually it's out of a ditch he's fallen into. We'll wait til the brother gets home - Tommy, he's been to the birthday party of a cousin of ours, Larry – and him and myself will cart Bowsie inside to his bed. Kevin here will bring you home. You'll never get a lift this time of night.
--That's really good of you-
--Sure you can't be walkin' all that way. You'd never make it
--Oh, you know where I live?
--We do o' course. How are you finding it? Tis a windy old spot round

the front of the mountain there. That's a good enough house though. Wasn't What do you call – the fella who built it - clever enough. A lot of people do up an old cottage a bit, but that place was just a pile of stones when he came there. You'd want to watch that loft with the gallery- type thing at the front though, the wood your man used on that wasn't so great...
--People talk a lot round here, said Kevin as they went out to his car. They don't mean any harm.They just like to know what's going on. Mostly, they'll always help you out too, not like in a city where you wouldn't know who's living right next door to you. The quare fella of the Lynch's is the best crack, he added. I heard he had a half dead ass in a car earlier and he drivin'a wagon load of tourists over the mountain road! They finally reached home at a quarter to four. Mercifully, Kevin said he didn't need a cup of tea and left them at the beginning of the drive. He'd re-assured Bill that The Doc had lived above in that valley for several years and never harmed anyone, and apart from the howlin' getting' a bit much at times, he wasn't any bother. He apologised for Mammy and said that was just her way and she didn't mean any harm. Cathy wasn't convinced.
--I reckon she's a sister to the Witch Hegarty, she said as they walked up the track.

Despite Kevin's re-assurances, Bill's heart nearly stopped when he saw Maggie and Lynn's bodies on the floor of their little-used sitting room. Lynn grunted angrily when he felt inside her clothes to ascertain that her heart was still beating.
--Geroff....bloody...... groper.....she mumbled. She rolled off the floor cushion she'd been propped on but remained deeply asleep. Bill wisely decided not to try and re-position her.
On her other side was a dishevelled Maggie, still fully clothed like her mother and in her sleeping bag which usually came out for summer camping and visits to friends' houses. He wondered what had been going on.
Then,to his dismay, he caught sight of a basket. A glance within confirmed his fears. That maniac of a baby, Mikey, was still here. Thanking God that he was at least asleep, Bill curled up very quietly around Lynn, gingerly pulled a tiny piece of duvet over himself, and shut his eyes.

Chapter Nine

Bill didn't get the sleep he felt he deserved. During the night he'd found himself mulling over the phrase NO PEACE FOR THE WICKED and assessing his behaviour in recent weeks. But but none of it seemed to account for the night's extreme discomforts.

Firstly, he was chilly, very chilly, with his back exposed to the draft from the door and half of him hanging off the floor cushion and lying on a bare bit of flagstone floor that the rug didn't reach. He was so tired that for a long time he couldn't make himself do anything about it, but at last he stumbled off to fetch some bedding, tucked himself up as best he could and pulled Lynn half on top of him. He had just gone off into a warm, blissful sleep when he felt himself being prodded violently. He regained consciousness with difficulty, slowly becoming aware that he was wet all down his underside. There was a ferocious row coming from Mikey who was completely sodden and eating his fists with hunger.

--I need to be sick. Lynn thrust Mikey at him and staggered off.
--I thought you only got sick in the afternoons-
Miserably, Bill felt the pee seeping through the front of his clothes as well as the back.as he tried to keep a grip on the flailing Mikey.
Lynn came back, looking wan.
--How can you just sit there! she exploded, Why didn't you take off his wet things!
--Well,I-
She took Mikey from him.
--Go and put the kettle on will you. I'll have to wash him.
The roaring didn't abate until they had got Mikey rinsed off in a basin and dressed in an old sweater of Maggie's and a towel. (At least he couldn't move much, trussed up like that, thought Bill). And then fed a couple of Weetabix and a bottle of milk.
--Isn't that a lot for a baby his age?
--Not Mikey. Nuala said that when she started him on baby rice the packet said to give two teaspoons. But Mikey polished off four tablespoons before he was satisfied.
--Do you mind if I go and change now? Bill meant it sarcastically.
--Can you collect up the clothes and nappies first, they need to go in a bucket to soak.-
Bill was going to swear at her but just then Nuala fell through the door, breathless and tearful.
--Sorry, sorry! We couldn't get back last night. Those youngfellas we had

a lift with wouldn't come out of their way off the main road to town. We had to stay the night at Maeve's. I got a lift out with the milk tanker. I'm sorry Mikey has you awake so early. Has he been okay? She took him from Lynn and pressed her face against his.

--Yes, fine, Lynn told her. Just had some breakfast....His plastic pants split so his clothes got a bit wet...

This gross understatement, with the stink of ammonia off everything enough to knock you over, was too much for Bill. He headed upstairs, threw off his pee-stained clothes, then remembered that the duvet was still downstairs. He pulled out some spare blankets and lay down under them. His skin felt vile- sticky and smelly- and he was too wound up to relax, though he desperately needed to sleep.

He heard Maggie getting up, and Cathy, who had at least got half a night's sleep, nobly asking to see her school books and My Little Ponies, and advising Lynn to go back to bed for a bit. He should be doing that, he thought. Lynn hadn't had a good night either and she had her sickness to cope with. But she'd been such a harridan in the night after he'd been so concerned for her that resentment got the better of sympathy.

Maggie told Cathy rather scornfully that she Didn't Play With My Little Ponies Any More, but could be heard rattling around in her school bag and chattering animatedly, and after a while the two of them headed off outside. Then Lynn climbed in beside him, bringing with her Maggie's nice warm, dry duvet.

They were both too stressed to sleep now but it was nice being cuddled up in their own bed.

Lynn was going to remark that they really should put the door on instead of the curtain, but thought she wouldn't risk mentioning that now. The proximity of her sister on the other side of the curtain in Maggie's room was awkward. Maggie was a very sound sleeper, but they didn't feel they could be intimate with Cathy so close.

Strange how they both wanted sex just because they knew they couldn't have it. Under normal circumstances they'd be more likely to lie in bed discussing whether it was worth trying to grow carrots again when the ground they planted them in just presented a blank Who, me? kind of face. Or whether Seamus had only been joking when he said that the cockney wan of the blow-ins- the wan with a man and two kids- was On The Game.

Lynn's mother had written, unbeknown to Cathy, to inform her that her sister was Very Depressed after a break up with her boyfriend, and she hoped they'd make her Really Welcome. She wasn't sure yet how

depressed Cathy really was, but she didn't think the sound of a couple copulating (Bill wasn't good at being quiet about it) would be therapeutic to someone who's boyfriend had just taken off with someone else.
 But they both needed the release and the re-assurance. And after a further few miraculously Maggie and Cathy free minutes, they relaxed.

This was more like a proper Sunday morning, thought Bill as he drifted off into a warm, post orgasmic sleep....
SHIT. It was Maggie, sobbing downstairs in the kitchen. Reluctantly Lynn dragged her head
off the pillow.
--Cathy will sort her out, said Bill into her neck.
--I'd better go, sighed Lynn, She sounds really upset.

Downstairs, Maggie, all blotchy and gulpy, ran to her, with a fresh outburst of crying. Cathy looked shaken too.
--We went to look at the garden, and there was a dog by the wall. It was whining, and foaming at the mouth, and then it fell over, having a real fit. I didn't know what to do-I was going to send Maggie to wake you up and run up to the Ryan's -but then it gave a howl and sort of stretched out...and died.
--How awful. Are you sure it's dead?Not just unconscious?
--Yes. It's eyes went blank and it stopped breathing. I checked that.
Cathy came over to Maggie and rubbed her back. Her face was still buried in Lynn's lap.
--At least the poor dog isn't in pain now, she said.
--Come on, said Lynn gently, trying to prise Maggie off, let's wash your face shall we. Here's Daddy.
Bill was normally good at being comforting fort he right length of time and then finding a suitable diversion. However, today he felt too jaded to do either. He braced himself as Maggie headed towards him with a fresh outburst of tears and heartbroken explanations of what had happened, headbutting him in the belly as she sought solace. He gritted his teeth. Lynn decided they all needed breakfast.
--We'll bury the dog afterwards, she said firmly.
Eventually, Maggie emerged from Bill's bruised stomach and decided that she could eat eggs on toast despite her state of mourning. Then she went off with Cathy to pick flowers for the lovely grave they would make.
--Which leaves me to dig the hole I suppose, said Bill mournfully to Lynn's back. She was washing up. I don't suppose the owner would be around to do it? What did it look like, do you know?
--I went and had a look it when I went out to the toilet. A border collie

type, hardly any white on it though. Small and foxy looking. It looked like poisoning to me, she added matter of factly.

She was a strange lady, reflected Bill, not for the first time. Often very practical about events that other people became emotional about. You'd think she could handle anything.

But then she could be so sensitive, weighing up every chance remark and giving it far too much importance, concluding, usually quite wrongly, that other people's thoughts were derogatory....

There'd been an incident last summer. They'd been in a bar where people were dancing, and one funny Oldfella had been pulling up various women to dance. They were all such neat movers, and they knew all the sets by heart. It made the so-called ceilidhs they enjoyed at home look pathetic-just a bunch of guffawing eejits ,occasionally managing to skip like rhinos for a couple of bars before they took a wrong turning and collided with someone else...

But now Lynn was self-consciously explaining, red with embarrassment, that she couldn't do that dancing. She made the mistake of saying she was English. She would have liked to go on to say that would love to learn, wasn't there a regular class held through the winter- but the oldfella had stuck his chin in the air and turned away.

A minute later she heard him complaining to his friend.

--Young gerrel there- he cocked his thumb in her direction and she was too miserable to be flattered at the mistake over her age- Young gerrel there, he continued loudly, and in a tone of disgust, Says she's too grand to dance, she's English!

Later, Bill, who'd been happily talking to all sorts of people, realised she was missing, and eventually found her, sobbing, under a tree in an empty field. When such hurts happened, all the other slights of years came flooding into her mind, and she wanted to avoid the rest of humanity for ever more.

At the same time, there were some things she felt strongly about and then she could be dangerously outspoken.

There was a fear in the back of Bill's mind that one day she would break out, resenting him for her dependence. Meanwhile, HE kept breaking out. His anger at the role he felt was forced upon him- boring Bill, solid, reliable, unoriginal- and his dislike of this image was apt to erupt at quite minor irritation.

A few weeks ago, Seamus had persuaded them to drive him to an encampment of benders and vans where he Needed To See Someone. Bill, already fed up with what he called The Secret Squirrel Bit, was going to refuse, when Lynn appeared and said she fancied a drive.

There was a young hippy there, cutting wood. Shirtless, tanned, all rippling muscles and as long and lean as an African warrior. To Bill's annoyance, Lynn decided she was going to take a photograph. And Birdie (Birdie! For God's sake...) grinned away at her and tossed his mane of hair about.
Bill hoped he had collected the biggest nits on his travels (he had spent the winter in Spain. And must be too off his head not to register the temperature change Bill thought cynically, as Birdie stretched himself and ran a hand down his black belly hair towards his low-slung trousers.)
Bill hoped he'd get pneumonia, and walked off across the hillside, fuming. His belly suddenly felt so paunchy it was a great weight to carry, and his tired, greying hair was sighing in his ears. It had been all he could do not to seize the posing prat by the dreadlocks and smash him face first into a rock...
When he passed on his return, he was still feeling nasty.
--Peace and love, Man, he snarled.
This amused Birdie, who plainly thought he was serious. Some sort of blitz-brained survivor of Woodstock or the Isle of Wight.
--Yea man, right on! he replied in a humouring tone.
Bill spun round and Caught Him Up By The T'roat, as Seamus enjoyed relaying afterwards.
Jesus, man, I won't be goin' there for a good while, let me be tellin' ye! And they all askin' me what I was doin', bringing that nutter up there with me!

--It's not one of Seamus's dogs then, sighed Bill, pushing away the humiliating memory, at least, there wasn't one like that last time I was down there, and I'm not walking down to see if he's got more since. He'd probably pretend it wasn't his anyway so he didn't have to bury it. I'd better do it. It might be weeks before we find the owner and the sooner Maggie forgets about it the better.
Yea. All that hysteria was a bit much. She wasn't like that when Haystacks died, mused Lynn.
There was a silence while they both remembered Haystacks. He was a huge buck rabbit. Lynn brought him home from the vet's one day. His intimidated owners had brought him there to be put to sleep. Lynn thought he would be an antidote for their neighbour's cat which had killed two bunnies belonging to Maggie. This fact had been hidden from Maggie but excuses for further disappearances would be hard to come by. Besides, Bill was going to get prosecuted by the RSPCA if she didn't act quickly. He had failed to catch the evil cat and have the simple

satisfaction of pulling its tail good and hard. It glided skilfully out of the way of stones he flung at it and then turned casually to assess him with its malicious gaze. Now he was threatening to set snares round the garden. Lynn thought he was sure to catch the wrong cat ,or someone's toddler, which could have a disastrous effect on her prospects at the vet's.
Haystacks turned up in the nick of time.
--Struth! gasped Bill, as he struggled to heave him out of a borrowed cat carrier. How could anything fed on carrots and lettuce get this big? When let loose in the run, Haystacks waddled, stiffly, with a Sumo wrestler's disdain, around his new domain. Then he lolled on his side, and made a sort of 'Plomp!' sound as he did so, like a huge eiderdown being squashed. His expression reminded Bill of something. That was it, that wretched story that Maggie had nearly driven them bonkers with when she had measles. I Want The Fierce Bad Rabbit! Let's have a different one this time, Darling- NO! I want The Fierce Bad Rabbit!

The cat never seemed to register that Haystacks was a rabbit. When it strolled through the run one day on a short cut to more exciting places, Haystacks came out of his coma and attacked it in such a way as to negate the idea that he could possibly be related in any way to such a gentle and timid species. Bill was cheering him on from the kitchen window.
--What are you shouting at, Daddy?
--Nothing, darling.

--Well, she'd had a bit of practice with the hamster dying first, said Bill. And Haystacks wasn't really a proper pet, he reflected. More like a Rottweiler. She couldn't pick him up and we couldn't let her stroke him.
--Remember how she cheered up when we said she should make that hamster a nice grave? She pinched those flowers out of Mr Longfield's garden that he wanted for the show....the poor old boy went mental.
--Oh yea...I'd forgotten that. It must have looked pretty horrible, this dog dying after being poisoned. Haystacks just faded away of old age.
--Oh yea? The day before he died, he was so still I thought he'd gone, and when I put my hand on him to check, he took a lump out of my thumb.
--Well, he wasn't ready, said Bill defensively. How would you feel if someone was all but planting you when you were still alive?
Lynn had always found Bill's intense concern and admiration for Haystacks irritating. She supposed he had lived out some macho

fantasy through the creature...
But perhaps she had been too hard on Maggie. And ought to help Bill bury the dog. He looked wrecked. He'd had no sleep to speak of and of course he'd expended all his energy on more pleasurable pursuits than the one of gravedigger which he now found foisted upon him.
--I'll come with you.

After two coffee breaks and a lot of sweating and grunting, they had finally scratched out a grave. Bill put the metal rod down on the pile of rocks they had levered out of the rough ground. They had got hold of a stiff, spittle-flecked leg each, in order to lower the dog down when there was a shout from the road. It was Seamus, looking all smug and jaunty. Today he was carrying a sort of cane and surveying everything with an affected Lord Of The Manor air.
--Hello! Howye.
--Morning, replied Bill unenthusiastically.
--Com'ere till tell ye! Seamus came alongside the wall, Ye'll never guess what Con Henchy is after doin!
He didn't give them a chance to try, but continued, Didn't he go and smash every window in The Doc's place last night! Anya -that's the German fella's wife, the family at the top o' the valley – was tellin' me this mornin'. She said the row was awful altogether, with Con ragin' and his wife screamin' at him to come away, and the kids cryin'. And The Doc going beserk howlin' all round the valley .
--We heard him didn't we, Bill reminded him.
Seamus was affronted.
--He'd hardly started then! Anyway, he continued with relish, the Germans were cowerin' in their cottage and all the doors locked and they afraid to come out until the Guards went up this mornin'. Jesus! he said suddenly, peering over the wall, What are ye doin' there? Is that a dog? Jesus! That's Con's dog! He climbed over the wall and inspected the animal which they'd had to lay out again while listening to him. He's been poisoned! he declared importantly, That's why he's foamy round his mouth! The Doc did it to another fella's dog a while back. Jesus, he looked up at them ominously, Con will go bonkers when he finds out.
--We won't tell him, decided Lynn, Let him think it got lost. Things are bad enough by the sound of it.
Seamus looked disappointed.
--Seamus, said Bill, Maggie was really upset about this dog dying, so I'd appreciate it if you wouldn't talk about it when she's around. And maybe we shouldn't mention Con and The Doc either. She's bound to hear about them at school but I don't want her to end up having nightmares

and be scared to go out to the toilet and all that. (He didn't mention the bad dream he'd had himself last night, as he writhed on the pee soaked cushion in the gale from the ill fitting door...The Doc had scrabbled at the window, sporting werewolf fangs and Marty Feldman eyes...Come to think of it, there wasn't much difference between the dream Doc and the daylight version....)
--Okay, okay, agreed Seamus.
--When are you collecting Meehaul? I think Maggie would like to come, said Bill, after they'd lowered the unfortunate dog into the grave, squashing in its legs with difficulty since there wasn't quite enough space, and Lynn was shovelling soil and stones over the last bit, watched unconcernedly by Seamus.
--Well it won't be today anyhow. I've to get wood. There's none left below.
--He hasn't any water where he's tied, said Cathy, who had just arrived.
--Arrah, said Seamus, after an appreciative Howye, he never bothers drinkin' anyway! I'll see ye so. Come down some time, he said for Cathy's benefit, and whistled his way off down the road.

When Bill next passed the bohreen, after walking Maggie to the bus a few days later, he saw that the tinkers had gone. He wandered down towards the caravans. He had resolved to keep his distance from Seamus for a while,but he was curious about the tinkers, the way they came and went, such a conspicuous presence so suddenly gone. They hadn't come by his place. He hadn't worked out what he would do if they tried to pull onto his land. Maggie had brought both her friend Majella and her big sister home one day. The sister had sat at the kitchen table with her homework. She was writing an essay about Itinerants . The new name was part of the drive to challenge old prejudices.
I don't like Nackers, the girl had written, They dont wash and there allways teevin things aff of desent people. And they dont treet there animals rite.
It was Majella's uncle who had been in the paper recently. A calf had fallen off his trailer. Tied, it had been dragged for miles..

There were some damp,sickly smelling bonfires of rags and tin cans smouldering along the verge. He was going to turn back, but the dogs spotted him and set up a racket. Nuala looked out.

--Oh, is it you, Bill. Are you looking for Seamus? He went off early, he's

gone doing something with Vinney. Will you have a cup of tea?
--Yes, okay. But I mustn't stop long. I've really got to do something about my van today.
There was something about Nuala, something wistful, almost an air of disbelief. Bill stepped up into the caravan.
--How's Mikey?
--Grand, thanks. He's asleep just now.
--I see the tinkers have gone.
--They have. They went off yesterday, like demons, heading for Limerick for a bit of company they said. I felt sorry for the old fella. The way the lads treated him. He didn't like it here at all. Tis a lonesome old spot! he kept saying, and they all batting him and telling him to shut up you old fool. Do you know the graveyard on the way to Conlon's Cross- the old deserted one? Well he wouldn't go past it at all. He was sure he saw a ghost there one time. Sorry about the smell. They always leave those stinking bonfires and the wind's bringing it straight in here.
--Why do they do that?
--I think it's all the old clothes. It's easier to burn them and beg a new lot than wash them. I might start doing the same! She glanced at a pile of grimy baby clothes. Bill saw that she had a bucket of water heating on the stove.
--Don't you find it lonely here?
--I do. I do of course. It's all right for Seamus, swanning off here, there and everywhere- she stopped. Is Maggie all right now? Did she forget about the dog yet?
--Yes, she's fine thanks. She decorated the grave with wonderful flower arrangements and holy pictures and had a great time. But she'd love to come and see Meehaul again. He's not in his old spot is he-we had a look the other day.
--I'm afraid he's gone, Bill. Seamus sold him to a farmer who wanted him for fetching wood. That'll suit him better, anyhow, he'll just pull the car around the fields and it won't matter how slowly he goes.
--But I thought he belonged to Christy?
--Well he did. But Christy has gone off and left us with all his animals. We can't manage them. Seamus has a crowd of dogs locked up in Christy's van down there and it stinks. They're getting really nasty because they're not getting enough to eat. We didn't have any money last week so Seamus sold the donkey.
--Ah well. I suppose food has to come first, for people and dogs.
--He only managed to bring a bit. Bones from the butcher. But it's hard dragging sacks all the way out here. He should buy a big case of tinned food really and get Tommy to bring it out...

--Will Christy come back?
--He might. We've heard he's still around, he hasn't gone far at all, he's just waiting for things to calm down. Seamus says he's trouble. We might move somewhere else on our own. Nuala actually felt a bit sad at this idea. Christy came from a big family and was relaxed and easy with Mikey, sometimes minding him for a few minutes.

As Bill walked back up the bohreen he saw Seamus coming towards him.
--Hi Seamus.I thought you were working with Vinney today.
Seamus looked at him suspiciously.
--I went up to the cross and your man never turned up. How is it you're down here?
--I was just passing so I called in for a minute. Bill realised Seamus suspected him of having designs on Nuala. While he was searching for the right thing to say to quell this myth, with the uneasy possibility that mentioning it might actually give it more substance, Seamus strode off. Bill was left feeling mis-judged and angry, particularly when he recalled the casual way Seamus was always pinching and squeezing Lynn and Cathy when his back was turned.

Nuala kept her head down,sorting through the washing while Seamus harangued her.
--Bringin' that fecker in here the minute my back's turned! Don't be bringin' him in here again,do ye hear? And don't be tellin' people all our business!

Chapter Ten

Cathy had been to the Post Office. There was a letter for Bill from the Emerald (Organic Food) Co-op. It said that the job he'd been promised as delivery driver was no longer available.
-- We expected to see you at the beginning of the month as arranged, and as there has been no word from you we have had to take on someone else. If you contact us later in the season we may be able to offer you some casual part-time work, read Bill. Cunts, he added.
--I thought it was a definite job, said Cathy. Didn't you have an interview?
--Yea. Last time we were over. And as soon as the house sale was definite, I contacted them and they were fine for me to start at the beginning of April. Then the sodding van packed up- but I wrote to them- Ah. He'd given the letter to Seamus-who was on his way, as usual, Into Town -thinking it would travel more quickly from there. Which it would have done if Seamus had remembered to post it.

Lynn and Cathy had dug a good bit of their own garden and got some seeds in under cloches. Bill tried to make admiring noises but was choked with anger about his kidnapped vehicle and the lost job. When they went inside for some lunch, he decided to go and sign on, something he'd been considering for a while but was now a necessity. He dragged the bike out of the shed, jumped on it and rode it like a tank across rocks and ruts to the road.
It was fifteen miles to town but it seemed further because the roads were so rough. By the time he arrived he felt purged and quite relaxed. Until he discovered that the office had closed ten minutes earlier and was shut now until the following week.
--Are ye after signin' on, Bill? It was Seamus, who always managed to know everyone else's business even if he was cagey with his own.
--Well....I was.....Seamus, you remember that letter I gave you a few weeks ago-
--Are you coming for a pint? Come in for a quick one, so.
Seamus seemed in very generous form and Bill was thirsty. They went into a small, dark room with a dying bit of a fire smouldering sulkily at the end of it. An old crone was out in the back room beyond the counter. The floor was of uneven stone flags and benches ran around the panelled

walls which were stained and discoloured from years of nicotine and splashed porter. There were warped and spotted metal billboards on the walls advertising Capstan cigarettes.

The drink after the long ride was very welcome. Bill let Seamus buy him another.

--Christy's back out the quarry, Seamus informed him. He's after buyin'a feckin' pony now!
And you should see the state on him. Lame and all sorts!
--What does he want it for? Can he ride it?
--Arrah, Jesus, no, the thing would fall over if you put an empty bag on it's back! Christy fancies himself at wheelin' and dealin' but he doesn't know a thing. And he doesn't think things through. Haven't I just got rid of a crowd o' dogs for him, and now he's after getting' a pony.
--Oh- you found homes for the dogs, that's good. Who-
--Well, you could say that, said Seamus hurriedly. How's Lynn ?
Bill didn't get a chance to answer.
--And her sister? Is she stayin' long more? Fine lookin' woman.
--Yes, yes she is, agreed Bill, though to his taste Cathy lacked Lynn's allure. She was blonde, taller and slimmer. Heads turned to admire her, but she didn't have The Something around the eyes, he thought loyally. The trouble was though-and it was one he'd never
experienced before, he'd always enjoyed Cathy's company but nothing more -only now....Maybe it was this Boring Bill hangup he'd developed driving some middle aged lust, or maybe it was her close proximity behind the curtains that had triggered it, but he was no longer indifferent to her attractions. Especially when she threw her just removed knickers down beside the too-short curtain that separated his and Lynn's room from the one she was sharing with Maggie. They were quite classy, silky looking ones, quite in contrast to the faded jeans and jumpers she wore. Lynn, who was a more feminine dresser than her sister, always wore a very functional style of knickers, he reflected.

He'd hear Cathy rustling around then and he'd started picturing suspenders and other items of lingerie he knew she couldn't possible wear under her jeans,but which appeared in his excited imagination nevertheless, and well – it was all getting a bit much and he was relieved she would be leaving soon.

Seamus was in the middle of a story and Bill hadn't heard a word. He was about to get up- a furtive look at his watch told him it was high time he got on the road if he was to make it back before dark and another day had gone with nothing achieved- when a little, plump, rabbity- faced man sat down at their table.

--Hello, hello, he fussed, How are you, Seamus. He held out his hand to

Bill. Ambrose Riley. Pleased to meet you, pleased to meet you. Just popped in for a quick drink you know. Hot day isn't it!
--Ah it is, it is, agreed Seamus dishonestly.
--Can I get you a pint there, Seamus? And Bill, what will you have?
--Well, I-
But Ambrose was off towards the bar.
--He's a business man. From The North, explained Seamus. He has a factory down in Shannon. He's got a rake of money. They call him Twenny Five Thousand on account of the way he's always boasting about how he just spent that much on a new car or a fur coat for his wife.
Towards the end of the next pint- again bought by Ambrose- Seamus asked him,
--Did you think any more about the garden? Now would be a good time to get it planted. If it's left long more twill be too late.
--Ah, Seamus, I did mean to talk it over with the wife. But we've had some big orders come in, and Maureen is coming up to her Leaving Cert this year...what with one thing and another...
--Oh. Only Nuala asked me to see you about it. Tis very hard for her ,with the baby, out the quarry there...His face took on a sad and wistful expression.
--Well,I tell you what, said Ambrose with alcoholic generosity, Come out and see us on Friday afternoon next week. We finish early then and do a bit of catching up at home. Anyway, must be getting on! he cried, swigging back the remains of his third double whiskey, Nice to meet you, Bill, Goodbye now. He scurried out of the door.
--He's gas, isn't he, said Seamus. He only came in here so that his wife and kids wouldn't spot him drinkin'. They're always tryin' to round him up, but they wouldn't think of lookin' in here. He's got a big old country house, with a lake in the grounds, and the old garden with a wall round it still there, only all overgrown -it hasn't been used for years. And a lot of empty stables. He said a while ago that Nuala and myself could do the garden and have the old coach house to live in.
Bill was in no condition to tell whether anyone was Gas or not. It would be nice to just curl up somewhere...He decided again that he really must make a move, but he didn't, and then Seamus's sister Maeve arrived.
--Are,there you are. Hello Bill, Howye. Paddy O'Loughlin said you were in here. Why didn't you call up to see us at home?
She looked quite like Seamus, only more wholesome,thought Bill. Same quite big nose (no beard of course), same gingery blonde hair (minus bald patch). Although she looked tired she had a similar jauntiness of manner. But it wasn't a swagger. He felt that her neat uprightness

reflected a character a lot more straightforward than her brother's.
--Listen. It's bad news with Mammy. You heard the hospital said it was cancer? They can't do anything more for her so they're letting her home.. The nurses will be in to help. You'll come and see her, won't you? Her eyes filled with tears as she subsided onto the bench next to Seamus.
--I will. I will of course, Seamus was saying, with his arm round her.
Bill thought that he'd better get another round of drinks.

It got dark on the way home and there wasn't much moon. He had no lights on the bike and he crashed a couple of times. When he finally got home, Lynn was in a frantic state.
--Oh,Bill,where were you?
--Sorry. Look, can you just let go of me for a minute while I put the bike away? I was in a hell of a mood earlier and I decided to ride into town and sign on, that's all. Is there any dinner left?
--But why didn't you tell me! And you've been gone hours and hours!
--Yea, I met Seamus and then all these people kept arriving when I was trying to leave. Sorry.
Shit. She wasn't going to sit him down and fetch his dinner and slippers, that was obvious. Not that he had any slippers, ah, he must remember, that would be an easy thing for Maggie to get him for Christmas. Sometimes he envied his father coming in from work and everybody waiting on him...you didn't ever get treatment like that these days. Especially when you'd only been to sign on the dole and not even managed to do it.
--Well,I've made a right fool of myself reporting you missing!
--You did WHAT? Bill was astonished.
--Well you just disappeared and I waited and waited – what if something had happened to you and no one had bothered-
--If something had happened I would have been picked up by an ambulance and the Guards would have contacted you. As Bill said this, he heard the word, Eventually.. tagging itself on.
--Anyway. What happened when you reported me missing?
--The Guards laughed their heads off!
Oh Lord, she was angry and close to tears. The hot dinner- never mind the being waited on, he'd already accepted that he'd be re-heating it himself – receded off the stove in his mind's eye as he braced himself for the rest of the story. He knew that if he took a step towards the house there would be a tirade about Unfeeling Male Indifference.
--It took me ages to get to the village, Lynn said accusingly. I'm glad Cathy was here to meet Maggie, that's all. I met Nuala down there. She

kept telling me not to worry, you'd only be having a drink somewhere-
--Shall we go inside -
--And I said you'd never go off drinking for hours and hours without telling me- She suddenly punched him in the stomach. He gasped. So she came with me to the barracks. We waited ages for the Guards to come back- they were off somewhere because some tinkers had a big fight- and then when they came in they just laughed!
--Oh dear. Well, let's go in-
Lynn was standing in front of him, blocking the exit from the shed, and kicking an old bucket in a very savage way.
--First they thought it was Seamus who we were reporting missing (kick, kick) And one of them said,'That fella? He's been around too long to get lost! (kick, kick) and they both just roared laughing! Eventually, one took the details, but he couldn't keep the grin off his face, as if I was completely neurotic. I came away feeling really stupid.
--I really am sorry, said Bill, pushing away the bucket and putting a tentative arm round her. He was relieved to feel her soften.
--I'm so glad you're back,Bill.
--Is there any dinner left?
--No there bloody isn't!

Lynn and Cathy were sitting in the little tussocky field at the back of the house. The Spring sunshine was beginning to have some warmth in it. They lounged against a big rock, Cathy with a bottle of cider. Bill had gone off with Jim Ryan, who insisted he'd have the van back in no time, he knew how to deal with the likes of Jo Kennedy.
--Why's cider so expensive here?
--Don't know. It's not very popular. I suppose it's all imported. No thanks, you drink it. Cathy, it's been great having you here, I'll really miss you.
--Yea, shame I've got to go. It was just what I needed, it's taken my mind off Phil completely. And it's been great seeing you. But actually, there are lots of things I want to get on with now. And I've used up all my leave so I've got to get back.
--What went wrong with you and Phil?
Cathy wouldn't look at her. Her head was down and she was picking at a hole in her jumper. She took another big gulp of cider.
--Everything. I shouldn't have hung on so long, but I haven't done very well at relationships so far have I....I just kept hoping things would change but every time I saw him it got worse.
He was always reading about some new theory on human behaviour and applying it to me. He used to wind me up on purpose then say it

wasn't *him* making me angry, I should be in charge of my own emotions -so it was my fault Then there were all these faddy diets...Once he wasn't eating fish and he sniffed me and said I had tuna Coming Out Of My Pores...Another time he was reading something about how the human brain developed and he said I had a Bicameral Mind...that meant like a primeval cave dweller so I got annoyed and then I got the shit about controlling my anger which was all my fault.
Then he found someone else...and told me all these details about, well, never mind.
--What a prat . Lynn hugged her.
--What's wrong with Auntie Cathy? Is she drunk? asked Maggie interestedly. She had just arrived. Nuala's coming up the track, she went on.

Nuala was struggling over the stones and rubble with Mikey in the pushchair. He was crowing and gurgling with glee at each new bump.
--Maggie, managed Cathy, Will you go and find some mugs? And bring the juice out.
Maggie ran off.
--She wouldn't have done that for me, said Lynn.
--That smug little sod …Cathy was muttering to herself.
Lynn remembered that Phil was shorter than her sister.
--And the bastard said I had Dormouse Orgasms! Lucky I had any at all with him.....Hi Nuala.
--Howye. There's a nice bit of sun in it today isn't there. I can't stop. I just came by to tell you Seamus and myself are leaving. Going over to live at the Rileys. Seamus is going to do their vegetable garden- keep them supplied and sell the rest.
--Oh yes. Bill mentioned that you might be doing that. Where is the Riley's place?
--Just the other side of the village on the back road by the grotto. We're going to live in the coach house where they kept the carts in the old days. It's a huge place but Seamus says we'll partition it off. Anyway, there's a great big fireplace in there and plenty of wood around. Will you come and visit when we get settled in?
--Oh we will. I'll miss you being down the road.
Seamus has invited a few people round to the quarry tonight. He's made a big fire ready outside. There are some musicians coming. Will you come down?
Maggie was back.
--Are you having juice or cider? she asked Nuala, splashing cider

messily into a mug at the same time, Can Mikey have some?
--Maggie! admonished Lynn, Babies don't drink cider. I don't expect he can drink from a cup yet either. Sorry we haven't got one with a spout, Nuala...
--That's okay, I've got one here with his drink already in it. Actually, he had a swig of Guinness the other night, he got hold of it before I could stop him, and he seemed to really like it. But we won't give him any cider now, she added hastily as Maggie was upending the bottle again.
 --I'll have that, thanks Maggie. Cathy reached over and took the bottle. That'll be great, thanks Nuala. .She knew her sister was like a zombie in the evenings, tired, pasty and pukey. But it was her last night in Ireland. And Vinney would be there.
--I might not stay very late, said Lynn, We'll have to bring Maggie if we all come -
--Oh, there'll be a good few kids there, said Nuala.
Lynn hoped they were young ones that tired early. She wouldn't be able to humiliate Maggie by dragging her away to bed, thereby reaching the blissful relief of her own, if all the other kids were allowed to rage around until the small hours...

Chapter Eleven

Nuala had been right, there were a good few kids at the party, along with Blow ins of assorted nationalities -even a couple from Australia- and some young locals. Seamus was in his element, telling stories, rolling joints, and dipping mugs into a big black pot filled with punch that he had on the less ferocious end of the fire.
--Have a drink, tis great stuff, he told them. Did ye bring some mugs?
Lynn brought them out of her bag and watched jealously while Cathy and Bill tasted the brew.
--Mmmm,that's lovely, said Cathy, What's in it?
--A bit of poteen, fruit, spices ,wine- As Seamus was telling her this, people were emptying in bottles of assorted brews.
A pot of vegetable stew was bubbling away, and set out on an old door were quiches and cakes, wholemeal loaves, salads and goat's cheese. Blow ins were competitive about their healthy home cooking, thought Bill, as he watched Lynn rather furtively add their contribution of some Quinnsworth crackers, Quinnsworth boxed cakes and Quinnsworth cheddar cheese. She hated cooking at the moment, and Cathy had been too drunk and maudlin to fulfil her promise of making a pizza.

Soon, a van pulled up and Vinney, the solicitor fellow with the bazouki and a couple of others got out. Seamus greeted them effusively and doled out drink.. The huge fire was like a beacon in the otherwise unlit night.
Maggie stood close to Lynn at first, looking shyly at all the kids dressed in dungarees and homespun jumpers. There was only one she recognised, the rest were in the Steiner school, or,officially at any rate, being Educated At Home.
Lynn didn't feel very comfortable. She had never liked getting stoned, and now drinking didn't agree either. She felt self-conscious,uptight and boring. Resentfully, she reflected that these people were actually very narrow-minded in their Alternative way: with an odious conviction about their own superiority to the rest of the human race. She thought she preferred the Ryans out of the people they'd met here so far. They were warm, decent, straightforward...then again, Jim had some very bigoted opinions...
The musicians started playing. She decided to risk a tiny bit of punch and as the night grew fully dark she felt safer and began to relax. It was great to be outside with a bit of a breeze at her back and the lovely heat from the fire warming her, the sky huge above and bright with stars. And

a session going on right in front of her.
--You're Lynn, aren't you? It was the girl who played the flute. I'm Mairead. How are you finding it, living here?
--Oh, it's lovely. We've had a few setbacks- Lynn didn't want to look like a moaner- But everything's slowly getting sorted out. We love the space and freedom, and the music...
--Well, you can't beat the sessions in County Clare! I'm studying in Dublin, so is my friend Bridie with the mandolin over there, but we come home whenever we can, to see our families of course, but also for the sessions. They're the best in the country.
--Mairead, said Maggie, Do you know where Christy's pony is? Mairead smiled at her and called over to Seamus with the same question.
--He didn't tie him properly, said Seamus carelessly, I think he's wandered up the bohreen, up the back here. He won't have gone far. But you won't find him in the dark.
--That's a shame, said Mairead to Maggie. You like animals don't you. Have you got any at home?

Cathy was perched on a log near Vinney and he was winking and smiling at her and making the odd quip in the brief spaces between tunes. Lynn noticed Nuala, standing back a bit from the fire, watching Cathy with an air of sad resignation. She hoped Nuala didn't fancy Vinney herself...but it wasn't jealousy she saw in her face, just an indefinable sadness. Mikey was balanced on her hip, clearly delighted with all the activity, especially the sparks dancing up from the fire and disappearing into the heavens.

Mairead's friend Bridie had joined her. They were talking about The Troubles. Someone local, an IRA sympathiser, had been suspected of smuggling arms up to the North, and the Guards had raided the house. When you moved to Ireland, the first advice people always gave you was, Don't Talk About The Troubles. The locals didn't talk about them much either. Lynn had her face turned slightly away, with an outward appearance of listening to the music, but she was trying to hear their conversation.
--I wouldn't blame him, said Bridie, He's got relatives up there. All those years of oppression, not having the vote, only having the lowest paid jobs and the worst living standards, then being massacred when you went on a civil rights march...then the British soldiers siding with the Protestants and making things worse- you can see why people support

the IRA.
--I could understand them blowing up that Mountbatten, said Mairead, he had some stupid old colonial title to remind us of British domination, what was it, Last Viceroy of India, Jesus..But a couple of young lads were with him...And blowing up innocent people in pubs...I know the UDA are as bad, but that doesn't excuse it. Ger Connolly says that it's losing them support down here. That and all the robberies. There were over two hundred last year, did you know that?
--It was a pub used by soldiers...I'm not sure Ger is right about the support. They banned the Wolf Tones from being played on RTE and they're still our best selling band. I think Haughey is worried that if sympathy is shown to the Republican movement the Troubles might spread down here. And he has to be careful of a backlash against the Irish living across the water. So he has to show the Brits that the rest of us are civilised souls and shocked at what's being done.
--But it's gone on for so many years. Some of it, I can't even think about. The women in Armagh prison that joined the Dirty Protest are smearing their period blood on the walls... ...I felt so sorry for that Anne Maguire, can you imagine it, losing your three kids....no wonder she slit her throat. No, it's all insane. There's no war that people fight ethically, war degrades everyone. And civil wars are the worst of all. Wasn't it beautiful when the Pop was speaking last year, I felt hopeful for a while after that...I memorised it: On my knees I beg you to turn away from violence . Further violence will only drag you down to ruin the land you claim to love and the values you claim to cherish....
There was a pause.
You're right about The Brits in general though, continued Mairead, They're awfully ignorant. I don't know what sort of education they get, but it can't be up to much. Ger was over there recently and he said they don't know the first thing about the Troubles, or who's who, they're only aware that there are some nutters with bombs called the IRA. No idea who the UDA are. They're terrified of anyone Irish, even if they're from the far tip of County Cork.. Ger couldn't get a room to rent anywhere! They none of them understand the issues at all. Especially not their part in causing it.
--None of it will end until the Brits are willing to listen and help put in a fairer form of government.
--They need to get rid of Thatcher. All she says is 'We Don't Talk To Terrorists' in that ghastly voice.
It was a good imitation. They both laughed.
--Did you get your essay finished? asked Bridie.
--Not yet. I was learning that new tune set and the whole day went by...

--Come on, let's go and play.

--Lynn, this is Pete O'Grady, and Annie. Bill had brought the Australian couple over to meet her. They're from Melbourne.
 The conversation was momentarily interrupted as a kid ran out in front of them, clutching one of their Quinnsworth cakes. The mother was in hot pursuit .
--Put that back! she drawled in an American accent, It's full of poison! Lynn studied her feet as the kid slouched past them again and sadly exchanged the cake for a fistful of nuts and raisins.
--My wife Lynn, Bill was repeating, looking at her anxiously.
--Oh, yes, sorry -pleased to meet you.
 Annie began chatting to Lynn in a very relaxed, friendly way. Her discomfort at her ignorance of The Troubles began to recede. Nobody normally mentioned what was going on
in the North. Her mother had been Worried of course. They had assured her, and themselves, that it was a different world down here. It was, and no one had said or done anything to imply that she and Bill weren't wanted, just the opposite in fact. But though you tried not to think of Cromwell, the Famine, or Thatcher, the more you learnt, the more ashamed you felt to be a Brit.
--Pete's ancestors are from Ireland, explained Annie, We've tried to trace them but we don't have enough details. We don't really care. We've managed to prove that the O'Grady who owns that filthy bar by the town dump isn't a long lost relation, that's a relief anyway!
--Are any of the kids yours? asked Lynn, as a rowdy gang were shooed away from the fire. They were trying to pull out a long blazing branch.
--No. We've been together quite a few years but we haven't been blessed. Though a lot of our friends told us we only had to set foot over here and we'd conceive instantly. We don't really want kids. We're quite happy the way we are. We're still into travelling- we're just having a six month stop here in a rented cottage. We couldn't keep uprooting kids. I don't know what Pete will do with his chickens as it is!
--Chickens?
--Yea, chickens! enthused Pete in his very loud voice, coming closer. He had a big, ruddy face. He rooted in his pocket and pulled out a package. With the air of a conjuror, he undid layers of paper to reveal an ornate box.. Carefully he opened it. Inside were eggs, wrapped individually in layers of coloured tissue paper.
--This is Ruby's first egg, said Pete proudly, lifting it up and inspecting it as if it was a rare jewel. Ruby is my oldest hen, he informed them reverently, She's a golden bantam. This, he went on, is Henrietta's -

--I keep hens, said Lynn. Marrans. We bought them here. I had a couple of Warrens when we lived in England but they were so old I just gave them to a friend.

She addressed her remark mainly to Annie, whose round friendly face was re-assuring. Pete meanwhile was gazing lovingly at another one of his eggs. Bill watched in perplexity. Of all the people present, these two had seemed the soundest, the least likely to bore the pants off you with lectures about your dietary shortfalls, the dangers of aspirin or the immoral story behind the jumper you were wearing. At least they hadn't done that, and now Annie was talking very interestingly about the Aborigines. She and Pete belonged to a support group that was trying to help them reclaim some of their land.

They were heading home now, said Annie. But she told them how to find the cottage they were living in and to be sure and come and see her photos some time. Pete spoilt it by adding,

--Yea, Ruby loves visitors!

The gang of kids appeared by the fire again. A couple had torches and they had been making expeditions off into the crag, where no doubt they were scaring each other witless with horror stories, making tentative attempts to flirt with the opposite sex, and eating Lynn's cakes which they had finally managed to steal. Maggie had palled up with another girl, and they had sidled up and joined the gang on their previous visit to the food table. Lynn was listening a bit anxiously to the screams and giggles coming from the undergrowth. The kids were clamouring for adult attention, now, all wanting to be first to impart some important piece of information. Maggie and a couple of others were extremely quiet though, and came and sat very close to their particular adults.

--MUM! JOHN! shouted a big lad with a cockney accent, There's a load of blood in the woods and there are dead things hanging up!

--Come off it! said John indifferently, You lot always end up scaring yourselves stoopid!

--Yea, go off and play! complained his mother.

But others had joined in.

--There is! There is! There's dead things in the woods down there! Come and see if you don't believe us!

A visible sigh passed round the adults. Someone got up.

--Come on then, which way is it?

A throng of kids, emboldened by his presence, shouted, This Way! Down Here! and crashed off into the crag. Arguments of, You didn't see it first, I did! And, You saw the blood but I saw the dead dogs! were continuing in loud voices when Seamus appeared.

--Where are ye goin'! Go on away out o' that now! That's Christy's van down there and you're not to go near it! He headed them off, giving the lad at the front a shove to re-direct him.
--Where is Christy? someone asked. Haven't seen him around lately-
--Arrah, he comes and goes, replied Seamus.
--But there's dead things in the bushes and my Dad's coming to see them! clamoured the boy.
--The kids have seen something and got the idea that- began the father but Seamus ignored him.
--Go way out o 'that now! There's nothin' in these bushes. Wasn't I down here this morning fetchin' wood. If ye can't control these feckin' kids then ye can take them home.
There were mutinous mutterings from the kids of 'Not fair!' and 'I'm telling my Mum and Dad' but they all came back. So did the Dad.
--Come on, Sam. Where's Emily? Right, in the car, we're going home. You needn't bother to call again, Seamus. He drove off, revving angrily.

The musicians were still playing and Seamus drained the last of the punch into their glasses. They were in a different world, with every tune telling its story and invisible instruments playing along with them.
Outside their charmed circle, no one was talking much, and more people began to climb into battered vehicles and leave.
Bill and Lynn, with a very quiet Maggie between them, walked up the bohreen and turned onto the road. The night was velvety. The tumbling walls were just visible. Occasionally the sweet breath of cattle steamed behind them.
--Put your big torch on Dad.
--This one's okay isn't it?
--Put the big one on, PLEASE Daddy! She was gripping his hand tightly.
--I brought a lantern. Here. Lynn got it out and after some groping found the matches and got it alight.
--There. Is that better?
Maggie didn't answer. The lantern had the effect of making the darkness around them seem denser beyond its small circle of light. She squeezed closer to Bill, nearly tripping him up.
--Those kids have been telling too many scary stories, said Bill, and launched into a jolly song. Come on Maggie, help me with the words. Old Noah, he did build an ark-
He and Lynn were keen to know what had been seen in the woods but had decided by unspoken agreement to leave it until daylight.

Although Maggie was extremely tired, Lynn had to sit beside her until

she fell asleep. Maggie made her sing Twinkle Twinkle Little Star, which she hadn't asked for since she was about three.
--I hope Cathy's all right, said Bill, when they were in their own bed, She should have come home with us.
--She's got designs on Vinney.
--Vinney! I've heard he's a right Derro.
--I don't know what she thinks she can achieve when she's leaving tomorrow. And its bloody cold to be shagging on the ground-
--Lynn!
--She'll have to kip on the caravan floor if she doesn't make it home.
--I suppose the Vinney thing is good really. A flirtation brings you back to life after someone's made you feel like shit, Bill conceded.

Tommy Lynch called next day with his taxi to take Cathy to Limerick station.
Maggie let him in.
--They're still asleep. They all got drunk last night, she was telling him.
--No we're not! shouted Lynn. She appeared, flustered and untidy.
--Sorry, Tommy, Cathy's not here. Could you go down to the quarry, and can I come too please?
Luckily Cathy had packed most of her stuff before going to the party. Lynn stuffed the last few things into a carrier bag and loaded Cathy's rucksack into the car boot, while Tommy stood smoking laconically.
--Can we go to the quarry then?
--Sure ye can, replied Tommy genially, But divil a train ever went from there!

Cathy was slumped against a log beside the still smouldering fire. A couple of bodies were still curled up in sleeping bags nearby. Cathy looked as if she'd been up a chimney. Even so, observed Lynn ruefully, she was young and attractive enough for the urchin look to have its charm.
--Cathy! Come on, you've got to leave for the train. You never slept there did you?
--No. I was in the caravan for a bit...but only on the floor...Is there another jumper handy? I'm freezing..
At the sound of the car and voices, Seamus had stuck his head out.
--Mornin! he called, smiling in his smuggest manner.
--Seamus, you couldn't make a cup of tea could you?
--I could not. There isn't any. Vinney and the lads came through the place like a plague o' locusts last night. There's no tea, milk, nothing. (Lynn liked the way he said that last word. Nu'un.) There's Nu'un left to

eat either.
As if to prove his point, Mikey could be heard bawling angrily in protest at the lack of breakfast.
--Herb tea then?
--There's nu'un. Vinney managed to pull all the herbs off the ceiling.
--Where are they?
--He pulled them off himself and chucked them on the fire. He's an awful eejit sometimes.

--I had an an awful night, Cathy told Lynn.
Lynn glanced over at Tommy who was now chatting away to Seamus and handing him a cigarette. He seemed to be in no hurry so she sat down.
--I thought you were getting on well with Vinney.
--So did I...But at the end of the night he just fell over in a heap! He's only just left actually and he didn't seem to notice me at all this morning...
--He was definitely noticing you last night.
--That's what I thought. I was beginning to wonder if I'd imagined it in my frustration, she said cynically
But anyway, you're leaving, so it's probably for the best. Shame you didn't come home with us. I was going to ask if you wanted to come but you looked so happy...Guiltily Lynn remembered her relish at having Bill to herself.
--I was happy....for a while.
--I came over and you didn't answer me. I know you hate me being Big Sisterly.
--I was happy. But after a while I realised I was incredibly stoned. I was like a lump of rubber, I just couldn't move. Or speak. Must have been that cake, the fudgy one. I sat and sat and I couldn't make sense of anything. It's a bit like that here anyway – nobody does what you expect them to, do they. And I felt, well...really Alone.
--I don't suppose anyone else would have made sense of it either, commented Lynn wrily, recalling the Dead Things and conversations overheard between some of the guests.
--I remember the crowd that were still here after you went home all got hungry and went marauding in the caravan, and Nuala was trying to stop them, and Seamus was saying, Arrah, they'd get more food in the morning, continued Cathy. They came out with eggs and bread. Someone asked me to move up but I couldn't. I think they'd been asking me and poking me for a long time before it penetrated as well...oh, God,

I hate being that stoned...I felt so STUPID...
Then I thought that someone had a flame thrower...After a while I worked out that someone had set fire to the frying pan, and they were pouring beer onto it to try and put it out....Then they cooked some sausages and the smell was terrible. In the middle of it, Seamus came over and asked where did they get the sausages because he didn't have any except some old rotten ones the butcher gave him for the dogs. So Brendan took them off the fire. They were still quite pink... - hardly cooked at all. Vinney had gone off for a pee or something and when he came back he just grabbed the pan and started chomping into them. They all laughed at first but then Brendan- he's the solicitor one, he's very well mannered and kind – told Vinney to leave them alone or he'd be making himself sick. Vinney just said, 'They're Grrrrand Man, Grrrand!' and carried on eating.
Tommy had come over.
--Is it Vinney? That fella has so much alcohol inside him he could eat a rotten horse and his stomach wouldn't notice!

--So you won't be coming back to see Vinney again.
They were in the bushes for a pee.
--NO.I smelt his feet last night. They'd all been making jokes about them but when he took his boots off- even in the open air, it was indescribable----sort of like rotting manure, only....rottener.
They both laughed and Lynn lost her balance.
--Bugger, I've peed on my pants....
--I still prefer him to Phil though, with all that crap psychology. Everyone here is so much more genuine and original. And spontaneous.
--But sometimes it can make you feel very misjudged and misunderstood.
--Yea. I'm quite relieved I'm scurrying home to safe predictable England. But another part of me doesn't want to admit defeat. You'll be all right will you, Lynn?
--I'll be fine, lied Lynn, then added more honestly, I wish you weren't going.
Tommy was beeping the car horn.
--I'll come back as soon as I can.

--Oh,Jesus, observed Seamus,who had come looking for them, Cryin' women! Will ye come on up out o' that now! He grabbed a big stick and brandished it, grinning. Or I'll give ye's somethin' to cry about!
Crying and laughing and wiping her face on her sleeve, Cathy headed

for the taxi. So did Seamus, promising over Mikey's roars that he'd be back with something to eat soon.

The taxi went off with a screech, swallowing the final Goodbyes, Take Cares and I Love Yous. Even Mikey was suddenly quiet, having fallen into an exhausted, unsatisfied sleep.

Lynn felt horribly bereft.

Chapter Eleven

Bill was admiring his van. He did this a lot. Jim Ryan had threatened Jo Kennedy with the withdrawal of the annual loan of his tractor if he didn't get the work done. There had still been a long wait for parts that should have been ordered months ago, and excuses from Jo like, 'Sure wasn't I in the middle of it when the (whatever it was he was using) broke on me!'
But there it was at last, parked below on a relatively dry spot at the side of the track. The problem now was scraping up enough petrol money to use it, but just having it there gave them a sense of being in charge of their lives again.
The first Sunday they had it back, they had been for a family outing, to the Craggaunowens, a re-structuring of a Bronze-age settlement. Lynn had left the sick stage of pregnancy behind her and was meant to be in the 'Comfortable' middle stage, before total Beached Whaledom arrived. She didn't feel comfortable at all, but it was great to be able to eat normal food, even if it had to be consumed in about fifteen doll's portions a day because her stomach was so squashed.
They all enjoyed the Craggaunowens. The grounds were peaceful and picturesque. Maggie ran about, crossing the wooden bridge out over the lake and exploring the fort-like dwellings, seeing where the animals were kept and how they made their clothes, then explaining it all to her parents.
On the way home they called in to a country hotel for a drink. There were a good few families there, all dressed in a 1950's sort of Sunday Best. Some of the children's outfits were remarkable: bow ties, frilled and flounced dresses, short white socks. Lynn resolved to make more of an effort on future Sundays.

Guard Hennessy appeared beside their table. He knew Bill now that he came to sign on at the barracks, after finally managing to catch the town office open and register there. Guard Hennessy was immensely tall, and swayed precariously from side to side, surveying them from one eye. The other seemed to have a life of its own. His huge feet, in gleaming boots, pointed outwards while his heels pressed hard together. They seemed to act as stabilisers, anchoring him while the rest of his long body lurched this way and that.

--I hear Mrs Lynch is not long for this worrld! he boomed.
--Yes, we'd heard she's very ill, poor soul, agreed Lynn. She leant back hastily as he loomed over her and some guinness slopped out of his glass.
--Tis a hard old life!
--Yes it is..
Lynn could feel Maggie vibrating beside her. She was struggling to master a fit of giggles. Her mirth was forcing its way out of her despite her valiant attempts to with-hold it. Her battle between the forces of spontaneity and good manners finally led to a volcanic trumpeting. This caused a considerable reaction in Guard Hennessy's focussing eye, which, teetering as it was at the far end of a sway, swivelled desperately for a few seconds as if trying to locate the cause of the noise. Then it zoomed back towards the people below and settled in to its normal disconcerting glare, evidently not connecting the odd sound with them at all.
--Must be like coming in to land in a plane, whispered Bill. Look out, Unauthorised pint landing!
They leant back hastily as their visitor over-reached himself, clutched the table to prevent himself falling right onto it and sent his slopping pint up the middle, where it played skittles with several empties. Bill had had the foresight to hang onto his own and keep it out of harm's way.

In the village, they called at Kelly's, one of the many grocery shops. They were all similar. It was a wonder they made a living. It was quiet now. Earlier there had been a crowd who came in for Mass and called there for papers and cigarettes. It was hard to believe the seemingly uncultivated, uninhabited land held such a hidden population.
At the counter they saw Seamus. He was lecturing an old farmer on the use of herbs. The farmer and his companion were regarding Seamus with the utmost suspicion, to the amusement of the young shop keeper, who kept asking questions to keep the entertainment going.
--So it's the chamomile is good for the fair hair? I'll tell the wife, so. And nettles are a good conditioner too? Is that right now? But what would you do about the stings?
--Your man is a badly fecker! muttered one farmer to the other on his way out, Them old herbs never did *his* hair much good!
Seamus noticed Bill and Lynn.
--Howye. Are ye well.
--Yea, pretty good. We got the van back at last, Bill told him happily.
--That's grand, so. Seamus turned back to finish his business at the counter. How much is that now, Michael? Is it now...Could ye put it on

the book for a few days? I know, I know, but I'll drop it in to ye on Thursday without fail. Thanks, Michael.
When Bill and Lynn had finished their shopping, Seamus was still inside.
--Why don't ye come and see the garden. Tis only a little way out the road.

On the way, Seamus asked could they just call at the Australian's place, just up that lane there, as he needed to drop something off. They had been meaning to visit Pete and Annie,so Bill turned up the track.
Pete and Annie were staying in a small ugly, bungalow, covered in brown pebbledash and surrounded by weed -strewn gravel where docks and ragwort were flourishing. Pete greeted them effusively and led the way inside. They went through the porch into a concrete floored room with wooden shelves at the side. Dust and feathers blew about the floor and a row of chickens peered at them. Pete sat down on an old chair.
--I was just giving the girls their powdering, he told them, taking an indignant looking hen and turning her upside down.
--What's that stuff?asked Maggie.
--Garlic powder. It keeps the pests off.
--Oh, does it? Maggie was all bright enthusiasm. Can we get some,Mum?
Lynn was irritated. She wanted a cup of tea.
--I've never had much problem with my hens.
--You will do, warned Pete, There are huge ticks in the grass here.
--Ye'll be too busy pullin' 'em off yourself to be worryin' about the hens, said Seamus. Is Annie in at all? You should go through and see her workshop, she makes grand jewellery. Tell her to put on the kettle there!

The rest of the bungalow was not much less lacking in comfort than the chicken's room. It was sparsely furnished and damp. Annie was working in a spare room which was her workshop, making a delicate bead choker. Around her were boxes of gleaming beads , her pattern book, parcels awaiting postage to shops in Dublin and London and two wooden
cases with chokers, bracelets and earrings displayed on black velvet, which she would take around festivals in the summer. Lynn was fascinated, it was such delicate and skilled work. She put in a couple of orders, one for Cathy's birthday present.
By the time they'd had tea and brack, and Annie had very patiently started Maggie off on a little bracelet of her own, insisting she didn't need that old frame it was set up on and Maggie was welcome to it, and Bill had joined Pete and Seamus in smoking most of the contents of the

package he had delivered earlier, it was well into the evening.

--We can't stop for long, Seamus, stressed Lynn.
--Just see the garden. And say Hello to Nuala or she'll be giving out to me for not bringing you in, he added cunningly. In through here, he directed Bill.
They turned in through an ivy covered archway and arrived in a gravelled courtyard surrounded by big pink walls. Through a gateway they could see a large park with trees and long lush grass, and in its midst a lake, somewhat diminished from its original grandeur, but still just large enough not to be called a pond.
Seamus headed for some big wooden doors past the empty stables. The inside of the coach house was like a huge cavern, with a new collection of rugs and hangings festooning the walls and ceiling. An area was partitioned off with suspended hazel branches which supported a screen of Indian bedspreads to form a separate bedroom.
A huge fire was blazing.
--Trow a few Tick ones in there, Nuala, instructed Seamus all the same. Hello Lynn, Bill, Howye. And Maggie -Hello Sweetheart. Seamus, have you got the shopping?
Lynn thought Nuala looked what her mother would call A Bit Off.
--I'd nothing to cook for the dinner. Did you get spuds, and butter?
--Don't be tearin' the head off me the minute I walk in, complained Seamus. I have it all here. Lynn, did ye see the carrier bag I was after bringin' from Kelly's?
An inspection revealed that it had been left at Pete and Annie's. Seamus had brought it in when they'd run low on butter for the brack. Nuala went and sat in a dark corner.
--We really must be going, said Bill. We'll come another time. Maggie needs to get home to bed, it's school tomorrow.
--Arrah, don't mind her, said Seamus, glancing over towards Nuala. The garden's only a step away. It won't take you a minute to see it.
Lynn decided to stay and talk to Nuala. Maggie was half asleep in a big saggy armchair.
Seamus looked suspicious but Bill explained that Lynn got very tired because of the baby, and they both headed outside.
--How's Mikey? asked Lynn, looking into his basket.
--He's crawling now. It's quite a business when he's awake – scouring the place! But he sleeps well with all the exercise.
--Do you like it here? It must be easier being near the village.
I -it's not bad. I can walk to the village but I don't go up there much. I'm

doing some work in the garden when Mikey sleeps in the afternoon...Sometimes we go into town, go to Quinnsworth and have something to eat in the cafe when he gets the giro. That's great, but most of the time I'm just stuck here.
--Doesn't Ambrose give you lifts?
--He did at first. But I'm not sure if he and Seamus are getting on very well. We do go and visit people sometimes.
Well....It won't be forever. Lynn looked for something comforting to say. Babies are a big tie when they're this age. She could see that it wasn't just Mikey making Nuala bitter and felt a bit ashamed of her platitude. But just then Seamus bounced in.
--Bill thinks the garden's grand! Ye'll never believe this, he went on, We're after seein' the funniest thing! We were coming back from the garden when the back door of the house flew open and out came Himself, lookin' all sporty, and a new tracksuit on him. 'Just going for a round of golf, just going for a round of golf – oh, Hello Bill, you must come in some time and meet the wife' says he. Golf my arse! In a tracksuit and it getting dark and all! And Bill believed him! Seamus was clutching his sides and even Nuala was laughing.
--Its just another way for him to creep off to the pub, she explained. We have great crack watching poor Breda trying to keep some control over his drinking. He's a terrible alcoholic.
Seamus was perusing some shelves above the table where the washing up bowl and saucepans stood.
--What are these buckets doin'up here? He lifted them down I had some grand Arrangements up there!
--I had to put them outside, to make room for the buckets. Seamus, you can't have buckets of fermenting fruit on the floor and Mikey crawling around eating it!
--Well it's your job to stop him. We're makin' some grand wine, he told his visitors. It has to Ferment Vigorously before it goes in the jars, he continued in important tones. You should keep Mikey away from the buckets, he told Nuala again. She raised her eyes heavenward.
Lynn could imagine the sort of touring demolition force Mikey must be when awake...
That individual began to stir in his basket.
--Oh, No..said Nuala, I thought he was down for the night.
--I hope it wasn't us that disturbed him, said Lynn.
--Not at all, he does wake up sometimes, said Nuala, giving Lynn a tired smile.
--Come on, my vigorous little fermentation! Seamus lifted Mikey out of the basket. The first of the vegetables should be in the delicatessen

soon, he called after them as they crossed the courtyard.
--Delicatessen, crikey, said Lynn. What can he be growing? Besides the obvious...

--Did you hear that bloke at the party talking about Mattie? asked Bill, as they drove home.
--No. What did he say?
--He was a local, Finn. Quite sound. Seamus wanted Mattie to come. Because he likes to get the old people to talk about fairies.
--The poor old boy. I'm glad he didn't come.
--Seamus wouldn't have been laughing at him. He genuinely loves to hear the old stories.
--I wouldn't want any elderly relation of mine exposed to the lunacy that went on down there.
--Maybe not. Anyway, me and Finn got talking and he said when he was growing up people regularly reported seeing fairies. But now they don't like talking about it because they think they're being made fun of. Then we got onto Knock. You know, the holy site in Mayo.
--Where the Pope went last year.
--Yea. Well last September was the centenary of the Knock Apparitions. This local girl saw Mary, Saint Joseph and John the Baptist standing by the church.
--Yea, yea...
--A local farmer looked over and saw a globe of golden light there. It was claimed that the vision was there for a long time and twenty five other people gathered and saw it too.
--Are you getting religious?
--No! Bill was indignant. Even if I saw that myself, I wouldn't find it any use to the world. I'm just thinking about things Seamus told me, about his childhood, and then all these old people genuinely believing they saw fairies...I think moonlight helps, no harsh electric lights in the old days...and I think you see what you believe in.
--Like when myself and Cathy used to scare ourselves silly watching old Hammer Horror films. I used to be petrified afterwards. I'd see ghosts and zombies out of the corner of my eye, and I'd be too terrified to look and check that they weren't really there.
--Kind of. If you're a kid and people tell you something exists though, you just believe it don't you. So you must be more likely to see it. Or let other things you are really seeing become that thing.
--Mum, whined Maggie drowsily from the back, I'm hungry!
--We're nearly home... Possibly. But there's a flaw in your argument.

How did the belief in fairies and whatever come about if no-one really saw them in the first place?
--No one could have seen all those three headed monsters and flying witches, but people believed it. Bill was reading The Name of The Rose.
--That was hundreds of years ago.
--Mum, are we having sausages?

Seamus was dancing with Mikey in his arms. Radio Clare was on. Andy Irvine was singing Paddy's green Shamrock Shore, his heart-wrenching version with a delicate mandolin backing.
Nuala was back in her corner, with a book she had finished last week on her lap. Nuala was thinking about Davy. Davy Flanagan. Of his beautiful, fine face, and his lovely voice. How she fell in love with him the first time she saw him, making a rallying speech to the mis- judged saviours of the world, the young hippies at the last Windsor Free Festival, before the police broke it up. And how she'd bided her time, but the bloke she was with didn't stand a chance. Of the four years they'd spent together, drunk on their own beauty, power and youthful zeal....

Chapter Thirteen

Mummy, wake up! There's a man digging up our vegetable!
--Mmmmmm?
A man! insisted Maggie, He's digging up our vegetables!
--I'll go and see, said Bill, stumbling around and pulling on his trousers.
It was early July. There had been a blissful week without rain and they had been for a few day's trip around the Burren coast.
Lynn had got some great photos. The landscape of tiny fields separated by untidy walls of rock, the sprinkling of cottages, the narrow, undulating road sloping down towards the sea, Fanore Beach with the normally spray- flinging sea as calm and blue as the Agean. And the hidden gardens of cerise -coloured cranesbill, late orchids, tormentil and harebells among the shimmering Burren rocks . They were now waiting to be framed or copied as paintings. And Annie had some contacts who might help with selling them. But you had to be careful.
--DON'T GO NEAR THOSE! she had shouted at Maggie as they explored the flower strew rocks.
A week earlier, Annie had ended up in hospital, she'd had some sort of allergic reaction after picking and sniffing some pretty, but very poisonous Monkshood.
--No need to scream at her like that...said Bill..
Lynn was feeling uneasy. Visiting the immense, powerful Cliffs of Moher with the sea pounding below had increased her nameless feeling of foreboding.
--Mum, you're squashing my hand! OW! Maggie had complained, I wasn't going anywhere near the edge!
Lynn felt so stiff compared to most of the people here, as if everything got out from her only through a kind of filter. They were so alive with their music dance, laughter and wonderful way with words which just poured out of them.
And she kept getting into awkward situations. The other day she'd been into Vaughan's shop, where they sold sewing stuff. She wanted to buy a reel of cotton.
Biddy Vaughan brought out swathes of material and was unrolling them all over the counter before Lynn knew what was happening.
--Is it a dress you're making? Or a skirt?
--Er....I really just wanted a reel of cotton.
--Sure, this is all cotton, it says on the labels, look it.
Several women gathered as interpreters before Lynn left, red in the face and with two yards of floral material which she was now obliged to turn

into a dress for Maggie - though God knows how when her sewing skills didn't stretch beyond re-positioning buttons - and what she now knew was called a SPHOOL of cotton.
Sometimes she ended up saying completely untrue things because it got too complicated trying to explain herself. She thought of friends who had gone off to live in foreign countries and despised herself for her cowardice. Bill said she was being over-sensitive. She'd go beserk if he said it was her hormones but he was concluding that at least the PMT had been predictable and maybe he'd been a bit over-optimistic thinking the pregnancy would be a smooth ride. He hoped that he wouldn't be bolstering her up forever, that when the baby came it would be a good ice breaker when it came to day to day banalities and surely she couldn't go wrong having a bit of a chat about teething and the like with the local women at the shop.

--HOY! shouted Bill, thinking simultaneously, Shit, I sound like a gamekeeper in a wax jacket.. What are you doing? (At least he hadn't said, Can I Help You?- a favourite of landowners over the water. It was always delivered in the worst Wah Wah tone and signalled intentions far from helpfulness. In short it meant How Dare You Take Two Steps Off That Footpath, You Scum.)
Oh Jesus, it was him: Con Henchy. And he was digging up his dog, or what remained of it.
--Look, began Bill, as Con, completely ignoring him, continued his work. (That's my fucking spade he's using! noticed Bill angrily.) There's no point in digging him up now. He'd be better off left here in peace...
He knew the dog was a bitch but he'd unconsciously adopted the He habit from Seamus. He looked on desperately as Con- big, red-headed, bristly and grunting- continued to shovel stones and clods.
--Plant something on the grave if you want., he offered desperately, And come back whenever you like-
(And have a mass said for him, he nearly added) He jumped back as Con heaved up a good portion of rotting dog on the end of the spade.
--LOOK. THIS IS MY LAND AND I WANT YOU TO LEAVE. I'LL GET YOU A BAG TO PUT YOUR DOG IN, THEN YOU GO.
--It's my dog all right, said Con to the air, and threw down the shovel.
--Hang on! cried Bill, What are you going to do with-
But Con was off, vaulting the wall and striding off down the road, quite indifferent to Bill and with a horrible intensity of purpose.
Trying not to look too closely at the job before him, or receive any messages from his nose, Bill set to work to re-bury the worm-ridden corpse.

--Just someone who thought we were doing Pick Your Own, he informed the curious Maggie unconvincingly. Stay over there! I thought I said you were to wait inside.

Luckily, someone else was coming along the road to distract her from the questions she was preparing to torment him with. A tinkle of bells heralded the arrival of a little cavalcade .

Coming along the road was a sidecar pulled by a big, feathery skewbald horse. It was driven by a vast, cosy- looking woman, and sitting next to her was a prim little Yorkshire terrier with a red bow in its hair. And a white goat, which was placidly surveying the scenery. Maggie was enchanted. Bill managed to shovel some earth over the grimmest portion of dead dog.

Into view came a second fine strong horse but this one was piebald and pulled a barrel top wagon with big wooden wheels. A very spry looking old man was walking beside the horse. He wore a black suit,collarless shirt and big black boots, and a pipe stuck out of the side of his mouth. They all pulled up at the gate where the horses stood patiently and the goat continued its cudding.

--Oh,God, tinkers, groaned Bill.

--You should call them Itinerants, Daddy, Maggie told him reprovingly. She was trying to pull him over to the gate.

Lynn appeared, wondering what was going on.

--Itinerants always sounds worse to me, she observed, as they followed their happily skipping daughter, Totally lacking in charm.

--Hello Missus, Grand Day Now, called the woman as soon as they were near.

--Yes it is.

Actually it wasn't. The sky was overcast and everything was grey and damp again. They had to keep the range going all day again to keep the chill off the house.

--The Missus has some Grand Clothes to show ye's, called the old man.

--Oh...I don't think we need any more clothes at the moment...said Lynn awkwardly.

--Ah,Ma'am, ye'll just have a look now, said the woman. His name is Sandy, he won't bite, she told Maggie, who was edging nearer to the dog, The ole goat won't hurt ye neither.

She had a kind face and she smiled at Maggie, who petted both animals in delight.

It was impossible to send them away and even Bill was no longer sure that he wanted to.

--Come in for a cup of tea, said Lynn, And you can show me the clothes, she added bravely.

The woman, whose name was Nan, heaved her voluminous person, which bulged like many melons under her brown overcoat, down from the car.
--Tis Cowld enough now, Missus, she said, contradicting her earlier statement.
--Yes, it is. I hope summer's not quite over yet, though.
On the sidecar were basins, pots, pans and firewood, also a couple of boxes of shopping. Tea, candles, bread and eggs were visible. And there were bin bags full of clothes which Nan had collected on her travels. The homeliness of Nan was very appealing...the lap you could lay your head on, the bow in the perky little dog's hair...So was the dapperness of Mickey, who, as Bill was already discovering, was one continuous story, each more incongruous than the last... and the animals had a sort of kind domesticity about them. Maggie wanted Sandy to come in too as he might be thirsty...

When the tea was made, Nan settled herself in a chair by the range, opened a bin bag and, slowly and unhurriedly, pulled out her wares one by one. Each crushed and stained garment was held up for inspection. Meanwhile Mickey drank his tea in long, loud slurps, commenting at intervals, and in complete contradiction of the reality of the ripped and buttonless items,
--That's a grand warm jersey for yerself now, Sonny! Ye'd be needin' one o' them when the cowld weather comes! Ah, look it, aren't them a grand pair o' shoes for yerself now, Missus!
Ah, a little jacket for the babba ye have comin', God bless him!
 Then he spotted a piece of harness that was hanging by the door.
--Here, Sonny, he said in a sharper tone, Will ye sell us that ole bit o' breeching there?
--This? I'm sorry, it isn't mine. A friend left it here.
--Well sure, if he left it he couldn't be wantin' it! I'll give ye a pup for it. I've a litter of terriers below in the wagon and they the best-
--I can't sell it until I've asked Seamus.
--Is it Seamus! And he an old acquaintance- Here Mickey was distracted as he caught sight of a lamp. Would ye swop us that ole lamp there, Sonny?

Bill was feeling close to despair. The morning had been disturbing enough, and now it seemed to his befuddled brain that he could not escape either selling something that he wanted to keep or buying something he did not wish to own. There was a knock at the door. Never had he felt so glad to see Seamus. He knew Seamus loved Wheelin'

and Dealin'.
Seamus entered with a rather affected, God Save All Here! which they knew only a few people a good bit older than him still used. But otherwise he seemed more subdued than usual
--What the hell is he wearing sunglasses for, thought Lynn. Outside it was now raining steadily.
--Hello, Sonny, are ye well. Ye're gone out o' the ole quarry below, then, Mickey addressed Seamus.
--We are, we are so. agreed Seamus. Christy is still down there, did ye not see him?
--Ah, we did so. He had an ole terrier aff of us. We were plannin' on stoppin' a couple o' days but wasn't that divil from Galway there ahead of us.
--Who's that?
--Your man they call Hatchet Johnny, him that has the big mark all down his head on account o' having the ole axe stuck in it that time.
--Jesus, is he there...
--There's been many a fight with that crowd. Me and Nan like a quiet life those times so we came away out of it.

--Christy's such an eejit, said Seamus to Bill, as Mickey began his sales pitch again. I hope he doesn't do any dealin' with the likes of them lot. There'll be trouble out of it for sure.
Mum, can Sandy have another biscuit?
God, Maggie, you've fed him half the tin! Offer them to our visitors please.
--Seamus, Mickey here wants to buy your harness, said Bill.
---I'd be wanting ten pounds for that, said Seamus promptly.
--Ten pound? cried Mickey, aghast, Tisn't worth two! I tell ye what, I've a grand pair o' work boots below, they'd do ye well, let me show ye's, I'll fetch them up-

The haggling began in earnest, peppered with plentiful insults of the other party's wares. Although Seamus had not actually had any wares in his possession when he came in, he laid claim, on returning from taking a pee, to a lamp which was hanging outside.
--I left it behind one time before you moved in.
Bill's understanding was that they had bought the place along with all its contents but he didn't bother to argue. He was too relieved to have retreated to the position of bystander, which he was now thoroughly enjoying.
Over an hour later, a sort of three-way deal was agreed. Mickey got the

piece of harness, the lamp purported to belong to Seamus, and a chicken. Seamus got a couple of quid and the boots -which proved to be new and approximately his size. And Bill and Lynn, so as not to hurt Nan's feelings, became the owners of the least stained baby jacket (which had unfortunately been dunked in boiling water at some stage of its life, giving it the texture of cardboard). They also, to their bewilderment, found themselves the owner of a pup, which would belong to Maggie but doubtless leave pools and poop and chewed things for her parents to clear up.

It had also somehow been agreed that Mickey and Nan could pull onto their land for a couple of days. Maggie clamouring 'Can they! Can they!' had not made it any easier to produce a good excuse as to why they should not. (Lynn now had her by the scruff of her jumper out in the toilet shed and was informing her in a dangerous hiss that she had better learn to keep her bloody little mouth shut in future.)

Seamus had really called in to tell them that his mother had died, and the funeral was at the end of the week. Lynn realised that the sunglasses were to cover his red eyes. They both said how sorry they were, and please give their condolences to the rest of the family, and of course they'd be there. Bill thought he ought to offer him a lift home.

--I don't know quite how we ended up letting those two come in here, worried Bill as he and Seamus sloshed down the track, I don't really like it...
--Arrah, they're harmless enough, said Seamus. Old cra'turs. he added affectionately.
The worst Mickey could do is loose his horses in your field- but sure, they're in it anyway- or steal a bit o'hay for 'em. And he's the great fella for tellin' stories. Nan too-she'll be company for Lynn. They won't stay long. They don't like to be long in the one spot. They'll never stop travellin' those two, they're the last of the old breed.
These words made Bill feel better, honoured even. He started up the van, looking ruefully at the petrol gauge. He couldn't ask Seamus for a contribution under the circumstances and mental arithmetic told him that there was only enough fuel to deliver Seamus home, and get back himself if he was very lucky. After that there'd be no more driving until the giro was cashed in three day's time.
--Bill, ye couldn't just- began Seamus on the way.
--I could not! snapped Bill.

It was nearly dark when he got back. The van was miles down the road,with an empty tank. He saw the sidecar, upended inside the wall, lit up in the glow from Mickey's fire. There was already washing spread on the nearby blackthorns. The ridiculous goat was sitting beside the fire, quietly watching the kettle coming to the boil. Beside it was a big black pot and the basin Nan had done her washing in.
There was a growl from under the wagon as Bill passed and a black dog slunk out. It was a heavily built, squash-faced beast that he hadn't seen before. He was glad to see it was tied.
He realised Mickey was sitting beside the fire as well as the goat, his pipe glowing.
--Hello there, Sonny, grand evenin!
It was true for Mickey that there was a bit of a break in the drizzle and a few stars were visible.
--Will ye have an ole drink now? he asked, holding up a bottle of whiskey.
Bill liked his face. It was lichened and leathery, but it wasn't ravaged with bitterness or savagery. Both Mickey and Nan, he was soon to learn, had suffered many hardships, but still they managed to remain joyful. They inhabited a timeless world that hardly distinguished dreams and fantasy from reality.
--I'll let Lynn know I'm back, then I'll come down again, decided Bill.
--She just went up herself. She was down here atin' bacon and cabbage with us. Isn't that a grand wee gerrel ye have. She was axin' to know could she have a ride on the ole hoss.
--She would! She loves animals. Well, I'll see you later.

There wasn't any dinner. As Mickey had told him, Lynn and Maggie had filled up on bacon and cabbage. Lynn made him eggs on toast and a pot of tea, which she set about draining herself. The bacon stew was delicious but it was also the saltiest thing she had ever eaten.
--They're a nice old couple, she told Bill, I don't think they'll cause us any trouble.
--I'm invited down for a drink, boasted Bill.
--I'll come with you. I'll just check on Maggie..Lynn suddenly didn't want to miss this opportunity to socialise. She realised that in a few more years it would no longer be available to anyone.

It was now quite breezy, with more rain lurking, but Mickey was still sitting by his fire. Nan was in the wagon. She heard their voices and called, Good Evenin' to ye,missus! So Lynn went over and looked up the

wooden steps through the open doors. She had seen inside the wagon earlier but it looked even more charming now, with the little squat queen stove blazing, and Nan sitting up in the bunk bed, wearing fingerless gloves and a great shapeless cardigan over a flannelette nighty. Around the sides of the wagon there were benches and underneath them were neatly fitted cupboards. On the ceiling there was faded patchwork material and photos of Mickey and Nan's large family.
--We were down round Shannon way a few days ago, Nan told Lynn after inviting her in, Near Durty Nellie's. You know that place?
--That's where they have the banquets isn't it.
You could take part in a medieval banquet,waited on by attendants with girdles and tresses, with harp music playing.
--Tis terrible busy down there. Tis terrible busy for the poor hosses those times. Then we were in Kilrush, There's a lovely quiet stoppin' place we have there, oh a lovely spot altogether-
Here she was interrupted by Mickey, coming in with a shovelful of burning wood to help the stove along.
--Are ye comin' out for an ole drink at all? he asked Lynn.
--It doesn't agree with me at the moment.
--Well,I've known a good few th'ole drink didn't agree with,but divil a one of 'em ever refused it! Ye wouldn't catch ME sittin' inside til I was asleep! And I've niver had a day's illness in me life! That's on account o' stayin' out in the air.

When Mickey had settled himself back on his milk crate, he addressed Bill. He leaned forward with his elbows on his jutting knees, and, taking his pipe from his mouth said,
--There's a field down Shannon Way, Sonny. And they say there's a Crock O' Gold buried under a tree there. Well,I had this hoss once and wasn't he always diggin! Oh, a terrible hoss he was for the diggin', sure didn't he wear out his shoes all the time with it!
He fixed Bill with his penetrating blue eyes. Bill felt a bit uncomfortable. He couldn't imagine what was coming next and whether a comment was required. Or what would be suitable if it was. But Mickey had gone on with his story.
--I tied that hoss undher that tree one night and in the mornin'- hadn't he dug a hole as deep as you'd bury a coffin!
Bill waited, expecting Mickey to produce some coins he'd saved from the magical crock..
--If we'd o' stayed another night, he'd o' dug up that crock o' gold!
It didn't matter that the conclusion of the story wasn't as exciting as it could have been. Mickey's animated speech was exciting in itself, and

his complete belief in the possibility of the crock being discovered was contagious.
--What happened to that horse?
--I got rid of him. Sure, I couldn't be getting' him the new shoes all the time.

Inside the wagon, Nan was pointing out various uncles, cousins, brothers and sisters, not to mention her own children in the tattered photos.
--That was me second little gerrel, Kathleen, she said, pointing at a faded photo of a child with thick curls and the same bright eyes.as Mickey She was drowned in an old well when we pulled beside a ruin. That was forty year ago and we've never been back by that place since. Oh, beautiful she was, ma'am, curly hair and all, and always mindin' the little fella, Johnny, for me while I was washin' or cookin'....There were tears in her eyes.
--I'm so sorry.
--Oh, there's been a lot lost on the road. But you never forget them. I had a brother killed aff of a horse, and we all warning him it was a wild divil and he shouldn't have kept him...And me sister lost two of hers, one with pneumonia he was after getting' from the measles, and Mary, that cut her leg and got the blood poisoning. Tis an awful thing to lose a child. When people are grown tis hard enough, but at least they had the bit o' life. We go through so much to have the babbas and then to have them taken from us... and they so young and believin' ye can make everything right. And maybe tis true that if Mary wasn't livin' on the road maybe the hospital would have helped her get better.
Lynn didn't know what to say.
But Nan was like Mickey. The conversation jumped about randomly. She had heaved herself off the bunk and made the usual brew of tea, sugar and milk all in the pot. She opened one of the little cupboards.
--Will ye have a little cake now, Ma'am?
--Yes please. You're very well organised.
--Sure, ye've got to have the bit o' comfort.
 --Do you think travelling kids would be better off in houses then? asked Lynn hesitantly. Would you accept a corporation house if you were offered one?
--They're better for some. Not for us, said Nan decisively. Twould kill us! And I know of people that got ill and died as soon as they stopped inside in a house! We were both born on the road and that's where we'll die. None of our children are in houses either, but they're all livin' on the town sites, and dhrivin' round in them vans and lorries. They've no interest in

travellin' with the wagons any more. Tis shameful,them places they have to stay on! We kept healthy, livin' the old way. But them places-sure ye wouldn't want to keep pigs on 'em.
The government thinks that that's how all the travellers will give in and go into houses. It's the young wans I feel sorry for. I 've had me life and I wouldn't want it different. There's no life on the road any more, but it takes more than going into a house to stop you being a traveller. There's not many that will be happy.

Outside, Bill, emboldened by the whiskey, was asking Mickey the taboo question, Had he had ever seen the fairies?
Seamus had recently asked an old fella in Moroney's bar the same thing, and been told to Feck Off for yourself and don't be thinking ye can laugh at me. Yet that tune, the Tarboltan, was supposed to have first been heard played by the fairies. And some musicians were said to have heard music in the sea or wind that they noted down. There'd recently been a radio programme about it.
Out here, gazing into the fire,with the horses munching nearby, and the glow from the wagon blending into the soft darkness around them, Bill wanted to absorb all he could of that past where such things had seemed so possible.
--I did not, Sonny! answered Mickey, rather to his surprise. I didn't see 'em. But me father did! His face lit up as always when he launched into one of his tales. He was comin' home – wid a dhrop taken, but still well able for himself – so he was goin' along, when Holy Mary Mother O' God weren't there two little men in red caps there inside a gate, and they hittin' and draggin' at each other like divils! Shtop yer fightin', he yells at 'em, but if he did, they just laffed. So in he goes, through the ole gate, to give 'em a hidin'. But they were gone back to the other side too quick for him to catch 'em. And that was how it went all night, they dodgin' back and fore til he was wore out and gev it up and went home.
Mickey paused for a swig of whiskey.
Bill thought he had come across this story in a book of Irish folk tales.
--I often HEARD the fairies sure enough, Mickey went on. Once, I was passin' one o' them forts. And I heard singin' from inside. And nobody there at all.
And one time, Sonny, oh,a good many year ago now, I had an ole ass. Well, Sonny, I never saw the bate of 'im in me life, afore nor since: he was as big as that hoss over there – and that's no word of a lie – and as STRONG, I tell ye, he could pull the wagon on his own and there's not many an ass can do that.
So this day, we'd come about twenty mile and it getting' dark, and

nowhere to pull in but an ole wet field with nu'un for wood at all. Well, in this field was a fairy fort, with a small little bit o' blackthorn growin' round the sides. So I harnesses up th'old ass and gets him to pull out the wood. But that wood, Sonny, it never burned at all! Just smoked and smoked, the worst I ever seen. And in the mornin' - Mickey leaned even further forward and fixed Bill with his gleaming gaze – In the mornin', didn't the ass drop dead, just like that. Dead as a stone! The fairies had that wood cursed so it wouldn't burn, he said with conviction, and twas them took the ass on me and all.

Lynn came and sat beside Bill. There was clucking from under the wagon where their hen had been housed in a wooden box. Lynn wondered if it would end up perched on the sidecar and basking in the warmth of the fire like the goat.
--How's the hen settling in?she asked Mickey, aware that this subject was probably an awful banality compared to whatever had gone before.
--Did ye ever see duck eggs now, Missus? cried Mickey, Why, Holy Mary Mother O' God, I never saw the bate of it in me life, afore nor since, there was a fella below in Kilkee gev me a couple and Honest to God! They were three times the size of that mug there!
Lynn, lounging comfortably against Bill, having a drop of whiskey after all and, finding it nearly as agreeable as in pre-pregnant days, having a drop more, wondered if he'd go onto goose eggs next. Given his gloriously exaggerated description of the duck eggs, unless a weightlifter appeared in the story, no one would be able to shift those boulders of incunabula at all....

--Seamus saw the Banshee once- began Bill.
--I never saw no banshee, interrupted Mickey, but just the other day didn't I see a fella who looked worse than the divil himself! Twas down Newmarket way, there's a big wood there, maybe ye's know it. Well I was collectin' wood when Holy Mary Mother O' God! This fella comes from the trees. Well,begod, his teeth must o' been – Mickey looked round for inspiration, and seizing a poker from beside the fire, measured off a six inch length – That size! he finished triumphantly. And that's no word of a lie! he added for good measure.

--Why are you crying? Bill asked Lynn later, when they were back in the house. But he knew. Soon no one would be left living the old travelling life. Tonight, with Mickey's star like eyes dancing from his grizzled old head, they had travelled aboard the wagon, creaking and clopping, around a different Ireland in a different world.

Lynn knew she wouldn't stick that life for a minute. (She wouldn't want the giving birth without gas and air for starters, let alone all the pregnancies...) Nor being frequently cold and hungry, and having her kids die...All that was just as stressful as living with the nuclear threat, video nasties and Thatcher.

Annie had remarked that she hated the way some of the Blow ins Romanticised The Miserable Lives Of Tinkers, especially the women. But there was a wonderful quality of innocence that Mickey and Nan had retained despite the times of suffering.. To the modern mind it might seem nothing more than a deplorable state of ignorance, but it allowed them to be far more accepting of fate,and far more easily pleased. Of course they'd never had to pay bills, but they wouldn't have ever got a giro either...

Ah, God, how exciting it must have been, travelling by moonlight Mickey had said, with the horses straining and frothing to cover the last few miles to the horse fair at Spancil Hill. The changing seasons, all the different places. Music, songs and stories.

Tonight, she wasn't going to remind herself of the dealing, drinking and inevitable fighting to follow. Yes, she was romanticising. And she would never forget this evening. Bright in her memory would stay the honeyed sweat of the horses, the jingle of harness, Nan about her business, big and cosy as an eiderdown, Mickey talking, talking, talking, his words running together like young fish in a stream, blending together hardship and joy, dreams and visions. A little education might be a fine thing. But today the nearly extinct skills of these people who had never been to school seemed of far more value.

Before Mickey and Nan left, there were a few more visitors. One was an old fella perched on his black bike like a vulture, with a tattered coat billowing behind him. He stopped to shake his fist at Mickey over the wall.

--Ye've been into my barn Mickey Donohue! He shouted, Takin' my firewood!And that's my hay ye have hangin' on the back o'your wagon! Mickey smiled cheekily and said, Tis a grand day, a grand day to be out bicycling!

--You stay out o' there or I'll have the guards on ye!

--I haven't seen him before, remarked Lynn.

--That's Jackie Hogan. I went past his place with Seamus. It's completely overgrown, you'd never know someone was living in there. We met him going up the lane to a well that was full of duckweed, Bill told her.

--Poor old man...
--Well according to Seamus, he has a fortune. Just won't spend any of it.

Jim Ryan passed. Normally he'd pull up and stop for a chat, but this time he gave Bill, who was repairing a piece of wall, the barest of salutes, and drove straight past. Bill didn't mention this to Lynn.

They spent another evening being transported to a different world. Maggie came with them, staying up late because it was a Friday night. But she wasn't her usual bubbly self, and at bed time she told Lynn that Majella was no longer her friend.
--She said I was friends with dirty knackers. Some of the others ran away pretending I smelt. I don't smell, do I?
--No darling, of course not.
--And she said, anyway you're all on drugs. You're not on drugs are you?
No. But some drugs aren't as bad as people think.
--What do you mean?
Lynn wished she hadn't said that.
--Well...aspirin is a drug but no one calls it that. So are wine and beer and whiskey but they are legal while some other things aren't. Some people don't think that's fair.
--They're Alcohol aren't they.
--Yes. Sometimes alcohol makes people behave very badly but nobody minds much because it's legal. But it's still a kind of drug.
– Is it? asked Maggie, interestedly, Because Majella's Dad drinks beer, so he's on drugs as well then!
--Well, it's no good saying that to her. People are worried because there are some Bad drugs around and that's what they've heard about. Did Majella say why she's decided we're all on drugs?
--Some kids that were at Seamus's party said hello to me. And Siobhan, this other girl, said, That's the Blow-ins from the Steiner school. Their Mams and Dads are all on drugs. And then Majella got all funny with me.
--What nonsense, said Lynn matter of factly, It sounds to me as if Siobhan just wants Majella to herself.
But t was all she could do not to shudder as the memories of her own sufferings in school flooded back to her. True she had never been bullied exactly, but somehow she had never been desirable Best Friend material. Not fashionable enough. Too vague and dreamy. And when everyone else - yes EVERYONE,even the most malnourished little

bitches imaginable beat her to it and managed to grow breasts - her social failure was sealed. At times like this all the painful memories leapt up and laughed at her and the humiliation was so acute it could have all happened yesterday.

There was the time when she realised that some sniggering boys were scrutinising her in the school corridor and to her horror she discovered on following their leering gaze that she only had one breast. The other wad of cotton wool had somehow escaped the bra she had desperately persuaded her mother to buy her and was on the floor near her feet.

Not long after that her friends pretended that a boy from the youth club everyone but her attended had said she sounded nice, and wanted to go out with her. They said he wanted to see a photo and she got all excited and brought it for them to pass on to him. Only to be told it was all a cruel pretence.

There was another time, when they had finally invited her to come with them. She had her mother driven demented. The poor woman (after getting home from work and cooking the family meal) was frantically sewing together the last seams of a new, fashionably long cardigan that Lynn felt she had to wear to be a tiny bit acceptable. Then someone rang and said, Sorry, there wasn't room in her Dad's car, perhaps next week...

That was teenager stuff anyway, Maggie was a long way off that...Lynn remembered earlier incidents and reflected that maybe she deserved to stay flat as a pancake until she was fifteen because she'd been quite a nasty child...She remembered being on a ferry to Belgium. On the deck was a big wheel, to work the anchor or something, and a little boy was standing at it, pretending to steer the ship and talking aloud of all the exotic ports he was landing in. Lynn desperately wanted a turn. 'I'll just sail her to Africa/ India/ Constantinopia' said the little boy. She'd got fed up waiting. She'd had a sneaky look round and thumped the poor little bugger as hard as she could. He'd ran off bawling...

She had to fight not to show her feelings to Maggie who seemed, thank God, more robust than she had been. (Lynn fervently hoped that would go for the chest department too.)

--It's nonsense, she told Maggie. Majella will forget about it in a couple of days time. Try not to let them see you're upset.

Great advice when she felt like howling herself. She knew she should be cheered but she was further stung when Maggie said,with some scorn in her voice, 'Of course I don't let them see I'm upset!

Next day around lunch time, a pick-up and a car with dodgy suspension pulled up by the gate and out piled Mickey and Nan's relations from Limerick.. To Lynn's relief, they kept away from the house (they looked nowhere as appealing as their forebears) but the three men took Mickey off for a bit of a drive in the car. A couple of women and several children stayed behind with Nan. Maggie stayed indoors, colouring with unusual concentration.

Later in the afternoon, there was a commotion. Looking down the track, Lynn saw that the bigger of the horses was harnessed to the sidecar, which was just being dragged through the gate as the horse plunged forward. Mickey was standing like a cowboy on the rocking car, whooping, yelling and waving a whip.
--LOOK OUT! yelled Bill,who was still pretending to be working in the garden but had been less and less able to concentrate. The sidecar caught the wooden gatepost, wrenching it out and continued to scrape along Bill's new section of wall, pulling rocks and soil onto the road.. The horse swerved and took off down the road in a clattering gallop.
The rest of the clan were taking no notice. They were by the fire, some arguing, some singing, one with a child on his lap. Bill stood open mouthed as the huge horse charged past again. As the sidecar jolted over the dislodged rocks, Mickey fell onto his back. The mad gallop must have ended at the forestry entrance at the top of the hill because it wasn't long before Bill heard the hooves coming back. Somehow, Mickey had righted himself and managed to stand up again. He was calling drunkenly, ablaze with whiskey and adrenalin, to ask didn't any of the childer want an ole ride.

Chapter Fourteen

Lynn was feeling horrible : worried about what to wear to the funeral, whilst knowing she had only one choice because nothing else fitted.
--Its all right for YOU, she snapped, when Bill said, with odious male matter -of -factness,
--Well if you know that's the only dress that fits, just shove it over your head and hurry up

Shame about the trees, thought Bill when they were finally leaving (a long time later than planned: Lynn had threatened not to go and he had realised that some serious cajoling and re-assurance along the lines of, You Know You Look Lovely despite that bloody great bulge, rather than pointing out brutal facts regarding the limited stock of available clothing, was urgently required.)
Maggie, too, was being a pain, all superior and critical of their lifestyle all of a sudden. And That Dear Old Man, ie, Mickey, had become That Bloody Knacker, he noticed. He told her not to swear. And decided she could clear up the next pool from the puppy herself.
Yes, shame about the trees, how Mickey had reached up and pruned all the available branches for firewood. His loppings had left them curiously bald and lopsided below a certain height.
Mickey and Nan had gone on their way quietly enough a couple of days after Mickey's Ben Hur act. He seemed none the worst and went up the road as jauntily as ever, leading the horse as always, and cheeking Jackie Hogan, who was screeching more complaints of theft and vandalism,with,
--Will ye sell us that ole bike now, Jackie!
--Go on away out o' that before I have the guards on ye! answered Jackie predictably, but he rode quickly away, recognising defeat.

Lynn was missing her sister. She had no idea that Cathy was, at that moment, hitching out of the town of Sligo,where she had spent an uncomfortable night on a dis-used railway track. Her companion was Elsa: crew- cutted, verbally strident and dressed in a man's collarless shirt and Doc Martins. At the Folk Club in Bristol, she had seemed quite interesting, and when it transpired that she played the violin and wanted to go to an Irish music festival the following week, Cathy was inspired and said she'd go along. She had no money but she'd just got a new job, and Elsa said they could hitch and not spend anything beyond the ferry fare. She could just fit it in before she started in the new job. She thought she would surprise Lynn with a quick visit on her way home. No point in writing, she'd arrive before the letter did. And she knew Lynn would be delighted to see her, she'd sounded a bit low in her last letter and asked if there was any chance she might come back over.

With them was Sam, Elsa's adenoidal son, who hardly spoke, especially if he needed a wee, which had caused consternation in several cars,and gazed blankly at the world through a veil of snot. The grey rubber tyre had come off Sam's big blue push chair somewhere on the route across Wales. Now the metal wheel rim was thick with tiny stones and gravel, giving the push chair a curious lurching motion. Cathy hoped that nothing worse would befall their conveyance because they relied on it to transport all their luggage -the tent, bags and bedding were piled behind and underneath Sam. She felt full of unease. It was only as they were leaving Dublin on a bus that she found out from Elsa that Ballyshannon, their designation, was right on the border. The IRA prisoners in the Maze had been on their dirty protest for two years. Thatcher continued to smile in her reptilian way and pronounce herself Un-moved. Feelings were running high, the Troubles were raging. Cathy did not want to be British and heading in that direction at all, but Elsa,whose politics were stuck in the era when women went down the mines (she had a few songs about that) and only knew Ireland as an antiquated place that didn't allow abortions, was unconcerned.

--There'll be people of all nationalities there, she assured Cathy, Anyway, who'd be bothered with two women and a little kid.

Cathy would have liked to go back but she didn't want to hitch on her own. She'd heard that, despite Ireland's reputation of safety, some poor woman in the County Kildare, had last year accepted a lift whilst waiting for her bus, and then been raped and murdered. Besides, they were nearly there now..

Bill had been cajoled into picking up a couple of people on the way to the funeral. One was the young solicitor, Brendan. He told them he was soon representing Vinney in a court case.

--He was driving with no insurance and he hit a motorbike. Being the fecking eejit he is,and worried on account of having no insurance he went and signed a paper saying he'd pay all the damages. Only they're enormous, so he can't. I'm wishing I hadn't taken it on. He's sure to make a holy show of me altogether.

Thanks for the lift, he went on, It's very good of you. Do you like venison? I've a freezer full of it out in my parent's shed, you can call over and get a piece any time. And salmon, if you want any salmon it's over at Frankie Daly's, you know, next to the big estate there...

Vinney was reluctantly gaining consciousness on Seamus and Nuala's floor. Mikey had crawled across him many times, enjoying the new obstacle challenge, but Vinney hadn't stirred. He had turned up the evening before and offered to take Seamus out for a conciliatory drink. Conciliatory on account of his mother's death, and also because he had offered Seamus work. Then, as so often, he had received a 'sub' from the old couple whose house was taken apart in readiness for improvements to begin and not yet got round to starting the job.
--Are you sure you should be out today? Seamus had queried, Only I saw Brendan yesterday and he's worryin' about your witnesses. You've to go and see them and tell them about the Case-
--Arrah, don't be Frrrreakin' me, Man! cried Vinney impatiently, Are ye coming for a drink or are ye takin' the feckin' veil?
--Just a quick one, said Seamus to Nuala.
--Vinney, attempted Nuala, You wouldn't sit with Mikey just for half an hour, so that Seamus and myself could go for a drink first? He shouldn't wake now. You could have a think about what you need to say and all that for the Case then-
--The Case! cried Vinney, heading for the door like a greyhound, I can't help ye Nuala, sure I have to see my witnesses!
--Just a quick one, affirmed Seamus again, heading after him.

Nuala knew there was no one in at the house. Ambrose and Seamus were already falling out and relations had deteriorated to the point where she avoided going over there as much as possible. She was no longer offered the use of the washing machine and Breda didn't chat to her as she used to. She and Seamus still went to the house to watch Fawlty Towers -God, then they forgot about other people entirely...Breda would be trying to put away another bottle that Ambrose had taken from the crate in the hall ('Excellent stuff, excellent quality! Bought it on a business trip you know!') and the daughter would be wheedling at him to buy her something or other. But she and Seamus didn't notice, they would have pains in their bellies from laughing so much. It was great.

But the bath...Breda had said a long time ago that she could use it, but the family were usually around, and anyway she was so used to squatting in the baby bath that she had almost forgotten the way most of the population in 1980 had become accustomed to keeping themselves clean. Now Mikey was asleep and she knew the family were off at some posh dinner. Seamus wouldn't be back for hours. She would treat herself. She gathered her wash things and headed for the house.

Inside, the décor was daunting. There was a huge kitchen with marble sideboards and everything of gleaming stainless steel. And a sort of Amusement Room which had exotic red wallpaper, a grand piano, a chaise longue, a pool table and a cabinet full of Waterford glass. The drawing room where they watched Fawlty Towers was vast, with two leather suites in it. She imagine the bathroom to contain a sunken pool, shell-shaped and oyster coloured, surrounded by bath oils and soft towels.
It was an awful shock when she rounded the corner of the stairs and the carpet suddenly ended. She was looking at a basin catching drips from the ceiling, peeling paint and a passageway to the bathroom that looked as if it had come off the set of that programme, The Addams Family. It was full of cobwebs and there were holes in the bare floorboards.
She picked her way gingerly along it and opened the bathroom door. Jesus,this couldn't be real. Everything was grey and flaky like rotten porridge- the walls,the carpet and the bath itself. On the sides of the bath was what looked like decades of scum and it was choked with empty containers which had once held bubble bath and shampoo. Plus hair. (No wonder Ambrose was so bald. They had discovered one blustery day that he wore a toupet)
Nuala hurried home.

Not only Vinney, but everyone in the village, had bought Seamus conciliatory drinks. Hence he was less cute than usual and unwisely brought Vinney home with him. Nuala had just got off to sleep after a very tiring evening with Mikey (the moon was full and that always made him lively) when Vinney put on the record player and commenced to leap wildly about the room.
Now they had all overslept-even Mikey- and were trying to make themselves respectable for the funeral before Tommy came to fetch them in his taxi.

In the funeral parlour, Mrs Lynch was lying in her coffin. Behind her sat the family, while the rest of the mourners filed around, murmuring prayers, crossing themselves, then shaking hands with the family and

saying, 'Sorry for your trouble.'
--Who's THAT? whispered Lynn to Annie, pointing to a figure up ahead of them in the queue, who was waddling along and bowing to those around him as if he was very important.
--Seamus warned me about him, Annie whispered back, He's a bit simple. He goes to all the funerals. Loves them. Thinks he's the priest. His father's very rich so they all tolerate it.
--Must be nice to have an endless free source of entertainment. Hey, he's gone round twice!
Lynn moved closer to Annie as the funeral freak re-joined the line in front of them and commenced to spray them with saliva as he told them, Thisssh way, thisssh way!
He seemed to think he was ushering them into his own party.
--Shorry for yer thrubble! he spluttered repeatedly as he yanked the hands of the family up and down so enthusiastically it was all they could do to hang onto their seats.
--Jesus, commented Seamus, rubbing his arm, then caught a black look from his uncle.
As Lynn and Annie were leaving, they caught sight of him diving in for a third time. Maeve, who had been sobbing a few minutes before, had exploded into a fit of giggles, which no amount of looks from Uncle Steven were quelling.
--He's known as Corpsy Kevin, whispered Annie. Lynn bit her lip in an agony of fear that she would laugh inappropriately and then wet herself: Her bladder wasn't great even when it wasn't squashed under a baby. She stared at the ground, trying not to see his goofy profile as, positioned right behind the hearse, he turned proudly from side to side, surveying the mourners. He made a great show of welcoming them to the church and directing them in. Most of the town seemed to be there.

When the service was over, they all trailed out to the graveyard, some in cars, many on foot. Nuala came over to greet them. She looked beautiful. She had put her hair up. She was in another ethnic dress but a black one. Lynn felt like a hideous old bag.
--Who's that man taking photos? she asked, thinking it might be a local custom. And feeling a bit regretful that she hadn't brought her own camera. There were some great faces here...
--Oh, that's Ambrose, said Nuala in disgust, Typical Protestant! No sensitivity at all. Would you like to come back to Maeve's house ? For refreshments.
--Oh,I don't think we should, that's just for family isn't it? Lynn did not

want to make any mistakes. What a good thing she had kept quiet about her immoral designs on the funeral-goers with her camera...
--It'll be fine. You can bet your life they'll be a good few in it that don't even KNOW anyone in the family. I'm sure you'll be grand just popping in for a bit anyway.
There was a hush except for Kevin spluttering a very mixed up prayer, while the priest tried to get down to some serious final business. Everyone made an intense scrutiny of the ground while he bawled out his words in order to be audible over his rival's gibberish and the sobbing of Seamus's other sister, who had come over from England.

At Maeve's house, sandwiches, cake and bottles of wine and whiskey obscured the table,and every shape and size of relation and well wisher was milling about. Bill had a glass thrust into his hand and was shunted about by the tide of humanity. People often struck up conversation with him as if he'd known them all their lives, but they always seemed to have a better anchorage than he did, and he generally got moved on before much of an answer was required.
Children scrambled under and between adult feet and legs, fought on the stairs and wrecked the bedrooms where they were feasting on pilfered sandwiches and cake.
Bill rather envied Lynn,who had gone off with Nuala to fetch Mikey from a teenager who'd been persuaded to mind him.. But he'd been instructed to keep an eye on Maggie (he hadn't a clue where she was) and besides, he was already too drunk to fight his way out.

--How's the vegetable selling going? Lynn asked Nuala. She thought that she ought to say something more about Mrs Lynch. She was often uncannily perceptive about people's thoughts and feelings, but simple banalities did not come easily to her. Perhaps some comment about what a nice funeral it had been? But that would be a downright lie. Anyway, Nuala did not seem exactly grief -stricken. Lynn knew she'd had hardly anything to do with Mrs Lynch, whose attitude to Seamus and his lifestyle had been one of total incomprehension and disapproval. So she gave up on trying to say the right thing, and Nuala seemed relieved to have escaped the claustrophobic house and any more talk about someone she'd hardly known.
--It's not great, to be honest with you. We started too late for one thing. Seamus grew a pile of that Chinese Cabbage, that was the thing that did the best, but nobody wants it. Breda quite liked it,but she could only use so much...You can't freeze it so most of it just went to seed. Some of the other stuff just didn't come up. Ambrose was meant to give us a lift into

town on Saturdays to sell stuff but he always seems to be going away - on business trips he says, but Seamus thinks he's off seeing some woman. There's nothing really to sell anyway. We're meant to keep Ambrose stocked up on vegetables but there aren't enough, so he doesn't want to pay us. So Seamus keeps using the few things that are growing down there for ourselves. And being near the village- well, Seamus gets invited out all the time. He spends more and he doesn't do the work for Ambrose.
--Don't you get out more, too?
--I did a couple of times. The daughter babysat. But I don't seem to have the energy. Having Mikey has changed things. I hate Seamus for the freedom he has but if I do manage to get out, I don't enjoy it. I'm too tired and I worry about Mikey. I feel all wrong without him.
--I know what you mean, lied Lynn. When Maggie was a baby, she'd had so much help (too much in fact) from her mother, and Cathy had been a doting Aunt whenever she came home. She had got out quite a lot, with the greatest feeling of relief.
--Are you sure you're not anaemic or something? That can make you feel really tired.
--I could be. I was on iron tablets before...Nuala glanced at her, then said quietly, I won't be there for ever. You don't know the half of it.
There were tears in her eyes.
--What's wrong? You mean...you want to leave Seamus? How long have you been with him?
--Only long enough to have Mikey...
--Where did you meet him?
--Carnsore Point festival. Well, I knew him from there. I sort of-fell into it all later..
--Shall we go in here for a minute? suggested Lynn. They turned off into a small, worn looking green with a couple of benches on it. Nuala talked hesitantly, not looking at Lynn.
-- I had this boyfriend in England, Davy. He was like me, he was from an Irish family but he grew up over there. We were together for four years. He was the most beautiful looking bloke I ever saw, artistic, musical...very political. We were kind of - powerful together. We did everything together and it was great. Well, for a long time...
Anyway, we weren't getting on very well, he could be a lazy bugger and I seemed to be doing all the work -we were living on a smallholding at the time - and then he started playing guitar in a punk band and I was jealous because he spent a lot of time practising with this woman. And I decided I'd had enough and just on a whim really I got a job over here.
--Was that with your Aunt?

--No, no. I used to come over and help my Aunt in my holidays when I was younger. She died, a good few years ago now. Quite suddenly. She had cancer and it just swept her away in a couple of months.

Nuala realised that Lynn, like everyone else, thought she was younger than she was.

-- This job was in a craft shop. I knew I'd made a terrible mistake, I was missing Davy like crazy and I was going to go home as soon as I'd saved the fare, but I made the mistake of coming up here for a day out. I met Seamus. I knew him and a couple of people he was with a bit from Carnsore and I thought I was being very cool getting a lift out to a session with them. Seamus was saying corny things about my eyes all night and buying me drinks but I didn't even like him. The thing was Lynn, we were miles away from town and I'd missed the last bus from there anyway. I couldn't get home. I was quite drunk and stoned and I ended up going back to his caravan, because I had to stay somewhere, and-and-

--You slept with him. But Nuala, you made a mistake, that doesn't mean you had to stay with him.

--I didn't admit it to anyone you see . I pretended it was what I wanted to do because I didn't want to look like a pathetic little eejit who'd been seduced. But I only slept with him because he expected it. The worst thing is that people always think I'm younger than I am. I hate that. And they probably think I was a complete innocent. But I lived four years with Davy and I had boyfriends before that. I never went to bed with anyone I didn't want to...even if it did mostly turn out to be shit. I don't know why I didn't say No. I lay there all night thinking how beautiful it used to be with Davy and feeling cheap and filthy. I wanted to walk out- but it was miles back to town and I didn't know anyone there.

 I had a big row from my boss, when I managed to get back-that was two days later because there were no buses on Sunday - there'd been this big order in, loads of heavy boxes to unload and I wasn't there, and the old bitch gave me the sack.. She wouldn't give me the rest of my pay either. I hitched up to some people I knew with tepees on the coast and stayed there for a while. No money, nothing. After a while Seamus came by and I ended up going home with him. There didn't seem anything else to do, he always had food and a good fire... I always had this feeling that I'd get away soon and it was all like a bad dream. It felt wrong all the time, there was no closeness, but he didn't notice...And I used to plan and dream of going to look for Davy. Then I realised Mikey was on the way...

--What about your parents? Couldn't you ask them for help? Have you got brothers and sisters?

--I've a brother, Michael, much older than me. He's in Canada now and hasn't been home in years. My parents went to England to have a better life. It was the worst insult to my Mum that I'd casually got myself pregnant. It's hard to explain but the way she carried on made it hard to be honest. I pretended that what I'd done was what I wanted, and I was happy...I'm so pathetic. My whole life is a lie. It's like a bad dream, someone else's dream that I got into by mistake...
Nuala was trying not to cry, Lynn hugging her.
Two women passed. They crossed themselves.
--That's the young one of the Lynch's, said one to the other. Sorry for your trouble, she said, leaning down to touch Nuala's hand.

--Oh, Nuala, what a mess. But listen, you have to start taking more charge of your life. You don't have to stay with Seamus-
--Who'd want me with Mikey? And I'm so tired. And no car or anything. Seamus has all the money as well. If I got a mile up the road it would be a miracle.
--You could come and live at our place, in a caravan.
--Thanks, Lynn, but I think I'll have to go much further away.
--Wouldn't your family have you back, if you explained things?
--They would help me, yes. My Mum sends me money sometimes and things for Mikey. But I don't want to go back and live with my parents after years of being independent. And I've disappointed them so much. They wouldn't be ashamed about me having a baby out of wedlock or any of that, although there's still girls over here being fecked away in the laundries for it... It's more about throwing away the chances they thought they were giving me.. They didn't approve of all the hippy stuff, but I was going to go to Art College. Myself and Davy were trying to get into the same one...
There was a long silence.
--I nearly had Davy's baby once, mused Nuala sadly, I miscarried. They say lots of first pregnancies end like that. I wish I'd stayed with him and been part of that big family. Married him, had kids with him....
--Would your parents have been happier if you married Seamus?
--I don't know. They're snobs really, they would have liked me to marry someone rich and educated. My Mum liked Davy. She's quite astute though, she could see his faults. But also I think she could feel the magic we had together. She'd be disappointed and maybe even a bit horrified if I ever took Seamus to meet her. Partly because he's much older than me. But she'd see through him in no time. Or rather she'd see through me...Do your parents like Bill?
--Yea, they do. They think he's a hero. It pisses me off sometimes..

They both laughed.
--I did think one time that I'd like to marry Seamus. It was when I had Mikey. You know how you hold your baby in your arms and you want everything to be right for them..Well I might have done it for Mikey. But Seamus is already married. In the Catholic church. So I had a lucky escape! She laughed,a bit bitterly.
--Oh.
--When I was in the hospital after having Mikey, I used to fall asleep in the afternoons. And I kept having this dream that Davy was the father and was coming to see me, with flowers, and this bracelet that he made me years ago....
 Nuala stood up and wiped her face.
--Mikey isn't the only child floating around either, she added. We'd better get on and fetch him, or your one will be thinking I got buried along with Seamus's mother...Sorry, Lynn. I shouldn't have told you all that I've never talked about it to anyone. You won't tell anyone will you?
--No. Of course not.
They started walking.
--Does Davy know about Mikey and everything?
--Yea. He phoned me up once when me and Seamus went to see my friend Kitty. She must have told him I'd be there. She didn't know Seamus was going to invite himself along. Mikey was only a few weeks old and Seamus was listening. We just chatted. I felt terrible. It was so good hearing his voice. But I knew I'd really hurt him having Mikey. And I couldn't undo it, or say what I really felt. And Seamus was bad vibing me as he calls it. He gave out to me for hours afterwards.
-- But you've still got your life ahead of you. You could probably get into art college when Mkey's older, whether or not you stay with Seamus.
Nuala said nothing.
--Where does Kitty live? Could you go and stay with her?
--She was my best friend over here, a second cousin. But she went to London, just after I arrived. I didn't know she was planning to do that or I might not have come over. That time myself and Seamus went to visit her, she was just back for a few days.

A girl was coming out of a door, looking flustered. She pulled a pushchair out. In the pushchair was Mikey, and he was yelling.
--Oh, Howye, Geraldine, sorry I'm late fetching him. Has he been okay? It was really good of you to have him. Don't worry, he's only roaring like that because he's hungry. Hang on, I'll find your money.
--Mam said I should take him out for a bit of air and see if I could see you coming and if not we'd give him his tea here.

Nuala gave Mikey a rusk. Geraldine bent and kissed him.
--He was really good fun til the last half hour, she told Nuala, we were all crawling around the floor with him and he loving it and roaring laughing. I've used up all the nappies, they're in that bag there. And his blue trousers. They got wet.
--That's great, Geraldine, thanks again. Bye now. Wave Bye bye, Mikey.

--Nuala...When you found out you were pregnant, did you ever think about having an abortion?
--Why do you ask that? There was hostility in Nuala's voice, as if Lynn was suggesting she chop Mikey's head off now. Yes I did, although I don't know how I would have got myself to England seeing as I couldn't get myself home in all that time....and no, I didn't want to do it. But it's not like I was risking being locked away and having Mikey taken off me. I can see why some people do it.
--I only wondered. Because I know someone who had one. And it really messed her up...They all go on about a woman's right to choose, and I always thought that was right. And I know some women are really desperate..But it seems to be quite casual. My friend went to a private clinic because she didn't want to be recognised by anyone local. I suppose if you're paying for it they're not going to turn you away. You get some counselling to help you make the decision but they just said, Yes dear, you can't possibly have this baby with all the difficulties you would both face. I think by that time she was having doubts and if she'd been told the things she told me afterwards....She wasn't religious. But afterwards...She said she had let herself be raped by the devil. She's with someone now, and she's got a little boy, but she 's never forgiven herself...In some ways, I like the firm moral stance that the Catholic church has-
--You WHAT? Nuala laughed cynically.
--Well, I know from what Seamus has told Bill and me that the priests used to live in luxury and take money and food from people who had nothing, but -
They had ended up in the little green again. Mikey was chewing at pieces of a funeral sandwich Nuala had found in her bag.
--You don't know the half of it, Lynn. It's the women who really suffer here. It's changing a bit now. An unmarried woman can get benefits. But not so long ago they just went in to the Nuns. The family signed them in. They didn't have a choice. There's still a terrible stigma about babies being born out of wedlock. What a load of rubbish! I hate religion! I can see why my parents left.. And the baby was taken away for adoption. No

choice. They're still open, those places. Or should I say closed. I don't know that much about it, it might be changing, but as far as I know you can't get back out...

--I didn't know, said Lynn lamely. Is that what you meant earlier? You said something about a laundry.

--They have to work in a laundry. For nothing. Punishment for their brief moment of passion I suppose. If they weren't in there after being raped. The women got the blame for that as well.

There was a silence.

--I'll never complain about my life again, thought Lynn. Even if there hadn't been much Passion in in lately. That side of things had been slow to take off with Bill. Maybe because she needed him more than she actually fancied him. But he was a lazy bugger in bed, she thought, and lacking in subtlety. It had got better. And then everything stayed sort of well oiled and ready. But lately, there hadn't been much communication between them, verbally or otherwise. Not even simple expressions of affection. The oil had run out.

Not long ago, she'd been out walking. Well, that had been her intention but she soon found herself lolling breathlessly beside a wall, incapacitated and infuriated. Her lungs heaved, her bladder was straining. The old heaviness, as if she'd been on a lurching, fume-filled bus all day, was back behind her eyeballs. After some unfortunately phrased comment from Bill as to her welfare, she'd stormed out, hating the feeling of dependency and helplessness and determined to prove that, as the books were always telling her, Pregnancy Wasn't A Disease. Suddenly, as she lay half prone and thinking vicious thoughts about everyone who wasn't as large as she was, Christy hopped over the wall in a hideous display of litheness, followed by a crew of dogs. He caught sight of her ('He had to look twice to see if it was really me or a big fat bin bag stuffed with tinker's clothes,' thought Lynn dismally) and gave an awkward greeting. His shirt was open and she saw a firm muscular belly, and Ooh, God, a lovely line of black hair leading-

Embarrassed at the pang this gave her, she kept her eyes on the dogs. She couldn't see the terrier that had been going to receive Seamus's comfrey treatment that time; there weren't any others that she recognised either.

Christy was as restless as usual and she always found it hard to understand his swift, impatient speech. They exchanged a few comments about the weather, the garden and Mrs Lynch's deteriorating health, and then he vaulted another wall and strode away, whistling. Young, lean, fit...

He left a tang of male sweat behind him that electrified the air. Lynn

longed to be light, slender, naked and smeared in it.
As she sat there, recalling this, the last elusive line of a poem she had been mentally composing for some time came into her mind.

Security

A leg, heavy with the weight of possession,
 crushes a belly.
Body-sodden air engulfs snores in a room
Black and smelly.
A good man is asleep. He is one who will never go away,
Because he knows how much she needs him.
He enduringly suffers day after day
Of lonely punishment,
Excluded from secret longings
And dark masturbating.

He is Family Life, solid, firm.
Mending bikes, listening,
lending an air of Discipline.
Breakfast, dinner, tea.
Snoozing with the telly (Bill had been fond of that in the old days)
It's not totally he-
He does it because she needs to live in the image
Of how it Should Be.

And when the longings get too much,
Or she screams resentfully that she Hates His Guts
He smiles benignly-
Dear woman and her silly stuff:
She blames him for Reality yet
She can't cope when she tries to be free.

They are kind to each other,
they don't scream and row,
Thousands of couples sink to
where they are now.
Love and guilt and their mutual pain
Hold them together.
This is all they can be.
So she beats back juice dripping,
Riotous hormones,

And quietly makes Silent Scream for tea.

And the night comes again.
A leg, possession-heavy, crushes a belly.
Body-sodden air engulfs snores in a room
Black, and smelly.
As the night's depths are torn by each
Outrageous grunt,
A woman sighs and turns, fantasies forgotten
To suck up comfort like some primeval runt.

--There's Seamus, said Nuala with some relief . She was regarding Lynn anxiously. Why had she told her all that personal stuff? The poor woman was in a sort of reverie, probably of total disillusion with her and the country of her dreams. Meanwhile, the sky had become increasingly sulphurous. Big drops of rain began to fall as they went towards him, relieved that in the rush to avoid getting soaked explanations as to why they'd been so long weren't needed.

Chapter Fifteen

Seamus and Nuala wers staying the night at Maeve's, along with many others. They were crammed uncomfortably into the bed of Maeve's little boy, who, in his turn, was crammed uncomfortably between his parents. Mikey was on the floor beside them, with the gap under the bed bunged up with a pile of coats so he couldn't roll under there in the night.
The scene downstairs had been high-spirited, with a drunken Bill shouting his praises for wakes and putting in orders for one of his own when the time came. Annie had observed in her kind, unobtrusive way that Lynn looked wrecked and Bill, though very affectionate and entertaining in his drunkenness, was no use to man or beast. She had invited Maggie to stay the night. She could help make some jewellery and, of course, feed The Girls.
Maggie went off with the briefest of kisses for Lynn. She hadn't taken kindly to being abandoned for so long. Or her mother crying in public. It made her feel insecure and resentful. With an embarrassed glance at her father she hurried towards the door before he could register that she was leaving and launch into some mortifying display.
Later Lynn, feeling bereft and foolish on behalf of both herself and Bill, drove home, while Bill alternately sang and snored beside her. She didn't actually have a driving licence but she had almost passed her test several times in the UK...

Nuala was nearly asleep, still remembering Lynn's words, 'Nuala, there's always our place, you could put a caravan there if you want to' and herself replying, 'Thanks Lynn', but reflecting that she'd never do it, she didn't have the energy or the guts, she'd need to go much further from Seamus, and sure, what was the point, it wouldn't bring Davy back...
She shouldn't have bothered Lynn with so much of her business. It had really set her off. Lynn had had a couple of drinks later and blurted out all that stuff about Bill being Insensitive and Just Like All the Rest, and cried. Luckily everyone was alternately crying and laughing so no one took much notice.
She herself felt purged. Nothing had changed, but despite her guilt there was great relief in talking to someone, even if they didn't quite understand each other. Now her cares were drifting away as sleep took over.
Until Seamus crawled on top of her, pulling the bedclothes off as he went....and then started scrabbling away in the bottom of the wardrobe, flinging out a whole heap of junk.

--Jesus, Seamus, will you mind Mikey down there! What are you doing ?
--Mammy probably had her money hid around the place. That's the way the old people did it. When my uncle Tom died, one o' the brothers found a rake o' money hid up the chimney. Maeve says Mam had nu'un in the bank. But my Aunt that went to America used to send her money all right. And she used to keep that in her wardrobe.
--But that's little Tom's wardrobe now. And Maeve would have shared it out if there had been any money.
--I'm just checkin'. And ye never know. People get crafty when there's money to be had.
--That's for sure, observed Nuala. But her irony was lost on Seamus, who went on with his story.
--Mammy was robbed of a lot o' money one time. My uncle, that's my father's brother, made a will. Givin' a certain amount to each brother that was alive on that day. He meant the day the will was wrote. My father was alive then, but he died before this brother -the one that was lavin' the money. Well the other brothers got it all, on account o' them twistin' it all about to mean that only the ones still alive when he DIED got anythin'. And they all knowin' that really my father's share should have gone to Mammy.
--Yea. I've heard awful stories of the most loving families falling out over who got what. But now you've checked that wardrobe, you'd better put all that stuff back before Maeve sees it. I'm sure she wouldn't rip you off, Seamus, she's far too decent.
As Nuala said this, a mental picture of Maeve's dour husband came into her mind, slouched in front of the telly and reading that horrible book he always had, Torture Through the Ages.
She didn't think much of him, but she didn't think he'd have the energy to search out the stashes of secreted money or the brains to distort legal documents.
Seamus got back into bed. They were just getting off to sleep again when there was a knock at the door. It was Christy.
--Sorry Seamus, Nuala, Howye, sorry to call so late. I just heard this evenin'. Here, have a drink for yerselves tomorrow. He handed Seamus some money.

Neither of them could sleep after this. They were squashed and uncomfortable in the little bed, there was still loud talking from the room below and the room was full of an ugly orange glow from the street light outside.
It was too late to go for a drink anywhere but Seamus suggested they just go out for a walk.

--I need to get out of this house. I'm all stuffed up from being inside all day. I can't wait to get back out the country. Is Mikey okay there?
--Yea, I don't think he'll wake. Geraldine did a good job with him. The whole family were playing with him and they've tired him out.
--Let's get out for some air, so.

They wandered along the deserted street with its grey houses, and settled on a low garden wall, enjoying the cool air.
--I saw the Banashee once, said Seamus after a while, On that doorstep over there.
Nuala regarded the ordinary step. She hadn't imagined that Banshees frequented Corporation houses.
--Honest to God. Twas when I was a young fella, still livin' at home in the house here. Myself and the sister -Eileen, not Maeve, she was too young - and a couple of friends, used to go to Limerick, to the dances. It was a lot more fun there. The old priest wouldn't be watching ye and movin' in if ye got close enough to see a girl's face, let alone the rest of her...That's what the priests used to do ye know, push ye apart with their sticks.
Anyway, I came back on this night very late. I was on my own, I think I got left behind somehow, I can't remember now. Twas very quiet, like this now, after the rain, and I strollin' along happily enough, when I came over all cold and shivery. I looked up and Jesus! Wasn't there an old woman sat on that step over there. And she combin' her hair – long, silvery stuff it was-and wailin'.
Jesus, boy, I ran out o' there like a hare. Straight upstairs and the brother Mossy thinkin' I'd gone mad altogether, jumpin' into bed with him like when we were kids! And in the mornin'- what do ye think? Mrs Moriarty that was our neighbour in that house there, died in the night! I'm tellin' ye,I wouldn't go out on my own at night for a long time after that.

Nuala loved stories like these. And because she felt guilty for badmouthing (that was what he would call it) Seamus to Lynn, she was now noticing all the things that she did like about him: stories,warm fires, his fry ups, his bacon and cabbage stews and pots of spuds, his humour, his affection for his country and its folklore, and his great sense of hospitality (well, on giro day anyway). He never shouted and he'd never hit her. True, he wasn't much cop as a contributing father- when he babysat she found Mikey trussed up in some very odd clothing, like two baby-grows at once, the legs from the one left dangling and the upper half of the other knotted around Mikey's middle. And he always handed him over the minute there was any sort of difficulty. But he did

fuss him and make him feel loved. Sometimes, it was annoying how easily he could make Mikey laugh. And Mikey was beginning to cry every time Seamus went out of the door (which he so often did) as if it was the end of the world...
And none of this – her frustration and isolation and disappointment- was really Seamus's fault, it was hers. His sister Eileen, the one from England, had remarked earlier about the girl they knew who was in trouble with Christy, 'It takes two to tango'. Later she had put her arm fondly round Nuala and said that she was so glad Seamus had Found The Right One now...

Nuala took Seamus's arm companionably as they headed back towards the house.
--It's only fair that Eileen and Jo get the house, she remarked, After her living here and nursing your Mam all this time.
-She should divide up some of the stuff, insisted Seamus stubbornly, And ye can bet they've all got money out of it some way or other!

It was just beginning to get light when Nuala was woken by a strange noise, a squeaking and squealing that she couldn't identify. Alarmed, she got out of bed, thinking that Mikey must be choking, or, despite the stack of coats, had managed to get himself jammed under the bed. But Mikey was sleeping soundly. She was just taking in, with a sinking heart, the sodden patches on the borrowed coats, when the door opened and in hopped Seamus.
He was in his long john suit which he liked to wear because it was the old country fashion he remembered from his childhood. Little Tom had asked why uncle Seamus was wearing a Babygrow. (To Nuala's great relief, Seamus hadn't gone so far as to try to sew himself into it last winter, as he assured her all the old people used to do. That was another good thing about Seamus, she reflected, he wasn't a SMELLY person, not apart from the welly socks anyway....Just a hint of armpit sometimes but never that greasy old smell some men got, no, he always smelt wholesome, cosy and -perhaps unsurprisingly given his fondness for a good blaze - of woodsmoke.)
Seamus had his hand stuffed between the buttons of his longjohns and was holding his genitals. His face wore an agonised expression.
--Nuala, Nuala, oh Jesus! He skipped out of the door, but soon returned, po-going violently.
--Whatever's the matter with you? Can't you keep still for a minute? And mind Mikey!
--No I feckin' can't! Aaaarrgh! It was that feckin' ointment!

--What ointment? Come back here, will you!
--Oh Jeeesus! That ointment I put on myself. From the bathroom.
Seamus had hopped halfway down the stairs but was now making his way back up again, having found no relief down there.
--I had an itch, so I put some cream on myself-
--Stop there a minute, ordered Nuala, Where's the cream?
--There, by the bath, gasped Seamus.
--Deep Heat Treatment For Rheumatic Pain, read Nuala, Jesus, Seamus,didn't you read what was in it?
But she knew that reading wasn't Seamus's strong point. Books didn't seem to have been present in the home when he was growing up. Once she'd been shocked when he couldn't use a telephone directory because his alphabet was hazy. He'd mis-read a sign on a van not long ago, replacing Diary for Dairy. She wasn't sure if he was dyslexic or just a victim of The Brother's brutal and in his case, useless, education. A while ago, she had started trying to teach him to spell. But he cheated, as if he still had to do anything he could to avoid a beating for getting it wrong.
--I did not. I told ye, I had an itch! Aaaarrrggh! Nuala, what will I do?Tis burnin' me to death!
--Maybe some cool water, suggested Nuala, I'll run the bath. She turned the taps on at full volume.
Seamus leapt in, still clad in his longjohns, but was soon clambering out again.
--What's the matter now? Careful! You're dripping all over the carpet.
--It feels worse in the water...Ah Jesus, I can't keep still. Nuala would ye fetch me my trousers there, I'll go out for a run-
When Nuala brought the trousers he was back in the bath. It went on like that for nearly an hour,with no solace to be found anywhere, until the heat of the cream gradually lessened its blistering attack.
As Seamus left the bathroom for the last time, Maeve appeared at the bottom of stairs.
--Er, is Seamus all right, Nuala?
--He is now, thanks, Maeve. He was a bit out of sorts. All that drink yesterday, and the grief. You know...

As Seamus and Nuala entered the courtyard outside the Riley's place, Ambrose appeared from the direction of the garden, looking hot, bothered and angry.
--Not now, Ambrose, advised Breda who had come out of the house

behind him, They're just back from the funeral.
---I want to see you later, then, Seamus, is that understood?
Seamus surveyed Ambrose regally.
--Ye need to calm down, Ambrose, he advised unwisely and in tones of immense superiority.
--And be like you! spluttered Ambrose in disgust. I'm a business man, I work hard for all this. It's my choice. I couldn't live with nothing like you, Seamus. And I'm not going to continue letting you ruin my property!
He hurried off, puffing audibly and calling as he went, 'Don't forget, I'll see you later!'
--Arrah, would ye look at the state o' that, said Seamus, watching the retreat of his short, overweight figure. It was true that he was a picture of ill-health: red faced, porky, stressed and suffering from constant indigestion and headaches due to jet lag and business lunches.

Nuala was aware that Ambrose's attitude was not unjustified. Seamus had lost interest in the garden and it was not yielding the produce that it should. Only a couple of weeks before, they had found black spots on the leaves of the spuds and in a panic lest it was the blight, Seamus had decided to dig them up. Nuala didn't think they could get blight any more but it was too difficult to get to the library to find out. The spuds were small but delicious. Breda got a few in her vegetable rack. When she passed Nuala hanging out her washing she commented, 'The potatoes are awfully small, Nuala.'
--Well, new ones usually are. They taste delicious though don't they, Nuala offered hopefully.
--But there's nothing left of them after I've peeled them, Breda complained
Nuala was astonished. And when Seamus heard about this, it had been his turn to be scandalised.
--Is it peeling new potatoes! he had cried, aghast, Honest to God, those two don't deserve any vegetables!
Seamus never peeled a potato, be it young, old or middle-aged. He covered them all with butter, herbs and a thick insulation of salt, and whatever else was on the plate was a bit superfluous. They were having a lot of potatoes-only meals at the moment, as they weren't making the expected income from selling garden produce. Seamus had been selling a bit of firewood lately to keep them going...

Cathy, Elsa and Sam were cruising through Connemara in the car of a laid-back American tourist. The lakes looked amazing, with blue sky reflected in the parts of the water that weren't thick with yellow lilies. In the distance rose mythical looking mountains. Cathy lolled in her seat, limp with gratitude and relief that they had been treated- apart from one incident,and against all the odds -so tolerantly in Ballyshannon and they were now heading safely South. She was still harbouring an idea of surprising Lynn with a visit but was increasingly anxious about inflicting Elsa on her. When she got back to Bristol she was never having anything to do with her again.

There had been, as promised, plenty of foreigners on the camping field at Ballyshannon, all playing, or learning to play, traditional music. The learners had their own circle. Elsa quickly drove away the group nearest to them by plonking herself down and commencing to grate away on her violin. She had one music book and she knew three tunes,or thought she did. Lots of people knew The Tenpenny Bit but didn't recognise it as played by Elsa. Undaunted, she gave them all her challenging glare, and said ,' Maybe you know this one then.' Someone suggested she try the workshop next day and she called him a Domineering Male Egotist. Besides Elsa, sat Sam, chewing at a lump of soda bread and Calvita cheese,their staple diet since arriving in Ireland. They had nothing to cook on. The bread and cheese was varied with cereal and sometimes they bought chips. They were losing weight (except Sam, who chewed unenthusiastically but steadily at whatever came his way.) With a diet so boring you didn't eat more than you needed.

The vacancy of Sam's stare was nearly as disconcerting as the ferocity of his mother's. Cathy joined the exodus from the musician's circle before Elsa began battering the ears of the last two bewildered German boys with her song about the girl who had lost her hair and all the skin off her knees from lugging coal carts up and down the mine shafts all day.

The German lads were nice. Especially the sweet one with curly hair. Cathy was sure they would have got together if she hadn't been with Elsa. She got a tune from them,which turned out to called Morrison's Jig. Nobody would stop to give her the name of it before, and by the time they did they were at the end of the set and had forgotten what they'd played, and then they were raging into something else. But the sweet German boy took the time to write it down for her to play on her flute. (When there was no one around. She was extra modest to make up for Elsa's gross ego)

The people in the shops were okay and the man on the door of the marquee where the concerts took place was friendly and seemed impressed that they had come All The Way From Bristol to hear the Irish music.

And one day they'd gone, a crowd of them from the campsite, to the wild and pure Rossnowlagh Beach. Elsa had actually spent twenty minutes playing with Sam at the edge of the sea, while Cathy, to her joy, managed to play along with a couple of tunes.

But Elsa was a continual source of embarrassment and her complete insensitivity was terrifying. Most people wouldn't need to know all about the history of a place to work out when feelings were running high and it was best to keep your mouth shut. But Elsa's politics said that women had kept their mouths shut too long. They had to open them as much as possible. They also had to drink in pubs without male escorts, and they had to drink pints.

Thus they found themselves in a bar, pints before them, surrounded by local men who were watching Thatcher on the news and cursing her to the heavens. A tribute was raised to the prisoners in the Maze.

--What's the Maze? Elsa asked loudly. She managed to sound contemptuous and bored.

--Shhh. It's another name for Long Kesh, the prison.

Thank God they had all erupted into a rebellious rendition of a Republican song. But one fella near them had noticed Elsa and was staring at them in an unfriendly way.

Elsa went for a pee, attracting curious looks.

--Sure is that a woman or a man or what? said someone.

--It's a woman who doesn't see the need to please ignorant men by dressing up- snapped Elsa, but she was interrupted.

--Sure we can see that! quipped someone.

--Ye feckin' English bitches, said the fella nearby. Cathy got up and fought her way towards the Ladies, scarlet and shaking. They needed to get out of the place before Elsa got them into real trouble.

As Elsa appeared, another toast was being raised.

--Oh, not again! she pronounced loudly.

--Elsa, we have to go, said Cathy, grabbing her arm, A message came from the camp site. Sam is awake and crying in the tent.

--Oh he always does that. He's a bloody pain. He'll go back to sleep after a bit.

Bugger. Stupid of her to hope that Elsa's maternal instincts would send her racing out of the bar.

--They said he's disturbing people and if we don't go back and see to him they're going to evict us.

--Fucking Nazi's!

--Yea, but we'd better go.

Cathy was terrified they'd be followed but they reached the camping field with no problems.

--Told you so, fast asleep, said Elsa after a quick glance at Sam. Wait til I find those cunts that were complaining...

Breda had driven off in her huge car to collect her daughter from some do or other. Ambrose was knocking loudly on the door of the coach-house.
--Come in, Seamus invited with an irritatingly large smile.
 Nuala's heart sank.
--Here, sit in there by the fire., Seamus gestured towards the blaze. Throw a few t'ick ones on there, will ye, Nuala.
Ambrose turned scarlet with fury as he took in the inferno and the piles of logs which were once his trees waiting in readiness around it.
--I don't want to sit down, and NO! I don't want some home-made wine!
--Seamus- said Nuala warningly. She folded up the paper she had taken from Maeve's yesterday. It wasn't much out of date. It was putting her off any dreams she might entertain of going back to England. The government was accepting one hundred and sixty American cruise missiles, the first European country to do so, and with no public debate. Thatcher was giving council tenants the right to buy their homes. But didn't you get a council house because you couldn't afford to buy? And move out of it when you could, leaving the house for another family less well off? Unemployment was at a forty four year high. And the miners were threatening to go on strike.
--I've come to discuss the destruction of my wood! spat Ambrose, his rabbity face twitching with fury. It's scandalous, scandalous! Almost the whole of the wood is gone! Just look at the size of the fire you've got here! We're in the month of August, Seamus!
--We've Mikey, sure, said Seamus self righteously, He has to be kept warm.
Nuala prayed that Ambrose wouldn't go and look at Mikey. She kept him in his vest most of the time, or topless altogether. Until she did that, he'd often woken up screaming, red as a beetroot and soaked in sweat.
--You're not to take any more wood from my property, do you understand? You'll have to get it somewhere else. The garden is shameful, shameful, it's a mass of slugs and weeds, Seamus!
--Well, ye didn't get us the Derris ye promised.
---'m a busy man, Seamus. I expected YOU to run the garden and be responsible for buying what you needed once it was started up. I can't continue to pay you for doing nothing and using up all my wood. You can stay here for the time being – until you find somewhere else to go. But don't expect any more money. You've made a laughing stock out of

me as it is!
He left, getting entangled with a bunch of herbs beside the door and beating them off with his lardy little hands as if they were a plague of locusts, before giving a final farewell of, 'Scandalous, scandalous!'
Then he knocked again. Nuala regarded the door with trepidation. Before Seamus could get there, Ambrose stuck his head in.
--And I'm taking back the chainsaw I bought you. Perhaps you'll do a bit less damage without it!

Lynn's garden was in a similar state to Seamus's and Nuala's. She tired easily, found it hard to bend and was demoralised by the proliferating weeds. Two rows of lettuces that should have been safe in the wardship of her organic slug pellets had disappeared. She looked up and saw Mrs Ryan coming down the road. 'I'll invite her in to tea.' she decided. They were well stocked up on nice soda bread and a fruit cake, having gone to town yesterday and done a big shop. And they could have boiled eggs, no shortage of those and the ones laid by her Marrans were rather fine.
Once, when she and Bill were out walking in some remote place, a woman, a complete stranger, had invited them in for tea. They had thought she just meant the liquid stuff, but rashers, eggs, bread and jam were put before them as though they were the prodigal son and daughter. And she gave them money and a bar of chocolate for Maggie. Lynn, most impressed by such hospitality, had vowed that she would start doing the same. But she had the problem of always feeling awkward when trying to entertain. Even frying eggs and slicing bread in front of anyone except close family made her jittery. And birthday parties were pure psychosis.
Normally, people also had the irritating habit of turning up when the cupboard was empty. But today she didn't have that problem. Moira Ryan was a very pleasant person. She would give it a try.

--Hello, Howye Moira- she called, when she realised it wasn't Moira Ryan at all. It was someone very similar in build and dress, but she had a bigger nose, smaller mouth, more wrinkles and an expression of pious disapproval.
--Oh...faltered Lynn, I thought you were Mrs Ryan, I mean Moira, she added, to show the miserable looking bat that she was on good terms with her neighbours, thank you.
--I'm her sister.
--Oh. Pleased to meet you. How are Jim and Moira? I haven't seen them

for a while. Are the boys enjoying their holidays?
--They're very well, thanks, said Poker- face stiffly. The boys are away this week. Jimmy has gone to help his uncle at Tournafulla in the County Limerick, and his brother is up in Connemara, learning the Irish along with the rest of his class from school.
--That's nice...Will you come in for a bit of tea? I was just going to have some myself and it would be nice to have a bit of company.
Lynn began to stutter as she made this little speech. Her companion's cold disapproval was un-nerving her. She brushed back her hair and deliberately flaunted her wedding ring in case suspicion about her and Bill's marital status was causing the bad vibe.
--Well, now, I'm in a hurry as it happens- But Mrs Ryan mark two followed her towards the house. She didn't comment as Lynn burbled about the garden and the goat they'd got at last. Inside, Lynn, clumsy in her nervousness, which was growing by the second, managed to put on the kettle and open the bread bin, not without sending the lid clattering to the floor. She shelved her plan to offer boiled eggs. She would probably scald herself.
--Will you have some cake? she managed, trying to smile hospitably.
 What was wrong with the old bag anyway? She was half inclined to tell her to fuck off, but she couldn't bear to see her visions of the Grand Spread come to nothing. Besides, if she did that, she would probably find that it was all a misunderstanding on her part and she'd just been too sensitive and reactionary as usual. She could hear Bill saying it.
--Oh, God no. Then Poker- face collected herself. I mean, I'm on my way to see someone. I'll just have the cup of tay thanks.
--Oh, said Lynn feeling flattened. Who's that?
--Our relation, Mister Keane, who lives below. He isn't well these days.
'A visit from you will probably finish him off,' thought Lynn. She remembered there was some Irish rule of Tea Etiquette. You were meant to refuse food the first time it was offered, something like that.
--Are you sure you won't have some cake?she enquired desperately, pushing the plate a bit closer to her visitor. Mrs Ryan's evil alter ego regarded it suspiciously.
'It must be the tinkers they're upset about,' thought Lynn, but she hadn't the courage to ask. Anyway, it was a good while since Mickey and Nan had moved on and they hadn't done anything terrible.
--The drugs! said her visitor suddenly, We don't want our boys having anything to do with drugs- Her voice had become hysterical, And that poor little girl of yours, to think of it-
Suddenly she was down on her knees on the kitchen floor, crossing herself frantically and praying that They (Lynn and Bill) wouldn't go

giving any drugs to their (the Ryan family's) boys. And God help her sister, she tried to keep them safe but with the likes of that fella of the Lynch's around the country, you wouldn't know what you could do to stop them mixing with the wrong types, Blessed Virgin keep these people from giving her boys any drugs and they with their lives before them...

Maggie appeared in the doorway, an aluminium bucket which was smeared with milk and hair in her hand. She was learning to milk the new goat and wouldn't allow Lynn to help her. In her enthusiasm she went out to milk the astonished creature of whatever it had managed to manufacture at all hours of the day.

--What's all this in the milk? Lynn would ask, Did you remember to wipe her with the cloth first?

--Yes, but she put her foot in the bucket, Maggie would answer, or, on one occasion, A bit got spilt but I managed to pour it back in.

--Ooh, cake! said Maggie now, Can I have some, Mum?

Lynn surveyed her daughter. In her grapplings with the goat that unique smell became strongly attached to her clothes, hence Lynn had insisted she keep an old set for wearing when they were staying at home. It was a long time since they'd been washed and now she looked at Maggie's hair, Lynn realised she hadn't reminded her to brush it lately. But her radiant countenance and obvious good health were surely the best indicators that she was well cared for and not fed morphine for breakfast.

--Ooh, visitors, remarked Maggie happily, coming in and spotting the woman kneeling at the far end of the table, Oh, she continued in some confusion, Are you saying your prayers?

The lady didn't answer but began getting stiffly to her feet.

--Would you like some milk? asked Maggie. Goat's milk is very good for you and I've just milked ours now so you can't say it's not fresh! I'll put some in a jug for you if you like.

--That's very nice of you pet, but we have some at home, managed Mrs Disapproving with a commendable effort at sociability, marred just slightly by the fact that she couldn't resist crossing herself again. She turned to Lynn.

--I'll say goodbye to you now, she announced and made her way with awful dignity to the door.

--Can I have some cake then, Mum? Maggie had already grabbed a plate and was brandishing the knife.

--That bloody old bag! blurted Lynn, and burst into tears.

Chapter Sixteen

--Perhaps we should go for a picnic, suggested Lynn.
Maggie was in a foul mood. The rift with her friend Majella was still upsetting her and she was mooching about, sulky and disgruntled. She answered her mother in a special tone of boredom and indulgence to let her know that a picnic held no interest, she was only going because she had to. And she was extra sulky because Lynn didn't think it was a good idea to bring Sandy.
Sandy was a sickly pup. She had just wormed him again and the effect on his already weak stomach had not been good. She wasn't sure what was wrong with him. But she was bracing herself for Maggie's accusations of murder in the fairly near future.
Lynn didn't want to go either. She was trying to force herself out of the apathy that being alone too much was causing her. And she was hurt because she'd expected that her parents or Cathy would have liked to pay them a visit by now. Her mother had written that her father's asthma was too bad to risk it at the moment. She had given long and amusing descriptions of all the kind female neighbours who came round to make a fuss of him; plus the pettinesses she had to put with in her choir and the power struggles within it. But spoilt it with remarks about Proper Nutrition and was a home birth Really Advisable in such a Remote Place. Cathy hadn't been in touch at all.
Bill had got a job for a few weeks, helping a couple of Blow ins they knew move house. And doing some building work on the new place. At that moment he and Jim Ryan were stopped on the road in their respective vehicles, Bill pleasantly surprised at Jim's friendliness as he passed over an open bottle of whiskey.
--Here, have a sup o' that for yerself, I'm celebrating.
--Oh?
--The old witch of a sister in law departs today! And if we don't see her for another fifty years it won't be too soon. By God, you're the lucky man, Bill, with the fine young one ye have to come visiting you and the wife.
He took back the bottle through his window and had another long swig. I've been drivin' the roads to get away from her! If I went to a bar she'd be at me for smellin' o' drink the minute I got through the door...
--Relatives can be a trial all right, said Bill, thinking of Lynn and Cathy's mother and his social worker brother. At least now they had to give notice before they turned up.
--This old stuff doesn't relax you in the same way as what the quare fella of the Lynch's is into, continued Jim, gazing at his bottle. Do ye see him

at all Bill? Ye couldn't get me a little piece for an old smoke could ye? Me nerves are gone on me! And listen, ye won't mention it to Moira, will ye, she's a bit old fashioned in that respect.

 .Cathy and Elsa's American host was touring all down the West coast. This wasn't the right direction for Lynn and Bill's but Cathy was enjoying the sense of luxury and relief too much to care. He bought them lunch in a luxurious hotel, and dropped them off at Doolin.
They walked the last mile down the road and Cathy thought it was the most beautiful place she had ever seen, with the little flower strewn fields divided by scattered walls and dotted with a few low, whitewashed cottages, a smell of wild thyme on the wind, and hedges of scarlet fuschia growing along the roadside.
They put up the tent on a little camp site, ate some soda bread and Calvita, and went for a walk..There was a sort of tail-end atmosphere in Doolin. Lisdoonvarna festival had recently taken place a couple of miles away (Cathy was cursing herself- if she'd known about that one she might have gone there with Lynn and Bill instead of getting herself into this mess with Elsa) and a lot of festival goers had obviously come over here too. There was litter blowing about, and it seemed as if everyone had finished their celebrating and gone home now, unless they were completely incapable of doing so. Someone, however, was managing to do more than sit in a sodden stupor, because when they returned to the tent they found that Elsa's sleeping bag- a very expensive one borrowed from her brother- and Cathy's waterproof coat were gone.
Cathy was shocked. She didn't expect things like that to happen in Ireland. Shame they didn't take Elsa's violin, she thought uncharitably... They'd spent an uncomfortable night with one sleeping bag spread over them all. Sam, who normally shared with his mother, had to go in the middle and made vile chesty noises.

Lynn didn't really know where to go for their picnic. She didn't want to climb a lot of walls. Up the road there was a long stretch of dark gloomy forestry to pass before you reached the cross with the turn off to the heavenly valley. Down the road there were several small tracks that she'd never explored between Seamus's bohreen and the main road a couple of miles further on..
--We'll just have to see how far I get and then find a nice field to sit in, she told Maggie, who answered with a melodramatic sigh.
--This looks nice, puffed Lynn a while later.

Despite Maggie's bored teenager act, her spirits had lifted. The lane they were looking at was quite well kept, with pretty white walls and a grassy middle. The day was fine, the trees still a dusty summer green. There was a stillness in the air, a hushed expectancy as if nature was waiting for Autumn to begin.
--This is where that old man Matty Keane lives, Maggie told her, It's the other end of his road. We can visit him!
--Oh, I don't know about that. We haven't been invited. Lynn was nervous. Moira Ryan's sister had been heading this way after the dreadful tea fiasco. She had probably filled the old boy's head with all kinds of scandal about them.
--Yes we can! insisted Maggie. He said,' Tell your Mammy, Any time you're passing, Don't forget now!'
It was good to see her bouncing with enthusiasm again anyway, so they continued on,
Lynn rather hoping that Mattie would be out, or the cottage hidden away somewhere too hard to get to.
They went on for half a mile and had the picnic on a grassy bank under an ash tree which provided great support for Lynn's aching back. She would be happy to laze here, read her book and then head home, but Maggie who had wandered on around the corner, appeared, calling breathlessly, 'Here's Mattie's house Mum! Come on, it's just around the corner!
Then she was gone and after a while Lynn knew she wasn't coming back and had no choice but to follow her.

Cathy wanted to get straight on the road. It was a long way to Lynn and Bill's and it did not lie on decent sized roads so it would be hard to get lifts. Also, since she now had no coat, she wanted to move while the decent weather held. But as they passed a bar, an oldfella in the doorway, said, 'Howye, Gerrels, is that a fiddle ye have there? Come in and give us a tune, so.'
Elsa, pint before her and the mysteriously orange- coloured lemonade and crisps provided for Sam, knew no inhibitions. She gave a ghastly rendition of what was meant to be a reel. There was more rhythm to Sam's crisp chewing.
--She's not bad, not bad, said the deaf old fella to the barman, Even if she does have a face like the back of a bus.
Elsa didn't hear him. Otherwise he would have got a savage lecture - What did he think HE looked like? SHE was Making a Statement to show she didn't have to Prettify herself to please men. Whether she terrified grannies or cracked mirrors was beside the point.

When they left the otherwise empty bar, Elsa was cheered by the Old fella's enthusiasm and the continuing sunshine and felt quite kindly towards Doolin again.
--We'll go down by the sea and play a few tunes, she announced. Cathy agreed, not without trepidation, but because she felt it would be good for Sam, whose needs weren't often considered.
There didn't seem to be much of a beach but they walked along a bit of cliff path and clambered along a rocky gully to be near the water. It wasn't a pretty or safe place- the rocks were black and slimy and someone had littered one part with crisp packets and broken glass. Cathy got out a cup and bowl for Sam and he ladled murky water from one to the other. No one was around so she took heart and got out her flute.
They hadn't been playing long when they heard manic laughter and the sound of glass shattering. Two male figures were stumbling across the rocks towards them. One – the owner of the bottle that had just been dropped – was shirtless and clad in combat trousers. He had black hair and bloodshot eyes. The other had a massive head of curls, a shambolic manner and a high pitched giggle, which he unleashed whenever the first one said anything. They came and settled themselves on the rocks close by.
Cathy thought the one with the red eyes looked psychotic.
--Let's go, she suggested quietly to Elsa.
--NO! Why should we?
Just lately, Cathy had been suffering from auditory premonitions of the next Ghastly Gaff Elsa would come out with, and with horrible foreboding, now waited for her to say, in best Playground Argument tones, It's a Free Country!
--Lovely day is't it, called Cathy brightly, before Elsa could open her devastating gob, meanwhile stuffing things into bags and noticing that Sam had fallen asleep with his face on the stones; and that, to escape, they'd somehow have to lift him, the pushchair and all the baggage over the rocks.
--Give us a fag, called Bloodshot Eyes rudely.
--No I won't, retorted Elsa promptly, Ask properly.
--Just give him one! hissed Cathy, Can't you see he's a nutter.
Now he was coming over the rocks towards them, mimicking a Royal accent (though God knows why, thought Cathy miserably, when Elsa's was anything but)
--Oh, AHSK PROPERLY is it? Like the English asked the Irish if they could take over our country and murder and starve us for centuries! What about Drogheda? Did the English ask the Irish if they could bash

out the brains of little kids or throw them into the sea to drown?
--I'm sincerely sorry for all that, began Cathy carefully, But it was a long time ago-
Shit. She had enraged him further.
--ALL THAT! He cried, That's all it is to you- All that!
Spittle was flying. The other fellow was giggling again.
Cathy was beginning to feel very frightened.

Lynn puffed after Maggie. At the end of the track the trees and bushes opened onto a yard that was a mixture of grass and cobbles. A stream flowed nearby and there was a lichen-covered stone bridge over it. Ducks, chickens and dogs came to meet them and cats began to stretch and yawn their way out of weedy flower tubs and holes between the walls. They were charming, even if all a bit dusty looking and aged.
--He won't hurt ye, he won't hurt ye, Mattie was saying to Maggie. He had appeared from an outhouse, a spry little man with bright berries of eyes, a shrewd expression and alarmingly bowed legs.
--Hello, Mister Keane- began Lynn. She was going to say that she hoped he didn't mind them turning up like this, but they'd been out for a walk, she hoped he remembered them, they'd met once at such- and-such, and of course he knew Maggie from the school bus-
But Mattie began talking straight away as if he'd always known them and they called every day. He went into the cottage, talking away and clearly expecting them to follow.

On the rocks, in the summer sun, The Eyes was screaming at them.
--That's all it is to you- All That! What do you think we're still fighting for? To get rid of you murdering, tyrannising British that starved our people in the famine and made them live like pigs for centuries! And have carried on suppressing the Catholics in the North and making their lives a misery!
--Honestly, said Cathy carefully, I am sincerely sorry. And ashamed- I have read about Ireland's history. But you can't hold us personally responsible.
She did feel ashamed, and she recognised some acute pain and personal involvement behind the deranged crusade they now found themselves the victims of. She thought she saw his face relenting a little in its hatred, but then Elsa had to speak.
--You needn't think you can bully us just because we're on our own.
He erupted.
--Is it bullying! he screamed, I've a brother in the Kesh, he'll show you

what bullying is! It's what the British army do, you arrogant fucking bitch! You come over here with the same old attitude, bastardising our music-
The Giggler loved this and let forth a volley of shrieking.
--We know we're not much good, explained Cathy, her mortification over her playing, which until now had consisted of unspoken doubt, now confirmed by this stark summary, That's why we came down here where we wouldn't bother anyone. Every one has to practice, she added hopefully, Anyway, we're going now.
--There's three year olds here that play better than that! You'll never be any good because you're not fucking Irish! You're fucking BRITISH! Your planet is Mars-the God of war! The sacking of Drogheda is, 'All That', to you, but how'd you like it if I bashed in this kid's head with a brick?
Cathy, though trying to keep up an outward veneer of calm, was sick with fear. Even Elsa suddenly realised that the situation was serious. Her maternal hackles, normally pretty deeply suppressed, arose.
--Don't you hurt my kid! she yelled, standing over the pushchair, wherein Cathy had managed to place the leaden Sam in hopeful preparation for flight.
--If you do that, said Cathy, You will be harming an Irish child. Spilling Irish Blood, she added, knowing he appreciated that kind of terminology. Elsa looked at her in confusion but mercifully kept quiet.
--An Irish child? The Eyes still held the rock, but he was wavering.
Elsa suddenly copped on.
--Yes, she said decisively, His father is- Paddy Tierney. From Galway, she added for good measure. To her shame, two desperate tears were running down her cheeks.
--Is it now, said The Eyes thoughtfully. Then he spotted the tears.
--That's pain! he cried ecstatically, That's real pain, like the women of Drogheda felt!
Now it was Cathy who felt like groaning, 'Oh, not again..'
--Here, give us a hand with this yoke, he instructed his crony, who took the other end of the pushchair without a word, even though a few minutes before he would happily have been party to a murder, We'll give ye's a hand to the road.
When they got to the road, a strange thing happened. The Eyes looked down at Elsa and took her face in his hands. He bent towards her.
"Oh, no!' thought Cathy, She'll never stand for that, she'll call him an Opportunistic Male Scumbag and kick him in the balls and he'll go bonkers again, we're all going to die!
Everything seemed intensified around them, the warmth of the sun, the colours of the gorse and fuschia, the little breeze, the sea sparkling below. The Eyes kissed Elsa. They looked weirdly beautiful.

She and Cathy never talked about this again.

It was quite dark in Mattie's house. The windows were small and full of cobwebs. The pall of smoke from the turf smouldering in the vast fireplace added to the sensation of ancient sleepiness.
Mattie didn't ask any questions. He seemed to know exactly who they were. He sat and talked, not to them exactly, sometimes he was thinking aloud, and he often addressed his remarks to the two dogs. The dogs were mis-shapen , with thick mats of fur on their rumps and ears. One of them had stinking breath. But they always stirred and wagged their tails in acknowledgement when he said their names.
The pot on the crane bubbled and the kettle was put on and off its hook, but otherwise nothing disturbed the soporific flow of Mattie's words. Lynn looked at Maggie,expecting her to be wriggling with boredom. But she was a picture of tranquility. A tabby cat had slid onto her lap and was now wrapping its long front legs around her neck. Lynn hoped it didn't have fleas. She started bracing herself to ward off the Cat Of Our Own which Maggie would no doubt soon propose.
Mattie was talking about the days when he and his wife rode about behind their little black pony Molly.
--Ah, Molly weren't ye the great trotter altogether! Ye got into town faster than many a baste twice your size! And at one time there were six children on that car! he added for Lynn's benefit.
--What are they doing now?
--Wait'll I see now....There was one went for a priest, and one a nun-she went off to Africa. I've two brothers married with families in Dublin and Americay, oh,wait a minute now, I think they died....And that feckin' Willie, he went on to himself, And he a blackguard entirely! No one of us has seen or heard o' him since 1950. And Maura- no, wait now, maybe she was a sister..
Lynn thought she should change the subject but Mattie did it for her.
--What will ye call the babba?
--I want it to be called Cindy if it's a girl and Barnaby if it's a boy, interposed Maggie, but Mum doesn't like those names. She shot her mother a resentful glance.
--Wait'll we see now, here's a bit o' silver for it, God bless ye. And where did I put it now?
Ah, I have it. Ye can have that for the ole goat. He gave Maggie a rather stiff collar. And aren't ye the lucky gerrel to own a pup as well!
Sure,there's no friend in the worrld like an ole dog, is there Jimmy? Would ye like a bit o' bacon now?

--Well, actually- began Lynn, who was feeling hungry again.
--There ye are Jimmy! And yerself, Gerry, ye'd be wantin' a bit too I'd say...

Maggie went outside with Mattie to help feed the ducks, hens and cats. It took a long time, with Mattie chatting to them all and remembering incidents in their lives. He put some grain in a tin and sent Maggie at the head of a line of ducks.
--See where their house is over there? Put the food in, then make sure ye've shut em up tight. Tie up the string on the door. Can ye do a good knot?
--I can tie my laces.
That'll do. Nice and tight now. You go on and do what's good for ye, he added, giving a loitering duck a guiding nudge with his foot.
--Why do they go to bed so early? asked Maggie.
--In case the old fox comes by. Or the good people - they like to play tricks, them old fairies.
When she got back, bursting with pride, he was down behind a grain bin in a dark corner, moving some bottles about. He gave her a wink.
--There ye are, gerrel. We'll go in and have a bit o' tay, so.

When they left, it was early evening. They were still charmed, but extremely hungry. Mattie had offered them stew, but never got around to dishing it up. The third time the kettle boiled, Lynn had quietly made the tea.
Outside, he was chatting to his long gone pony again.
--Off with ye now, then, and don't be treadin' on old long ears up there! Ye mind his house in the long grass, do ye hear me now, Molly!
--Well, Goodnight- began Lynn, suddenly feeling nervous. His ramblings had been bizarre, but perhaps now they were going to spill over into fully fledged insanity. She turned towards the lane.
--Sure and ye don't have to be goin' all round the road above! cried Mattie. Molly there will bring ye the quick way along the bohreen!
Lynn wasn't sure what to do. There was a silence. Then Mattie appeared to forget about Mollie and the bohreen that there was no sign of. He began advising her that if ever Bill wanted an old bottle he still had a few left, and it the best in the county, and put through the worrem twice, whatever that meant,. And then he waved them on their way.

There were strange old men tucked away all over the place, reflected Lynn. Even if it was women who officially lived longer. All those Poor

Widow Women must have committed suicide at the antics of their Shan Omadaun sons. Jesus, here was another old boy, coming down to visit Mattie. That would be company for him, even if this one was even more shambolic than usual..
UGH! God, that was vile...
This old fella had a small black sheepdog on a piece of frayed baler twine. There was, of course, plenty of the stuff about his person : holding his coat together, holding his trousers up, and so on. But when Maggie went to pat the timorous dog, she saw that its personal piece of string was embedded in its neck. The skin had grown right over it in one place. At the end of this area, the string had bitten in deeply, leaving a crimson groove encrusted with a perpetually disturbed and pus-leaking scab.
--Oooh, Mum, his neck, his neck! Maggie looked anxiously up at Lynn, expecting her to take action.
The dog's owner had already said the customary, 'Grand Evenin" and 'Are ye after visitin' Mattie? I'm just goin' that way meself,' and was going on his way.
--Excuse me, ventured Lynn. My daughter is worried about your dog's neck. She thought the interference might be more acceptable if she made it on Maggie's behalf. Did you know the string is cutting into him? Shall we help you to get it off?
Maggie was muttering darkly about calling the RSPCA , which Lynn didn't feel was very tactful. She gave her a look and Maggie muttered more loudly. Lynn made a resolve to clout her at the first opportunity. Anyway, she didn't think the RSPCA operated here. And shouldn't they be more concerned for all these poor old men with their homes crumbling in on them and no clue as to what the community nurses at home liked to call Personal Hygiene? Perhaps all the crops of blackheads and crusty clothing she'd now seen had given her a sort of famine fatigue, but it was more probable that pity wasn't needed because these old people seemed happy in their grimy eccentricity. They had a dignity and character that was lost to many of the elderly at home, who weren't expected to do - anything. Except- clean, fed and safe albeit -sag in front of a huge television and be prescribed anti-depressants if they didn't show enough enthusiasm for returning the odious chit-chat of their carers.
Neighbours and family were far more helpful here, and most of these old characters turned out to have someone looking out for them, even if helping them wash was a long way down the list. She'd seen the Ryan boys riding this way on their bikes with provisions for Mattie, and Jim brought him loads of briquettes and sometimes gave him rides into town.

In fact Mattie never seemed short of lifts. She sometimes saw him in a car with some other old fellas, going to Mass.
This other one with his dog, though...he was several degrees more degenerate than Mattie, and if there was a benevolent eye looking out for him at all, it certainly hadn't travelled as far as his dog. Lynn longed for the satisfaction of removing the string, cleaning away all that pus and getting the wound dressed with a nice clean bandage. (This was a bit optimistic, she reflected, but maybe Mattie had a reasonable rag somewhere,and some sort of antiseptic, a bit of foot-rot spray perhaps, hadn't he said he kept a few sheep until recently...)
The old fella's gaze rested on the hideous spectacle of his dog's neck for a few seconds but he didn't seem to think there was any problem. He made a few frustratingly unrelated remarks and then said,' Goodnight to ye now,Missus,' and wandered on.
--I'll speak to the Ryans about it, Lynn told the furious Maggie. They're sure to know him.

When they got home Lynn saw, with a sinking heart, that they had visitors. A van belonging to some friends of Seamus was parked on the dry patch. Seamus was no doubt within, having got them to bring him out here. She had been finding the days lonely with Bill away, but feeling as huge and ugly and at this minute, as dizzy and tired as she did after the walk home, the last thing she wanted to discover was that one of Seamus's Rent A Crowds had taken over her home. Now she would be denied an evening of quiet companionship with Bill. And more to the point she wouldn't be able to piss in a bucket beside the range. Damn.

Inside the house were Seamus and an intense young man with thick auburn hair and burning eyes. He should be playing the part of a rebel in some film, she thought, his eyes alone would clear a path through all the dirty Saxon Strangers.....Jesus, perhaps he was involved in something now...
He was talking about killing things all right, but the enemy appeared to be goats. And other assorted wildlife that he had already had the pleasure of finishing off. They were smoking in the house, which was not allowed. And persuading Bill that he should come hunting with them.
--There are some grand goats runnin' wild in the crag, enticed Seamus, Good milkers and all.
--We've got a goat now, explained Bill, sounding relieved. But he was not to be let off so lightly.
--Sure, when ye've caught 'em, ye can sell 'em, declared Seamus.

--Who to? asked Lynn, but nobody answered her.
Bill eventually agreed to Go Along ForThe Craic in a couple of day's time.
Lynn, infuriated, went upstairs to kiss Maggie goodnight and didn't come back down.
She would lie down with her library book. The town library was wonderful. Discovering all the great literature not available over the water made the insomnia the baby was causing almost a pleasure. Such life, descriptive imagery, divine honest rudeness, outrageous behaviour and pure originality. Lynn was devouring it all with relish. The only trouble was that it made her feel even more stiff and boring than she already imagined herself to be.
On Maggie's shelf, she noticed the prize that her daughter had brought back after her stay at Pete and Annie's. Occupying pride of place in a pretty little cup was a blown egg, with a faded paper heart underneath it, on which Pete had inscribed, 'Ruby Loves Eric.Their First Egg.' It wasn't very nice to blow it then, thought Lynn nastily.
Oh, BUGGER. She had forgotten to bring up the bucket, and she already needed a pee...

Chapter Seventeen

The day of the Goat Hunt came.
--You'll really be out of favour with Jim Ryan now, said Lynn warningly, as she saw Seamus and the flaming haired Paddy, who she had mentally dubbed Wild Man, coming towards the house. Bill gave her an irritatingly smug look, then hastily re-arranged his expression as he saw her face darkening.
--We're not going near his land, he assured her. I'll just go this once. Perhaps I'll make some money out of it.
Lynn grunted. She sensed that Bill did not believe what he was saying.

Wild Man had a couple of Wild Dogs with him. And a great knobbly cave man cudgel.....
Another fellow had come too, with thick glasses and a real bog accent, all ssshh and throaty noises. This was Frankie Daly, the one that Brendan poached with. He had brought a placatory piece of salmon for Lynn. Maggie had gone off to play with the children of some German blow-ins they had got to know.

The hunters left, Bill with a furtive and hasty kiss, and Lynn was left with a lonely day in front of her. She seethed with resentment. She didn't exactly want to go and catch goats but she hated those who were fit enough to do so. As for Bill's -pathetic – behaviour...She started a letter to Cathy. When she described things that shocked or infuriated her in a funny way for her sister's benefit, they all became more acceptable. And then she regained her view that she was privileged to be here.

Cathy, Elsa and Sam had spent the night just outside Mallow. They'd arrived in the dark after getting a lift in a truck and gone in through an open field gate. It seemed like a field but when they lay down in their envelope tent (they had lost the poles and pegs somewhere) they found some sort of rubble underneath them. Maybe the land was going to be built on soon.
They'd run for a while along the little road at Doolin, then Elsa had stood in the middle of it and stopped the first car that came along by blocking its passage with the pushchair.
--We need a lift. We've been in some trouble.
The woman was young and pretty. She looked at Elsa as if she suspected her of just having robbed a bank.
--I don't think we can help you, she said with relief in her voice, glancing

at her new husband and clasping his hand for support, We're on our honeymoon you see, just touring down the coast and then crossing on the Killimer ferry to Kerry.
--We'd be really grateful, began Cathy.
--That'll do, said Elsa, opening the back door.
They had been firmly ousted from the car near Tralee. Their hosts were going out around the coast and Rosslare lay unarguably in completely the opposite direction.
--Where's the most uncomfortable place you've ever slept? asked Elsa.
--I slept in a launderette once. It wasn't too bad, but someone flung me out at two in the morning, said Cathy reluctantly. She tried to avoid talking to Elsa now because Elsa always said things that annoyed her
--Mine was a phone box.
--How can you sleep in a phone box?
--Well, you don't stretch out on a mattress, Cath. You just sit curled up on the floor. You don't sleep much but you nod off for a few minutes. Then you get terrible cramps that wake you up again. The floor was bit damp and pissy but it kept the worst of the rain off, she added.
--I'm never doing this again, said Cathy, If I haven't got the money to drive my own car or at least buy tickets on public transport, I'm not bloody going. We've got to get to Rosslare today or I'll lose that job. Shit, I'm going to be two days late now . I already told them my sister had gone into labour early...
--You shouldn't work for capitalist scumbags that sack you for being a day late.
--Elsa, it's a new hostel for homeless people, not the stock exchange! They have a rota and if I'm not there it throws everyone else out-

Lynn was relieved to hear the footsteps and voices at the back of the house. The light was dim, both outside- it was well into the evening- and inside-they were down to the paraffin lamps again. The nightly gang of delinquent crane flies were queuing up to fry themselves on the lamps and a few exhibitionists had turned themselves into burning torches. Peering out of the porch, she could just make out the shapes of Seamus and company as they came across the rough ground behind the house and climbed over the wall. They were having a struggle. Wild goats must be hard to handle. Somewhere in the distance, she could hear a kid bleating frantically.
They were carrying the first goat. Seamus was taking charge.
--Pull him over this way, he ordered Frankie.
Seamus had remarked that morning, when Frankie went off to relieve

himself, that your man wasn't quite the full shillin'- nu'un really wrong with him, but he came from a huge family and was a little bit simple. He was certainly useful for doing the carrying, observed Lynn. She realised that the goat they were dragging – a massive, hairy, smelly thing- was dead. When Seamus, with a proprietorial air, turned on the big garage lamp that was kept hanging in the porch door for emergencies, she saw that the creature's throat was torn and bloody. Seamus gave her a cheerful, 'Hello Lynn, Howye. Ye wouldn't put on the kettle there, from a primeval face streaked with crimson warpaint.

There was an unpleasant vibration in the air made up of rank male sweat (perhaps she didn't like the stuff so much after all), the metallic tang of blood, the pungent cheesy smell of puck goat, fear, adrenalin, hormones...

At the back of the group, like one of the lesser schoolboys in,'Lord Of The Flies', came Bill.

--This'll make a grand skin for your floor, Seamus was saying, as he nailed the reeking thing onto an old door they'd stood up in one of the outhouses. The hair was long and coarse and the skin itself so thick and tough that it was a difficult task. Frankie and Bill were trying to keep it flat against the door for him.

--Now th'old fat is scraped off, ye need to rub in wood ash, to make him soft, advised Seamus a good while later.

--Don't use that stuff there! warned Bill, That's a bucket of shit I forgot to take down and bury.

--Jeshush, and I after puttin' my hand in it.....said Frankie.

--Lynn, ye wouldn't throw a few spuds into the pot. And ye could fry up Frankie's salmon with it, tis beautiful with a bit o' butter and garlic. And would ye make us an ole cup o' tay there. When Seamus was trying to get you to do something, his speech became more Irish than usual. It was generally quite continental on account of mixing with so many different blow-ins.

--We had a grand day's huntin' altogether, he continued, Did ye see the old puck goat on the door there?

--His skin you mean?

--Sure, it's a great size, 'tisn't often you get one that big. He'll cover a good bit of floor for ye.

--That's very kind of him.

--Well,that's your man finished, continued Seamus contentedly, stuffing some hoofs and entrails into Lynn's bin.

--Well and truly, commented Lynn drily. But she knew that sarcasm was

wasted on Seamus and disapproval would only register when the door you slammed actually hit him in the face.
--We skinned the other one above in the crag, but twas nearly dark when we caught the old puck, so we had to bring him along as he was. Jesus,I'm starvin',would ye mind if I had an old cut o' bread, went on Seamus, already hacking a slice off the loaf on the table, We were nearly killed carrying him (He didn't seem to be to be able to help making unfortunate puns) and he a ton weight!
--How come you didn't catch any live goats? Lynn asked when she had her back turned, pushing the salmon about in the biggest pan. I thought you were looking for nannies.
--Sure, the skin Paddy is bringing home with him is off a nanny.

The others trooped in,looking pagan and demonic. Bill couldn't meet her eye and she suddenly felt sorry for him.
--Where's the one that was bleating? she asked, recalling the juvenile cries she had heard earlier, You haven't killed that one as well?
--He's in the van, Seamus told her. Nuala can have him for a pet.
--Shouldn't he be with his mother? She could hear the kid now, shouting away in the distance with desperate high pitched Maaaaaa's.
--Arrah, she was no good, only one dacent tit on her, replied Seamus disinterestedly, while Bill, head down, decided to continue washing his hands a bit longer.
--All the same, persisted Lynn, he must have been getting something from her to survive. He's certainly missing her now. Why don't you let him go – if you put him back over the wall they'll probably find each other eventually.
--He can't find her sure, she's in the van!
-- Then why is he bleating so much? Lynn was confused.
--He means that her skin is in the van, said Bill, keeping his eyes on the floor.

– Where are them feckin' dogs? demanded Frankie suddenly, and he and Paddy leapt up and made for the door.
--Probably tearin' the t'roats off each other,s aid Seamus genially. Jesus,they're mad altogether, your man can't stop 'em at all! If ye saw the way they pulled down those two goats....We would have had another one if that old gobshite Jim Ryan hadn't come giving out to us.
Bill winced. Seamus went to investigate the howling that was coming from outside.
--Paddy's just puttin' the dogs away in the van, he informed them, an amused expression on his face. He's tyin' em up so they can't get to the

kid. They were after havin' a go at your goat, what do ye call, Tessie. Bill groaned.

In some ways, Bill could not deny that he had enjoyed the hunt, and this made it harder for him to face Lynn in her disgust. Lynn reflected that this need to go killing things was another deplorable area of maleness about as bizarre and pitiable as the taste for girly mags. What she needed was a few other women to sit and feel superior with.
Bill couldn't explain how walking out into the wildest, most impenetrable terrain had been exciting, with the conversation all of events outside his experience. Frankie talked about Shhtrokehaulin' salmon by moonlight and dodging bailiffs. They recounted various antics of friends and neighbours and found each more funny than the last. Paddy had a bottle of whiskey which they drank from as they went along. Under its influence, Bill rather enjoyed Seamus's cheekily familiar conversation with Jim Ryan when they met him digging out a ditch at the back of his land.
Seamus then began talking about what the German family had discovered when they first bought their cottage at what Bill had thought was the more normal end of the Heavenly valley.
--They were diggin' round the side of the cottage -they were goin' building an extra room on it – and didn't your man find a skellington. Of a baby.
--Didn't lots of babies die in the old days? asked Bill hopefully.
--Twasn't the only one, said Seamus ominously, There was another below, where the old garden used to be.
He paused importantly and Bill knew he was meant to offer another suggestion and whatever he came up with, the answer would be Wrong.
--Were they children that died in the famine? he tried. But Seamus ignored him.
--Th'old couple that lived there, most people thought they were married. But they weren't, they were brother and sister. You got a lot o' that out the country one time, twas hard for people them times to find someone to marry. That's why so many went to be priests and nuns. And you got a brother and sister stayin' on together and people kind o' forgot they weren't husband and wife.
--It would take more than other people forgettin' before you'd catch ME lookin' at me sister! remarked Paddy, whose sister was uncommonly spotty.
--Anyway, continued Seamus, not approving of the interruption, The

Germans gave these babies a Christian burial-
--What did they put them in to move them to the graveyard? asked Bill, the whiskey having dulled his normal sense of delicacy.
--They didn't go to the graveyard, can ye imagine the priest - Seamus took a pitying breath and began again.- That fella from Teepee valley in Wales was over at the time and he a kind o' priest, so he helped them.
--Jesus, commented Bill, knowing he'd be safe with that one. His mind was full of questions. How did the Germans know how old the bones were? Couldn't the babies have belonged to an earlier family- before the brother and sister - and simply have died of consumption or something? Maybe there was a perfectly good reason- everyone else being too ill perhaps, or maybe the family were just too poor- as to why they weren't taken to the churchyard to be buried. But he sensed that it wouldn't go down well with Seamus,who was so enjoying the drama. And he had a nasty feeling that on this occasion, Seamus was probably right.

When they started running after the first goat, racing and jumping over the rocks, dodging through the blackthorn and hazel bushes,clambering over ancient but still solid walls, Bill felt wildly exhilarated. Bodhrans pounded and ancient clannish marches played in his head.
He hadn't really thought about how they were going to catch the goats but had vaguely expected to corner them somewhere then pull one out. Possibly, that had been an option for the rest of the tribe too, but when the dogs went in like wolves at the throat of the slowest goat -she was waiting for her kid to catch up – little effort was made to stop them. Paddy, with brutal practicality, was in there slitting her throat before Bill had really taken in what was happening. Frankie pulled out a plastic bag and put a few choice cuts into it. The raw body and the rest of the guts, apart from the bits the dogs had been given, were left steaming unpleasantly on the rock with the flies already gathering. Soon, they were loping on in search of more excitement.
The kid, which Bill had been ordered to hold while the skinning went on to keep it safe from the dogs, sniffed plaintively at what was left of its mother, then decided that following the skin was a better bet, and ran after Paddy.
Bill managed to scoop it up again and catch up with Seamus.
--Look, I thought we were going to catch live goats.
--Sure, ye have one there!
--I'm going back now.
Bill tightened his grasp on the kid. He decided he had better bring it home with him before the dogs -or the people -managed to savage it.

--Arrah, come on, we'll get you a goat, promised Seamus. He thought this was all Bill was concerned about and he was sulking at the distraction of the murder on the way to his goal.
Come on and don't be cribbin',I said we'd get ye a goat...

Bill tried to leave. He wandered through the crag for a long way, with the kid struggling and yelling. Then he came to an area where the walls seemed to be endless. He couldn't see the point of dividing up this land into so many fortress-like cells for him to clamber in and out of. Who had farmed here years ago, and how in the hell could you graze sheep or cattle decently in such tiny enclosures? Now they were eerily empty except for the shivering grass sprinkled with harebells,cat's ear and dancing butterflies and the air thick with the droning of myriad unseen insects.
Eventually, he met up with Seamus, Paddy and Frankie again and admitted defeat. He hung back as they chased another group of goats and the dogs grabbed one by a hind leg and probably broke it before she managed to struggle away over a wall. He got the blood all over him when they came across the old puck, who was lying alone, clearly trying to die with dignity, and the dogs went in in a frenzy. This was pure bad luck, he tried to explain to Lynn- nobody knew that the puck would be lying there, and Seamus and Paddy had been running after a couple of nannies at the time with every intention of bringing them home to a life of cosy domesticity...
Bill beat at the dogs with a rock, hitting one on the head.
--Jesus, commented Seamus, coming up behind him, Bill's after tryin'to kill your dog, Paddy!
Paddy arrived, knelt by the goat, and whipped out his knife.
--He's half dead anyhow, and the dogs have torn his throat, he told Bill when he tried to argue.

Chapter Eighteen

--Jesus, would ye look at the way he's takin' the corners! Could ye put your foot down a bit there, Pat, and see if we can get close enough to get his attention!

Seamus, riding in his cousin Pat's car, behind the caravan that Ambrose Riley had been obliged to purchase to get rid of him and Nuala, was horrified. It was Mike and Tricia Hehir's old caravan. The one that had inspired Christy's appalling attempts at carpentry. The one with the ornate black range and carved bookshelves and bunks in it. They had sold it because they had managed to buy a cottage in Roscommon.
A fellow from a farm, in a red tartan beret, was towing it for Seamus and Nuala. All their belongings- except Mikey- were inside. They had never realised that tractors could go so fast....

Seamus hid his face in his hands as the caravan hurtled round a narrow bend and collected a deep dent and lengthy scratch from the wall it had just dismantled. Pat beeped his horn frenetically but Red Beret either couldn't, or wouldn't, hear. They went on a couple of miles, then he took a short cut across a corner of waste ground where a lot of rubbish was dumped and the back tyre of the beautiful caravan burst and went flat.
– Oh, Jesus, Jesus, will ye stop him somehow, Seamus beseeched Pat. Pat accelerated dangerously and for a brief moment managed to squeeze up alongside the careering tractor. Seamus gesticulated and shouted frantically. Red Beret saluted happily before the narrowness of the road forced them to pull back again.

The caravan rocked wildly from side to side and began to shed pieces of tyre. Seamus shut his eyes. It was his dream to own such a caravan. And it was swinging along the road disintegrating in front of them.
--Arrah, I can't bear to look, he said, when they arrived on the piece of common he'd picked for their new dwelling place, a good many miles away from the Riley's. It was an uneven grassy area where some sort of mining had taken place in the past. A tiny bohreen ran through it. On the the other side of this was a lake.

Seamus didn't attempt to speak to Red Beret, just held out a ten pound note, then headed for the caravan, bracing himself for the worst.
--Com'ere! called Red Beret, Your man told me twenty pound, not ten.
--Go back and ask him for more then, said Seamus, fondling the other ten pound note in his pocket and thinking to himself that he was entitled to keep the rest towards the damages .

Maggie ran in breathlessly.
--There's a pony by the gate, come and see!
Bill thought she meant a stray and wasn't best pleased to realise he had been lured down there to see some passing tinkers beating along a poor old crippled black creature. With a sinking heart he realised it was Hatchet Johnny. He didn't want to get into any sort of conversation but Maggie - who was getting very bold of late and, he decided, needed a good talking to- ignored him and ran ahead, where, to his fury, she was asking Johnny himself where they were going. Bill felt obliged to go and keep an eye on things. One of the three big lads who were whacking the pony told her, in that fast snappy way of speaking they had,'The Knackers'.
Maggie was confused. Surely the pony was already with the knackers? But she couldn't ask because you weren't meant to call them that.
--Would ye sell that ole caravan by the house there? Johnny asked Bill.
--No.
They'd just got it, cheaply enough, and were thinking of having a tenant, maybe someone with a child so there'd be company for Maggie. To Bill's relief, Johnny and crew seemed to be in a hurry and the question had been asked out of habit rather than any real interest. They continued on their way, whooping and beating the sweating pony, whose head yo-yo'd up and down with the extent of its limping.
--Dad, that's the pony Christy had, said Maggie.
--Yea,I thought it was... Bill knew what was coming.
--Can we buy it? You said I was going to have a pony when we moved here.
Oh Jesus, so they had.
--I haven't forgotten, Maggie. But we meant a decent one that you could ride. And I'm afraid we can't afford it at the moment. So don't start nagging, he added, noticing her expression. He headed away quickly, to the sanctity of his shed and his stack of wood. The unusually long dry spell was due to come to an end. Autumn would be on them before they knew it and with the baby due in less than three months time he wanted to know that the house would be warm for the whole winter. The work at Patsy and Sinead's had grown in to a regular couple of days a week and he was doing some delivery work for the Emerald Co-op, so he didn't have that much time at home now. And privately he was glad. He had a laugh with Patsy and Sinead, and at the co-op there were all sorts of volunteers from abroad. The conversations were interesting and the volunteers were enthusiastic and optimistic.
Lynn by contrast seemed to be getting grumpier by the day. She had been very reluctant to attend the anti-natal clinic. She loathed being

poked about with, as she referred to it when complaining to Bill. In fact she had recently had a nightmare in which indifferent doctors had opened her up with a can opener. That was about the measure of it, you had to queue up with a load of huge women and they all looked like stupid heifers and it was awful to know you looked just the same. And at the end of the line your body got groped and let known that its only significance at present was the succour for what it carried and your privacy and dignity did not merit any importance.

They'd been out to a doctor on the coast a while ago, one recommended by some friends because he was keen on homeopathy, to see if he'd deliver the baby at home. Mike and Tricia had delivered their own baby, which was their third, but neither Bill or Lynn had the confidence to consider that.

Lynn did not much like the doctor; he didn't say much and seemed nervous. But he hadn't said No outright. And Annie had introduced them to a lady who was a trained midwife but not working now due to having young children of her own. She was keen to promote Home Births and had not only the knowledge but a lot of useful kit like waterproof pads and a clamp for the baby's cord, kept from the hospital supplies in the hope of opportunities like this one. It was all a bit disorganised though, and Bill was channelling his uneasiness into laying by stores of wood and hiding emergency cans of petrol. The latter was so that he could keep his fuel gauge on the near-empty mark for the benefit of Seamus, who would not then be able to co-erce him into being his taxi man and cause him to be absent from home when the crucial time came. He expected that at least he'd have to drive to the phone box at Conlon's Cross, and possibly to the hospital itself, and he was determined to be properly prepared.

In the shed, he began to saw frantically. All this had reminded him of Maggie's birth, how he'd sweated with horror at Lynn's pain and wanted to run away at times, but she'd had a grip like a pit bull's on his wrist, so he couldn't. Oh yes, it was far out and wonderful when Maggie finally arrived but, and he was sure Lynn would agree, a good part of that euphoria was down to sheer relief that it was over. For many days they worried because Maggie was so restless and wakeful, and they were nearly demented from lack of sleep. The joy of parenthood did not make its appearance until a good while later. And he could never have imagined what a lot of work it all was, and how alarming it was when she cried and they didn't know why. When she cried when they were out shopping or something, the agitation it caused him was terrible, and people always seemed to look disapproving when your baby cried, as if you shouldn't have brought the bloody thing -whoops, his baby daughter

-out of the house.
Nor could he have imagined how many hurdles dogged the smooth path of development- teething, and inoculations .With the literature from the surgery threatening that if you left your child Unprotected -and how ominous that sounded, as if you were leaving her out on a rock for the jackals to devour – she would probably end up blind, deaf and paralysed; while the alternative lobby were warning that the good health now enjoyed by Western nations was the reason why diseases had disappeared, rather than the other way round, and you risked damaging your child's immune system and giving it brain damage if you accepted the chemicals pushed on you by the Capitalist Establishment who were paid to sell such poisons.

 The sheer worry of Responsibility, the permanent problem of trying to make the right decisions- when to call the Doctor, whether to twist the arm of that kid that was sneakily treading on Maggie's toes behind its back or Speak Reasonably to it, and the over riding problem of how to let your kid try out its walking, socialising and other skills without running life -threatening risks, made the worry immense, however rewarding child rearing might be at times. Sometimes he wouldn't mind escaping from New Mandom at all...

Seamus opened the caravan door, with considerable difficulty because it was now so mis-shapen. He flinched.
– Oh,Jesus,tis ruined entirely, he told Nuala in tones of complete abjection.
Red Beret, who had been preparing to argue his case,decided to leave.
--The wheel has carved through the wheel arch, continued Seamus,and all the shite off the road is gone up inside. Everything is ruined. He sat down on a rock to roll a cigarette. Nuala subsided beside him with nothing to say. The last couple of weeks had been awful,with the bad vibes at Ambrose's sapping her, not to mention being locked out of the house and not being able to use the washing machine...Thank God Mikey had fallen asleep in the car and wasn't staggering around out here where there was all manner of rubbish sticking up through the ground and little streams for him to drown in.
Pat's girlfriend, Rose, a big hippo of a girl who had a wonderful amount of energy for conversation and practical matters alike, took charge. She looked inside the van.
--I don't think it's too bad, she told them cheerfully, It's more mud than anything else. We can wash that off. Have you any buckets or bowls?

Ah, I can see them...If you two go and get them filled from the lake there, she said to Pat and Seamus, Nuala and myself will make a start on getting everything outside.

The stink of the mud and manure on the pile of pots, pans and bags was awful. But the connection from the gas bottle to the stove was still intact. Rose got the kettle on.

Seamus spotted some flat blocks upended in one of the many depressions in the ground round about and he and Pat managed to shove them under the van to stabilise it a bit where the tyre was missing. Then Rose put them both on Rinsing duty. After a bit they just carried everything to the lake and swished it around in there and Rose and Nuala gave the things a final wash in some warm soapy water. Most of the clothes and other stuff were in plastic bags and had stayed safely protected inside. The interior walls were another matter, but Rose determinedly got to work on those too. After a while, Seamus cheered up a bit, and went inside to nail some pieces of wood he'd found over the gaping wheel arch.

--There's lots of useful stuff lyin' around this place, he remarked. Nuala however was regarding the Useful Stuff with increasing horror.

Maggie appeared in the doorway, brandishing her Building Society book.. How the hell had she found that?
--Daddy, I'm going to buy that pony! she informed him.
--Don't be daft, said Bill rather cruelly, his present tensions making him less indulgent than usual.
--But there's enough money in my book so it won't cost you anything, and you said I could have a pony-
--A decent one, Maggie. One that you could ride. That pony is old and lame. There would be vet bills and a lot of worry for nothing.
He hoped she wouldn't demand that they went in search of the decent one then. They had no money to spare and he regretted the daydreaming they'd indulged in in her presence.
--Mum said I could! She told me to come and ask you. PLEASE, Daddy-
Bill was not gullible enough to believe this one. Lynn, too busy being Uncomfortable to want to deal with Maggie's pleas and accusations, had simply resorted to the age- old, 'Ask Your Father.' Bill thought this should be outlawed. Especially if he had to change nappies and all the rest. But then he reflected that he'd recently said,'Ask Your Mother' on an occasion when he'd felt too weary to argue.
Unfortunately, it had given Maggie false hope. And extra weaponry to fuel a further session of wheedling, fatally aided by the big grey eyes

looking moist and reproachful at the hurtfulness of adults who made promises they didn't keep....

Half an hour later, Bill got into the van. He knew Johnny wouldn't do business with an English Building Society book, so he'd collected up the spare cash, some tools and whatever else he thought might clinch the deal. He'd ended up feeling very sorry for Maggie, after he'd ordered her sharply to stop looking at him like that and they'd talked properly. He had explained that they did really mean to get her a pony, only not just now. And Maggie had burst into tears, sobbing that nothing was any good Just Now.
Recently, in town, when she'd been standing on her own, waiting for Lynn to come out of a shop, two boys, who seemed huge to her, had suddenly appeared. They stood very close to her so she couldn't escape.
--What happened to our dog? demanded one.
--What dog?
--Our dog! We know she's buried on your land. You told Bernie Gallagher in school.
Maggie didn't even know the names of the people raging about in the Heavenly Valley, let alone that Con Henchy had two sons..
--It died so my Dad buried it, she said, perplexed.
At this point, Bernie herself had luckily come by.
--Lave her alone ye big galoot! she said to one of them. That's all she knows. Now get lost!
--All right Bernie, no need to ate the heads aff us, we were only askin'!
--We didn't touch her, complained the other brother in aggrieved tones as they backed off.
Their father was too busy in his war with The Doc to explain anything to them so they had simply wanted information. They had said Hello quite nicely a couple of times since. But Maggie's present mood made her want to dwell on the shock of the initial encounter.
And various other factors had influenced her present opinion as to the Awfulness of life. There was the discovery of the Puck's skin on the shed door, not to mention skidding on his guts which a fox had re-distributed during the night. And the death of her pup, which had suffered from permanent diarrhoea and died soon after Lynn had banished it to the shed: which circumstance Maggie considered to be the cause of its death rather than any long term health problem. And lastly there was her mother's lassitude and lack of energy and interest in herself.
--I gave up my Adopted Donkey, Maggie pointed out to her father, So this would be a good thing to do instead. You thought it was a good idea

for the Horse Sanctuary to help Poor Ill-Treated Animals, so why have you changed your minds now?

Actually, when Lynn's ancient Aunt Fiona had paid for Maggie to Adopt a Donkey for a year, Bill had been heartily sickened by the letters they received, ostensibly from Daisy the donkey herself, enthusing about how nice it was to be Gambolling In The Meadow and Eating Clover with all her new friends. But he supposed that such sentimentality was necessary to enable the good works to keep going.

By the time Mikey woke up, Seamus was scorching the hides off them all with the beautiful black range blasting at full capacity. And kicking and cursing at Diddy, the goat kid, who kept trying to join the company inside. The heat inside was too much to have the door shut against him, but for once Nuala agreed that the fire was needed to dry everything out.

They hadn't been able to call at a shop on the way as intended. But Rose had found a packet of semolina and was determinedly cooking it for their tea. Outside there was still a pile of muddied clothes and some smashed crockery, but they could see that, with another wash, and if you avoided looking at the wheel arch, the caravan would be almost back to its original condition. The horrible scratch and the four foot dent they'd just have to live with...

Immediately Bill and Lynn (who had emerged, guiltily and too late to offer him support) had agreed to buy the pony - if they could - they both regretted it. Doubts assailed them that indulging Maggie was the right thing to do.

Lynn had felt terribly guilty as she heard the tail end of Maggie's outpourings. She had been a neglectful mother and Maggie's innocence had been destroyed by the sight of corpses and death....But as she saw Maggie quickly regain her spirits as Bill went towards the van, she reflected angrily that it was a part of growing up to find out that life wasn't perfect and you had to make the best of it. And that sometimes adults could see that a course of action was plain stupid. She cursed herself for not being firmer. (And for not leaving the decision entirely to Bill so that she could blame him for the inevitable outcome.)

Dealing with Hatchet Johnny might encourage him to come back again- an ominous thought. And not only Johnny but half the neighbourhood would soon be laughing their heads off at the eejits who'd run after him to buy a half dead pony. (Johnny hadn't even tried to sell it to him, thought Bill grimly as he drove along, he didn't think even the Blow ins on the hill there would be daft enough to buy that old crock...) The news would go around and there would be all sorts of jokes made at their expense. And oh God, thought Lynn, not vet bills, she'd give it a dose of wormer but that was all....

Thus it was that Bill drove after the tinkers with gritted teeth, Lynn slammed her way indoors and locked herself into a cupboard with her photos, and Maggie, wishing she hadn't been so persistent, because her parents had been right (and at least they'd still been speaking to her this morning) slunk away into the goat shed. She no longer wanted the poor pony but it was far too late to say so.

Chapter Nineteen

Bill and Lynn were having an almighty row. They didn't do this very often. Quite often their disagreements ended with them both suddenly laughing at the ludicrousness of what one of them had just said. So its ferocity was a shock- to them, but particularly to Maggie, who was woken up by it.
Bill had come back late and smelt of drink. He had told Maggie in a none too friendly way that he had bought the perishing pony. But as he'd only caught up with it miles away, and the poor creature was exhausted, he had only managed to lead it as far as Mr Keane's. (After which he had to trudge back miles to fetch his van). Maggie could go along and fetch it in the morning (if it was capable of walking any further, which after his own experiences today, he rather doubted.)
The atmosphere was so bad you could hardly stand up in it. Maggie slunk guiltily up to bed. Nobody offered to come and read to her. There was no electricity at the moment but nobody lit her lamp either.

Maggie fell asleep but was aware now and then of raised voices below. Both were blaming the other for giving in to her. They shouted louder and louder. Her Dad was yelling, 'Laughing stock! Just Needs A Bit O' Feedin'! That's what that fucking knacker said to me!'
Daddy, who had carefully explained why you should call them Itinerants.
--Christ! Bill continued wildly, I'd like to put a dent in the other side of his head for him!
He went on to mimic some more of Johnny's uniquely transparent sales cliches, until he was interrupted by Lynn, saying in a bored tone, 'You're useless at an Irish accent.'
Maggie could almost see her father's eyes bulging, the way they had when he'd suddenly picked up that man with long hair by his neck. She stiffened in the bed.
--At least I try, retorted Bill, They all think you're a stuck -up cow.
Lynn was stung by the horrible truth of this: it was the curse of the shy to be labelled 'Stuck up'. Bill was a bastard for rubbing it in.
--Ha! She scoffed, Look at the messes you've got us into!
--I didn't get into a fucking mess today! I went and bought your spoilt daughter a pony if you remember! Bill realised he was leaning over Lynn in what would be described in a police statement as a Threatening Manner. As he strode away, seething, Lynn shouted, 'Oh, so she's MY daughter now is she! Trust you to put all the blame on me. And don't boast about BUYING HER A PONY when it's a poor old rescue job,

please. It's a wonder she felt sorry for it at all with all the cruelty she's witnessed around here. It's a wonder she didn't nip out and skin it! she finished venomously.

Bill was infuriated by this remark. It not only reminded him of the shame of the hunting expedition but had the added sting of implying that he had irretrievably damaged his daughter. At this minute he wanted to tear away over bog and crag, bursting out of the moral jail imposed on him, slicing up goats and pregnant women as he went.

--YOU BITCH! he roared.

Maggie, rigid and shaking, heard a huge crash below. Most of the time she hadn't been able to hear all that was being said, but the boiling hatred of both parties was so penetrating she thought that people round at the other side of the world had probably been unable to carry on with whatever it was they'd been doing (especially if it was sleeping....)

Because the house was built into a sloping piece of ground, Maggie's window was only a couple of feet above the rough bank behind the house, although there was a bit of a gap between the wall of the house and that which held back the land in the ambitious hope of also doing the same with the damp.

For some while she had been considering ways to stop her parents arguing. They were locked in battle, oblivious to her, and the shouting was horrible. She could pretend she'd wet the bed, something she hadn't done in several years, but which she remembered always elicited a comforting, matter of fact, It -Happens- To- All -Of -Us- response, being tucked back in to a nice dry bed and if she was lucky, being read to. But she couldn't quite bring herself to deliberately pee in her pyjamas.

If she went down, they might feel guilty and be kind to her. But they both seemed to hate her at the moment. They would probably just both yell at her instead of each other.

She began to feel angry and decided she would go outside, in the hope that they would spot her wandering about and think, 'How awful, we've driven Maggie out into the night, let's go and say sorry and we'll all have cocoa.'

The defiant part of her, which considered that her parents should be arrested for their bad behaviour, felt that, even if it lacked the glamour of climbing down an ivy covered trellis with a properly alarming drop below, going out through the window was at least a protest.

Once out on the uneven bank of rubble, brambles and rough grass at the back of the house, Maggie didn't know what to do. It was chilly and the wet grass was already penetrating her shoes, which she'd put on, along with her jumper, so that when her parents found her, they'd know she meant business and they would be satisfyingly guilty that their dreadful behaviour was going to drive her away. Shame she couldn't get her wellies, but they were down by the door.

It was spooky out here, with little flusters of wind and the eery light you got when there were no street lights, just that of the moon, which was slicing in and out of the clouds and casting odd blue, flickering shadows. When Maggie was feeling safe, she loved that light. At other times, it seemed as if their house was a tiny vulnerable island surrounded by a chaotic disordered spirit which seemed to roam about here in the roadless, dark bog . She didn't like the bog. She wished they lived in a place with little green rocky fields all around it. She shut her curtains and she had her lamp when the electricity wasn't working. But the lamp had a life of its own and could be almost as disconcerting as the moonlit expanse outside, sometimes growing and casting shadows that could turn into all sorts of nasty things, sometimes worrying her by threatening to go out altogether.

 One night, after Bernie and some others were telling scary stories at school, she had lain in terror lest the lamp go out. Her mother had shown her how the wick worked when the lamps were having their clean and re-fill of paraffin, but she wasn't meant to touch it herself. Maggie thought she faced a choice between setting herself on fire or being plunged into a room full of vampires. She could have called her Mum on that occasion - she had been normal then - but there was her pride, she'd never been scared of the dark before, and everyone kept stressing that soon she would be a BIG SISTER...Plus her parents were getting very crotchety about Adult Time lately, fed up with her now they spent so much time at home, she reflected bitterly.

It hadn't been very nice, stretching across that deep gap between the window sill and the bank beyond. Now she was out here, Maggie longed only to be safely back in bed, with Lynn reading her a story. There hadn't been much of that lately, either...Lynn was always too tired...

The gap looked deeper and darker from this side. She started scrambling down the bank . Brambles tore at her legs and there were places where there were rocks, and uneven stones that slid underneath her. She slithered on her backside down onto the track that petered out at the edge of the bog. She found her way around the side of the house and opened the door of the goat shed, rattling the chain that hung on the back of it as loudly as she could, hoping that someone would come out. Tessie sat chewing away indifferently, with her odd goaty grin on her face and didn't bother to get up. She was a bit lame now and liked to lie down more than she used to. But the hair was growing over the scars where Paddy's dog had mauled her leg. The vet said she had been lucky the bone wasn't broken, but there'd been a row of horrible black stitches and Tessie had to have medicine as well. Despite her injured leg, she had been very good at wriggling around to avoid swallowing it.

The argument inside the house had passed on to the timeless topic of money, or the lack of it. Bill had foolishly and very unfairly insinuated that if Lynn had been so concerned about preserving the stuff, she shouldn't have gone and got pregnant. The row exploded into an uncontrolled inferno.
--How DARE you blame me! If you'd been able to mend your own vehicle like any normal man I would have got to the clinic and not ended up in this state! You useless, cowardly bastard, trying to put the blame on me!
--And if you knew the slightest thing about mechanics, you silly bitch, you'd realise it wasn't a little job I could do with a screwdriver and a couple of spanners! You want me to do all the women's stuff with you but you don't bother to learn the first thing about how an engine works.
--Well you could have got it moved a long time earlier if you hadn't been getting stoned with Seamus all the bloody time!
Both parties were geysers of intense malice and resentment, spitting out thoughts that they didn't even know had been festering away inside them. Each warped idea seemed to pass on its disease to the next. Events and situations neither had previously recognised as problematical got portrayed to the other as totally unbearable.

Maggie, dejected and ignored (her reflection that her parents wouldn't care if she was carried away by one of Paddy's dogs, was, at that moment, quite accurate. They were making so much noise they wouldn't have heard a howling pack of wolves coming to devour her) wandered back behind the house, tears running down her face, bracing herself to clamber up the bank and re-enter her window.
Suddenly her mother screamed, 'I HATE YOU SOOO MUCH! ' and there was another crash. The feeble bit of light from the lantern inside went out.
--What the hell did you do that for, you daft cow -

Maggie found the bank and began to feel her way up it, trying to avoid

rocks and brambles. She became entangled and began to cry as she pulled them off her hair and face, feeling blood flowing form the scratches. The bit of moon had disappeared behind the clouds. Her window seemed to have moved. She went further around the bank, lost her footing, and rolled down the slope, bashing her knees and then her head. She landed on her side in a horrible, squelching, rotten -smelling piece of bog.
After a long time she managed to stand up.. She knew there were deep holes out here, holes you couldn't get out of. But she couldn't just stay here...she blundered slowly forward.
Then the half moon came out again. There seemed to be a row of whitish rocks ahead of her. She staggered towards them. She tripped as she came up against a sort of step. Then she felt the ground become a bit more solid beneath her feet. She sank down against one of the rocks, not caring any more about the wetness seeping through her clothes. She sat there a long time.

When she opened her eyes again, there were movements on the rock opposite her.
She thought there was a tiny man made out of a leaf, jumping about, then pausing to survey her with gleaming, penetrating eyes. She had a sensation of flickering smiles and wreaths of women's hair; and leaping and floating herself as old men with bumpy knees fluted and fiddled. And then a lump on the side of the rock became a grouchy old face and grinned at her, not very nicely. Maggie shut her eyes again.

The row finally abated around two am, with both parties slumped, shocked and exhausted in their chairs. After a while, Bill lit a candle and said, 'Cup of tea?' and Lynn said, 'Yes please' which felt very good. He carefully made his way over the broken glass to the kettle.
Dragging themselves up to bed, they were simultaneously smitten with a desire to see Maggie, not just the customary goodnight peep to straighten the covers if necessary and sneak an extra kiss, but a strong urge to cuddle her close, bury their faces in the sleepy warmth of someone unaffected by adult cares. There was a moment of re-awakened tension as they collided on the narrow landing on Maggie's side of the loft, then Bill got a grip on both himself and Lynn's hand and they went in together, both having made the generous resolve to let the other have first cuddle.

Guard Hennessy was on the phone to the barracks in the town. It was

three thirty AM. He was badly hung over from celebrating the victory after the Hurling match. He didn't actually live at the barracks. He'd been tracked to a back room of Donnelly's bar, from whence he'd failed to make it home, by a distraught Lynn. Now she had driven off again to help her-whatever you called Your Man, because none of these Blow ins were married - look for their lost child.
Sergeant Quin was on the line at the other end and none too happy about being brought from his bed.
--It's that eejit Hennessy, he told his bleary- eyed wife, What the feck are they doin' letting him make phone calls? Tis Australia they should have sent him to, not just Cloonagh to be plaguing the daylights out of us!
Guard Hennessy explained that the English Wan had lost her child.
--Which Wan would that be? asked the Sergeant crossly.
--They live on the hill above Conlon's Cross. The place that used to belong to the German fella. You were visitin' the barracks that time she came in complainin' she was after losing her hus -I mean her man.
--And now she's lost the child? What is she after doin' with them at all? the Sergeant inquired rather unfairly.
--She found himself, he wasn't lost at all. But the child is gone out of her bedroom and the window left hanging open. Hatchet Johnny was in the townland lately. Oh, and your wan is about to give birth any minute, he added for good measure.

Streaks of pink light were already creeping across the sky when the group of Guards arrived equipped with bright lights and wearing wellingtons. One was despatched to take a statement from Lynn who was in a state of collapse in the kitchen.
--Don't go upsetting her now, the Sergeant had warned, or you'll find yourself with another child to replace the lost one.
The young guard thought it was going to be very hard to ask the woman about her missing child without upsetting her .He approached the house with trepidation.

Bill was out in the bog, howling in anguish. Moira Ryan was with him, trying to bring him back to the house. Jim had set off to see if Christy or any of the few other people in the neighbourhood had seen Maggie. Dermot and Jimmy, who had woken with all the activity but been ordered to stay above in their own house, were peeping over the boundary wall, determined not to miss the action.
--Hatchet Johnny is meant to have taken her, Jimmy, the older one, told his brother.
--What would he want with her? asked young Dermot in surprise, Sure,

he has a crowd o' kids already!
His brother, usually a hive of information, declined to answer.
--Come along here - keep your head down! We'll go over to the old road, we'll have a better view from there.
--But we're not allowed-
The old road was a taboo place. It had once existed as a kind of causeway through the bog but now it was deep under clumps of sedge, murky pools and fallen rocks. Birches and rowan saplings had moved in. The wet ground had gradually swallowed it up. There were only a couple of places where you could walk on it and feel that the surface was firmer than the squelching morass on either side. But they weren't allowed out there in that area of the bog. Their Da said that there had been bridges made of wooden planks one time, over some of the deepest parts, and these would be rotten now. If you walked on them and they collapsed you would never be seen again. If he ever had the money he'd like to rebuild it. It would be a much quicker way to get to Mattie's.
--I know a bit that's okay. Come on!
Then they saw the lights of their father's car coming back up their track.
--Quick, said Jimmy, Run! If he catches us out here he'll tan the arses off us-
--JIMMY, DERMOT!
--Oh, Jesus. Tis all your fault, I didn't want to come out here in the first place! whined Dermot.
--Get in the car, lads, ordered their father.
They got into the back seat in shamed silence. To their surprise he turned and ruffled both their heads affectionately.

The unfortunate Hatchet Johnny was at that moment being released from the town barracks, wearing an expression of aggrieved innocence that was for once genuine. No one had believed that he could be responsible for Maggie's disappearance, but the necessary questions had to be asked. So he had been dragged out of his bender and taken in.
 The over zealous young officer managed in the space of a few minutes to move Guarda-Itinerant relations a long way back down the ladder which they had been laboriously climbing under Sergeant Quin's guidance.

Maggie screamed. Something was coming, some animal. It was getting a little bit light now and she could see it, a big dark thing coming towards her. She could hear its hooves sploshing and its snorty breathing. She waited, rigid with terror. Something sniffed her and snorted in fear, and came back and sniffed her again. Its breath smelt nice, like sweet hay. It was a pony.

Around five thirty the three guards re-convened at the house, to await the organisation of a more extensive search, involving local people and a contingent of guards from Limerick, who had dogs. Lynn became hysterical at the idea of anyone hunting Maggie with dogs, but was assured that these would be firmly controlled, were highly trained and would never be allowed off the leash. Another cup of tea appeared before her, treacly with sugar. It seemed to be the agreed antidote to her going into labour, and she had never been plied with so much of it in her life. When there weren't all these blue suited strangers striding about, she could pee more or less where she liked (although, for obvious reasons there was an understanding that a certain radius around the door was left alone). With the current lack of privacy, she had made several trips to the bucket in the shed and now she set out again.
She perched on the plank seat, a bit gingerly since the bucket beneath was extremely full. She winced as a bright light shone in on her as a hopeful guard, double checking the outhouses- which she and Bill had explained were the first places they had scoured - had one last look.
--Oh, very sorry, Ma'am, will you excuse me, he said, hastily turning his beam elsewhere.

Then Lynn heard another voice. From the goat shed next door.
--Mum.....is that you? Mum....
--She's here! The guard was suddenly shouting. His tone held amazement and a degree of scorn as he concluded that the daft parents couldn't even search a shed properly. He was also surprised that another of the guards hadn't done so, because generally they never trusted anyone's word about the state of things and double checked anyway.
--Let me see her, let me see her! shrieked Lynn, trying to push past the two guards now shining their lights into the goat shed.
Maggie's face was scratched, and covered in dried snot and the streaks of tears. Her forehead was bruised. She was wet and muddy.
Lynn bent down beside her and hugged her.
--Oh, Maggie, Maggie, where have you been?

--Let's get her inside now, Ma'am, interrupted Guard O'Rourke. Best leave all that til later. We have a female officer on her way, she'll want to

take a look at her-
--No! She's not going anywhere!
-- She may want to send her down for a check up at the hospital. Only if it's necessary. We have to do what's best for your wee gerrel. Come on, Pet, he lifted Maggie up, Let's bring you inside.

As the main group of guards drove back towards the town in the early morning mist, they mulled over the night's events. The more humorous ones saw it all as great joke. Some were resentful at the wasting of their time and energy, and one was extremely hostile because such a cock up would never have occurred if, as was well known, all these blow ins weren't off their heads on drugs.
Guard O' Rourke was apparently dozing. But behind the lowered head and closed eyes his mind was churning. He had looked twice into that shed, and apart from the stupid mug of the goat blasting its cabbagy breath in his face, he knew well there'd been nothing bigger than a mouse inside. It was all very strange. The young girl had looked odd as he'd carried her inside. You'd expect her to be frightened or sobbing with relief (like her mother, Jesus, that one knew how to caterwaul). But she'd looked contented and only vaguely surprised at all the guards milling about.
Maybe she was Traumatised, unable to react. He'd once had to mind a poor youngfella who'd seen his father fatally injured. He had been completely blank-faced- white, stricken and silent as if some tap to all his functioning had been turned off so as not to endure the unbearable. But Maggie didn't look like that....She looked, despite the dirt and dried snot, as though she'd been somewhere wonderful and in her mind was still there. Drugs, that must be it. The lads were all saying that the likes of these were on the drugs. She must have had some of her parents' drugs. What luck she'd found her way back to the goat shed like that, after they'd been miles over the bog and somehow missed her. But that strange look on her face. He'd seen it himself and HE wasn't on drugs. Or had they slipped him something in the tea maybe?

No one else was concerned for anything beyond breakfast now. They'd had a wasted night with these daft blow ins, but they'd have many a story and joke to tell over a pint out of it. Sergeant Quin was still up there with a female of the Limerick force who was specially trained to deal sensitively with such matters (she had just been putting the kettle on as he left) They'd be keen to make sure that the wee gerrel hadn't been molested of course, but after that they'd probably encourage the whole family to get some sleep.

There might be some follow up to check that the parents were capable of doing the job of rearing a child. He himself thought the English couple were decent enough. They were actually married too, though not in the Catholic church of course.

When they had found Maggie, everyone was talking or crying as they'd gone triumphantly into the house. He'd set her down in an old armchair and gone back outside to have one last look. The goat was at the far end of the shed, cudding away as always. He looked at the depression in the straw where Maggie had been sitting.
 Then he had heard hoof beats and looking up to the rough ground that backed onto the expanse of bog behind the house he discerned a black pony, springing over the uneven ground, muscles rippling, coat gleaming, trotting briskly towards him in the dawn light. It whickered,then fell to cropping the grass.
He must have been watching it for a long time, because, exposed now in the full light of morning, he realised it was not rounded, strong and supple as he had thought, but knobbly, dull -coated and stiff, with a backbone that stood up like a piece of ply.
It was all very strange, but if you tried to explain it, perhaps it wouldn't amount to much..

Chapter Twenty

Lynn and Bill were still in a leaden, exhausted sleep at lunch time, when Maggie, overheated and short of oxygen, squirmed her way out from between them, the only place they could bear her to be before they dared to sleep. They both became aware of her moving and became instantly alert and panicky.
--Where are you going? demanded Bill.
--For a wee, said Maggie in surprise, I'm getting up now. It's too hot in the middle of you two.
--I'll come with you, said Bill hurriedly.
--Bill- warned Lynn.
But Maggie seemed pleased.
--You can come and see Molly. Molly, my pony, she went on, seeing Bill's perplexed look.
--Oh, you're calling her Molly are you. But she's down at Mister Keane's, remember?
He glanced at Lynn. The female officer last night had been satisfied that Maggie had not been assaulted and was not hypothermic. She had voiced her concerns over the stress that could have caused her to want to leave the house alone in the dark, and said that she would be contacting the school and checking Maggie's medical records. They would understand that these things must be done to make sure that children were protected because you would be shocked at what went on. But she thought from what she had seen that they were normally a loving family and trusted that they'd ensure this wouldn't happen again. Now there were a few things they should be aware of. Maggie had some bruises and though they weren't serious it was possible she might have banged her head, and could be concussed. Sometimes that came on later. If they noticed any slurring of speech, if her vision was affected or she had any memory loss, they must get help at once. Here was the number of the hospital and the person to ask for. She would be giving them a report so they'd know the details.
Bill had a slightly shivery feeling. He told himself Maggie had had a strange night and was bound to be a bit confused. He thought he would ask some test questions to see she wasn't concussed.
--Can you remember what you had for your dinner yesterday?
--What?
Lynn repeated the question for him. She was terrified that if they had to take Maggie to a Doctor or the hospital, she would be taken away from her and put into care or whatever it was called here.

--Sausages. Meat ones. With spuds and our own cabbage, that horrible stuff that's all hard and had a slug in last week. Maggie shot Lynn a resentful look.
--And what's your middle name?
Maggie sighed.
--Charlotte. I HATE Charlotte. I wish I could change it to Cindy, Mum! You said you were going to Look Into It, but you didn't do anything.. And my names not Margaret, it's Margot like Gran. Why?
--Just in case you banged your head last night. Sometimes it can make you lose your memory.
Maggie gave him a scathing look.
--I'm going out to see Molly. She brought me back in the night. Well,I suppose it was morning really, it was all blue and sparkly...
--Maggie, said Bill carefully, I think you're a bit confused. Look, let's go and have some breakfast, then we'll all go down to Mister Keane's and fetch her. But she was very tired yesterday, we'll have a look and see if she's able to come today or she needs a bit more rest.
Lynn, un-nerved, was shoving on her clothes in a parody of the Dressing Race at her primary school sports day. Maggie's joyous conviction about her nightly transportation and the pony's whereabouts were worrying. She was desperate to forget the anxieties of the night and its unanswered questions, almost frantic to indulge in the comforting normality of cooking breakfast.
She got three thick rashers sizzling on the gas stove. It was no good, she just had to have meat at the moment, and the other two were being very good about it, they understood the difficulties of cooking two meals at once and w ere enduring the new diet quite without complaint (the meat aspect anyway, she thought, smiling to herself at Maggie's description of their cabbage) Then Bill and Maggie came in, the former plainly in a state of shock, the latter looking aggrieved.
--That pony found its way up here in the night, said Bill, I would never have thought-
--I TOLD you, Dad, She was on the little road near where I saw the fairies and I managed to get on her from the wall and she brought me home.
--Well,that's great, said Lynn desperately, Now we don't have to go all the way to Mister Keane's to fetch her. She hacked slices of bread, sending the butter dish skidding across the table. She kept thinking that if they all sat down and started eating no more inexplicable pieces of information would emerge. They were all extremely hungry and she got her desired respite for a couple of minutes before Bill spoilt it.
--I wonder how that bag of bones got through the gate? he mused, It

was still tied shut. She must have scrambled over the wall somewhere..I'm amazed she managed to walk all that way as well. I left her down there was because she literally couldn't go any further. She sat down on the road a couple of times...Old Mattie must have fed her some magic oats!
--She didn't go over the wall, Maggie insisted at once. She came up that little bohreen behind the house. It goes all the way to Mister Keane's. I could see the little bridge in the distance, the stone one near his yard.
Her face was earnest as she looked at the distress on her parent's faces and mis-read its origin. I'm very sorry about last night, she told them,dropping her eyes to her plate, I didn't mean to worry you.
It was true that she had quite forgotten the revenge aspect of her behaviour. The awful tensions that had prompted her exit from the house, the terror of her blunderings in the bog, had been wiped away. She only realised from the reaction when she was discovered in the goat shed- and how exactly she'd arrived there she couldn't remember, that they had been desperately worried, and then been told off by a police lady.
--That's all right, Darling. It was all our fault. We shouldn't have been shouting like that should we. But never, never, go out on your own again, will you.
Maggie promised and there was a bit of a lecture about Strangers and Bottomless Bog Holes,followed by hugs and kisses. But still her parents didn't look happy, especially when she said, Will you come out, and I'll show you where Molly brought me up the little road? hoping to cheer them up.

Nuala was rinsing her washing. Mikey had great aptitude for getting grubby now that he could crawl at high velocity and hang onto furniture to reach down whatever he could get a dumpy paw on.
Diddy the goat kid was with her as always, skipping about and Maa-ing at her unceasingly because it was near his feeding time. In fact, he Maa'd most of the time, it never seemed to penetrate that only three bottles of milk per day were forthcoming. He was a nuisance getting under her feet - today he had jumped onto the rinsed washing- but he made up for it with his innocent playfulness. She loved his neat little hooves, sweet enquiring face and soft baby coat. She especially loved him when he was sucking at his lemonade bottle of milk. Jamesie from the farm above had given her the big teat to go on it, they used them sometimes for calves or lambs.
The place where they had the caravan now was known as The Mines.

The ground was covered in a pleasant-looking green sward, but it was very uneven in places, and there were lots of narrow, but quite deep rivulets flowing towards the lake, some of them springing from the ground.

The bohreen went on past the farm above and linked up with several similar ones, dotted with isolated cottages. At the far end of The Mines there were the remains of some sort of ugly brick buildings and several collapsing fences which encircled deep holes. On the surface, the place was pretty, but there was an atmosphere of instability. There was a continual movement as years of dumped rubbish thrust upwards through the ground, and despite Seamus's efforts at landscaping his new premises, rusty metal, broken glass and rotting carpet had a nasty habit of re-appearing. Now Seamus was erecting a sort of corral of woven hazel branches around the caravan, to make the place safer for Mikey to play in.

Nuala was relieved that the weather had turned rainy again. There had been a couple more exceptionally dry weeks after the move when the streams and the spring up the road where they got their water threatened to dry up entirely. The lake became a brown sludgy pool with a huge swarm of malarial looking mosquitoes hanging over it, and there had been a nightly argument over who sieved out all the tiny fish that got caught in the drinking water.

Christy had turned up a few days after themselves, pulling his caravan with quite a smart looking white van.

--Jesus! Not that feckin' eejit! expostulated Seamus, as Christy became recognisable behind the steering wheel, He's got some cheek if he thinks he's pullin' on here!

Then he went out and greeted Christy like a long lost brother and entered into earnest discussion about the best place to park. Christy's van had a rubbery look to it, perhaps due to the damage caused by losing all its innards. Christy decided to put it alongside a thick hedge that marked the edge of the Mines. He seemed to be smitten with the same territorial need as Seamus, spending a couple of days building a haphazard wall around the other three sides. The wall encompassed the van too, which Nuala thought was odd.

Now Seamus had come to tell Nuala that he and Christy were just off for a walk. They were enjoying themselves lately, discovering old untenanted cottages full of loot which could be sold to antique shops -

flat irons and churns to use as flower pots- not to mention items they could use themselves. Seamus had an ancient bike with huge wheels. And some grand pieces of harness put by for his next session of Dealing.

Sometimes Nuala went with them, but today she was going to join Mikey for an afternoon snooze. First, she had to go and beat up the terriers whose turn it was to be left behind under Christy's van. They were terrible for yapping. She had found a great stick for the job- one of those long poles for opening school windows. She wondered if some lads had stolen it and dumped it out here as revenge on The Brothers; anyway, it was ideal for reaching under the van and prodding the little sods when they wouldn't shut up. That job done, Nuala got onto the bunk above Mikey, and was soon fast asleep. But it wasn't long before the yapping started up again, incessant and hysterical. She spent a couple of minutes sleepily devising tortures for the noisiest and ugliest dog before she noticed that there were other sounds -the mooing of cows and their snorty breathing, heavy footfalls and people shouting. She got up and went to the door.

Outside, the brothers from the farm, Jamesie and PJ, were trying to get their cows back into a group. Something had frightened them and they were trampling wildly among the scrap metal and rocks, with the brothers sweating and swearing behind them.

--Get back there will ye, y'old bitch! roared Jamesie, Oh, Howye, twas the cow I was speaking to, he grinned as he caught sight of Nuala.

He was nice, she thought wistfully. Good looking. And that kind expression always on his face. He always gave her a smile and said a few words about the weather when he passed, and something extra,like, Was she managing all right with the water. Once he'd asked her was she happy here and she'd wanted to cry because of his look of concern and interest. He wasn't meaning just the water, firewood and so on, but herself. Herself, stuck here with a man a lot older than herself (when he was here at all, which wasn't often), that she didn't love.

--Oh,tis grand, she replied bravely, but when she tried to meet his eye he was still regarding her in that special way, and she had to look away again.

PJ, the older brother,who had a wife and kids above at the house, stormed up. The three cows he'd been following had veered off up the bohreen in the wrong direction.

--Will ye tell Seamus all this old junk has to come down! Would ye look at the feckin' state of it! he shouted in exasperation, gesturing in outrage at the wattle fence. It was one of Seamus's cleaning days and it was hung all over with vividly coloured rugs and blankets,Tis no wonder the

feckin' cows are terrified to go past it, tis like a feckin' fairground! He aimed a kick at the fence.
--Sure,it isn't Nuala's fault, Jamesie reminded him.
PJ was making quick work of demolishing the fence which Seamus had spent a day erecting. Nuala hastily gathered up the precious rugs and put them in a neat pile. She didn't want Seamus directing her to Give Those A Good Beatin' and Airin' when he came back.
--Can ye spare a minute to help fetch those cows back? Jamesie suddenly asked.
PJ gave him a look that said, Messing with the hippies now, is it.
But Nuala was already glancing into the caravan to see was Mikey still safely asleep, and Jamesie had turned away to hide the bit of a blush that was creeping over his face.

--- Where've ye been? demanded Seamus when Nuala got back. There was a kind of glow about her and she was unable to meet his eye. Mikey was crawlin' around in here on his own! And while ye've been off gallivantin', some fecker's after destroyin' the fence!
--That was PJ, said Nuala, picking up Mikey and busying herself with his soggy trousers so that she didn't have to look at Seamus, The cows were frightened of the fence so he took it down. I had to go and help round them up.
--Well don't go near that old fecker again, he can round up his own cows, do ye hear me. Helping him! After he vandalising the place! he continued in disgust.
--I was helping his brother. It was only PJ giving out about the fence. But they really were having awful trouble with the cows going in all directions. Jamesie is very nice, she added loyally.
Although she tried to sound matter of fact, Seamus, with his ability to know people's business before it happened to them, and who could always sniff out information that might cause discomfort if repeated, immediately pounced.
--Oh, so Jamesie is Very Nice is he. Well, ye can stay away from the snidy fecker. If he comes round here again I'll flatten his nose for him.
--He has to come past with the cows, argued Nuala. She was burning with guilt. It had been blissful strolling down the bohreen with Jamesie. He hadn't seemed in any great hurry to catch up with the cows, and by the time they cornered them in a gateway several fields up, they were chatting and laughing...
And such a kind look on his face as he glanced down at her. Ah God...Black, black, black is the colour of my true love's hair, that song came into her mind as she watched him going round behind the cows to

turn them. As they met up again behind them their arms touched briefly, skin against skin. His was covered with soft black hair. They looked at each other, just for a second, but everything seemed stilled. Then the lead cow took off, and they followed, both shocked and quiet.

Nuala went all the way to the farm with Jamesie and by the time they got there they were laughing again, like maniacs said PJ's wife after, in reproving tones. Nuala had looked in to check on Mikey as they passed the caravan and, God forgive her, the thought came into her mind that if she didn't have him, this feeling with Jamesie - and she knew he shared it too- could be free to grow into the type of love she'd had with Davy. She'd been embarrassed, coming out of the caravan again and he waiting on the road for her, but he asked Was The Little Fella Okay with just the sort of concern he showed when he asked about her. It was lovely, the way he looked at her. Big dark eyes, very steady, with thick black lashes. Ah God, perhaps he wouldn't mind that she had Mikey and they could be together...

Nuala had an instinctive awareness of when Mikey would wake and an Overdue bell was penetrating the floaty layers of joy, re-birth and excitement. She saw that Jamesie couldn't invite her in for tea because the glowering disapproval of his brother would be too much for him. He looked wistful as he said Goodbye. She couldn't have gone in because of Mikey but she felt hurt.

She also felt obliquely hurt on his behalf, because of Mikey's existence. Fate was not going to allow them to comfort each other, but even with this bitter knowledge in her brain, Nuala floated home, unable to resist the flickering pathways of promise, and the colours that had flooded the day and made it beautiful. She had a longing image of Jamesie's face before her, laughing in that kind crinkly way. And resting on her naked breasts.

Chapter Twenty One

Brendan called to the caravan one evening, with beer and the tale of his humiliation at Vinney's court case. Christy came over as well and Seamus, in his favourite role of host, stoking the stove and cooking the week's food supply for his guests, was scarcely recognisable as the interrogator who had tormented Nuala.

--Vinney made a holy show of me altogether, Brendan told them, head in hands at the mortifying memory.

--Were there many in court? asked Seamus, as he tended his frying pan.

--There were. A whole crowd of drongos Vinney brought in from somewhere. He can look well when he chooses, but he was drinking all week, and he standing there with those old rags he wears for trousers and his feet stinking like a sewer! Brendan took a comforting swig of beer. And all the riff-raff he brought with him - all cheering! The judge took a dim view of it and asked hadn't they a comb between them. And only one witness turned up. The rest were gone away to Dublin. Vinney didn't even look for them until the night before the case.....To be quite honest with ye I don't think all the witnesses in the world would have saved him look in' the way he did. He's got to pay-

Even Nuala, who had retreated to a corner where she was outwardly darning Seamus's solidified sock, and privately cradling Jamesie's spent body against her own, was awoken from her reverie and gasped at the hugeness of the fine.

--Arrah, don't worry yourselves, advised Brendan bitterly, he hasn't any money, so he can't pay it. He'll pay what he can - a few pounds a week. They might try to take away his tools, he'll have to hide those..

The conversation went on to the exploits of Bill and Lynn.

--I heard the Guards are keeping a watch on them, said Brendan, cheering up at the thought of the whole of the Limerick force searching about in a bog for a child who was all the time in a shed by the back door. Seamus was a bit put out that it wasn't himself telling the story to Brendan, but by the time it ended he was rolling about clutching his sides, along with Christy.

--The brother was passin' that way yesterday, remarked Christy, He says they're after buyin' that old pony of mine back off Hatchet Johnny!

This amused them for another ten minutes. Seamus, howling with mirth, was about to make disparaging remarks about Bill and Lynn's intelligence, when just in time he remembered that Christy had made the

same mistake. He wondered why Christy now thought it so funny. He concluded that Christy was now feeling superior, having made a surprisingly good deal swopping the pony for that van out there. Whereas whatever price Bill and Lynn had given for it, if it was more than the cost of a can of dog food, would be too much.
There was a knock on the door. Frankie Daly was outside, having spotted Brendan's car parked outside. He was hoping for a lift home after a busy evening's work.
--Hello, Howye Frankie, greeted Seamus, Jesus, th'old nights are drawin' in now aren't they.
--They are, they are now, agreed Frankie sagaciously while Seamus studied the gloom for a minute.
Brendan greeted Frankie and handed him a joint. They got into discussion about which worms made the best fishing bait, and the new game keeper down at the manor.
Meanwhile, Nuala dreamed.

--The Henchy boys aren't in school any more, Maggie told Lynn, as she fiddled with a multi coloured, crotcheted hat – a present from Patsy and Sinead- that was attached by its strings to the handle of the baby basket. Everything had been ready for ages and Maggie had got tired of re-arranging the little sheet and blankets and looking at the clothes. They seemed to have been waiting forever.
--Oh, are they ill? asked Lynn, then added hopefully, Or have they moved?
After Mickey the tinker had done his Ben Hur act up and down the road that day, and knocked down the wall in passing, Bill had discovered that a portion of extremely rotten dog had surfaced, and had to bury it yet again. She would be profoundly relieved to hear that Con or The Doc, or better still both, had left the area.
– Orla says their Da's in prison! And their Mam has taken them away to live somewhere else, Maggie informed her importantly.
Lynn noted the, 'Orla says', and was pleased that Maggie's tentative new friendship was enduring thus far. Bernie had seemed a bit too knowing for comfort, plus being apt to cast Maggie off when there was more exciting company. Orla was actually a rather stodgy, undesirable girl who had attached herself hopefully to Maggie and seemed to find her glamorous. Maggie- wherever she was living- had always been one of the scruffiest kids going, so it must be her English accent that impressed Orla. Maggie- who was trying hard to lose her accent- much preferred the lively company of Bernie, but as it tended to come and go,

it was useful to have Orla to fall back on.
--Does Orla know that for sure?
--Everyone knows! replied Maggie impatiently, Their Da attacked The Doc for poisoning his dog and he nearly killed him! So he's gone to prison! Mum,what's a cleaver? she asked with anticipatory relish.
Lynn told her, with a mixture of distaste and relief. This was the first time that Maggie had come home from school chattering and not distant and pre-occupied. It was just a shame about the cause of her return to earth...

Lynn was still uneasy. Inexplicable events were fascinating until they happened in your own life...
Bill had followed Maggie outside on that morning after her adventure to be shown the pony that was meant to have rescued her from the bog. His face was tense. He wanted to be fair, to hear her story as she thought it had happened. But he didn't see how it could have done. As she spoke all sorts of emotions raged through him. He felt like shaking her for taking her ridiculous fancy too far as she told him guilelessly that she'd seen the fairies Mattie had told her about on a rock on an invisible road in the bog. Then he wanted to murder someone (Who? Seamus?) for leaving their LSD where his daughter had managed to ingest it. Then he wanted to hurt himself, chop off his hand, for driving the poor little kid to leave the house in the first place. Whatever the cause- whether it was the stress inflicted on her with the move or their row or both, she could be developing schizophrenia, his child had a Fragmented Mind, or someone else had got into it, Jesus, like that film, The Exorcist...
– I was on the little road and she came sploshing along, and she sniffed me. She was scared of me first, I don't suppose she expected me to be there, and it was only a tiny bit light.
--But there isn't any road, said Bill, perplexed.
--There was last night. When Molly came, a nice warm light came around us and I could hear a noise...not like bells but like a really tiny tinkling, sort of tickling my ears...Molly was hot and steamy and she smelt nice. She was shiny. She was pawing the ground and dancing a bit-
--You mean limping-
--No, dancing around.
--And you followed her back here?
--I rode her! She's really comfy, Dad. I just knew it would be okay to get on her. I stood on the rock and she brought me all along that little green road that's over there-
--Where? asked Bill, realising that an edge of sarcasm had crept into his

voice. Damn. He was no good at this, what did the fucking social workers call it, Being Non Threatening. His brother George liked to go on about it,plus Not Asking Leading Questions that put ideas into peoples' heads rather than getting at the truth as well...But since his brother George had become a Social Worker he had a term for everything, he spouted jargon like that pissing mannikin thing in Belgium shot stale water. Surely he, Bill, a decent honest human being, could do better than that.

--I can't see it now. Maggie peered out at the bog, crestfallen. But it was there last night. A little green road and it was higher than the bushes and pools of water either side. There were some white stones along the sides..

Lynn would be better at this, thought Bill. Wasn't she always trying, sometimes nonsensically it seemed to him, to keep things pleasant and smooth for Maggie. Ah,there she came, heaving herself over the wall and perching there like Humpty Dumpty, gasping. He felt slightly repulsed. Then he was taken over by guilt and, as well as relief that he would never be pregnant, a desire to sort all this out so that the baby could be born knowing its family weren't all about to be certified.

What was that Seamus had told him once when they were in town. They'd passed a plump, sad looking old woman who'd regarded Seamus only vaguely when he greeted her. When she had shuffled on her way, Seamus told him that she was only the same age as himself, but when she was younger her family had signed her in.

--Signed her in? How do you mean?

--Into the mental hospital. On account of her being too wild - going off to dances in Limerick, staying out late...her father used to puck her all over the road sometimes. And I saw him hit her with his stick, but it didn't stop her.

--But surely you can't put someone in a mental hospital without a Doctor saying they're ill?

--Ye can here. Bad girls and sometimes lazy sons just got signed in. Their parents just asked the Doctor. And if ye'd seen her then! Nu'un wrong with her in the world, a beautiful girl altogether and as sane as you and me! I've heard they're changin' things a bit now. They have to do checks on people. They can't just keep them in there. So some like your wan are coming out. But she's fecked from being in there so long, tis too late for her.

--That's where Maggie met Molly on the little road, Bill pointed out helpfully to Lynn, gesturing at the untidy expanse of bog. She gazed at him in perplexity. Bill nudged her, trying to convey that Maggie must be humoured or they'd never get to the bottom of this. Unfortunately Maggie saw it. She felt hurt by their doubt. She could sense that the lovely memory of her meeting and the ride on the warm, safe pony was going to lead to endless, disapproving interrogations. In her mind she began to replace it with a sulky wander in the bog and a chilly sleep when she'd found her way back to the goat shed. She needed parents who were kindly disposed towards her and not wondering whether to haul her before one of those people she'd seen in films, who asked people that they thought were mad lots of questions. . Realising that your parents were actually a bit afraid of you, when you had always turned to them for strength and security was dreadful.

--So you managed to get on her and she brought you up here? asked Lynn. It was true that the pony was muddy all up her legs. But she couldn't see how she could have carried Maggie. And with not even a bridle on her...

In another dimension, down a long, long tunnel with darkness swiftly closing over it, Maggie saw herself climbing on to Molly's firm, well muscled, back. The dawn light was bright, making the stones on the grassy road glow, and the pools alongside gleam. And suddenly she felt completely safe and happy. Molly's coat was sleek with youth and fitness and a sweet steam came off her. Maggie thought she heard music but listening to it was like trying to catch the sound of birds' wings. Over there, in the distance, she could see Mister Keane's cottage and the little stone bridge she had noticed when they stood in his yard. Molly began to trot and Maggie was glad they'd made them ride bareback sometimes at the stables back in England because it helped your balance and understanding of the pony. But it was a most comfy trot. She held onto Molly's thick mane but didn't feel as if she would fall off. It was wonderful.

She remembered sliding off Molly who had stopped and started cropping the grass up at the back of the house. She wanted to get her a treat, a carrot or something from the store at the back of the goat shed, but by the time she got there she realised she didn't feel at all well. She noticed that there were voices coming from the house, and blue lights down near the road. Then she collapsed on the straw. When they found her later and carried her inside, lots of people were talking, but it didn't matter, it was like a foreign language coming from miles away.

Suddenly, Maggie burst into hysterical sobs. Lynn tried to comfort her but she broke away and stumbled towards the emaciated, hunched pony. She tried to sob into its thin mane but it laid back its ears and shook her off. She felt the dry, brittle hair and glimpsed the fat white lice

that peopled it, before, with nothing to lean on, she toppled to her knees, howling.
They had left the subject alone after that, though Bill and Lynn could be observed at times peering at the pony or across the bog in serious, but unrewarded, contemplation.

A couple of weeks later, when the weather had long turned back to a permanent soft but very wetting rain, they thought they would be safe venturing out for a drive to the village, to have a drink perhaps and get a couple of things from the shop. They wanted to soak up the normality of other people's lives. Or was it, thought Lynn, to soak up their unconcern at the abnormality of life around here...
Perhaps they'd call on their German friends on the way back. They could ask their advice about the pony's medical needs.
As they were going into the shop, a younger girl from Maggie's school appeared.
Howye Maggie, she said in a slightly lispy voice, Are ye okay? I heard ye got lost or something.
Lynn and Bill exchanged looks.
--I'm all right, replied Maggie, I just wanted to go for a walk and my Mam and Dad thought I was lost. She produced a conspiratorial, eyes heavenward expression to emphasise the stupidity of parents.
--I heard the guards were lookin for ye and all!
--Yes they were. But they went away when they realised I wasn't really lost.
--Come on then, Maggie, interrupted Lynn, impressed at how well the interrogation was being handled but still anxious on Maggie's behalf.
The questioner was an untidy little girl in a funny old fashioned dress that was very faded, a knitted cardigan done up on the wrong buttons and wellies. She had a simple face and big glasses. She stared with hungry insensitivity and Lynn could see she would like to ride her battered bike down the street, squashed sweets in one hand, the other ringing her bell to announce the sensational story,'Come'ere till tell ye! Guess who I was just talkin' to!
She cast slightly nervous glances at Bill but followed them inside the shop, approaching Maggie again as Lynn looked at the bread shelf.
--Com'ere, is it true ye slept in th'old shed with the goat?
God, thought Lynn, next she'll be asking if the guard really shone his torch in and yer Mam with her knickers down..
--I did sleep in there for a bit, said Maggie, It was dark you see, she continued quite patronisingly, And I couldn't find my way back to the house.

--Goats smell! declared the young one.
--Go on away now, Lynn told her, rather weakly because the wretched child was sure to be related to someone in the shop that might take offence if she was unkind to her. She got a myopic stare for answer and no movement except for a slight shuffle of the wellingtoned feet. Lynn's suspicions were proved correct as the man behind the counter called out.
--Is that you, Kathleen! Come over here for yourself. How is Mammy, is she better at all? Well now, you give her this - mind how you carry it now, wait'll we see, I'll put it in a carrier bag for you. And this is for yourself, don't eat it all now, will you, there's the good gerrel, save some for later. Off you go now!
--Don't mind her, Maggie told her mother, She's only in High Babies, she continued disparagingly.
Kathleen turned to go, but she managed to sidle close to Maggie again.
--Ye shouldn't go out in the dark, she told her importantly, Ye'll be taken by the fairies!

Going back up the street there was, as always, a sensation that they were passing through a tunnel of animated talk which broke off and then resumed again when they were at a certain distance. Seamus had explained it didn't mean the talk was about them, just that people were curious because they were new, and really they should stop and pass the time of day a bit. But just now Bill had to admit that they were bound to be the hot topic of conversation.
--They'll soon forget about it, he told Lynn re-assuringly.
Maggie now seemed as cool as a cucumber, un-nervingly so. She was only a kid after all but had told her story with such casual conviction it was a bit disconcerting.
Luckily, another topic of conversation was dominating the local news, and that was an approaching gale. There had been a bad one the previous year, causing all manner of damage. A whole pile of caravans somewhere up the coast had been picked up by the wind and flung in a smashed-up heap several fields away. Bill and Lynn decided to forego their visit to the Germans and go straight home. They hadn't much stock to get in, apart from the hens and poor old Molly, or any hay ricks to tie down (Far From the Madding Crowd was one of Lynn's favourite films...Bill was incensed at her hypocritical leering at that classic sexist pig played by Terence Stamp; but he endured the re-runs because he was in love with Julie Christie) . Around here, there were still people who had those sort of hay ricks...and Bill and Lynn felt the instinct to make all safe.

On the way back, they called at the Post Office. There was a letter from Cathy.
Lynn settled down with a mug of tea before she opened it.

Dear Lynn,
I'm really sorry not to have been in touch for so long.
I have a confession to make. I actually came to Ireland at the end of July, long story but it was a complete cock up..It was a spur of the moment decision (Never Again) so no time to write first. I wanted to come and see you but I couldn't get there. I was travelling with a complete drongo who got us into all kinds of trouble. Well,maybe it wasn't all her fault, we had bad luck, and there are a lot of nutcases over there- Be Careful!
Everything went wrong (will tell you properly when I see you – will you be back at Christmas?Hope so) and I had to get back as I was due to start a new job. (I was two days late but luckily they let me off)
On the funny side, I can claim to have slept in some very strange places. The last one was the worst. We came off the ferry at two in the morning, went into some old barracks place in Pembroke. We lost the tent pegs somewhere so were just lying in the tent. There were trees above us and all these crows flapping about all night, and screeching at each other, quite spooky! Worse thing was when we got up-all covered in bird shit!!
I'm working in a hostel for homeless people (all men.There's a lady tramp around but I don't know where she goes-I don't think there's any place for women). It was set up by a local person, but we get a bit of funding from the council. We have four men in the hostel at the moment but expect more when the weather gets cold. Most of them are very mistrustful and only come in when they're desperate. Some of them won't talk at all. There's a strange old boy who has a supermarket trolley and it's full of bags. All the bags are stuffed with other bags. He won't let go of it, he has to have it with him all the time. We only got him inside once. He usually sits all night in an underground car park.
Some of them are really interesting, one is a war veteran who was on the Atlantic convoys. It's terrible that he's ended up like this. But I live in hope- things can only get better (especially when we get rid of Thatcher). In twenty years time there won't be any more tramps on the streets.
And no Nukes either I hope. The CND rally against the missiles at Greenham was powerful, it was really good to be with all those people united against the lunacy. Kinnock spoke really well. There was also lots of good music from various people playing while we were marching.

Mum told me Maggie has a funny old pony. That's nice. Hope the goat is still giving milk and M is managing to bring it indoors in cleaner condition! I have written her a letter of her own.
You must be fed up with the wait now- and excited that it's nearly time for the baby to arrive! Are you still arguing over names or have you decided now? What has happened with the Home Birth idea-are you going to do it?
Give my love to Bill and say Hello to Seamus and Nuala (expect Mikey is walking now?-that must be fun!!!)

Loads of Love,
Cathy xxxx

ps. I met someone. Don't want to say too much at moment given my past disasters but all is going well so far.

Lynn felt tears prickling her eyes. Cathy had been so near, and she hadn't known. She fell to reminiscing about her sister. What an odd thing Families were . You grew up in a unit, loving, and sometimes hating (there'd been a fair bit of that with her father) each other. Your parents worried, made sacrifices and did their best for you. (Again, she thought her father had made a meal out of the worrying, to show her mother what had been inflicted on him) Throughout childhood you were being prepared for having to go out into the world where you had to find someone else to love, and create a new unit of your own. But there was always an ache for the old one, and a feeling that you'd broken their hearts by going. It must have been nice in the simple times when old people sat by the fire in the family home and helped mind the grand children. (Not that she could picture her Dad doing that) One day Maggie would turn her back and go. How would she stand it? Perhaps if Maggie was a really obnoxious teenager (she really couldn't imagine it but friends had assured her they'd had the same faith in their lovely kids and the dreadful metamorphosis just happened, whatever you did), it might be easier to face it...
She and Cathy used to do nearly everything together. Cathy, though younger, was always bolder. When they started going to the stables,and began to spend all their time there, Cathy was the one who took the ponies in and out to the field, cantering bareback on one and leading the other, hair flying. Lynn remembered the pattern of dust and hair it left on the backside of her jeans. She had a weird feeling she'd seen that pattern very recently. She got up and went to the porch. There was still a smelly heap in the corner- the filthy clothes they'd taken off Maggie after

her night in the bog. She'd been meaning to wash them, or, now she'd left them festering too long, burn them. Gingerly, she lifted up the jeans, which still had Maggie's pyjamas inside them. They were going mouldy and were stiff from all the murky water they'd absorbed. They were solid mud until well above the knees. But on the seat and upper legs, the crescent pattern with its margin of dust and black hair left by bareback riding was plain to see.

At The Mines, the ever vigilant Seamus was thrusting his feet into his wellingtons, which he kept under the caravan step. Hatchet Johnny was outside.
Johnny jumped out of his truck and was over to Christy's patch like a rocket.
--Where is he? he demanded, after trying the door of his erstwhile van and finding to his fury that it was locked. He rapped in a frenzy on the caravan door which fell open to reveal that it was frustratingly unoccupied.
--Where is he? Johnny demanded again. His words snapped out like castanets and he seemed to find it impossible to keep still, darting and sniffing around like a cross between a shark and an intensely excited lurcher.
--He's off hunting, Seamus told him.
--I want my van back! declared Johnny fiercely.
Seamus was aware of two other tinkers getting out of the pick-up behind him. He was relieved to see they were only youngfellas, of about thirteen and fifteen years old. But even so, his heart was racing and his mouth had gone dry. Blast Christy to hell.
--I thought ye made a deal, he ventured cautiously.
Johnny ignored this.
--I want my feckin' van back! Where's that feckin' bollix hidin'?
--I told ye, he's away huntin'.
Johnny suddenly made a run at the wall Christy had erected and began pulling it down. But Christy, as if in expectation of this occurrence, had used some pretty hefty rocks - purloined from one of the farm walls, and the cause of a further deterioration in relations with PJ. He had also put in posts and chicken wire for re-enforcement. These weren't very stable and Johnny, if he had been able to slow down and apply himself more methodically, could have taken out a section of wall big enough to back out the van out in ten minutes, even if he wouldn't have had the keys to get inside it. In his rage he was incapable of thinking logically and went and gave the van an enraged kick, denting it severely.

--That fella! I'll hit 'im in the head with a brick, so I will! he spat. He vaulted back over the wall and stormed back to his pick up. The two lads, who had been wandering about looking for scrap, only managed to get themselves half into the vehicle before it took off. They finally got the doors closed as it skidded round the bend above by the farm.
– Oh, Jesus...Seamus told Nuala miserably, He'll be back again...

Christy was at home when Johnny came back. Seamus was hiding behind his curtains, listening intently through the open window. Johnny was again demanding the return of his van. Christy was ignoring Seamus's advice and insisting that a deal had been made and the van was his.
--Jesus Mary and Joseph, groaned Seamus, Christy has even less sense than I thought. Stay inside Nuala,and be ready to run to the house above and call the guards. I'll see can I distract your man before he tears Christy apart.
As he went out, Johnny was not responding well to the logic of Christy's argument. He was pacing back and forth, making dangerous little darting movements as his loaded, furious energy threatened to explode.
--Give me back the horse then, said Christy, We made a deal. Give me back the horse and you can have the van.
--Jesus....Seamus groaned again. Now Christy was calling the creature a horse. But while he was trying to lure Johnny away from Christy by offering him pieces of harness, dogs, lamps and, in desperation, his new jeans, a miracle occurred. It was in the form of a very battered car, bulging with Johnny's relations.
--Will ye come up out o' that! roared the driver, There's a gale comin' in! Come on will ye, we're all movin'!
--Tis true for him, said Seamus to Nuala, watching with relief as the two vehicles careered away, Th'old wind is savage. We'd better let the range out, he decided as the caravan did a little buck as the wind got under it, I'll just let the kettle boil there, then I'll chuck everything that's burning away outside.
Christy appeared at the door.
--Any chance of an ole cup o'tea there Seamus, I'm out o'gas.
--Ye'll be out of a head on your shoulders if ye carry on the way ye're goin', Seamus told him.
--Would you go on away out o' that now, Seamus, snapped Christy angrily, We made a deal-
--Arrrah,deal my arse, twas obvious somethin' wasn't right. Do ye think he'd be givin' a grand van like that away-

--He traded it for the horse!

--Horse my arse. What would he be wantin' with that feckin' thing, and he with a herd of fine big horses above on the Galway road? Sure and haven't ye seen' em for yerself! He just wanted a place to leave that van on account of being in some kind of trouble with it. It was stolen most likely, or maybe he did a robbery in it, sure isn't it obvious to anyone but a feckin' omadaun like yerself!

--Ah,would ye feck off for yourself! retorted Christy, Hasn't he gone away now, and I still have my van. If I was listening to yerself I'd be after giving him me caravan, dogs , money and all by now!

Chapter Twenty Two

Seamus and Christy were stopped from coming to blows by the caravan jumping again, much higher than the last time.
--Did ye feel that! said Seamus nervously, If she takes another lep like that we could come off the blocks altogether. Lookit! Now the range door has come open!
Seamus made for the caravan door, meaning to fetch the shovel from outside and remove the rest of the embers from the range. But he had great difficulty opening it against the wind, which was now howling. Once he got it past a certain point he found it snatched from his grasp and flung open so that it crashed violently against the caravan's side.
--Tis terrible out there, he told Chrsity and Nuala, Would ye hang onto the door for a minute, Christy, while I get these ashes out- He battled his way back in with the shovel.
--Twould be safer to leave them in, they'll burn out soon anyway, pointed out Christy. But they had never heeded each other's advice, and it would take more than a transatlantic gale to make Seamus start doing so now. He scooped out a shovelful of embers and half a glowing briquette and attempted to take them out through the door. The wind blew most of it back inside and they all had to jump about to put the sparks out. Mikey roared laughing at the funny people but Seamus was mortally depressed over a hole which had been burned in his favourite blanket, a patchwork affair, magpied from some Dutch people who'd been around last year...

Smoking a joint and drinking tea, they forgot their disagreements as the storm raged and battered outside. It had reached a really intimidating strength. They had Radio Clare on, but the batteries were running down, turning jigs and reels into slow airs played on untuned instruments. Mikey was pulling and dragging at everything in sight, missing the spell that Nuala usually ensured he had outside. Even when he only stayed in his push chair, the different sights and sounds gave him something to think about and he came back calmer.
Things began to bang on the sides of the caravan. Twigs and branches were being hurled by the wind. Nula was terrified it might heft a telegraph pole at them next. The line of poles that went to the farm were already leaning at all angles.Then their home took a series of shaky jumps just like an unruly horse.
--Seamus, Nuala clutched his arm nervously, We won't tip over altogether will we?

--Ah, God, no!
But then the caravan began to leap like a rodeo horse instead of a slightly frisky one.
--Christy, said Seamus hurriedly, Maybe we should go over to your caravan. Tis much more sheltered over there with that big hedge alongside. And it's not sideways to the wind like this is.
--Okay so, agreed Christy.
--Nuala, will ye wrap Mikey up there, instructed Seamus, to her irritation. She had been sorting out Mikey's things for several minutes but he always had to say it, as if she'd take him out naked otherwise.
They fought their way out and the wind attacked them. Bent almost double, with air, water, leaves and branches rushing all around them, they stumbled across to Christy's caravan. Seamus heaved the door open. They raised their heads.
It was very odd-looking inside. Everything seemed to be in motion. The walls were billowing gently, the floor was undulating and, above the stove, where they hung on a string to dry, a collection of socks were dancing a frenzied polka. Slowly they lifted their eyes.
--JESUS! exclaimed Christy, stunned, The feckin' roof is after blowin' away!

Eventually, after a respectful silence, Nula asked, What'll we do- go up to the farm?
--Is it them cunts! We will not! Here, take Mikey a minute. Seamus dumped the little fellow in her arms, We'll go the other way, up to Paddy Hines's place. I was in school with him. We can get a lift into town and stay at Maeve's. He had to bawl to make himself heard as the wind gusted around them.
--You'll have to carry Mikey, Nula yelled back, I'm not able for him all that way!
--Can ye not put him in the push chair?
--Not in this, he'll be drowned altogether!
--Arrah, come on will you, we'll all be drowned if we don't move! put in Christy, The sister has one o' them plastic roofs on hers, he added unwisely.
--Arrah, one o' them would never stay on in this! said Seamus quickly, before Nuala could start giving out to him. She'd told him to get one last week, only the money she thought they could spend on it was already owed to someone, so he couldn't. He tucked Mikey inside his coat as much as he could, and, almost blinded by the driving wind and rain, they set off.

The gale, as they struggled up the bohreen, was awesome. It was all they could do to move against the wind. The rain beat into them and Mikey's curls were plastered to his skull and his back soaked, despite the raincoat Seamus was trying to hold around him. As they fought their way at last into the nearest farm building, he sat dead still, gazing out, now that his face was released from his father's armpit, with huge, amazed eyes.

They were in the dairy, a horrible metal place with puddles on the concrete floor that smelt of chemical sterilizer. The air was chilly and the stainless steel tank and pipes were covered in drips. The wind made a ghostly booming noise as it slung itself against the metal doors and raced around the empty tank.

--Stay here, said Seamus, I'll see if I can find Paddy.

Christy took Mikey and amused him by tapping on the pipes with a stick and singing. He was good with kids, having a crowd of younger siblings and already being an Uncle to a couple more. But if they'd only gone up to Jamesie's farm instead of coming here., thought Nuala. But maybe not...she wouldn't want to be there with Seamus, it would be far too awkward. She'd been thinking a lot recently about Lynn's offer of a place to live. She was worried. She was hardly feeding Mikey now. The weaning onto a bottle had been a sort of accident, she'd only wanted to get him used to taking the odd one. The first time, he'd hated it, he'd refused it and cried , then he'd got desperate, started sucking and fallen asleep from exhaustion. But then the English woman, the one that Seamus kept saying was On The Game, told her that breast milk was sweet so it was best to dilute condensed milk which babies preferred the taste of. The minute she gave Mikey the odd bottle, her own milk had started drying up. She felt quite sad about it, but she had more energy. Her worry was that her periods had returned. At least,one had. That had been a good while ago, and there should be another by now, but maybe they weren't regular when they were just coming back. Oh God, please, please make it come soon and she promised then she'd stop living this lie, she'd find the strength and and start again somehow. She'd have to let Jamesie know where she was going so he'd come and see her....Ah God, if she could just bask in the radiance of one of his smiles again for re-assurance. But Seamus was Keeping An Eye. All the time. When Jamesie went past with the cows he was watching, if she went for a walk he had to know where she was going...

Jamesie was so gorgeous...he was probably sitting in a bar now with some girl who didn't have any complications laughing at his jokes....

Seamus and Paddy appeared. The wind brought them flying through the door and pushed Paddy up against his tank.

--Howye. Are ye well or are ye drownded! said Paddy when he got his breath back. Lookit, I don't want to be drivin' into town in this. There are trees down and all sorts. But I'll take you into the village.

--Grand,so, agreed Christy.

The roads were hardly recognisable,with water gushing in all directions and mud and stones strewn all over them. Outside Heaney's Bar, the sign was swinging crazily and creaking and groaning. There wasn't a soul in sight up or down the street, but the bar door opened when they tried it. Heaney's kids, who had the day off school, had taken it over in the absence of customers. They were at that moment trying to bring two dogs for a walk around the tables and chairs. The dogs, knowing they were normally strictly banned from the bar, were trying to escape before someone realised their mistake and walloped them with a beery tea towel.

--Is your father here at all? asked Seamus.

One of the boys ran out through the door at the back.

--Dad, Dad, there's a man in the bar.

Eamon Heaney appeared, with water streaming off him.

--Hello,Howye Seamus, Tis terrible bad weather isn't it, lads. I wasn't expecting anyone in today.

--But ye'll give us an old drink there. We're after being blasted out of the place above, and hasn't the roof of Christy's caravan blown away altogether.

--Well,I was trying to cover the hay I have in the barn a bit better. The bloody rain is getting in there.

--Well, could ye not pour us a drink,and then I'll come and give ye a hand.

--I wasn't planning on opening today, sighed Eamon, Tis the kids have the door unlocked on me. But he began to pull a pint, and expressed no surprise when Seamus asked could he give him the money again as he'd managed to leave it behind in the chaos.

They spent most of the day in the bar. At lunch time two little girls brought them a plate of sandwiches, which, they explained proudly, they were after making themselves. At five o'clock, Maeve's husband came to fetch them. By this time Mikey was black from crawling on the floor among cigarette butts and the grime off muddy boots. Nuala had run out of nappies and he was wearing a sweatshirt like a huge football in his plastic pants. It was heavy, so the whole lot kept falling down. He had just pee'd cataclysmically -the result of Heaney's little girls continually plying him with orange juice and coke - and the arrangement, being at half mast, had failed to catch the deluge. Mikey managed to crawl through the pool before anyone caught him.

Maeve's husband surveyed the scene with distaste. His expression grew sourer when Seamus asked him could Christy have a lift into town as well, and he said little during the drive.

Maeve was great though, she gave them both a nice tea and ran to a neighbour to borrow clothes and nappies while Nuala put Mikey in the bath. Later, Seamus made his usual announcement of Having To See Someone and went out.

--Mikey looks as if he's down for the night, said Maeve later, I'll keep an eye on him if you want to go and find Seamus.

Nuala just walked- through the Fair Green and around the dark streets with the wind buffeting her and the dismal drizzle into which the rain had now subsided soaking her. People were out, despite the gloomy evening, glad to stretch their legs after being huddled inside all day. You could tell that the storm was over now. There was a half-heartedness to the wind. God, she'd been frightened this morning. In the town it had been nothing more than an inconvenience but for a while out there at The Mines it had looked as if it was not only the caravan that was going to blow away but Mikey who would be torn out of their arms. In fact the caravan could have blown away for all she knew, no one had been back to look at it yet...

Maybe they'd get a Corporation house, all colourless. She regarded the streets where everything seemed dirty, grey and wet. It was only early Autumn with months of worse darkness ahead. She'd come out for air. And to think about Jamesie. But she couldn't picture him so well now or recall his voice. The gloom had got into her soul.

Chapter Twenty Three

--We'll have to move out o 'here for the winter, Seamus told Nuala, There's feck all wood in it.
The weather was bright and frosty. The blue sky had a hardness to it and there was a bite in the morning air. The hedges were heavy with haws and spiders webs. At night the sky was brilliant with stars. When they woke in the mornings there was a layer of ice on the ceiling just above their bunk where the condensation had frozen. Seamus always got up bravely to light the range and warm the place.
--I'm killed, he complained now, Traipsin' all over the place to find a few sticks of wood! Anyway, I don't like livin' beside them old feckers – he nodded in the direction of the farm house - they're always bad vibin'! There's a good spot I'm thinkin' of, out in the forestry. No one will bother us there.

That was for sure, thought Nuala, as she surveyed their new home. It wasn't just forestry, not neat rows of conifers as she'd expected, it was woods - tangled, ancient woods with its roots in a swamp. They were parked on a verge dotted with the usual tinker's junk. Behind them, the sodden, gnarled trees and briars collapsed into stagnant brown pools. Across the road was one decent field, then an expanse of bog, then more rotting woodland.
--Grand isn't it, said Seamus.
Nuala didn't answer.
--Put on the kettle there will ye, wait'll I turn the gas back on, there ye are. Look it, what ye need to do is unpack all this stuff, and arrange it nicely, and give the rugs a good beatin' will ye, they're full of dust. And would ye put on a pot o' spuds there, I'm starvin'. I've to get wood....
Saw over his shoulder, Seamus squelched away.

A few nights later, when Nuala was in bed up in the bunk (she was no sooner out of it than she was climbin' back in again, Seamus had confided to Brendan not long ago, she was always feckin' sleepin', and no conversation out of her, ye might as well be talkin to that pile of wood, at least that would crack and sizzle at ye...) and Seamus was nursing the feeble bit of flame in the range (the wood was a bit damp but it would soon dry now he had it stacked), they heard a vehicle. Seamus was instantly at the window. This was a rare occurrence. The night was black. There wasn't a light from any house and the nearest street light was miles away. He could see headlights travelling on up the hill.

He went back to the range. The temporary cessation of his duties had allowed the flame to die to a feeble flicker. They were out of firelighters, having used an uncommon amount in recent days. There wasn't even a bit of milk carton left to assist his efforts.

--Well feck it anyway, he remarked.

The next minute, the whole caravan was filled with bright – intensely bright – light. Seamus, who had been carrying out his ministrations by candlelight, shielded his eyes in shock. It was as if the sun had fallen in on top of them.

--Jesus, Seamus, what is it? called Nuala anxiously.

--It's that crowd in the car. They've a light for spottin' foxes. Do ye hear that now- that quacking noise? That's to call up the fox.

--I don't like it! I hope they don't come here all the time...said Nuala, who was still only a shaky voice from the bedroom, Seamus! What's that now? It sounds like bullets!

Terrified, Nuala leapt from the bunk and in her panic missed her footing, breaking a mirror that stood on the wheel arch.

--Jesus, Nuala, mind yerself will ye, said Seamus, that was a grand mirror I got from that cottage near-

--I've cut myself.

--Wait a minute, I'll get the toilet roll. Mind that rug there, will ye, there'll be an awful stain if blood gets on it.

--There's no toilet roll left. Look in Mikey's bag, there's cotton wool in there.

The bullets whizzed across the hill while they ripped up a nappy and bandaged Nuala's arm. She was in a panic that the caravan, not to mention the people inside, would be hit.

--Sure, they shone that big light around didn't they, so they know we're here, said Seamus. But he reflected privately that knowing might not be the same as caring. Even after the car pulled away and the night enfolded them in darkness and solitude, he couldn't relax.

In the morning, Seamus was grumpy. About the wood not lighting, about there being no eggs or rashers for breakfast and it still two days until he could get the giro, about Mikey smearing shite down his last pair of clean trousers....And about Diddy, who foolishly leapt into the caravan just as he opened the door to go out.

--Ah, will ye look at it! he cried in disgust, grabbing Diddy by his collar and hoiking him into the air, Filthy footmarks all over that skin!

--Up, Did up! cried Mikey, pointing and chuckling.

--Next time he goes up, said Seamus, he won't be coming down. He'll be

hangin' from that tree over there.
--Seamus, will you put him down, pleaded Nuala, he's choking! He only jumped up because he's looking for his bottle, he usually has it by now but I -
--Bottle my arse! Don't be wastin' any more milk on him and he the size of a bullock! Shit anyway - look at the state of this rug.
--Its only a bit of mud, Seamus. When it dries it'll brush off easily enough. Can't you move it from the door though, a white rug is hardly going to stay clean in winter, there's bound to be some mud coming in. I'll put down some papers-
--Ye will not. I want the place lookin' decent.
Seamus held Diddy at arms length and gave him a boot onto the road.
--Up Did Up! cried Mikey ecstatically.
Diddy stumbled to his feet, shaking his head, and tottered away.
--I've to see someone, announced Seamus, pulling out his bike from behind the caravan.
--But Seamus-
--I'll bring back food and briquettes, he called over his shoulder.

Another regular occurrence at the forestry was the Beagle Hunt. A group of farmers in black coats, caps and the regulation tall wellingtons chased a pack of baying dogs about. The beagles in their turn chased foxes, hares and, once, a beautiful stag. It bounded right past the caravan, passing within a couple of feet of Nuala who was outside, muscles rippling under its silvery winter coat. It had a broad chest and fine antlers. The whites of its eyes showed as, snorting and panting it hurtled towards the half buried boundary fence that separated the boggy woodland from the road. It tried to leap over but got entangled in the wire and crashed onto its shoulder with a heavy thud. Frantically it struggled up, tore its way out and headed off into the trees. Nuala could only hope it wasn't too badly cut.
For days afterwards, stray beagles could be heard baying in the woods opposite, and sometimes they saw them still splashing through the bog, following some scent or other that made them forget all thought of food and rest. Far behind them, men called and cursed, until at last they were all accounted for.

Annie and Pete called one day, and invited herself and Seamus to come for a drive and a drink. Nuala didn't really want to go. She'd lost the ability to converse through lack of practice and now, instead of feeling pleased at the prospect of company and different scenery, it all seemed too much effort.

She missed Christy being next door. Even though he and Seamus had often fallen out, she could always have a chat with him, and sometimes he would mind Mikey for a bit. Christy had loaded his belongings and (thank God) his dogs into his van and driven off in the direction of Rosslare the day after the gale and not been heard of since. The remains of his caravan was still out at The Mines, disintegrating in a horrible mess of warped panels and fluffy cladding that was no doubt driving the cows to take off for Galway.

Nuala hardly got into town to renew her library books. She occasionally managed to get hold of a paper. Sometimes she wished she hadn't. The prisoners in the Maze were on hunger strike now, saying they were willing to die for their beliefs and their right to be treated as political prisoners. At times, Nuala had reflected on what would be the worst way to die -not that any of them were ideal, and she didn't have a death wish, it was just one of those odd trains of thought that seemed to afflict the human mind from time to time. She had always thought dying in a fire would be the worst, or maybe drowning...But to starve yourself to death, Jesus...She'd read about the force feeding of the Suffragettes - totally ghastly. She wondered if they would force feed the prisoners in The Maze..In England, the 'Yorkshire Ripper' had killed yet another woman; a poor student who had been returning to Leeds university after attending a seminar had been beaten with a hammer and stabbed with a screw driver.

At the moment the only thing Nuala liked doing was sleeping but she had no good excuse for turning down the invitation so she had to go.

God, the ease of life with a vehicle- especially one like this camper van where you had everything with you -and the sheer comfort of it, sailing through the countryside...Nuala began to feel glad she had come out. They drove into the grounds of one of the ruined mansions once inhabited by the English gentry. The shell of the huge house stood, gaunt and eerie, with the floors and the roof quite gone and only the empty fireplaces, clinging to the walls like gaping mouths, to mark where the different storeys had been.

They got soaked exploring the walled garden, wading through sopping grass and a tangle of weeds. Pete sank into a pile or rotting apples. They found three vast greenhouses, with their glass long broken, and timber all decayed. Brambles bound the wooden shelves which had once been stacked with plants, and all but buried the brickwork paths that ran between the long-lost beds outside.

--Do you know anything about this place Seamus? asked Pete, Was it

burnt in the Troubles or what?
--I think it was, all right, said Seamus, but you should ask Frankie Daly if you really want to know the history. I know it was fired one time but the family didn't leave it until a good bit later. There are a lot of these places around...Like the one Ambrose Riley is in, the old fecker!
--It's sad to see it all gone to ruin like this, said Nuala. It's ghostly isn't it. You half expect the gardeners to come around the corner with wheelbarrows-
--And doffing their caps to the gentry, poor sods! put in Pete, whose politics didn't allow for this kind of nostalgia.
--Its a good thing those days are over, said Annie, but Nuala's right, I have the same feeling, that just around the corner they're all still buzzing away, weeding and watering, carrying huge armfuls of flowers into the house to decorate it for the ball... It's an awful waste isn't it, shame some of us couldn't get together and rent the garden, get it all going again..
Pete was about to make a cynical remark about it being a ball that those workers would only squint at through a crack in the curtains if they were lucky, when Seamus interrupted.
--Ye'd go round an awful lot o' corners to find anyone around here! Will ye come on for yourselves for the love o' God and let's get a drink. If the ghosty gardeners didn't get there first and drink it all on us, he added.
Nuala was often irritated by Seamus's inability to consider anything seriously, but she was grateful for this intervention. It was a melancholy old place and what she wanted now was a nice hot whiskey in a bar with a good fire- and someone to take an attraction to Mikey and play with him for a bit so she could enjoy it in peace. She'd hoped to tire him out on this excursion but she'd been unable to put him down, much to his annoyance, because he would have got saturated in all the long grass and tangled weeds.
--Lets go and see my ancestor, suggested Pete,who hadn't taken offence. He was all G'Day, I'm Easy Going, unless chickens - which could do no wrong - or children – who could do no right - came into it, observed Nuala somewhat uneasily as she fought to keep her grip on the writhing Mikey.
--My ancestor, the great Dan O' Grady, continued Pete with a big grin on his ruddy face.
--Oh Pete, pleaded Annie, not there! Lets go somewhere cosy and cheeful for God's sake. --Wait'll ye see this, tis gas! enthused Seamus to Nuala.
--Why do you call him your ancestor?Are you really related? asked Nuala.
--No! laughed Annie,They just have the same surname. We did do a bit

of research but its not the same branch of the family.

The bar run by the man Pete jokingly referred to as his ancestor was situated beside the town dump. On its other side was the slaughterhouse. They parked beside a high mesh fence which was decorated all over with rubbish plastered there by the wind. A screaming crowd of seagulls and carrion birds rose briefly into the air, before returning to their scavenging. Also scavenging were a crowd of tinker kids, swarming over the undulating expanse and loading their spoils into a battered pram.
--I'll just pop in here and see is there any meat for the dogs, Seamus told the others, leading the way into the slaughterhouse yard. They followed dubiously. Soon they passed a great pile of dismembered limbs and slimy corpses.
--Jesus, Seamus....said Nuala, Do they always leave the old stuff around like that?
--That must be against the law! pronounced Pete loudly. A rotting calf was staring at him from the top of the pile.
--Will ye keep your big mouth shut now, for the love o' God, ordered Seamus, Here comes Chopper Tierney, ye wouldn't want to upset him. A fellow covered in blood and with every class of knife hanging off his belt was approaching.
--I'm going to the pub, said Pete. Don't get any ideas about bringing any of that stuff in my camper. The answer's NO!
Annie and Nuala scuttled after him. As they rounded the corner the sickly reek off the dump blasted them. You wouldn't know which establishment was worse.

Dan O'Grady was behind his bar watching a television. He was a dour looking person. They weren't sure for a long time whether he'd noticed them or not. Eventually he decided to look up and ask what they wanted. The choice was limited to cider or guinness. He was waiting for a delivery.
They sat on a bench near the miserable fire, where a few lumps of turf gave out about as much heat as a candle. The walls were stained with damp and soot. They pulled their bench out to try and get nearer the heat, but soon retreated because of the smoke. They were the only customers and at least Mikey could toddle around without coming to harm. (Annie reflected that there must be some horrendous germs on the floor, with all the frequenters of the dump and slaughterhouse

traipsing over it, and the proprietor not the type to have ever washed it in his life. But she kept her thoughts to herself. Knowing Pete's attitude to kids it was probably safer for Mikey to stay at a distance.)
Seamus was telling them how Brendan Cassidy had met Bill, Lynn (and she as big as one of them things, a Whatdoyecall-a barrage balloon) with their kid in the middle of Limerick city. He asked were they after visiting the maternity hospital, but they weren't anywhere near it. They said that was where they'd been all right, but looked a bit shifty. And when he passed the place where he'd first spotted them in the street he saw it was the door of a private Doctor, some sort of psychiatrist type.
--We're after drivin' em mad! roared Seamus, slapping his thigh.
--The baby must be due any time, said Nuala, turning to Annie. I hope they don't go trying to induce her. They seem to be doing that more and more. I'm sure its just for their own convenience.
Nuala hadn't seen Lynn in a long while but she had received a postcard, sent to the bar nearest to their current parking place. It had touched her that Lynn had made the effort to find out where she'd gone. It was a treat to get mail. The only other people who wrote were her mother - rather stiffly – and Kitty. Seamus had an awful habit of opening the letters as it was usually him who picked them up. She couldn't entirely blame him. She knew that his mother had pounced on any rare letter that came through the family door. It was regarded as her property until she had made sure there was no money in it. But did Seamus *have* to make his pronouncement every time that Kitty was an Old Hooer and a Dirty Bitch and there was no way she was coming to visit. Lynn had put the postcard in an envelope, addressed to her.

Hi Nuala, it said,

Heard you had to move after the gale. Hope you are in a nice spot now. We had a bit of damage to the roof but Bill managed to fix it. It scared me though-hope we don't have any more! I'm staying close to home now, feeling huge and fed up-can't wait for this baby to arrive. Hope we'll be bringing him/her to meet you soon -and please do call if you can ever get up this way. Offer still stands, Love, Lynn
Seamus was annoyed that it was addressed only to her. She read it out to him, omitting the Offer Still Stands and hoped he'd be satisfied. He read a couple of lines himself just to check there was nothing suspicious, then luckily gave up the effort.

Pete, who, if he didn't like kids, was positively phobic about maternity talk,especially when it threatened to encompass the actual process of

labour, took a huge slug to finish his pint and leapt up.
--I'll get another round. Same again is it, haha.
--Oh Pete, let's go somewhere less depressing now, begged Annie.
--I don't want any more cider, said Nuala, It makes me too windy.
--Windy? queried Seamus.
--It makes her fart, you dope, said Pete.
--Just have a half will ye, said Seamus, I'm just going outside to see is there anythin' worth havin' off the dump. Then we'll go on somewhere else.
--See if there's anything at all nice to drink will you then, Pete, sighed Annie. She gazed despondently at her empty glass.
--Ugh! Look at that, Nuala!
Nuala glanced over at Dan O'Grady but he was still gazing indifferently at his television while Pete hovered, trying to catch his attention. Annie's glass had a green ring around it and so, on inspection, did the others. Eventually Pete came back with the drinks and some crisps.
--These are probably off the dump, remarked Annie, I'll be guinea pig, Nuala. If I'm still alive in ten minutes time you can eat yours. Pete, have you seen the sides of the glasses?

Seamus came back, looking smug.
--I got a grand bike for you Nuala. Those tinker kids were just after fetching it out so I offered them a couple of quid for it. It has a seat for Mikey and all, it just needs a bit of mendin'.
--Where is it? Nuala was pleased. It would be nice to go riding around the countryside.
--I left it outside, by the dog bones. Pete, would ye give me the keys and I'll put the bones inside- there's a couple of dogs sniffin' round out there.
--I told you, said Pete, sounding amiable but firm, I'm not having any stinking meat in my camper.
--Arrah, tisn't stinkin' at all! Tis good stuff, from inside. And in a bag, insisted Seamus.
--We may as well all come now, said Annie, We're not drinking these.
--Why not? demanded Seamus.
--The sides of the glasses have got green slime on them, Annie told him.
--Give me that. Seamus took Nuala's glass, Tis grand, sure! So saying, he emptied it down his throat. The others were gazing at the green ring, Annie and Nuala snorting with laughter, when Mikey toddled up and threw a handful of used matches and ash he'd been busily collecting from assorted ash trays into Pete's drink.
Annie could see that, although Pete hadn't been too keen on finishing his drink after seeing its green trim, his stunned silence and darkening

countenance meant that he was highly offended, and thought that Mikey, who was grinning from ear to ear, should be punished in some way. A familiar train of thought went through her mind: good job she didn't want kids; what if one day she did; it would be the end; or might he be different with his own, that often happened....

Meanwhile, she hastily offered to change Mikey's nappy. She had enough experience of Mikey to know that you could never change his nappy often enough. She whipped him up and bore him off just as he was about to knock over Pete's polluted drink in an attempt to retrieve his booty.

Annie liked the company of kids now and again (like the time she had had Maggie to stay) and it gratified her to give the odd bit of assistance to tired parents. Nuala's relieved look made her feel good. She discovered that there was no Ladies toilet, and the Men's was outside. She had to deal with Mikey in the back porch which was full of old crates and bottles. Mikey, oblivious to the handicap of his trousers and plastic pants being round his ankles, was determined to climb the pile of crates. He was like a wind up toy, she reflected, he just moved constantly, never still for a minute - poor Nuala - until he suddenly keeled over. He would go from hyperactivity into deep sleep in a few seconds. He was an endearing little chap, with his head of curls and his happy spirit. But also the most exhausting kid she had ever encountered.

As they were about to come back in, Mikey struggling to free his hand from her grasp and go in search of new adventures, and the sodden nappy in a carrier bag - which she realised from the wetness on her leg must have a hole in it somewhere - a truck pulled up in front of Dan's. Mikey pointed excitedly. He loved big vehicles.

--T'actor! T'actor! This had apparently been his next word after Dad. He had not yet mustered Mam. As Annie obligingly admired the truck through the open gateway, her gaze alighted on an old trough half hidden in the unkempt grass at the edge of the yard. It was full of duckweed. And glasses.

Nuala appeared.

--Are you all right with him, Annie?

--Yea, we're fine. Mind the bag though, there's a bit of a hole in it.

--Annie...

--Yea?

--Are you and Pete married?

--No. Why?

--Well, I hoped...You see I'm not feeding Mikey any more, and I really don't want to get pregnant again, but it's hard to get anything to stop it here.

--I thought they just legalised contraception.
--They'll only give it to married couples.. I thought if you'd been married maybe you could get me something.
--I got a years' supply of the pill before we set out on our travels. I'm sure I heard someone say that the doctor gave her the pill as a period regulator and people get round it that way. Have you tried?
--No, but I'll have to.
--Or if there's someone you know that's coming over, they could just bring you a job lot of condoms. They're not exactly hard to hide.
--Yea..I just don't know anybody that's coming over at the moment.
Nuala didn't mention the sick fear she had inside that it might already be too late.

As they were leaving, the men from the truck were just coming in. Farmers by the look of it, who probably called regularly after dropping off a few animals next door. Dan actually stirred himself and managed a few comments about the weather and the hurling while he produced more of his glasses with the special pattern on them according to which way they'd lain in the trough.
Nuala suddenly realised that it was PJ and Jamesie and felt herself blushing horribly. The bar was near the door and they'd have to pass right by them going out. PJ saw them first and gave a very curt, minimal nod. Nuala was at the back. The others had already passed, Annie leading Mikey. Nuala hardly dared look, she felt so self-conscious, but for a second she raised her eyes. Jamesie turned, he was going to smile she thought and he began to, but then all sorts of confusion passed over his face- irritation, frustration, sadness, resignation... He said a quick,Hello Nuala, and he turned away.

Chapter Twenty Four

Nuala woke to a horrible griping pain in her belly. She'd had it most of yesterday but now it was worse. She realised she was bleeding, heavily. Oh, Thank you, thank you.. But she was frightened. She wasn't sure if this was really a miscarriage but it was a long time since that last period she'd had.
Seamus was already up and rattling the range. She could hear rashers sizzling. Mikey stomped into the bedroom, dragging a sodden nappy and the ineffectual plastic pants, which he was trying to shake off.
--Nuala, called Seamus, Will ye come on out of that and see to Mikey. He's drippin' all over the rugs! I've to go out in a minute.
Nuala only had two inadequate sanitary pads. She took one of Mikey's nappies off the shelf above the bunk and stuffed it into her knickers. She screwed up the sheet and threw it into the washing basket. She couldn't get her jeans on. She looked for a skirt.
--Nuala, will ye come on, I've got to go.
Sh shambled out into the living area.
--Be sure and keep the range going there, instructed Seamus, who had a cut of bread folded round a rasher in his hand, And give the place a tidy will ye. I've to meet Willy O'Connor at the cross.
Nuala was worried. There seemed to be an awful lot of blood. But she didn't want to tell Seamus because she had never told him her fears about being pregnant. Seamus hated anyone keeping secrets from him,and he would think she had been Plannin' Tings (she could hear him saying it so clearly)- like an abortion, rather than simply not wanting to face reality. And she would never hear the end of it. Seamus didn't notice her much these days (That was partly her fault, pushing him away, losing herself in books and sleep.) He hadn't noticed the subtle changes in her body. He certainly wouldn't know when her periods were due. As long as the rugs were tidy and the range lit she could have got a tattoo all over her face or be wearing a space suit.
--Are you going anywhere near a shop?
--No. He's picking me up, then I'm helping him with stone pickin' while there's nu'un growin' in the field. There's a rasher and an egg for you in the pan there and we've plenty o' bread. We'll go into town after I get paid, have a day out. There's a couple of quid in that old mug there, if ye really need anythin'. You could go on your bike to the village, take Mikey with ye, twould be a nice ride.
--Yea, I might do that...
Nuala managed to get Mikey dressed and rinse the messy sheet before

lying down, too shaky to do any more. She couldn't go up on the bunk with Mikey awake, so she lay on the long seat. Mikey came and bounced on her.

Jim Ryan was looking at Molly's teeth.
--I know about Not Looking A Gift Horse In The Mouth, but what do you actually look for when you want to know their age?
--Hold her tight there, Bill and I'll show ye.
Jim pushed back Molly's lips to reveal her none too clean teeth.
--Now. When a horse is young- up to five years old- he has baby teeth, just like a person. By the time he's five, all the teeth are permanent. If you looked at a two year old, you'd see that all the milk teeth were there and the sharp ones at the front might already be showing a bit o' wear. After a horse is five years old, you have to look for how worn his teeth are, and the shape of 'em. The ones at the front, here, the incisors they call them, they slope out more and more as he gets older. And the shape of the teeth changes. They start off egg shaped, then they go more round. If I see all the front ones with round surfaces, that tells me a horse is about seventeen years of age. But after that, they'll go from round to triangular.
 He pushed some more of the looser slimy, half chewed grass off Molly's teeth.
--Now, he went on, I know Molly is over sixteen years of age- well, that doesn't take much science, God bless her -but going back to her teeth now, if she was younger than that, I'd see a sort of little hook on the back outside of her teeth. But that wears off and is gone by about sixteen years. Do ye see this, now, he continued.
Bill peered.
--Can you see she has ridges up and down her teeth. Those only start at ten to twelve years. If they've come on all the back teeth, that shows the horse is at least fourteen.
Jim let go of Molly's mouth. What I didn't see, Bill is a thing called Galvin's Groove. He was a horseman from Australia in the last century. Now that groove, Bill- it's normally brown- that starts showing when a horse is about ten years old. It'll grow down, and be all the way the length of the tooth by the time he's about twenty. But then it starts to go again. So at twenty five a horse will only have the groove on the bottom half. And by the time he's thirty it'll be gone.
--Is that right, now, commented Bill, impressed.
--The last thing is that, the older a horse is, the more narrow these front ones, the incisors, get, and the more they slope forward. Like a feckin'

crow's beak, eh, Molly!
Bill winced.
--It's my guess Molly is about thirty five years old. God knows where she's been. Probably starvin on some tinker encampment for years. If she'd had better care...But they only look after the ones they can use and she has that lameness- that won't go, Bill. I don't think Maggie will be ridin' her.
--We knew that when we bought her.
--Funny she's called her the same name as Mattie's old pony. I never saw her- we only came here fifteen years ago- but I've heard enough about her over the years! For all we know this could be her.

By the end of the day the worst of the bleeding was over. Nuala had shoved three nappies into the range. There was a horrible smoke leaking into the room. Mikey was filthy and cross. Diddy was bawling and bleating desperately outside. The door opened.
--Howye. Did ye put on a pot o' spuds? Willy's given me some sausages and stuff- He stopped. Jesus, Nuala, the place is freezin! Why did ye let the range out? Did ye not bring in any wood? I left a pile outside for ye. Look at the state of the place, nu'un done at all!
--Sorry Seamus. I'm not feeling well. I've got my period, a really heavy one. I'm a bit better now but I've had awful pains.
--Arrah...Seamus was silenced, I'll make ye a cup o' tea. Meadowsweet, that's a good painkiller.
He went to put the kettle on.
--Jesus, Did ye not bring any water in either!
As he came back in with a freshly filled bucket, he remarked in disgust, Ye need to keep the half door open. I've told ye about that. It smells like them old fires the tinkers leave after 'em in here!
Nuala was drained and indifferent to everything, but was grateful when he handed her a mug of herb tea. He had put a lot of honey in it. It was good, it revived her.
There wasn't a single washed or dry nappy in the place but she thought she'd keep this information to herself for a while.

Chapter Twenty Five

The Doctor from the coast -Doctor Moroney -was listening to Lynn's belly through a black ear trumpet. He looked very young and very worried.
--The contractions should be stronger than this by now, he told Bill, I'm sorry but I think the best thing is for your wife to go into hospital.
The two midwife friends, who had turned up ready and prepared as soon as they got Bill's phone call, exchanged disgusted looks.
--Is there a phone nearby? continued their deadly serious Doctor.
No, Bill told him with satisfaction, It's three miles away. At Conlon's Cross.
It was only two hours since he'd been there himself, to ring the midwives. He had been shaking with excitement and fear and amazed that the phone worked and that both women were able to come at once. Even though, they assured him, there'd be a good while to wait yet.
--Look, tried Bill, We really wanted a Home Birth. Is there something wrong?
--Not at all. But the contractions are very faint. And under such circumstances, when progress is rather slow like this, there is a danger of stress to the baby. I'm aware that it's a fair distance so it would be wiser for your wife to go to the hospital. now.
--I'll go, said Lynn wearily.
--I can drive them, there's no need for an ambulance, offered Kate, one of the midwives.
--She'll be safer in the ambulance, insisted Doctor Moroney, and began giving instructions on what Lynn should take.

When he'd gone out of the door, and Bill was collecting up a nighty, hairbrush, sanitary pads and other essentials, Mary erupted.
--The man is terrified! Did you see him shaking! she cried in exasperation, There's nothing wrong with you at all, Lynn. ---All that needs doing is to give it a bit more time, then see if the waters need to be broken properly and things would get going nicely.
Bill suppressed a shudder. He would never forget that bit from last time, Lynn's innermost regions being attacked with a bloody great knitting needle thing....
--I'm really sorry, Lynn, said Mary, taking her hand, I was looking forward to delivering this baby. I'll be along to see you in the hospital anyway. Now don't worry, tis nice enough in there, modern and all.
--Is your little girl going to be okay? Do you have someone to mind her?

asked Kate. Do you want me to phone anybody for you?---
--That's kind of you but no thanks. Maggie is staying with our neighbours. They'll pick her up after school.

The Ryans had been very kind and decent since the night of Maggie's disappearance. Lynn was surprised and relieved that they'd offered to have Maggie because although The Aunt was extreme, some of the things she'd come out with- the drugs,etc - must have been discussed at the house above. She didn't realise that now, in the general euphoria of seeing her on her way, the Ryans were happily indifferent to the faults of their neighbours.
Moira Ryan was determined to make Maggie welcome. She had been taking great interest in all she was doing (Did you now, Pet, isn't that grand!), fussing over her and remarking to Lynn or Bill, 'Ah, the cr'atur!' . Jim too always asked how th'old pony was doing and how the goat was milking. (The pony was filling out after two doses of wormer and there was a bit of a gloss coming on her coat, now that the layers of louse powder were no longer needed. The arthritis, no one could do much about). She was either eating,or standing rather morosely under an ancient apple tree. She didn't really like attention, in fact she obviously found it irksome, shaking off stroking hands and laying back her ears. But anyway, Maggie never went near her, concentrating her attentions on Tessie, who she liked to take for a walk after school.
On the subject of her adventure, Maggie insisted to anyone at school who made enquiries that she had been for a wander in the field,ended up briefly in the bog, then been into the goat shed on her way back because Tessie was making a funny noise.
Bill and Lynn had learnt that the subject was not to be approached but although they longed to forget the whole disconcerting and humiliating business, they thought that Maggie might suffer from suppressing the story she'd first told them. And that their family unit might need outside help to repair itself. Hence the visit to the shrink-where Maggie told her story so well they came away with the definite impression the man thought that her parents were neurotic and he'd like to find her some better ones. And the Family Therapy, which Bill had walked out of half way through, denouncing it as American Crap.

Now, at last and ten days overdue, the long, uncomfortable, boring wait was at its end. But, bumping along in the ambulance,with her contractions rapidly worsening, Lynn was longing to be back in the middle of last week.

The house had been peaceful, the midwives so relaxed and re-assuring---until that gibbering Doctor Moroney had turned up. Now the siren was blaring and they were tearing around corners in a way that implied she must have something seriously wrong with her. Bill tried, between being flung from one side of the lethal vehicle to the other, to re-assure her. They got as far as the outskirts of the town, and were told that they'd go into the hospital just to see how she was getting on, before carrying on to the Maternity Unit at Limerick.

Lynn didn't get that far. After one of the vile examinations she so hated, she was told that there wasn't time to travel any further. Bill managed to stop the nurses giving her an enema, something she'd been worried about.
--Look, she's been shitting all night! he told them rather pointedly, And she doesn't want to be shaved either -
Then, to his fury, he was barred from the labour room with a curt, 'Sorry we don't allow men in here.' Both nurses shortly emerged and went busily off down the corridor without giving him a glance.
After a few minutes, Bill crept to the door. It sounded as if Lynn was on her own in there. He couldn't hear any conversation, or encouraging voices. Or, for that matter, the inevitable grunts and groans. But every now and then someone inside was ringing a bell. As he furtively began to push open the door, an old harridan of a nurse appeared and barred his way.
--Now, we told you, there's no one allowed in there but medical staff.
--But my wife is ringing a bell! There should be someone with her!
--I'm just going in to her now, his tormentor informed him, in a tone completely devoid of haste or interest. It was infuriating.
Bill then heard her telling Lynn, 'There's nothing we can do to hurry it up, Pet, you just have to wait a while longer, in a tone suitable for addressing a two year old.
Lynn was, as the hag spoke to her, being overcome by another huge contraction and was therefore unable to reply. If she had been, she would have explained that, whilst she appreciated that she hadn't quite reached the 'pushing' stage, she was at that desperate point - in hellish pain but not actively involved in bringing about its end by working away, squeezing and straining to push out her baby. And she would desperately, *desperately,* like someone - even you, you fucking old witch - to keep her company, hold her hand and tell her it wouldn't be long now. Briefly, she saw the door open again after The Hag had left her (patting her back patronisingly on her way) and Bill's face appear. A short struggle took place and she saw no more of him.

At last a couple of midwives appeared, and, after another vile examination, invited her to try pushing. They gave her the mask for the gas and air as well. Lynn had hoped her second child would come more easily than her first, but no such luck, it was the same old grind, and Jesus, they nearly split her turning the baby's shoulder or something just at the end...
Then suddenly, with a wet slither, there he was, a little red bum sticking up rather forlornly.
--It's a boy, dear. Well done.
And for a minute he could endure the business-like ministrations of the midwives while she savoured the miraculous cessation of pain.
They put him in an incubator for a minute and switched on the overhead heater above her bed for her because she had suddenly, after all the sweating, started to shiver. They brought her a cup of tea, and at last allowed Bill in. He burst into tears of frustration, fury and relief, burying his face in her salty neck. The staff wisely retreated.
--I missed it all, blubbered Bill, For three fucking hours those cunts wouldn't let me in! I was threatened with the Guards, told to go and drink tea! If it wasn't for that little shite Moroney leading us up the garden path this wouldn't have happened, we would have gone to Limerick and I would have been with you-
--Well, you're here now. And here's your son. Lynn felt rather distant from Bill's suffering. I'm sure he'll appreciate your presence much more from now on, rather than when he was being squashed and pulled about to get him out of me. And to tell the truth, Bill, don't be offended and I know you're my husband, but -I felt embarrassed last time. I know its natural and women give birth every day, but I hate the fact that people have to watch me do it. I wish I could sneak off somewhere and do it under a bush ...I really missed you at the beginning, it was really lonely, she went on, But the rest, well I'd rather you watched a documentary than me. Look at his nice hair, she continued proudly, but Bill's expression was glazed. He'd been saved from the torment of witnessing Lynn in her pain, but he'd imagined it anyway, and been denied any way of channelling his anxiety. He'd also missed the high of seeing the actual appearance of his baby.
Last time, they'd cried together in relief and exhilaration. This was much more impersonal. And now how here came two officious nurses to shepherd him off and assist Lynn - minus her baby- to the ward, For A Good Night's Sleep.

Lynn couldn't sleep at all. First, she wanted to pee. It was night and the rest of the ward's occupants were asleep, so she couldn't ask the whereabouts of the toilet. They'd given her an episiotomy, sprung it on her right at the end when she was in no state to argue, just told her, 'The baby's head is a bit large for you, so we're just going to make a little cut.' The stitches hurt and she wasn't sure if it was safe to walk. She rang her bell. A nurse came and assisted her to the toilet. She sat there for a long time, pondering on the gross distortion of words that described what they'd done as a 'little cut'. The pee seemed nervous of venturing out near the damaged landscape, lost its way and stung like hell. She shuffled gingerly back to her bed.

At two AM she was still awake, buzzing with excitement and aching to see her baby - hold him, feed him, love him. Where the hell had they put him? He was probably awake, needing her. He would need a feed! (The Hag was probably telling the poor little sod they Couldn't Hurry It Up, dear) Lynn got out of bed and headed for the corridor. A nurse soon apprehended her.

--You'll see your baby in the morning, she said unsympathetically, You can't wander around waking the whole ward. I'll get you something to help you sleep.

Bill had finally made it out into the cold night air. Depressed and exhausted, he'd been unable to find his way to the doors on the ground floor for some while. On his travels, he'd realised it wouldn't do for him to turn up at the Ryans, who'd naturally expect him to be jubilant and would want to Wet The Baby's Head with him, looking as deranged as he must do at present. He had a suspicion Maggie would still be up, despite it being way past her bed time, wanting – well, he wasn't sure. Glowing descriptions of her sweet cuddly sibling, re-assurance that she was still loved, or his full attention while she related Tessie's latest antics. He suspected it would be the latter. Anyway, he'd better look presentable. He headed into a Men's toilet.

There wasn't any soap, or a plug in any of the sinks. But at least he could rinse his tear-streaked face. And get rid of some of fibres of cotton wool which a nurse had given Lynn to mop her spouting breasts with from his hair.

A man came out of a cubicle in dressing gown and slippers. He shuffled up to the sink beside Bill and hawked a hideous lump of phlem into it. Bill recognised him as the person who had given himself and Cathy a lift after their night in Geigan's that time.

--Oh,er, Hello, Bowsie isn't it, said Bill wearily.

There was a silence, wherein the other man's bulbous and already highly coloured face turned from scarlet to a deep and volcanic purple.

--Jesus, thought Bill, He's having a heart attack! He looked frantically towards the door, unsure whether to shout or run for help while his mind stayed an unhelpful blank re the First Aid courses he had attended in the past.
Bowsie was toppling forward. But as Bill put out his arms to catch him, he found a lumpy finger jabbing hard at his throat and Bowsie Flynn's bloodshot eyes glaring straight into his own. His breath stank like a bad drain. He jabbed again.
--Is it callin' me a Bowsie ye are?
--I thought that was your-
--No one calls me a Bowsie, do ye hear! I'm Mister Jack Flynn!
Showering the paralysed Bill with more unwholesome droplets, he launched into a tirade about his Dacent Forebears and Family, Respected Throughout The County.
--We've never before been insulted by foreign upstarts, ye that are takin' over the country, God Save us!
When at last he loosened his grip a fraction, Bill made a bolt for the door. He ran like a hare down the corridor and dodged past two women who were smoking just outside.
--Jesus, what's wrong with your man! said one to the other.
--I saw him earlier, going up to Maternity with his wife, said the second woman sucking hungrily at her cigarette.
--Sure, she must have had quinns to frighten him like that!

Lynn took the sleeping pills but still she stayed awake. At four thirty, a woman from the bed opposite came over to find out her name and what she was in for. She had five kids but she was after having a miscarriage and she was sure it was God's punishment for something.
--You're very lucky to have five children, said Lynn, although she wouldn't have fancied the idea herself at all, Some people can't have any at all.
This didn't seem to comfort the other woman much.
--Perhaps it's just your body needing a rest for a while, said Lynn, Sometimes miscarriages happen because there's something wrong with the baby, which is a good thing really.
She wished the woman would go away. She didn't want to hear about anyone's problems just now, she wanted to dream about her baby (and being able to walk without gasping, and eat normally, and feel attractive again)
She regretted making her observation about miscarriage, because for the next hour, Mrs Kennedy quizzed her, making serious inroads into

that sense of joy and reverence that had made insomnia seem almost a privilege. Lynn had to pretend to go to sleep to get rid of her.
Shortly after this, the nurses came round with the medicines, and, complaining and groaning, the ward came awake.
--Hello, Cra'tur, said a tough looking woman in the next bed, What are ye in for?
--I had a baby, said Lynn, feeling rather insulted. Her anxiety got the better of her, But I don't know where they've taken him! He must be starving!
 She was scrambling out of bed as she spoke, determined to rescue her offspring from his kidnappers.
--Arrah, don't worry, said the woman with dismal finality, They'll dump him in yer arms soon enough, and twenty years of thankless work ahead of ye! Ah sorry, is it your first? she continued, seeing Lynn's crestfallen face, The first ones are a bit o' joy aren't they.
Lynn didn't correct her because a nurse was approaching with a baby in each arm.
--Which one do you want? she teased Lynn.
'Give me my baby NOW, thought Lynn, or I'll scratch your bloody eyes out..'
--That one, she managed to growl before she snatched him.
The other baby was a wan looking specimen, pale and sad looking, if such an observation could be made about a person less than a day old. It went to a tired-looking woman in a bed two places up. She handled it gently but entirely without enthusiasm or affection. The closest it got to a cuddle was when it was winded. When it went off back to the nursery Lynn thought the look on its face was unmistakeably one of resignation. Later, a huge family of siblings arrived and Lynn understood the woman's fatigue. She felt happier for the baby as it was enthusiastically passed around and fed its bottle by one of those capable girls who had been born with Big Sister stamped on her.
It was awful being parted from her own little fellow, who had fallen asleep after his feed. It was hard not to punch the nurse who firmly wrested him away, spouting rubbish about how he'd have more peace up there in the nursery, and they couldn't have babies waking up all the other ladies on the ward, now take yourself off for a wash, the Doctors will be round soon.
Mrs Tired was in the toilets, feebly ringing out her face flannel. She told Lynn that later they would go to a different place -more of a rest home- run by the nuns. There was not the space to keep patients who weren't really ill here in the town hospital.

Breakfast was being splattered out by two incredibly spotty girls when they got back. They lobbed globular lumps of porridge into bowls that looked as if they'd already with-stood the frustrated ravings of generations of patients deprived of decent food. The girls hacked up bread and spread it with marge -there was no jam or marmalade - and threw it onto plates.

Lynn had heard the talk about the hospital food - and the spotty girls- but she had assumed the stories were exaggerated. Surely it couldn't be true that they brought the soup round right after your mid morning drink?

--The food is much better at the Nun's place, whispered Mrs Tired, looking sadly at her bowl of goo, Ye'd think you were in prison lookin' at this stuff

The Doctors arrived.

--Come'ere Doctor, Mrs Insomnia Kennedy in the bed opposite asked at once, when it was her turn, Do ye think the miscarriage is me body's way of tellin' me it's needin' a rest from havin' babies?

Lynn squirmed in her bed. She busied herself rooting in her wash bag for an invisible item and listened uncomfortably for his answer.

--Not at all, not at all! said the Great Man decisively, if your body can conceive a child, then it's perfectly able to do the rest of the job. Sure, weren't women's bodies designed to bear children! he concluded smugly.

Lynn thought the design was far from perfect. But efforts to alter the prototype were usually more for the convenience of hospital staff than the owners of the Perfectly Able bodies. Mrs Tough and Cynical voiced her thoughts for her. 'Ah would ye feck off for yerself! ' Lynn heard her mutter.

Bill and Maggie arrived in the middle of the morning, Maggie proudly bearing a bouquet of flowers. So did the pimply pair of girls who proceeded to lay out cutlery and slosh soup about. Most patients refused it, still being half way through their morning cup of tea.

--You'll get the rest of your dinner in an hour's time, Mrs Tired informed her resignedly.

Lynn shuffled up the corridor with Bill and Maggie to admire their baby through the nursery window. They had missed the ten o'clock feed and wouldn't be permitted physical contact with their new relation until later. In any case, as they were soon told by a nurse, visitors shouldn't really be in until the afternoon. They did look a bit, well, Germy, reflected Lynn anxiously, as she cast discreet glances at her loved ones. Although of course hospitals had the effect of making anyone who came in from the outside world look a bit muddy and hairy...All the same, she hoped they'd washed their hands, and maybe she could ask Bill to make sure Maggie took off her goaty jumper next time...

She was watching Maggie carefully, hoping that she would be proud and fond of her little brother. New born babies weren't that appealing really, except to their creators...There was one up here you'd swear should be in the ape-house at the zoo...

--Which one is he, Mum? asked Maggie, peering through the glass at the row of plastic containers, Why are they in those sandwich box things?

Bill was relieved that Maggie had saved him the embarrassment of having to ask which of the new entries was his son. He felt he ought to recognise him, if not from the brief encounter the night before, then by some power of parental intuition. This however, was proving reluctant to perform its task.

--They're called Bassinets I think, Lynn was telling Maggie, There wouldn't be room for a whole lot of big cots. And those are easier for the hospital to keep clean .

Bill was thinking, 'Jesus, I hope its not that one at the end, it looks like a monkey, all long and red and scrawny...

--Look at that one's lovely black hair, is that him Mum?
--No. The one next door. He's got fair hair, said Lynn rather reproachfully.
--That's him, that's Ciaran, confirmed Bill happily.
--Why's he got felt tip on his head?
-What? Oh. That's not felt tip, it's a kind of bruise.
--Did the nurses drop him? Maggie looked angry.
--No. It's a bruise from me, when he was pressing on the cer- a part of my insides before he was born. It'll go away soon.
--Oh. Yuk, remarked Maggie matter of factly, Dad, can we go to the shops now? she asked, after a further brief glance at the sleeping infants.

Loving, protective, jealous, intolerant, indifferent -Lynn realised that Maggie would be all these things at different times but right now there was nothing more to keep her interest. It was nice though that, half way down the corridor, she asked Bill to wait a minute and ran back to Lynn to give her a big hug. Maggie's hugs bordered on the divine, she had away of wrapping a soft warm arm round your neck.....they were best when she wasn't in the hairy jumper of course, but even so,as she whispered, I love you,Mum, Lynn felt a glow of perfection. All was right with her world. Except the fucking stitches of course, making the trip up the corridor feel more like a trek in the Hymalayas. Hot and shaky, she retired gratefully to her bed.

Chapter Twenty Six

--Ah, here ye are.
Lynn looked up blearily and saw Seamus.
--Congratulations. Jim Ryan told me ye were in here and the baby born at last. A boy, that's grand, so.
– Thank you. You must have just missed Bill and Maggie going out It's very nice of you to come and see me, she continued, but in truth she felt embarrassed at being in such a mess. Her skin had gone all rough and blotchy from the heat in here, and she'd been asleep, and suddenly she felt like crying though she couldn't think why.
--I'd have come anyway of course, said Seamus, But I'm really here on account of Nuala. She's in the ward below. She had a chest infection.
Oh dear. Sorry to hear that. I'll go and see her if I'm allowed. Bill will go anyway.
(Whoops, that was probably the wrong thing to say. Even if Nuala was trussed up and wheezing in a hospital bed, Seamus might not like other men visiting her.) How long has she been in here? she asked quickly.
(Come to think of it, she wasn't that keen on Bill visiting Nuala either. She felt so unattractive at present, with her skin like red sand paper)
--A couple of days. She was bad there for about a week at home, then we got a different Doctor out, and he signed her straight in.
--Where's Mikey? Lynn found herself glancing about involuntarily. The image of Mikey which had come to mind – chortling gaily as he clambered over her, digging his little blue -booted feet into her tenderest regions - was not pleasant.
--Arrah, he's grand, said Seamus, mistaking her concerns, My sister has him. He's not allowed on the ward but I bring him below on the car park where Nuala can see him out of the window. We've a grand cottage now, he went on, You must come and see it, tis by the river. There's a grand garden, room for loads of stuff. I'm already getting' it ready for plantin' in the Spring. Do ye know anyone that's lookin' for a caravan?
A nurse bore down on them.
--Is that fella still here! She cried in fairly good -humoured exasperation, Haven't I just chased him out of the ward below and now I find him up here!

Underneath them, Nuala had finally got a place on the ward. For two days her bed had stood in the corridor. She had the most dreadful headache. Her brain felt as if it was inside a pressure cooker somebody had forgotten to put the little steam-letting valve on. But when Maeve had attempted to give her a 'luke -warm sponge down' as advised by the Doctor she had shivered so violently that that her teeth clattered uncontrollably, and Maeve, thoroughly alarmed, had covered her up again. The Doctor had given very few pieces of advice. His general attitude seemed to be that Nuala was ill because she was a dirty hippy. Maeve had been shocked at the state of her – so weak she could hardly lift her head off the pillow, and smelling strange, a sweet sickly smell like dead flowers.

--How long has she been like this? she asked Seamus, who had been up in his garden, dreaming of its bountiful future. He had the music turned up extra loud so he could enjoy it out there. Nuala was writhing as it battered her head like a shower of meteorites. Have you had the Doctor out again, Seamus?

--He came all right, the day before yesterday. He said it might be Brucellosis. On account of the goat's milk. But Paddy Hines- that's who we got the goat from - says he's talkin' rubbish, Paddy's family have always drunk goat's milk and you don't get Brucellosis from it anyway. Or it might be Glandew- glandew – wotsit?

--Glandular fever?

--That's it.

--Well, did he do a blood test or anything to find out?

---No. He did say the medicine wasn't working yet and he might change it, but he didn't come back when he was meant to.

--Seamus- Maeve was nearly screaming at his unconcern- Would you turn the music down! Nuala has a headache!

--She always liked White Mansions, said Seamus,affronted, I was up the garden, sure, I can't hear it unless I turn it up loud. There's a grand big garden here, did ye see it yet-

--I'm going to call Doctor Brady, said Maeve. Mikey's waking up there Seamus. Will you mind him now and I'll go over the road and see can I use the phone there. Thank God you're in the village now.

When Doctor Brady arrived, he immediately arranged for Nuala to go to hospital. She couldn't remember how the days had passed before that as the fever had eaten at her and she got hotter and hotter and daily more weak and disorientated. Rose had come out a couple of times to help mind Mikey and Maeve had taken him home with her on several occasions.

Nuala had experienced flu -like symptoms before, but this time she couldn't shake them off. The cottage had been very cold. There was something wrong with the range, perhaps that had something to do with

the chill that got into her. Seamus was out most of the day so it didn't affect him so much.
She was shivering and sweating with her head throbbing away, aided by Seamus's indifferent use of the record player, when Vinney suddenly loomed up beside the bed, scaring the life out of her. He'd only come to invite her to,'Thrrrry Some Rrrrrrhubarb' and wave a spoon under her nose. He didn't appreciate how ill she was either.

When Nuala got to the hospital, the attitude wasn't much more sympathetic. She was sitting in a wheelchair, still in a small room on the ground floor where her details were being taken. It was a long wait. She told the nurse that she needed to go to the toilet.
--Down that way, answered the nurse indifferently, Past the big doors on the right.
Nuala had come here in an ambulance. She had not been out of bed in a week, except to lower herself shakily onto the bucket beside it. She was only wearing a nighty. She struggled up out of the wheelchair and stumbled up the public corridor, in her bare feet and trying to hold a blanket round her shoulders. She was as weak as water and shaking in the draft. When she came out of the toilet she couldn't remember which way to go and eventually collapsed, to the interest of all the passing visitors. Eventually, the same nurse came along wearing an expression that told Nuala what a nuisance she was, and scooped her back into the wheelchair.

The corridor where her bed was parked was bedlam. Especially at night, when the nurses bashed bed pans and medication trolleys about. And laughed uproariously and most unprofessionally at the antics of the patients. They argued mockingly with an old lady who had stitches all over her shaved head, who was also a tenant of the corridor, and had suffered a brain haemorrhage. She was constantly trying to get out of bed - which was a thing with bars on the sides like a child's cot- to do jobs on her farm, and had loud conversations with dead relatives. It was heaven when Nuala heard she'd got a place on the ward, and even better to find herself in a kind of annexe where they put recovering patients who didn't need too much attention.
The antibiotics were at last beginning to work. The fever had gone. There was a blissful cessation of pain in her skull. But she was completely exhausted. It hadn't been Brucellosis,or Glandular Fever, just a very severe chest infection. When they x-rayed her,they told her she had a Shadow on her lung, but hadn't explained what it meant....her lung

was still full of muck she supposed.
There were two diabetic ladies in the annexe. One was young and very knowledgeable about her condition, keen to get herself, 'stabilised', and go home. The other was Bridie, a huge woman from out in the country somewhere. The only thing she wanted to do was eat, and sugar content did not enter her greedy calculations. One evening, they got scones for tea. Bridie wasn't allowed one of course, but she badgered the nurse with the trolley so much that she laughed and said, 'All right, Bridie, I'll give you a half of one. But don't be letting on to anyone!'
After this, Bridie got two more scones for herself from patients who didn't have much appetite, and another from a timid lady who did but was too frightened to say so, and then went round clearing up up all the odd pieces and leftover jam. The jam, having been deposited onto the plates by the two spotty girls, had not been distributed in genteel amounts. Later, Bridie collapsed in a heavyweight heap. The nurses had to come with special gadgetry to lift her back onto her straining bed.

That night, Nuala was involved in a little drama of her own. The nearest toilet was a fair way down the corridor, so she had a bed-pan underneath her bed. The kind nurse with the scones had given it to her when she first came up here. But whatever way she tried to get off her high, hard bed on this occasion, she slipped and fell with a crash onto the slippery floor below. The bed pan clattered.
--Jesus,Mary and Joseph! cried someone. Everyone seemed to be awake and commenting and two nurses came running.
--Bedpan, is it! cried one, after hearing the story, There's no need for a young one like you to be falling out of bed trying to use a bed pan! You're well able to WALK to the toilet!
Nuala knew there was no point in saying that she could have equally fallen if she was going to do that. The nurse marched off with her bed pan. As she began her hike to the toilet, an excited Bridie was explaining to a couple of other patients who were out of their beds to enjoy the entertainment, "Didn't that young gerrel over there -Nuala her name is – take a flying leap out of the bed and end up in a heap on the floor!

The toilets and bath were in one room. The bath was full of sheets or something left to soak. As she sat on the toilet, someone tried to come in. This usually happened because there were only two toilets and the locks were broken. Despite this, and the bullying attitude of some of the nurses, Nuala wasn't sure if she wanted to go home. She missed Mikey, but the thought of caring for him again was daunting. She quite liked her bed in the corner, the world going on below the window, the comings and goings on the ward all at a comfortable distance. She read, and slept and had no desire to do anything more.

Chapter Twenty Seven

--There were two ladies here one time, and they the best of friends, they were always together.
Father McInerney was telling one of his stories.
The ladies on the ward loved it when he came round. Lynn had been surprised at his joviality. She had expected him to talk only of religion. She was a little uneasy, and careful to laugh only when the others did. It was lovely here at the Nun's place, and very peaceful at this end of a long, majestic corridor that had a statue of the Virgin and flower arrangements along it. The meals were good and there was a spacious, clean bathroom, in which Lynn had got into the habit of pampering herself for a long while each day.
On Sunday the other ladies went to Mass. Lynn felt as if there was a bit of a hole in her life, and they must pity her for her lack of spiritual direction. But nobody mentioned it, and although she worried that Father McInerney must be on the look out for those in need of guidance in such matters, he had never done more than ask how she was and crack jokes. The rest home was populated by extraordinary characters. Father McInerney could safely tell stories about those that had passed away. They were fond stories anyway, and names were never mentioned.
---We'll call the one old lady Mary. Well, on this day, Mary was telling her friend that she'd had cornflakes for her breakfast, when -we'll call her friend Katy - Katy got very agitated and started calling Mary a liar. Poor Mary was bewildered. 'But we did! she insists. 'Oh you wicked liar! says Katy again, You never did hear the corncrake before breakfast!

When Lynn was in the toilets one day, an old lady- wearing a coat and hat and carrying a handbag- started talking to her.
--I'll be going home this afternoon.
--Oh, that's nice. Have you been here long?
--Five years, dear, the old lady told her, putting a hand on her arm, I had a little dog ye see, she went on in a confidential tone, And he gave me a weak heart with his pullin' and draggin' at the lead all the time. But I'm better now.
When Lynn mentioned her encounter to the other ladies in the ward, and said how nice it was that the lady was going home, they all rolled about in their beds.
--She's been here for about fifty years, not five! She says that to everyone!
Lynn wished she could develop a better sense of humour, was less

gullible,and could tell when people were joking. She felt a bit isolated and disorientated -from the Catholicism, the humour,the slightly cruel way people laughed at each other - and the culture of bottle feeding. The other Mothers sat companionably gossiping at feeding time, their babies held at arm's length with their bottles stuck in their mouths, while the nurses drew the curtains around her and she sat alone breast feeding Ciaran. In one way, it was blissful, just herself and him in delicious intimacy. The last feed at ten o'clock was the best when she knew there wouldn't be any visitors hovering awkwardly outside her curtains. Ciaran was for some reason at his most wakeful then. She would commune deeply with him, gazing into his blue eyes which he was a bit lazy about opening the rest of the time. And eat biscuits and other goodies people had brought her. It was great to enjoy sweet things again.

But otherwise - it was weird. Outside, an unusual fall of snow had made the surroundings of the rest home -lawns stretching away to a wood of pine trees- surreally beautiful, and the presence of nuns, Father McInerney, the statues and holy pictures were in one way soothing. But also a bit threatening, and a constant reminder that she was a misfit. She looked at a religious book from a shelf in the hall and was amazed at the complexity of sin grading. She wanted to get home to the heathen normality of Bill and Maggie. She was beginning to wonder how she would cope. It was such a lazy existence here - you hardly saw the babies, they were kept miles away, arriving on a long trolley at feeding time, already washed and rolled up in pink or blue flannelette, all on their sides and facing in the same direction. Once, one of the others had been sick on the back of Ciaran's head... The mothers were not invited to help in their care and night feeds weren't mentioned. No one else seemed concerned, they were always laughing away about life...her mistake with the old lady had become a good story for the visitors.

'Didn't your one over there, Lynn, she's English, believe every word she said, the cra'tur! Divil a dog that one ever had! She won't be goin' anywhere-with or without anything on a lead!

One afternoon, Lynn decided to go in search of the mysterious nursery. When she found it, a nurse was busy preparing the babies for their ride on the trolley. The little girl with the gorgeous black hair, who belonged to the small lady nearest to Lynn, was just having her topknot brushed up into a quiff, before being rolled up at high velocity in her piece of pink flannelette. When it was Ciaran's turn, he began to cry.

--Can I hold him?asked Lynn, as he was being popped neatly but indifferently onto the trolley.

–You can, Pet, said the nurse, seeming rather amused, But he'll stop in

a minute.
Lynn picked him up but then felt ridiculously self conscious and doubtful of her ability to hold her own son - although she and the others had of course had to carry the babies on and off the bus and along corridors when they'd come here, newly sliced up...That felt like years ago. She put him back on the trolley and didn't ask, as she'd intended to do, what happened when the babies got hungry in the night.

Nuala was back home in the cottage. As Seamus had promised, the range was now working properly. Seamus was busy painting a big old dresser he'd brought in from the shed outside, and pinning up pictures or nice pieces of material wherever he found an empty piece of wood or wall. The walnut chest of drawers in the bedroom would look as if it was riddled with woodworm for ever more. Mikey was pulling at her shirt, crying, 'Where Did, where Did! excitedly, and making little forays to peer under furniture and behind the door.

When they arrived home from the hospital, Seamus had sat her in the nice chair by the range and fed her tea and brack. Maeve was already there, with Mikey. Nuala held out her arms – and Mikey turned his head and burrowed into Maeve's chest. Nuala felt anguished tears rising.
--Its all right, Nuala, said Maeve quickly, They do that when you've had to be away for a while. Tom did the same to me when I had my appendix out. It's like they can only have one person looking after them at this age, that way they feel safe. He'll come round, just give him a bit of time, and then he won't want to be parted from you for anything.
Nuala, a little comforted, drank her tea and basked in the warmth from the range.
--Where's Diddy? she asked Seamus, suddenly registering that there was no bleating, either inside or out.
--Arrah...Seamus looked sheepish, Arrah, Nuala, he was gettin' to be too much of a nuisance around the place, jumpin' on the furniture and all. And he would have ruined the garden.
There was a silence. Then Seamus brightened up.
--Lookit. I saved his skin for your chair.

Annie had sneaked in behind Lynn's curtains and was making disrespectful comments about a system that should be promoting breast feeding but instead seemed ashamed of it.
– Well, not totally, said Lynn, Several of the nurses have told me what a good thing I'm doing. And I quite like the curtains. There are a lot of men

wandering in and out you know.
--Do you? laughed Annie, I suppose it must be awkward being the only one. Lynn, have you anything I can eat?I've got a jewellery order to finish before Christmas and I was working away this afternoon, and Pete was out-we just met up to come here - so I sort of forgot to stop and eat anything.
--There are biscuits in the locker if you can find them. Sorry it's a bit of a mess..
--I see what you mean! Annie rummaged through toiletries, books, half written letters and half eaten snacks. When are they going to let you out? You've been here an awful long time. It can't be very good for- Annie sought for the right words -family relations. She finally emerged from the locker with a packet of Goldgrain, on which she kept her eyes focussed.
--I know. I'm dying to go home. There's nothing wrong, they keep everyone in for ten days. It's the opposite of what they do in England now-that's like a conveyor belt, you leave about as soon as you can stand up again. But they're making this longer because of this freak snow. I think they're worried the babies will be too cold when they go out of here. They might be right when it comes to our place...Maggie's fine anyway. She keeps bringing in things she's done at school, and little pictures for Ciaran. Moira Ryan started her on some knitting but I don't suppose that'll last long... She paused. Bill is -Bill's being a bit of a pain actually..
Annie carried on munching her biscuits in a non committal fashion.
--He seems to be in a kind of sulk. Lynn continued. And I'm, well I feel a bit strange and spaced out at the moment- it's this place,with none of your normal things to be getting on with, and they don't let you do anything with the babies except feed them --and I want some solidity. I don't want to be fussing over a big spoilt kid when I've got a real one to be worrying about.
Annie murmured, 'Dodgy..' but she was down in the locker again and Lynn didn't register her comment. So Maggie's okay then? she asked as she emerged with a bar of chocolate, Do you mind if I have some of this Lynn?
--No, carry on.
--Its all died down after her Night Out hasn't it. I haven't heard any talk anyway, said Annie.
Annie was the only person Lynn had confided in with all the details of that night.
– Yea, everything seems to be okay. She handled it so calmly. After that first time when she began to tell Bill, she wouldn't let anyone get the

slightest sniff of what really happened. Perhaps she doesn't know herself. But she seemed to make a decision to lie about it...or just forget it- if you can forget something by just deciding to. It did worry me, but we've just left it alone since then.. She thought she saw the fairies though, and she swore that Molly - that decrepit pony-sort of rescued her and came along some magic road through the bog to bring her home.
--Yea...well there aren't really any logical explanations. If she went on admitting she met the fairies she'd have psychics hassling her, kids teasing her, Blow ins turning her into a Guru, psychologists questioning her sanity.... (Lynn blushed) She's chosen the only safe way really. I'm sure she doesn't mean to hurt you by not confiding in you. I think you should leave it alone now. Forget it.
--Yea. But Lynn couldn't help continuing to muse. I think she was probably a bit concussed. She did have a bruise on her head. And Mattie had filled her head with his stuff about the fairies. One thing though, she did ride Molly out of the bog- I would never have believed it but later I saw the marks on her jeans. You can see when someone's ridden bareback.
--I know, I did a lot of it. My Mum was always complaining about the state of my trousers, smiled Annie.
--You expect to protect your kids, and when its something you've caused yourself-
--That's right! said an odiously cheery voice, and the ruddy face of Pete thrust itself through the curtains.
--Ruby's chicks were nearly taken by a fox last week and if I hadn't come out when I heard her squawking for help... I wouldn't have liked that on my conscience! Myrtle flapped up into the rafters and got stuck. She's going to need a lot of help to get over the height phobia it's given her.
--Yea, like shoving her off her perch, said Annie, Is it okay to eat this, Lynn?
--Yea, fine. After a pause, Lynn added loudly, God, Annie, you're not pregnant are you? And took great delight in watching the colour drain from Pete's face, They say you only have to set foot here, look what happened to me, she added.
After Pete had gone off to charm the nurses with his chicken stories, which, having only met him once before, they were still finding amusing,
--That was cruel! laughed Annie.
--Sorry, I couldn't resist it.
--Lynn, if you think back, there were probably lots of things you didn't tell your parents about. I know there were lots of events in my life that they weren't let in on. And as Maggie grows up, there'll be all sorts of things she'll choose not to tell you about.

--I know that....

Lynn and Cathy had enjoyed endless freedom as kids, growing up in a part of Surrey that was gradually being engulfed by housing estates, new roads and a gravel mine, but which provided, until the machinery arrived, empty fields, overgrown orchards and dis-used pigsties, through which they wandered, making camps and collecting slow worms, frogs and newts.

They had also played on the army land miles away from home. Kids weren't supervised then. You just came home in time for tea. They'd been down into underground storerooms lined with sandbags and trespassed on part of the Assault Course. There were often rival gangs of kids, or terrifyingly large teenage boys making horrible threats. Lynn remembered a time when some of them invaded her latest Camp. One of them set a spider alight with his cigarette lighter. He also used the word, Bollocks. She hadn't a clue what it meant but thought it the most horrible word she'd ever heard and pictured a big pile of steaming dog turds. Another time, a crowd of them had spent all day converting a dis-used pigsty into a Camp (which meant that now it had a chair, a saucepan and - the piece de resistance- a drawbridge made of rusty corrugated iron lowered on baler twine). The dyke over which this contraption was lowered had taken all day to dig and had necessitated the loan of a pickaxe, but was in fact only six inches deep. As they were admiring their day's work, two big boys appeared. They demolished the drawbridge with one resounding kick, then told the terrified workers that they were Trespassing and would be Prosecuted if it wasn't all put back to its previous condition by morning. Once, the same boys had told their friend John that they would wrap burning rubber round his legs if he ever came near their fire again. Horrible tortures were always being threatened and fights were hard to avoid. As well as this, older girls were always talking with scary relish about Rapes and Assaults. Adults were distant. Unless you were really distressed about something, you didn't consult them. There'd been all sorts of incidents her parents never heard about. But they weren't inexplicable.

--But she did tell us. We just didn't believe her. What do you think really happened? she asked Annie.

--It's not complicated, said Annie promptly, She was pissed off at you two. She went out to show you how much you'd upset her. She got lost in the bog. She thought she saw fairies. There could be endless explanations for that - it was moonlit, Mattie had told her the place was heaving with them, she'd banged her head and might have been a bit concussed or whatever - and lastly, she was was scared out of her wits. Then she met up with the pony and managed to get on it. Lucky that,

wasn't it. Horses are pretty good at finding their way home. I thought I was lost once, I went too far out in the bush, I thought I knew where I was but the track I was on just got more and more overgrown and then fizzled out altogether. I turned round and I went all over the place, trying to find the right way and getting more and more confused and worried. In the end I just gave my horse his head, it felt to me like he was going completely the wrong way, but he took me home.
--But it wasn't Molly's home, Lynn persisted, even though she was beginning to feel stupid and neurotic, She'd never been to our place before. And why was she in the bog?
--She obviously didn't like the grass at Mattie's! I expect he forgot to close a gate, he's meant to be a bit doolally isn't he. It was probably just luck that she ended up coming to your place. She probably didn't like the bog any more than Maggie did, I expect she was as pleased to see Maggie as Maggie was to see her. Lynn, you can't explain every single thing logically. I've a friend who saw a ghost. I don't believe in ghosts, but I believe her if you see what I mean. The experiences of so many different people can't all be put down to insanity, that's for sure. There aren't logical explanations for everything the human mind experiences and we don't yet know the half of what it's capable of. One day all might be revealed but until then- just stop bloody worrying.
Annie finished the second bar of chocolate.
--That horse I was telling you about is called Swift, she told Lynn, He's on a friend's ranch at the moment. I can't wait to ride him again, he's wonderful, almost telepathic. He's fast - you never have to push him- just a bit scary sometimes because he's quite nervous. But it's all genuine, he'd never do anything just to try and throw you off. He never bucks or rears. But he does snort at things, and shy.....If he's really got the wind up I just get off and walk beside him for a bit. I like just walking along with him almost as much as the riding. It won't be long now, she added, We should be home by midsummer next year.
--Oh, Annie! Are you leaving Ireland?
--Yea, don't look so shocked! We only came away for a year, to have a look round and see what we could find out about Pete's family. We'll be around for a few months yet though and we'll see you again before we go. I've got some jewellery orders to finish- besides the Christmas ones, I've got to get those out of the way first -t hen we're hoping to have a look at Scotland before we go back to Oz. That reminds me, I've got some new contacts for you to try with the photos. I made a list but I forgot to bring it, I'll have to send it to you. And the chickens will need a home if you want them.
--Doing well, isn't he, asked Lynn's favourite nurse of Annie, who had

been stroking the back of Ciaran's downy head while she talked.
--Yea, he's a sweetie, and I'm sure he's twice as big as last time I saw him, Annie agreed as Lynn handed him over. She still found it hard not to punch the nurses, even this plump smily one, when they took him away for the night.
--Time's up, I'm afraid, the victim of Lynn's homicidal thoughts told Annie, Have you been feeding that man of yours properly? He doesn't seem his normal self tonight.
-I've something lined up for when we get back, Annie told her, Chicken Curry.
-Ah, he'll enjoy that, he looks like a fella would have a great appetite, smiled the innocent nurse, Hurry on then, Pet, or we'll have to find a spare bed -Sister Carmel is up the hall and about to lock the doors.
The nurse bustled off and Annie picked up her jacket.
--Don't forget now - Stop Worrying. Enjoy your family, she hesitated, And Lynn...Look after Bill a bit.

Chapter Twenty Eight

Lynn had expected the house to have some sort of face lift in honour of Ciaran's home-coming. He was dressed for the first time in his own blue cardigan and leggings but the importance of the occasion registered for him not in his clothes but the realisation that his milk supply had suddenly become readily available. He was making up for the deprivations of the hospital routine and the chill and shabbiness of the house had no effect on him. But Lynn felt insulted on his behalf.
--A few people came to celebrate last night, Bill commented guardedly as he saw her glancing around.
--Oh. Who was that then?
--Just some Germans. They're Woofing for a couple of months.
Bill hurriedly emptied an ash-tray which he'd overlooked during the morning's hungover cleaning session.

Maggie rushed in from school, cheeks glowing.
--Mum! You're back! I've been thinking about you all day! I wanted to come to the hospital but Daddy said I had to go to school- she shot Daddy a specialist scowl- Did you see your room? I put flowers in it.
Lynn wondered whereon earth she had found flowers in late November.
--Brigitte brought them last night, went on Maggie, Those dried ones that everyone grows. They're really pretty-can we grow some next year?
--Who's Brigitte?
Bill was loudly riddling the range.
--The German lady who comes here, explained Maggie.
Lynn noticed the plural.
Maggie came towards her, about to hug her, then felt awkward with the baby between them.
--Oh, look, he's got his little blue jacket on! she exclaimed, settling for a snuggle against Lynn's side, Isn't it sweet! Mum, can he sleep in my room?
--Perhaps when he's older. At the moment he wakes up in the night and has to be fed and have his nappy changed.
--I wouldn't mind! I could come and call you-
--Wait until he's older. But perhaps he can come and have a sleep in your room in the daytime.
Lynn was delighted with Maggie's enthusiasm and affection. It made up for the un-named air of awkwardness and hostility between herself and Bill. Gratefully, she carried Ciaran upstairs, following Maggie to admire her flowers, and trying not to reflect on their origin.

Brigitte. Pronounced Brigitta. It sounded hard and brittle. It sounded like Bitch. It had Git in it, thought Lynn nastily.

Nuala was all but choking on the alien stench of hot plastic and petrol. She might have been sick if her stomach hadn't been left behind during Breda's wild acceleration onto the Limerick road. Her heart, which was already beating with terror and excitement, had made a further lurch at the prospect of getting into Breda's powerful BMW after she had stuck out her thumb. But, guilty as she felt for endangering Mikey's life this way, she would at least be off the road before anyone saw her and reported back to Seamus. Breda certainly wouldn't be communicating with him, and if she did mention to anyone that she'd given Nuala a lift, she should be safely on the boat before the news got back to him. And at least Breda wouldn't be hassling her for a Kiss For The Old Ride, like the farmer who'd brought her down to the big road.
--Hello Nuala .Hello Mikey. Hasn't he grown, Breda had said politely, I'm going down to Shannon if that's any help.
--Yes please, replied Nuala, I'm going to visit a friend for a few days. Breda eyed the two bulging bags she was struggling with.
--You need such a lot of stuff with a toddler, don't you, was all she said. Wouldn't it be easier to catch the bus?
--I was going to, but I missed it, lied Nuala, clutching Mikey as they took off with the velocity of Concorde.
--Oh, have they changed the times? I thought it went at ten thirty. There was an uncomfortable silence. Nuala couldn't explain that she had only enough money for the ticket as a foot passenger on the boat. Breda didn't make any further comment,but conversed pleasantly, with no animosity, but no understanding of Nuala's world.
 Nuala found it hard to concentrate. She regarded the back of Breda's thick neck which cascaded over her collar like a lobster -coloured landslide. She promised herself that, if they got out of this alive, she'd turn straight for home and never leave it again. She shut her eyes as Breda began a determined attempt to overtake and narrowly missed an oncoming lorry that hooted long and loud. If Breda noticed her nervousness at the rushing Shannon traffic after the quiet existence of the last few years, she wasn't prepared to change her driving style. But she was tactful enough to avoid mention of either Seamus or Ambrose. Later, she asked where Nuala's friend lived.
--Just beyond Tipperary, said Nuala,knowing that was on the route to Rosslare,and praying that she wouldn't be asked any more questions.
--I'll take you through the city and onto the right road, said Breda,

heaving the wheel with her bulky arms and sailing onto a roundabout to a chorus of beeping.
--Thanks, said Nuala weakly.
As they passed through Limerick she gazed in awe at the acres of clothes she could see through the window of Dunne's Stores, the queues of traffic and all the busy people. She felt a bit better now that the car had to travel more slowly and Mikey had fallen asleep.
--I didn't see you before you left. I wanted to give you something for Mikey, said Breda,when she opened the door for her. She firmly pushed some notes into Nuala's hand.

Nuala stood beside the road, considering what to do. Maeve, had been out to the cottage to tidy it ready for her home-coming from hospital. (Seamus had been indignant. He didn't approve of the type of tidying that reduced the photogenic appeal of his house-hold, however much more safe and convenient it might make it for other people.) Maeve had brought Kitty's letter, for once unopened, to the ward.
Kitty was in London. Life was great, there were lots of other Irish people, she'd been on benefits, it was quite easy to sign on, but now she had a job. There was this great place called The Roundhouse where all these brilliant bands played...If Nuala ever wanted to come over....
She had enough money now for a train ticket. No, it was best to keep it for a train ticket across the water, that was where she'd been dreading hitching. She felt dwarfed by fear. Looking down at Mikey's curly head as he slept in his push chair she was overwhelmed with guilt. Seamus was out for the day, digging over someone's garden. She could be back before he knew she'd been anywhere. What did she want to go back to England for with its Cruise missiles, Yorkshire Ripper and the press hounding the unfortunate girl that big ugly eejit of a Prince was going out with.
Life with Seamus was okay. They went for nice walks...he had great admiration for the pictures she occasionally painted. Recently they'd been recording old Irish stories together on a cassette player. They could play it for Mikey later on, or they might give it to Tom as a Christmas present. They'd had a laugh with the sound effects- the hooves of the Coppal Bawn, leprechauns banging away at their shoes, running water, and thunder, bits of fairy music..And he was Mikey's father. She turned the push chair back towards the city centre and hoisted one bag onto her back. The other was hanging on the push chair,weighing it down so much that she couldn't let go of it or it tipped backwards like a seat on a fairground ride.

Now she felt utterly defeated and hated herself. And she was afraid that Seamus might have come home early and found her gone. Or that, with his unerring ability to sniff out the smallest deception, he would, if she went back, find some clue, even if she was there quietly cooking the dinner, to give away the devious plan she had been intent on earlier in the day. God, wouldn't he give out to her...

Miserably she turned into a bar to use the toilet. She hardly noticed her name being called, but when she finally looked round the nearly empty place she saw a very good looking young man, smiling at her a bit uncertainly. A bit broader than of old, shorter haired. Same fine, noble features. Davy.

Mikey, the angel, was still asleep. Davy had bought Nuala several drinks and, while the winter gloom descended over the afternoon outside, told her about his family and how he came to be here.

--I got into Art College- Plymouth. I'm in my final year now. I'm doing the odd trip over here in my holidays on a driving job- yea, I passed my test. Remember that instructor we had when we were both having lessons? Orange Utang.

They both laughed.

Well I decided he wasn't much good and changed to someone else. He wasn't much better looking but I got through first time with him. Did you pass yours?

--No.

--But you can drive on a provisional over here can't you . I love it! Some of the driving is insane, but it's kind of good natured. That would never happen in England, it's strangling in red tape. And there's a lot of discontent at the moment, Thatcher privatising everything., killing off the mining industry, plus we've become the target for a nuclear missile strike...Art is a great way to challenge the system, some of us are putting on an anti-nuclear exhibition at the moment... But it's very hard to make a living out of it. I'll probably always do another job as well. I was really lucky to get this. It was thanks to my old man actually, best thing he ever did for me.

--What do you do exactly?

--Bring some art and craft supplies over to some small businesses and take some of their stuff back to buyers at home. It started off as one trip but it's developed lots of offshoots. I bring some wholefood supplies to some people living out on an island-I don't go out there, just meet them in Galway. I give people lifts and make a bit of extra money for myself. I have a breather when I come over here, then I go back ready to fight

again. Sometimes I have enough time to stop for a couple of days and see the relatives. My Gran's still up there in Connemara.
--How is she?
--She fell over back in the summer. That shook her up a bit. But she's still managing, still in the old house. The neighbours look after her. I love that house. The big old bed's still there. I remember her putting us to sleep in it as kids. I always felt safe in it,s afer than anywhere else in my life. She's still full of spirit, likes to know what every one's doing..Well, you know, you met her that time. She's asked after you a couple of times actually...I told her you had a little boy, that confused her a bit...Davy glanced at Mikey, He's a good sleeper isn't he.
--That's what happens when he goes in a car. Nuala was going to add that she would pay for it later, but kept quiet. She didn't want to remember Mikey at the moment.
--How are the rest of your family? she asked.
Much as she had liked them, Nuala didn't at this minute care at all how they were. She was flooded with hundreds of memories and longed to talk about their past life together. But just listening to his voice was good.
--Mum's well. Life got easier for her with the old man when we started living together and I got out of the family home ..and now Maria is in University, so more space all round, although there was never the kind of friction with her that there was with me.... Claire and Richie got married and they've got a baby. John, that little boy you used to make a fuss of, is unrecognisable, he's like the incredible hulk! And Aileen's in High School now.
Oh, his beautiful voice, how good it was to hear it again. And to look at him and remember how it was to fancy someone every single minute of every day. Although,she wasn't feeling that now. She was just feeling safe.
 --Why are you in Limerick then Nuala? Do you live near here?
--No..I'm on my way to visit Kitty. I'm going to stay with her in London for a bit .I haven't seen her for ages.
--How's - Seamus isn't it.
--We split up. Nuala made it sound as if the split was old and the visit was an organised holiday.
Seamus would be home by now, tweaking cushions into place and sniffing for a pot of spuds.
--Where are you going now? Nuala asked.
--Waterford. I'm staying there for a couple of days, with a mate. I can give you a lift down there if you want, it'll save you lugging all that baggage about. You can get on the train there, you might be able to get

a refund on some of your ticket.
Nuala didn't tell him that she didn't have a ticket. Davy looked at his watch. It looked quite expensive. He never used to wear one.
--We'd better get going though or we won't make it in time. Did you realise it was this late?
Nuala didn't answer.
--Well I know a good B&B down there if we're too late, and you could ring Kitty from there if you need to, let her know you'll be on the morning one.
Nuala, who hadn't contacted Kitty at all, let all this wash over her. Davy made everything feel easy. She smiled at him gratefully as she got into the car.
--Will Mikey be all right on the back seat there? Here, I'll shift these boxes up a bit. Good job you met me on the way back or you'd never have got in. They're getting me a van soon...
--It's good to see you again, he concluded.
It seemed that God was blessing her decision after all.

Mikey seemed drugged by the travelling and hardly stirred.
 With the drink relaxing her, the warmth of the car and the feeling of being so unexpectedly cared for, Nuala dozed off.
 When she was awoken by Mikey trying to scramble through to the front seats, she felt different. What the hell was she doing..Davy stopped the car so that she could get in the back to change Mikey, and cast amused glances while she fought to keep him still for two minutes. Then he remarked that they'd better get on, they should make it to the station in time but he'd promised to phone someone at eight and he wanted to get to his friend's house where he knew there was a phone that worked. As Nuala groped about in her bag, finally finding Mikey's bottle of juice and a pulverised sandwich, she reflected with increasing anxiety that he hadn't actually said anything of a very personal nature at all.
They stopped in a dark gateway for a pee. That was quite intimate, thought Nuala. Mikey had climbed onto the driver's seat and was nearly exploding with glee as he bounced about at the wheel. Nuala lost her balance and sat down on a bramble, peeing on the corner of her skirt.
--Are you all right? asked Davy, laughing and reaching out a hand. She remembered all that his hands used to make her feel. And simply being hand in hand whenever they went out. There was nothing now -except this overwhelming need to be looked after, to have this awful lostness taken away. They got back in the car. Nuala sat in the back, so that she could restrain Mikey.

--Don't suppose you like Ian Dury do you? said Davy over his shoulder.
--It's not my favourite, but it's okay-
--I've still got all the old stuff. I'll never go off Horslips...Davy was raking through a box of cassettes with one hand, Not sure I've got it with me... He put in a cassette, Planxty.
Somewhere in the next ten miles Davy told her she must come and meet his girlfriend before she came back to Ireland. They were living in Plymouth but they were often up in Surrey. She wouldn't know Rowena (Rowena! Nuala had always hated that name, along with Fenella. It wasn't logical or fair but it instantly conjured up a picture of an immaculate blond with a deep, self assured voice, who always knew what to say and would smile at her in a patronising, superior way) She wouldn't know Rowena, she wasn't one of the old crowd, they'd met last year when she moved from another course. Davy caught the look on her face.
--She's not at all posh if that's what you're thinking, he said easily, She can't help what she was christened. All her mates call her Rosie.

Planxty had got to, As I Roved Out.

If I married the lassie that had the land my love,
It's that I'll rue until the day I die,
When misfortune falls sure no man can shun her,
I was a blind fool, and it I'll ne'er deny.
Now at night when I go to my bed of slumber
Thoughts of my own true love run in my mind,
When I turn around my love to greet her,
Sure instead of gold tis brass I"ll find....

Davy went on to tell her that Rosie was great, had an amazing voice- it was really gutsy, but not harsh- and they had formed a new band. He'd brought her over to see a bit of Ireland, in the summer. They'd been to Lisdoonvarna, had a great time at the festival,and then been to stay with his Gran. She'd loved the wild mountainous places like Connemara, and done a couple of powerful paintings. She'd got those moody colours when the weather was changing to perfection. She didn't really go for traditional landscapes, she just painted Moods.
--I've got a photo of her in my wallet, I'll show you when we get to the station.

Nuala had never expected to reach the station. She didn't know what she'd been expecting. She felt like one of those wild animals on documentaries that had been shot with a tranquiliser. Her eyes were still open in a glazed stare, her features frozen into a horrible grimace of a smile. She sat in numb silence while, unheeded behind her, Mikey pulled things out of the bags.

At the station, Nuala cried and started blurting everything out. How sorry she was, how much she'd missed him, how she hadn't been able to talk the time he'd rung her at Kitty's, how she used to dream it was him coming to visit her after she had Mikey and it was horrible waking up.
--I'm eternally sorry for leaving you.
Davy was embarrassed. He manoeuvred her to a quieter part of the platform.
--I missed you so much, it was all a mistake---
--You've explained that, and I understand-
--All this time-
--Nuala, listen. What we had was great. But we were very young when we got together. I'll never forget those times. But it ran its course. Remember what it was like towards the end? Now you're only choosing to remember the good bits, that's human nature, but we were driving each other insane. And there was always a clash between you wanting to escape society by finding the rural idyll and me wanting to challenge it head on. It wouldn't have lasted. I'm with someone I love now. I'm sorry it didn't work out between you and Seamus-
--It was all a sham with Seamus! All the time I wanted you.
Nuala's black fear dwarfed her memory of the feeling she'd had for Jamesie, or the hope of any relationship that might yet happen and brighten her future.
--You knew my address, said Davy bitterly, then continued hurriedly, No, sorry I didn't mean that-
He took a deep breath, and Nuala through her pain and fear, recognised that he was preparing to leave her.
--Look, I can't stay with you any longer. I'm sorry you're so unhappy and I'm sorry if I've made things worse. I didn't realise you still felt like that about us and it was stupid of me to offer you a lift-
--It wasn't, it wasn't- Can't I stay with you tonight? We could talk some more.
--No, there's no point.
Davy broke away to rescue Mikey, who was toddling happily towards the platform edge.
--God, Nuala! Haven't you any of those rein things? You've got to mind

this fella, do you hear? Hold onto him now.
He took Nuala's soggy face in both hands.
--Listen. Things will get better, they will. It will be good for you to be with Kitty, have some fun with her. I didn't know I was going to cause you such trouble when I saw you in that bar. You knew where you were going then-
--I didn't. I would have gone home to Seamus but for meeting you.
Davy was quiet for a minute, digesting this.
--Well, you have two choices. Carry on and see Kitty, you can talk things over with her, and maybe you'll see more clearly what you want to do. You can always decide to go back to Seamus. You can write to him, or ring somewhere and get a message to him. Say you just needed a break... Christ! Why am I telling you that when you just buggered off and I never heard a thing from you-
He stopped.
--I don't want to go to England when you're here, said Nuala.
--Your other choice, Davy continued, is to get the train back the other way and go home now. And Nuala- Don't think I wasn't hurt to death when I heard you'd taken up with someone else just like that. I was in pieces. But something good has come out of it. And it could for you too. You're still young and beautiful. And talented. Start drawing and writing again. Look after Mikey, now, he's a great little kid. Here.
He pressed money into her hand.
--Nuala, I'm going now. Don't think I don't care, but it won't do any good me hanging around. Good luck, Nuala. God Bless.
She had never heard Davy say, God Bless. He walked away as firmly as he could, and Nuala, in later reflection, had to admit that it was all he could do. She stood on the dirty platform, a jelly of hopelessness and remorse, hot relentless tears coursing down her face. But, as Mikey made another bid for the platform edge, she saw it through her haze and somehow moved to retrieve him. She gathered up her jumbled bags and dragged everything to the waiting room, where she dug out Mikey's bottle of juice, scraping off a blackened pulp that was once a banana. She found his toy tractor embedded in a Yoplait carton and managed to clean it fairly well with the loo roll she always carried.
The next train through was the one for Rosslare. They got on it.

Chapter Twenty Nine

Bill was driving Maggie down to the cross in the mornings. The weather was atrocious- lashing rain and wind had taken over from the brief cold spell they'd had while Lynn was in hospital.

Lynn usually stayed in bed, trying to catch up on sleep lost to Ciaran's frenetic night feeds and bouts of colic. At ten, he woke her, moaning to himself preparatory to setting up a full scale bellow. It was another hour before she'd got him fed, changed and settled so that she could wash the sticky milk and baby puke off herself and get dressed. There was a stinking heap of washing and a bucket of nappies to deal with and Bill had forgotten to bring in the briquettes from the shed. Outside, the rain was a solid sheet.

Upstairs, Ciaran, though he he'd seemed sound asleep, started fretting again. She needed some breakfast,or rather, lunch. Where the hell was Bill? He was meant to bring back some groceries and some urgently needed sanitary towels...

At four o'clock, with the dark already settling outside, Bill arrived with Maggie.

--Did you get the gripe water?asked Lynn.

--Hello Bill, have you had a good day... I think so. It should be there somewhere..

--You think so? Don't you know if you got it or not? Well you didn't! It's not bloody here! Lynn was outraged, Well you can walk about with Ciaran when he screeches tonight then!

--I will, said Bill and began to quietly unpack the rest of the shopping..

--Dad, what's Woofing? asked Maggie.

--Work Experience On Organic Farms.

--Oh. Couldn't we have someone here for Work Experience? Then Mum wouldn't get in such a bad mood.

--I'm not in a bad mood because I have to work! said Lynn, although actually a Lot Of People don't know that looking after a baby is work, she continued acidly, I'm in a bad mood because I'm stuck here and can't get out and Daddy has been out all day and not got things he knew were important.

Bill chose not to comment on this, signifying that she was being very petty and childish to slag him off in front of Maggie.

--We haven't got a farm, he explained to Maggie, and we don't grow enough yet to give Woofers the the kind of experience they'd want. Anyway, most Woofers don't come in winter.

--Oh. Why is Brigitte here then? asked Maggie interestedly.
--She's stopping with Patsy and Sinead for a few weeks but really she's on her way to work in a Steiner community, where they help people who are handicapped. It's based on the same idea as the schools, he continued (quite unnecessarily, thought Lynn), The man who started the schools was German, so a lot of German people come to work in them.
Lynn was irritated by the patient explanation. What she wanted to know was why Maggie was asking about fucking Brigitte again.
--You saw Brigitte today did you? she asked her.
Bill interrupted angrily.
--I gave her a lift. She was hitching in that rain, soaked to the skin.
--And of course you wouldn't have stopped if she was dry, with her beautiful hair blowing in the wind.
Lynn had by now obtained descriptions of the shapely shampoo advert with a crinkly nose and a charming way of saying Wegetables. She realised Brigitte's presence at Patsy and Sinead's had been influencing Bill's enthusiasm for helping out over there for some time.
--It looked very beautiful wet, actually, Bill couldn't resist saying.
Lynn regretted being in her soft bulky ethnic slippers. She had a very strong urge to kick him. She persisted in her interrogation.
--So how come she was with you when you went to pick up Maggie?
He must have been with her most of the day. Bill seemed unperturbed.
--Maggie, go on up and take your wet things off. And don't just chuck them on the floor. If they're not muddy bring them down to hang on the range. I said I'd run Brigitte back to Patsy and Sinead's but there wasn't time to go out there before the bus would arrive. So we picked up Maggie first, that's all.
So Patsy and Sinead had seen Bill driving Brigitte about (wasting their precious petrol) and so, she realised, had their friends on other occasions. Annie had insinuated as much. And even the disloyal Maggie mentioned her with a sort of casual, fond familiarity.
-Stop trying to make me feel guilty, Lynn, said Bill coldly, Nothing happened. You can't expect me to stop talking to all other women. Anyway, he justified himself, she's only a kid. But intelligent. And good company. And FUN, he added with mean emphasis, I won't drive past people stuck on the road just because I'm married to a paranoid old bitch.
 He stomped out.
---She isn't PEOPLE! Lynn screamed after him, She's a big-titted (here she had a mental flash that these two words could be made out of the letters in the bloody girl's name as well) blonde that you're very obviously AFTER!

But she was only bawling at the relentless rain. Bill was a diminishing blob in the distance.
--Mum! Maggie was calling, Ciaran's crying...
Still seething, Lynn headed for the stairs.
--Your tits are nearly as big as Brigitte's now, Maggie informed her comfortably as she arrived in the bedroom.

Davy was looking at a sketch. It was of Nuala. She was washing at the sink in the little bed sit where they'd lived for a while. Her head was on one side, her black hair pushed back over one shoulder. She was naked from the waist up, wearing a white petticoat that she often had on under her long skirts. He put it back carefully at the back of the portfolio where he kept his oldest stuff. Then he went to ring Rosie.
--Hiya Rosie, Are you all right?
--Yea. The band practice was good. But I'm just about to go out, CND night, remember? Has that watch I gave you stopped? She was smiling, he could tell.
Davy glanced at his wrist. It wasn't a new watch, her brother had a spare.
-- I got held up. Sorry.
--When will you be back?
--Tomorrow night. I've a present for you, Gorgeous.
They both laughed. It was a joke between them. She had a very demanding little sister who always asked visitors if they had brought her a present.
– No, I really have.
There had been some new jewellery in one of the craft shops. Fine beadwork. He didn't like most of it, those African type colours were too gawdy, but he'd spotted a necklace with a matching bracelet in blues, greens and purples, those moody mountain colours she'd painted, with a background of deep brown to match her eyes.
--Oooh, great, I can't wait. And I can't wait to see you, Davy darling.
--I love you. See you tomorrow.

After his day's work digging over the field- and a very muddy affair it had ended up being-Seamus had bought the ride-on tractor they'd seen in Keane's for Mikey. He would have to sneak it into the house to hide it up to the loft room by going in the side way by the river. But when he got home, Nuala and Mikey were gone.
 Maeve had come out to see him next morning, driven in Tommy's taxi. She told him awkwardly that they'd had a phone call. Nuala was in

England and wouldn't say where.
The tractor was green, with a trailer and chunky red wheels. Mikey's first word had been T'actor....Seamus's tears dripped into the trailer.

Lynn's mother was delighted to hear that she and the children were coming home for Christmas. Her father affected enthusiasm too but privately hoped he wouldn't have to participate too much. He was never keen on Christmas, especially when it was made chaotic by visitors. He wouldn't mind telling Maggie a few of his funny stories and he'd volunteer for the washing up and distribute drinks on the day itself. But after that he hoped to retreat to his Ham Radio equipment in the little room he insisted on calling, The Shack'.
If getting away looked as if it would invite disapproval, he could always fall back on his stock excuse, 'The Old Chest's Getting A Bit Tight'. He suffered a lot with it, but being asthmatic did have a few advantages.
--I think there's been some sort of a rift with Bill, Margot was reporting now, looking round the Shack door. He hoped she wasn't going to interfere too much. Lynn had made her bed..
--But she couldn't say much over those awful phones..
Lynn's mother was well educated, well-travelled and generally open minded. But she had never understood Lynn's fascination with Ireland and now the usual tone of slight disapproval was in her voice. She had a way of putting a tiny emphasis on her words. Her Capital Letter comments, Bill called them.
--I hope they don't have a Rough Crossing, Fred, she said now.
Grandad sighed as he realised that the distant, exciting signal he was trying to tune into was lost, replaced by what was known to the initiated as Bubble and Squeak.
--That Irish Sea is infamous.
Well everyone knew that. Their ferry last year had been unable to dock due to the rough sea and they'd sat for hours waiting to enter the harbour. It was a strange holiday. They'd driven around the South coast, visiting Youghal and The Blarney Stone. He'd developed a liking for hot whiskeys and the Irish landladies, who fed him huge fried breakfasts and showed great concern for his asthma. But it seemed an empty sort of place and after the two days with Lynn and Bill, he was delighted to get home to decent plumbing and his Jazz records. Margot was charmed by the hospitality but not much else. She thought the music was Frenetic. (At that point she hadn't heard any slow airs) Later she summed up her overall impression to Lynn with, 'It's all so...Unkempt.'

The crossing wasn't particularly rough and the night was fairly dry. The train travelled through slate roofed Welsh villages in the small hours of a romantic-looking moonlit night. The rhythm of the train was soothing after the judder of the boat, which had been horribly crowded with people going to see their relations across the water. They were all, apart from those nursing babies or being sick, smoking, drinking and singing the worst of raucous old songs.

In the carriage, Lynn lay back, next to her sleeping children, and looked forward to the luxury that awaited her. She wasn't going to think about her last conversation with Bill, when she'd told him that she was going to England for Christmas.

--Oh, aren't I invited then? he'd asked nastily. Who's going to milk Tessie?

--I need to think things over. Tessie's nearly dry, you can get away with milking her every other day. I'm sure Brigitte will help you.

--Ha ha. Well don't think too long, and if you find Tessie gone when you get back don't blame me.

Lyn was unable to say exactly what she wanted, beyond a desire to get away from the relentless bad vibe that tainted the whole house, and be spoilt for a while. As so often, she'd had to make a humiliating request for money from her mother. Her father had told her on the phone how Worried her mother was about her being so far away and Living That Kind of Lifestyle. He was good at the capitals too, reflected Lynn, but he just liked winding people up. Just now she craved her mother's devoted, capable love, even if it would eventually make her feel inadequate. (The fact was, she WAS inadequate, it was just easier to hide it from herself when she didn't see her mother's sociable, popular, fulfilled and reasonably financed life)

Her mother would help with Ciaran, make her meals, read to Maggie. She would notice when Lynn was stuck and needed something passed to her, she would say things like, 'Oh, I've put that little pile of clothes from by the door in the washing machine...' Washing machine. Lynn sighed with grateful anticipation. The elderly gentleman opposite, a widower who had been reluctantly invited to spend Christmas with his daughter and her husband in Reading, hastily re-arranged his trousers. He had been furtively admiring Lynn for many miles and he was disturbed by the look of rapture that lingered on her sleepy face.

Nuala was holding Mikey's hand. He was awake again. The street lights bothered him, amongst other things. It took a long time to get him off to sleep and if she loosened her clasp on his hand before he was deeply unconscious, he'd be sure to pop up again, in just as lively a state as he'd been an hour ago. He wasn't having anything to do with the cot Kitty had borrowed for him. He'd stood in it, screaming defiantly for several hours, so now he was back on some cushions on the floor. Mikey was afraid of the vacuum cleaner and he ran in terror when Kitty's neighbour used an electric drill. But he loved the traffic, particularly the big red buses. There was a park not far away. Although the graffiti and some of the people that sat on the benches were depressing, Nuala took Mikey there every day, taking a tea towel to wipe the wet swing seats and slide with. It was very hard to keep Mikey out of trouble in the small flat where Kitty's friends left hot drinks and cigarette lighters lying about on the floor.

The landlord of the flat had made sure that she was Just Visiting, and she'd realised that when Kitty issued her casual invitation, she hadn't expected it to be followed up so quickly or with any idea of permanence. It was good to be with Kitty again. One night she'd found a friend to babysit and they'd gone out to a pub where there was a band playing. They came home laughing as explosively as they used to. But then Nuala discovered that Mikey hadn't been asleep at all. He had been busy, shredding up a tampax and several cigarettes and mashing them together with lipstick. He had distributed this colourful mixture around the room. It was impossible to forget for very long that her stay with Kitty had to come to an end, after which she would be homeless.

She would never forget her journey here. Her total exhaustion, mental and physical.....the kindness of people on the way....especially that woman, Mary, on the boat. Mikey was determinedly wobbling up and down, grinning at all the passengers who were trying not to spill their trays of scalding coffee and soup on him. Nuala had to follow him and, once they'd passed the seating area with many a near miss, steer him away from the stairs, which resulted in continual battles.

Before they boarded the boat, the train had held an equal number of hazards. Mikey had been delighted to discover that the doors opened obligingly as you crawled up to them, and he could, if he was quick, travel on to the next carriage before his mother caught up with him. Apart from being embarrassed at the filth on him, Nuala was worried that his little fingers would get caught where the two adjoining floors slid over one another. But when she tried to keep him on the seat, he kept climbing up her and trying to escape over the top, or he'd be heading off forwards across the table. She thought it would look better if she took off his blue wellies if he was going to do that. To her horror she found that his little feet were quite soaked with sweat. His damp socks left little prints as, chuckling with glee, he made off up the aisle again. They were

soon blacker than Seamus's range polish. Mikey came back to her, trying to hop and saying, 'Pull sock! Pull sock!' urgently. The sodden, filthy articles were hanging off his feet, so Nuala left those off too.
That woman on the boat, Mary, had been so kind. She seemed to understand Nuala's plight when she came and sat by them. She bought tea and called Mikey a Little Dote. She took him off for a long walk, washing his face, hands- and feet -somewhere on the way and buying him a toy boat from the shop. She seemed to have charmed him because he sat on her lap then, while she amused him with an endless supply of rhymes, games and tickles.
Mary chatted about her family, and found out, without asking too much and making Nuala get emotional, that she was visiting her friend and possibly staying on in England. She gave Nuala her sister's address; she ran a boarding house in Somerset, and sometimes took people on to help with the cleaning and the breakfasts. Before she left to rejoin her husband who was drinking in the bar, she gave Nuala a paper.
--You keep it, I've read it. They've ended the Hunger Strike. A couple of them nearly died but it looks like they'll pull through. They've been promised some concessions. Isn't that a load off our minds right before Christmas.
There was another saviour Nuala would never forget. They had arrived on a clanking, grimy, bewildering platform in the early hours of the morning. Mikey was grizzling and wriggling horribly. In later years she couldn't picture the face of her saviour with the Mars Bar, but what she did remember was the wrapping coming off a big brown rectangle and it descending towards the mouth of the astonished, then blissfully silenced, infant. What matter if, to add to the finishing touches of his dishevelment, he had a river of goo down his front and his hands looked as if they'd been dipped into Cadbury vats when Kitty finally found them. He was quiet. And sitting still.

Frankie and Brendan called on Seamus to see if he was coming out. They meant poaching. It was a clear night with the moon nearly full and a frost glistening. Some of the blow ins had invited him to a Solstice Party tomorrow night, in recognition of the real Pagan origins of the festival soon to be celebrated. He thought it would be better craic than Mass and the dinner he'd have in a few days at Maeve's, but he didn't feel his usual enthusiasm, even though he'd be able to sell a good bit of blow. But the empty cottage was desperate. Every now and then he'd find himself crying. He put his coat and boots on gratefully. Probably the lads wouldn't notice if he was crying out there in the night.

Maggie was enjoying herself. She'd been to the cinema with Gran, and although she loved her baby brother, it was very nice to have the attention of someone who wasn't always being distracted by his needs. Gran bought her new trousers and a jumper (she knew better than to suggest a dress) to be put away until the proper day, and a book on Goat keeping. Maggie sat in the bus, happily reading her book and planning to spend any Christmas money she received on items for the Basic First Aid Kit which the book claimed was essential.

They'd got the bus into Winchester because Gran Didn't Think They'd Bother Grandad Today. Mum had come too but gone back earlier. She said the heat and the reek from the perfume testers in the overcrowded shops made her feel ill.

Mum was in a funny mood. They went out for a nice wintry walk, with Ciaran in his sling, but otherwise, she was being very lazy, reflected Maggie. Like lying about on the sofa in a borrowed dressing gown. Maggie could distinctly remember her mother giving out about people who Slobbed About Half The Day in Dressing Gowns, that was why she didn't have one of her own. And Mum seemed abnormally indifferent to what she was eating. She no longer kept an eye on Grandad (who liked sweets- treacle brittle and humbugs were his favourites) or tried to stop Granny Margot coming out with her favourite maxim, 'Leave Some Room For Pudding'. Her habit of not noticing when you spoke to her had got worse as well.

Lynn had forgotten what living with mod cons was like. Everything so clean, smooth, luxurious. You just popped the clothes into the washing machine (as her mother had quietly done when they arrived, remarking with that tone she could never keep under control that they smelt so, well, *Smoky*), turned on the cooker with no worry about whether the gas bottle was nearly empty, flicked on the lights, picked up the telephone. Tasks that took all day were accomplished in minutes.

The countryside was very pretty, if a bit manicured. There were nice walks along the Drover's Road and beside the river. The pub they visited was full of old farm tools, harness and horse brasses, all polished up and never to be used again. People came and had lunch, wearing green wellies and expensive country clothes and laughing loudly as if all the world should be admiring their wit.

Cathy arrived, happy and animated. While she and Lynn cooked dinner together, she told Lynn about Martin her new boyfriend, and the hostel. Their father had poured whiskey with reckless generosity and before long they were giggling stupidly over the bizarre behaviour of some of

the sleepers. They were referred to as sleepers but in reality it seemed to be the last thing most of them actually did.
--I shouldn't be laughing, spluttered Cathy, mopping up some sauce she had just spilt, I'm normally so angry over the injustice in our society...and scared- because some of them are nuts, or sometimes they're really angry ...I'm not really meant to talk about them but if I didn't I'd end up cracking up myself and it's good to have a laugh about it all from a distance. There's this other bloke, called Bonzo, and-
--*Bonzo?*
They caught each other's eye and were spluttering again.

Upstairs, Gran was bathing Ciaran, and Grandad was wiring up a series of Lego windmills, powered by a large battery and interlinked with a series of elastic bands. It was outwardly for Maggie's benefit, but they had a comfortable agreement whereby she wrote lists of items to be added to her First Aid Kit (her vision had now expanded to include happy pictures of herself administering to numerous flea ridden, emaciated and deformed animals) while Grandad happily added new connections, his eyes glowing.
It was very comfortable here with her family, thought Lynn. The easy familiarity, the help with the kids, no shortage of anything...and able to enjoy alcohol again, she reflected happily as she wobbled out of the kitchen to inform those upstairs that the food was ready.

Chapter Thirty

Bill rang, late, when he knew that Maggie, and hopefully Lynn's parents, would be in bed.
--I've a call for you from the Republic of Ireland, said a woman's voice, and the soft, neat accent immediately filled her with the old yearning and dis-satisfaction with Britishness.
--Lynn, it's me. Bill always said that. His voice was faint and the line crackly.
--Where are you? asked Lynn, picturing him in the phone box at the end of the village, with the Grotto behind him and then the lonely, moonlit road bordered by endless crag. Of course, it was the same moonlit night outside the house she was in now, but you didn't experience it in the same way. There was no need to go out for a pee or fetch wood, and the street lights cast a continual murky orange fog.
--I'm in Geigan's, Bill told her, I came with Seamus, he added unwisely. 'Ha!' thought Lynn, her tenderness evaporating,'That fella...And that bloody Brigitte's probably around too.'
--How did you get all the way over there?
-- With one of Brendan's friends. Just about everyone seems to be here tonight. It's the last session before Christmas. I just spotted Jim. Are you having a good time? enquired Bill with lame desperation.
--Lynn could hear Geigan's in the background now, and visualise the smoky interior; pollution you had to swim through, the assorted characters, the laughter and the banter, a group of local couples getting up to dance, the music, which was, though all that way away, making her spine tingle.
--Yes, thanks. The weather's okay so we've been getting out for some nice walks. Maggie's got a new goat book. Yes, Gran let her have a couple of things early. Cathy's here now - She was being carefully impersonal.
There was loud cheering at Bill's end and familiar cries of, 'Mighty, mighty!' and, 'Good man yerself!' and so on.
--Lynn, I miss you.
She felt a glow of longing and relief moving through her, but all that came out was,' Oh, she's left you on your own has she?' But she was wishing she was there in Geigan's with him, she hadn't been to that particular session yet,and now she felt well again, it would be great to go. She'd resign herself happily to a week of itchy eyes and the sore throat that would follow.
--Lynn, I love you. I've written you a letter. Please read it -

Bill sounded desperate, she realised with relish. In the background she detected the voice of Tom Flannery, the old fella who made it his job to give out about everyone and everything, but especially The Brits.
--Feckin' Thatcher! he was saying now, She won't pay to be in the EEC and the rest of us have to make up for it!
He had been going on about that since the announcement back in May that Britain's payments were to be reduced. As Lynn understood it - not that she wanted to defend the loathsome woman of course - but as she understood it, Germany and France had picked up the bill. But she wasn't completely certain, she read things in papers but the details remained peculiarly elusive when she needed them.
--Tom, said Bill, in a tone that was both exasperated and amused, I'm trying to talk to my wife.
Lynn, still wondering in frustration why it was that she could never remember facts properly, suddenly realised that the pips were going.
--I've no more change, said Bill, I love you -
It felt as if he had fallen over a cliff. Why hadn't she heeded Cathy's advice. They'd been talking earlier, before they got pissed on their father's whiskey.
--You do tend to pounce on Bill without thinking things through, remarked Cathy, I honestly think he's doing his best. Maybe if you could explain what you want without being sarcastic...
--Yea.I know. But you'd think he'd realise without having it spelt out.
--He's not that kind. But he's one hundred percent decent. You can't have everything. Tell him you love him a bit more often.

The next day- Christmas Eve -she rang the Ryans, who she knew had just had a phone installed after someone in the family died and left them some money.
--Shame it wasn't herself, Jim had remarked to Bill.
Bill was shocked until he followed the direction of Jim's gaze and was nearly knocked down by the evil force field emanating from a photo of the sister in law - that old bat who had given Lynn such a hard time -which stood upon the dresser.
--Oh, Lynn, is it yourself, enthused Moira Ryan with her customary warmth, How are you? And your parents, are they well? And is Maggie enjoying herself, ah, the pet! And the little fella, is he sleeping any better? Isn't that grand. Bill was in to us yesterday. He'll be over at Patsy and Sinead's just now but you'll know that of course. Tis good for him to have the company when you can't all be together.
The warmth of her tone, the straightforwardness of her enquiries and the lack of suspicion that she and Bill might be apart for any other reason

than the pressure of family duties brought tears to Lynn's eyes. She knew that, if she talked about the problems between herself and Bill, Moira would show a great deal of insight and wisdom. This had happened before when she had found herself unexpectedly blurting out her troubles to local women who'd invited her in for cup of tea. But the result was that she was left feeling like a petulant teenager. It wasn't that they were patronising, they weren't in the least. But they seemed to have such maturity, although Annie would say it was just that their convent school upbringing had trained them to accept a woman's lot and be a faithful wife. Lynn wasn't sure about that. She remembered that as a kid you thought that all adults possessed such maturity and wisdom. Now she thought it was largely illusory. Particularly among the blow ins. The members of the Alternative community looked here and there for Fulfilment, tried to Rediscover Themselves, took off with each others partners and dragged their kids along. They gave great thought to giving their offspring names like Billberry or Sunshine, made sure they were breastfed and didn't wear nylon. Some were very skilled growers or crafts people. Most were capable of keeping a fire going and stocking the cupboard with whatever food they'd been persuaded was good for them that week. And when a kid was clobbering its friends, some sort of guidance would be issued - but with a huge variance of style. It was horrendous, they'd seen some of the travelling crowd who drank too much simply punch their kids on the ear and shout, Fuckin' shut up!' The stoned types might manage to say, 'Leave it out!' in a half amused drawl, while the most affected would deliver a long lecture on the folly of violence.

Well, of course, all the Blow-ins were different. 'We're all Pioneers,' she'd heard someone claim, 'exploring different lifestyles... above all getting away from the old damaging, constricting, war- mongering, greedy ways to something more Spiritual.'

Within the home, your own bread was an essential requisite, goat's milk and home made jam were further passports to acceptability, and it was also helpful if you made clothes, spun or died wool (with vegetable derivatives) and made cheese and sold herbs to the Wholefood store. If you made a rice pudding it would need to be an Indian one with cardamoms and exotic things in it, and you'd make a point of explaining that it was sweetened with apple juice.

Herbal healing was sacrosanct. You kept meadowsweet for headaches and chamomile and valerian to help you sleep. Even when you could see that some poor dog was dying of septicaemia you mustn't mention antibiotics, but let everyone enjoy themselves making poultices and tinctures.

It wasn't that Lynn didn't believe in it all, she did. All this stuff was good, and satisfying. But she hated being constantly lectured to. Above all she wished she could sometimes just give Maggie some bloody baked beans for tea without looking over her shoulder.

--Bill rang me yesterday, she was pleased to tell Moira Ryan, But we got cut off. If you see him please give him my love. And you could tell him to reverse the charges if he rings again.
--The lines are very busy just now with everyone ringing home for Christmas. I don't know why Bill didn't come up here. I told him he must come and use our phone. It's such a blessing, Lynn. God knows we've waited long enough for it, it was such an expense getting the ESB up here we thought we'd never have it, but with Jim's Uncle leaving the bit of money...Anyway, he'll ring you again, of course he will, and if we see him we'll drag him up here ourselves and you can have a good long chat without getting cut off.

--It's George, announced Lynn's mother in a carefully neutral tone. She was avoiding her eye. At times like this, she and Lynn were prone to unfortunate giggling fits and the results had at times been disastrous. She bit her tongue and went out to the kitchen.
--Oh Christ, began Lynn, then realised that Bill's odious brother had been right behind her mother and escape was impossible.
--Would you like a drink, George? asked her mother, who had gained control of herself and re-entered the room. George asked for a coffee, then settled himself opposite Lynn in a deliberately relaxed pose (one big foot resting across the other knee) and arranged his features into one of concerned interest.
Lynn mentally said Goodbye to the drama she'd been watching. She'd inherited her father's contempt for television. But well, it was Christmas, she was aching to talk to Bill (why had she been so horrible to him, perhaps the way she'd enjoyed letting him grovel like that would drive him away for good - into the rounded young arms of Brigitte) and she needed to be distracted. As well as simply bloody lazy for a bit. She didn't turn the TV off. She felt suspicious and distrustful as to why George was there and it didn't incline her to be polite or encouraging. Unfortunately, her mother did it for her, when she arrived with the coffee and a plate of mince pies. The News had come on. She glanced at Prince Charles. He was frequently being featured at the moment, with his engagement to Diana Spencer imminent.
--He's so -*gauche*, she remarked, I hope he manages to take his left

hand out of his pocket when he gets married!
  She made some small talk then tactfully went upstairs with coffee for Fred.
Lynn fervently hoped that Ciaran would wake up, bawling, or that Maggie would arrive and clamber all over George (he'd hated that when she was younger) chattering obliviously about goats. But no such lucky interruption took place.
--How are things? asked George.
--Fine, smiled Lynn innocently, Ciaran's feeding well, and we think he just smiled for the first time, it's a bit early to tell but it really looked like a proper smile. Maggie's enjoying herself...
How DARE he come here like this.
--And what about between you and Bill?
None of your fucking business.
--Fine, declared Lynn airily.
--Bill suggested I speak to you.
*The Bastard! Of all the underhand tricks....*And she couldn't think why. Bill loved his sister but he loathed poor old George.
--Bill does understand that you're feeling Disempowered at present, continued George seriously.
--Oh ,right.
Funny how the features were the same but George was so unattractive. The mouth too small, the nose too big, the expression so pompous...He smelt rotten too, stale and cheesy, if she had her way she'd hang him on the line for a couple of days..
--And that the resentment this causes has become a Barrier to Communication.
  George was dying to Utilise his Intervention Strategies in order to Facilitate Meaningful Dialogue. He hoped that his brother and his wife would let him Use His Own Role Creatively in doing this. After all, his training could be useful in many areas and his own family were at the moment as much in need of guidance as those on his caseload.
--Would you agree that you are feeling Disempowered? he persisted, Stuck in an isolated cottage...Lack of social contact doesn't help to increase self-confidence or independence, he suggested in a sympathetic tone. He hoped that he was showing Empathy.
--Neither does your husband looking at someone else's tits.
Damn! It was good to see him flinch but she was being drawn in,despite her resolve to give nothing away and get rid of him as fast as possible.
--And Bill's as dependent as a two year old, she added, remembering the letters and forms he'd whined about recently until she'd sorted them out for him.

--Bill felt REJECTED, Lynn. He felt that he couldn't give you the support you needed-
--Too right.
--And holding totally different Value Bases as you do-
George wasn't quite sure about that bit but he loved the term.
--Do we? Oh yes, perhaps I have been a bit keener than him on the bacon recently.
--It seems that it was becoming impossible for you to Relate Meaningfully.
Why doesn't the daft bugger realise he's just wasted three years training learning to state the glaringly obvious in grandiose terms.
--Coming home with the shopping would have been good enough.
George, wearing a look of weary patience, tried another tack.
--There's Maggie to consider. An Ongoing Situation of Hostility can be very damaging to a child.
Lynn remained silent, hating him. George too remained silent. He knew that periods of Reflection and Contemplation were as important as talking.
--There is not an ongoing situation of hostility, said Lynn at last, Just a bit of a bad patch. I came here to enjoy Christmas with my family, so now if you don't mind-
George remained rooted as solidly as ever in his chair. He told her in his calm, measured tone that there was something called Family Therapy.
--It's just a suggestion. It often helps to talk things over frankly with a Mediator. I'd be very happy to fulfil that role.
--I'm sure. Ciaran's crying so I'm going upstairs now.
There was a silence during which it was patently apparent that Ciaran must still be sound asleep. George rose reluctantly. If only Bill had confided in him earlier. (Not that he had done, he'd been drunk, and rambling and had dialled George's number by mistake.) But from his brief comments George had been able to Gain Insights. If he had known about these Issues earlier, he might have made an Intervention that was Pro-active rather than Re-active...
Lynn's mother appeared.
--Oh, are you off, George?
--Yes, I must be going, Margot. Lovely to see you again. If I can be of any assistance -
--Ah, would you fuck off for yourself, they both heard Lynn say from half way up the stairs.
George knew you had to expect Challenging Behaviour from people under stress. Margot reflected that the man was a complete nincompoop. But she would have preferred it if her daughter expressed

herself in a way more reflective of her true intelligence.
George left, hoping that, despite her Defensiveness, Lynn would consider his offer. And realise that he hadn't been there just as an Advocate for Bill, but as someone who could help Facilitate Meaningful Dialogue, help them both Come To Terms with the situation and Find A Way Forward.

At Annie and Pete's house in Ireland, Bill, dishevelled and desperate, was being soothed by Annie over his mistake on the telephone.
--If Lynn thinks I asked that twat to go and see her she'll never come back! he prophesied in anguish.

Upstairs in her parent's house, Lynn, seething with rage and head boiling with clever comments she should have made, grabbed paper and pen to write a nasty letter to George. She would never send it (the imbecile would probably find he didn't have enough in his Pot Of Resources to cope with the truth and kill himself) but it might relieve the worst of her tension and allow her to sleep tonight. Maggie passed the door. Mum was muttering, Fuck, fuck, fuck.

By Boxing Day, the atmosphere in the house was deteriorating.
Cathy had gone. Martin came to pick her up after the Christmas dinner. She was back on duty that evening. Martin was good looking with a gentle smile. He was friendly and relaxed. He immediately started telling Maggie silly jokes.
--What does Tessie like for breakfast?
--Um..hay?
--Maa-malade! What's Tessie's favourite game? Maaa -rbles! Who does Tessie love the best?
--Me?
--Nope. Maaaa-tin! No, not really. She told me it's Maaa-ggie.
There were little secret looks always passing between him and Cathy which made Lynn a bit uncomfortable, not to mention jealous. She told herself sagely that that stage wouldn't last much longer..
--It seems Awfully Harsh that you have to go to work on Christmas Day, Granny Margot was saying to Cathy upstairs where she was helping collect up her things.
--Mum, I've explained all that. I was lucky to be here for the dinner. And yesterday evening. Christmas is our busiest time, when we get extra people in off the streets for a few days.
--Couldn't you find something less demanding to do?
--No, said Cathy firmly, It's the best thing I've ever done. Plus it's how I

met Martin.
There was a hole after they left, with promises to come to Ireland in the Spring, and Maggie clinging onto Martin until he got into the car.

Now Grandad had retreated to The Shack, leaving Granny Margot to deal with two lots of people he'd jovially invited round for drinks in an earlier fit of sociability.
Maggie was growsy and tearful, and Lynn was beginning to feel stifled and increasingly desperate to talk to Bill. He rang while she had just popped out for a short walk.
--Did he say he'd ring back? Or I should ring him somewhere? Where was he? She demanded of the bemused and then resentful Maggie.
As well as missing the chance to start sorting out her relationship, she'd been denied the pleasure of eavesdropping while Bill had to pretend to be overwhelmed with joy at Maggie's present of a tweed tie carefully chosen from the Beleek shop.

Nuala was sitting beside Mikey, holding his hand again. He was so nearly asleep...if only Kitty and her boyfriend in the next room wouldn't keep hooting at something they were watching...
How plain the room was, well of course it was a tiny box room, unused, but all the rooms were like this in this building, where Kitty knew several of the other residents. Smooth pale walls, cold ceilings; no dusty beams or corners, not a herb or dried flower in sight. Floors tiled or neatly carpeted; no goatskins, no cushions, no multi-coloured blankets. Empty window-sill and table;no stones, no bones, no ferns. No fireplace surrounded by buckets, logs, pots or hissing kettle. Just the stifling heat from the radiators.
It was odd how much she missed Seamus. It wasn't just because she could tell that Mikey was confused and missing him. It was the familiarity, and the cosiness he put into a home,even if he did drive you mad with his fussing about it all.
She realised that she loved him in a way. Couples who'd been married a long time were Comfortable together; they fitted around each other like an old glove, well, an old sock it would be in Seamus's case. They couldn't rekindle the passion of the early days very often,but sometimes it came upon them again. And they had their good memories. With Seamus, she had the Old Sock kind of love without having experienced any passion, or stored up any romantic memories to fortify it.

It was all her fault. She should never have gone with Seamus in the first place. Now she had done an awful thing, taking Mikey away. But Seamus would never leave her in peace if she was any closer. She was fearful of the responsibility for Mikey and all the insecurity that lay ahead. But she couldn't go back. Kitty- and Davy- had told her she was intelligent and attractive. And she had her first giro in her purse.

Chapter Thirty One

--Lynn, there's a parcel for you.
Lynn could hear the reluctance in her mother's voice. She knew her mother loved having her here. Besides enjoying teaching Maggie things and playing games with her, she appreciated having Lynn to laugh and chat with, and it was true that they did get on well. But she never felt properly adult. It wasn't that her mother didn't treat her as one, it was more that, by being so capable, socially and practically, she made Lynn more aware of her own failings. It was too easy to shelter under the veil of her Mum's popularity and easy manner, never having to make the effort herself.
A degree of pressure was being applied.
--I Do Wish you'd stay here. I could give you So Much Help. And the playgroup they have here now is Awfully Good...
Hence the tone with which she produced the parcel that she knew was from Bill.

Lynn, I'm sorry I was such a cunt to you, Lynn read. She hastily refolded the paper and went upstairs to read the rest.
I felt like I wasn't needed. When you had Ciaran it came to a head but it started a long time before that. Everything I did seemed to be wrong.
I know you think I slept with Brigitte -This was left unfinished and he started again.
I think you know I slept with Brigitte. It was only once. I felt so bad about it I couldn't face you. But also I felt very angry with you for making me feel guilty (I know that's not fair) so I kept being a cunt but not wanting to be one.
Lynn smiled at this.
I thought you had driven me to it but I suppose that's not fair either. I'm not making excuses Lynn, I will always regret it but honestly it was just a bit of drunken fun. I just wanted to feel happy and young and carefree again for a night-
--So I make you feel old, laden and boring, thought Lynn, Thanks.
There wasn't any of the deeper, more spiritual feeling I've always had with you. When I woke up I wished she wasn't there, I asked her to go. Then I kept thinking that I should have been kinder-
--Why? thought Lynn, why be so kind to a bloody little bitch who casually wrecks our relationship (and could have found any number of YOUNG, GOOD LOOKING blokes without PAUNCHES to sleep with, she added

to herself cruelly)*I knew that she was leaving soon and I didn't want her to go off feeling she had been used-*
Lynn couldn't help raising her eyes towards the ceiling at this noble statement-
I wanted to make her feel all right, partly because of things you've told me about the way men have finished with you, and that Phil bloke with Cathy - you can either leave someone feeling destroyed or you can make the effort to leave them feeling all right about themselves-
--But that's ME, thought Lynn indignantly, the likes of Brigitte don't deserve all that consideration!
She was furiously jealous that Bill should care so much about the bloody girl's feelings. Throwing in all this - typically mis-directed - New-Man-Tuned-Into-Feelings stuff at this stage! The pain at the thought of their intimacy was knotting her insides.
I just wanted to say Goodbye to her in a kinder way but I knew you'd go mad if I told you I was going to see her. I was going to Patsy and Sinead's to find her but she was on the road hitching in the rain as I told you. All I did was buy her a drink and explain about my feelings for you and wish her well-
Shouldn't she know he had feelings for his wife, or did she think it was a loveless Arranged |Marriage? Or did she, Lynn, look so frumpy, ugly and bad tempered that Brigitte didn't suppose for a minute that anything affectionate, let alone sexual, happened between them (But how had she supposed that Ciaran arrived?)
Lynn was doing suspicious sums in her head.
Bill and Brigitte would have got to the village by ten. He had to buy the bit of shopping, true, but he must have sat with her for hours.
Bill would later admit that the charm of the crinkly nose again began to over- ride considerations of commitment and the bonds of spirituality. He felt that he deserved some kind of reward for resisting its huge power, but all he got when he arrived home was Lynn tearing the head off him for not getting Gripe Water - which he was sure he had bought, and later found where it had fallen out of the carrier bag on the track. And no thanks for getting the sodding sanitary towels either. He didn't mind putting them into a Quinnsworth trolley but buying them in small shops was different; and she would want some funny kind that he'd had to ask for in several places and it had been embarrassing. He didn't see Irish men buying sanitary towels.. With big families there was always another female to do it. Lucky sods.

Lynn, please come back. I miss you so much and I promise I will never, never be unfaithful again.. PLEASE BELIEVE ME. Christmas was shite

without you and although I have been going out I am very lonely. My life is nothing without you and Maggie.
He went on to say how beautiful she was- as a person, and yes, in looks, even though she never believed it, lots of people had said so and asked after her. And what a great kid Maggie was and that was because Lynn was her mother.
And he missed Ciaran.
He must be changing so fast. Please bring him home, Lynn. Or if you want me to come over there, I will. We could move back for good if that's what you want...I want to be with you and I want so desperately to hold Ciaran again-
Lynn's cynicism had almost entirely evaporated but it made a brief re-appearance as she wondered if this desire to hold Ciaran now encompassed the small hours of the night.
There was a parcel, wrapped in thick wads of the Irish Times. Lynn hoped for something romantic, but layers later, saw that it was small, flat and bottle-shaped. She began reflecting in disgust that all men thought of was alcohol. There was a message wrapped round it on a page from one of Maggie's school books.
Don't use the English sort. It makes them grow ears like Prince Charles, she read. Mystified, she peeled off the last layer to reveal the missing bottle of Gripe Water. There was a PS. *Have kept your present here hoping you are coming back...*

The festivities already seemed distant and sad and that empty, after-Christmas feeling was settling on them all. It was that time when you had to get yourself together and back into a routine or succumb to the urge to commit suicide. But Lynn wasn't inclined to book their tickets home just yet. She was enjoying the rest, and a mean part of her felt that, even though she was longing to see him, now she was sure of Bill's affections it wouldn't hurt if she stayed just a bit longer.
She had qualms of conscience-she knew he hated milking Tessie, who he had running battles with. And he was out working as well-helping Jim feed his cattle, and Patsy do some bits of building work. And she was aware that Maggie was behaving oddly, and Grandad was running dangerously low on Bonhomie....Cathy had squeezed her hand before she left, nodded in their father's direction and whispered, 'I wouldn't stay too long. He hasn't changed that much'.

Bill had managed to ring a couple of times, once from the phone box at Conlon's Cross- a call which didn't last long on account of the usual problems with levers not doing what they should and crossed lines- and once from the Ryans.
--What have you been doing? he asked.
--Well, not much. Ciaran takes most of my time and I'm quite tired still.
--But he's sleeping through the night?
--Sometimes. We're getting there. I don't think he'll ever be as good a sleeper as Maggie was though.
--She was terrible! Bill laughed. Have you seen anyone? Besides Cathy?
--I don't seem to get on with English people any more. Its weird. You feel comfortable with the voices at first, but everything else is so different from the way we live now...
But actually, Dad was really good yesterday, he took us out to see his friends who live in an old house, sort of faded and dusty, but full of lovely things. We had to walk the last bit because their drive was too dodgy for the mini -some of it had washed away in the heavy rain they had just before I came over. He said it was too far for him to walk so he'd wait in the car. And he said, Be as long as you like, I've got my warm coat on and the radio and I'll blow the horn if I'm in trouble. We didn't stay that long and Sylvie, the woman, took him mince pies and tea, but it was good of him all the same. I sometimes forget how bad his asthma really is, and all the times he spends waiting in the car because people have dogs he can't go near, or he's just too breathless to move.
--I remember.
--This couple keep hens and they gave us some chicks. Silkies- they're tiny! I didn't even know you could hatch chicks in winter. They've kept hens for years and they've got all sorts of unusual ones. But the people in the new houses keep complaining about the noise the cockerel makes, you wouldn't believe it.
--I would. That's why we left.
--How are things there?
--Cold. Frosts all the time. They're all saying they've never seen anything like it but that's probably an exaggeration. The house is bloody freezing when I get home..But don't worry, when I know when you're coming back I'll stay in for a couple of days and make the range behave itself. I've been at Patsy and Sinead's nearly every day helping with the building. Brigitte went off ages ago, he added after a pause, But don't worry. I'll *never* make that mistake again, with her or anyone else.
--I know. I believe you. It was my fault as well.
--I don't know if that's true...but thank you...I've some good news

actually. Patsy and Sinead are going into partnership with Emerald and we can do the same thing if we want. Its a sort of co-operative, almost like a mini Common Market. I've got all the bumf on it here, I didn't send it on because I thought you'd be on your way back any time. We could have volunteers as well, Patsy's been telling me about it-
--I don't want volunteers. I don't want people I don't know living with us.
--But that's the point. They become people you DO know. Good people. You get all that extra help and their skills and their company. And you don't have to pay them.
--I don't understand why they want to come and work for no pay.
--They don't work flat out. They have a holiday as well. And they learn new skills - if this plan works out, they'll be learning how to make chairs.
Bill decided that was enough on the subject of volunteers for the time being and went on to Patsy's recent ideas for a traditional furniture workshop.
--Sounds great, said Lynn, realising she had sounded rather unenthusiastic so far. Then a thought struck her.
--Bill,what happened to those chairs that were in the barn when we first came? I wanted to bring them in and replace the two that are wobbly. I looked after the hay pile went down but they didn't seem to be there any more.
Bill had a nasty recollection of Seamus claiming them as his own one day when he'd been distracted and not feeling like an argument. He decided to continue with the subject of volunteers after all. She'd have to get used to the idea, he'd need a team of people working on the chairs and in the garden, which would be much bigger than at present.
--Think about the help you'd have. You just have to feed them. You can ask them to babysit or whatever you need, it wouldn't just be help in the garden.
Bill wasn't totally sure this was right. And it had suddenly occurred to him that they'd need somewhere to sleep. Maybe they could just borrow them from other people for the odd day to begin with.
--Could they do the cooking too? asked Lynn hopefully.
--Of course, said Bill blithely, though he really hadn't a clue. I heard a sad thing in Kelly's yesterday, he went on. That old man - the one you saw when you went to visit Mattie that time- well he was in Quinn's the night before, sobbing and crying because his dog died. Of blood poisoning. He doesn't look it, but he's almost blind. He only used to walk between his place and Mattie's because he knew the way so well after all the years they'd both lived there -
--But what place? There isn't any other house down there.
--Well there is actually, I'm not sure where exactly. It's probably like

Jackie Hogan's place, so buried you just don't notice it. Otherwise he only got to Quinn's once in a while when someone fetched him in a car. He couldn't see that the string he led the dog about with was cutting into its neck. He was really upset that he'd caused its death. When Jim and some others went down there to take him some food and things they found his house in an awful state. They're probably moving him into a home.

--Oh dear. I wish I'd said something. I really didn't know what to do..I promised Maggie I'd ask the Ryans and then I just left it...Shit, she's coming down. Don't tell her, Bill, will you. And don't tell her you punched Tessie in the face, she added in a whisper.

--Of course I won't! But I'm going to pull Tessie's ears off if you don't come back soon.

--Bye Darling. I'll ring the Ryans to let you know exactly when we'll be arriving.

She handed the phone to Maggie who gave her a hostile sort of look.

Nuala was in the room she shared with Mikey at the B&B near Taunton, reading her mother's letter again. This morning she had been painting a wall in one of the rooms, a nightmare with Mikey below and trying to get at the paint pot. She could only do the higher parts that he couldn't reach, the rest she'd have to finish when he was asleep. There weren't many customers this time of year, just the odd contract worker, so she had to help with all the jobs there weren't time for in summer. Deep cleaning the whole greasy kitchen was next on the list. Mrs Billings was nowhere near as kind as her sister on the boat and she didn't like Mikey. The sight of his curls seemed to offend her, she tutted at his frequent demands for Bocky Juice. And she kept making criticisms to the effect that he was not a Real Boy like her grandsons. But this room was okay, although Mrs B was already hinting that she'd have to go to the smallest one when more guests started turning up. Luckily the woman went out quite a lot to the shops, Bingo and the WI.

Nuala and Mikey were going to a Mother and Toddler group. And on the High Street she'd got chatting to a lady who was campaigning for CND and been invited to a Folk Club. It was held in a local cafe and it would be all right to bring Mikey for the early part of the evening at least.

The letter gave her a lovely warm feeling. It had arrived at Kitty's just before she got the coach down here.

Dear Nuala,
I have been so worried about you. Davy's mother rang me, and told us

he met you going to the ferry, and you might have left Seamus. Is it true? I hope you are at Kitty's as I don't know where else to try. It took me a while to get her new address, I hope this is the right one.
Nuala, we really want you to come home, and live with us. We hardly know Mikey and he is our grandson.
The cheque is to get him a Christmas present (hope you get it in time) and something for yourself, and there should be enough for your ticket home, but please ask if you need more or are stuck for money. As you know, Christmas is always a bit strange because we think of M -and you! - but we managed to enjoy it . There was a party in the hall on Christmas Eve organised by Mrs Phelps. You'll know what that was like- we didn't stay too long! We are both well.
I won't give you all the news from this end now as I want to get this in the post.
Please write, or better still, ring us and let us know how you are. Hoping very much to see you and Mikey soon,
All my love,
Mam xxxx

Nuala had rung her Mum when Mrs Billings was out. The old bat would probably check her bill and notice the call later on, but she might not even be here then. She was going to visit them soon and meanwhile she'd send some photos of Mikey that Kitty had taken.. But oddly, the letter had strengthened her resolve to stay here, at least for a while. Mikey had a big new dumper truck, a red plastic potty (that was proving a bit optimistic for the time being but he also had a stock of disposable nappies that didn't leak when he was asleep) and the rest of the money was in the bank. And she knew her parents were there if she needed them..

Lynn's father had mellowed in his old age and Maggie had seen a much better side of him than Lynn and Cathy. When they were teenagers, he used to rage about the house, complaining about strange things. One of his stock phrases was, 'Filthy snotty handkerchiefs left everywhere!' He went on for hours once he'd started while their mother tried to calm him. Now and again she gave them a little talk, explaining that he couldn't help it, it was the effect of the steroids he had to take for his asthma. And he'd had a rotten childhood.
Downstairs he was at this minute beginning to shout hysterically.
--I always knew this would happen! Landing on us with another baby! Filthy shitty nappies everywhere! I won't have it!

Cathy's present to Lynn, besides some essential oils, had been a big bag of disposable nappies. Lynn realised she had forgotten to put the last one in the bin after changing Ciaran in the kitchen. What an absurd, but predictable exaggeration, she thought indignantly. Firstly, it was one nappy, singular. Next, it wasn't shitty. Babies didn't really do proper shits until they were on solids. Not the objectionable type anyway. And she was only here for a holiday (even if she hadn't been so sure about that when she'd first arrived)

There was a knock at the front door and the shouting stopped. It was Jean, one of the members of her mother's choir, with her young grandson. The child was what Lynn mentally categorised as a Biscuit Kid - indeterminate fair hair, no outstanding features of any kind, boringly clean, pallid indoor skin. He wore new Christmas clothes from Mothercare And he carried a large plastic machine gun. It was in primary colours to appeal to his age group, but it was very definitely a machine gun.

Lynn's mother, quite unruffled despite the recent tirade, ushered them in and made introductions. Lynn went to make coffee. Grandad passed through the living room, smiling jovially and bidding Jean a Happy New Year.

--The old chest's a bit tight today actually, so I hope you'll excuse me, I'm going to lie down for a bit.

--I don't think I'll be able to come to the practice this week, Jean was saying when Lynn came back with the coffee, I'm helping my daughter with Harry until he goes back to playgroup. They're starting late because of the hall repairs.

--Oh, I quite understand. We've decided to leave it until February anyway. Several people have had that awful cold. Would Harry like a biscuit?

But Harry had already grabbed two. He took a miniscule bite from each then dropped them on the carpet.

Maggie had appeared, still in her pyjamas, and was looking indignant.

--Go and get yourself some cereal, said Lynn hastily.

--But I'm not hungry yet -

--I don't think he likes Malted Milk, said Jean indulgently, He's very fussy about his food. Here you are, Harry, try this one.

Lynn dived across the room and helped Maggie towards the kitchen. Another biscuit had bitten the dust. Jean was in full flood.

--Oh, they're very good there, Harry can already count to twenty and write his name, and do up his coat zip, they teach them so much. My daughter wants to get him into that new nursery school though, she

doesn't want him to be behind when he starts proper school and they stay there for the afternoon as well so its just like real school, they do so much better if they start learning to read and write early, and of course she can get back to full time work then, she's making the house so nice, she wants to buy all new furniture, the kitchen's already done, oh it's lovely, but she wants those corner sofas...Only Harry would have to have his dinner there and they might not do anything he likes.
Lynn's mother was giving her daughter a look that meant, 'Keep quiet,she's my best Alto.'
--Last week I made him his favourite dinner, continued Jean obliviously, but he wouldn't eat it. So I asked him what he wanted and he said, Sausages. So I cooked those but he got all upset, threw them on the floor he did, because he didn't mean those, he wanted the Pinky ones. That's what he calls Pork sausages,bless him, the Pinky ones. So we had to go to the shop and get some, didn't we Harry? But it wasn't sausages he meant at all, not on their own, it was Pizza-you know, that new type with the Salami sausage on it! He was making such a fuss we had to go back again to get one-
--Mum doesn't like army toys, remarked Maggie loudly from the doorway.
Lynn felt uneasy. She only did it occasionally, but Maggie had a disconcerting knack of making loud, profoundly uncomfortable statements. Which were doubly awkward because they were undeniably true. Once she'd told someone they were having dinner with that her gravy Looked Like Snot. And she'd been in an odd mood lately.
--Oh, Harry has Action Men too, said Lynn's mother quickly, Don't they do all sorts of things like Polar Exploration and Deep Sea Diving?
Harry was pointing his gun at Maggie. She stuck out her tongue.
--He's got all those, all the Action Men, said Jean, And for Christmas he had a big new set of guns and tanks and a new -
Harry suddenly erupted in to life and set about blasting them all into imaginary oblivion, accompanied by loud machine gun noises, kicking biscuits out of his way with macho swipes.
--You're all dead!
--He needs his arse kicked, announced Maggie,suddenly and irrevocably.
There was an awful silence. Even Lynn's mother,with her great social skills couldn't find a way to change or soften this uniquely Irish and truthful statement.
--Maggie! That's extremely rude- she finally mustered, Say sorry-
But Maggie was running upstairs. They heard her burst into noisy tears and a door banged.

ynn followed her. The encounter had epitomised all she felt was wrong with modern English life. It was materialistic, greedy, wasteful. There was a paranoid parental machine that whizzed kids around from one highly organised educational pursuit to another as soon as they could crawl. Kids were too clean. They never had time to play with the great free gifts of imagination and improvisation and only saw their parents at weekends. She'd seen the Ryan boys playing army but they ran about at the edge of the bog with old bits of wood, hiding in muddy holes and shouting Achtung and Gott in Himmel and phrases she remembered from boys comics in school. Horrible comics actually, but it all seemed quite quaint now. Of course, they were older, with their own land to play on. That was another thing-there was so much -gloriously unkempt! -space in Ireland.

But there were men with real guns running and hiding in the bogs in the North. If it ever got resolved and peace was restored, would kids in future years play, Troubles, she wondered.

Jean seemed mindless, but she did sing, so perhaps she wasn't completely....Never mind the Arse Kicking, Jean would probably tell her friends that Maggie needed her face slapped.

Suddenly, Lynn wanted desperately to go home. Her new life was real and wholesome and satisfying and she was going to go back and make it work. Welcome these volunteers (as long as they didn't look like Brigitte, maybe they could make it couples only) and help Bill get this furniture thing off the ground. And try harder to sell her photos. And not be paranoid. And be more loving to Bill.

She tried to cuddle Maggie, after she'd pulled her into a sitting position from where she had her head buried under the pillow.
--We're never going home are we, Maggie burst out, We've been here for ages and ages and you're never going to let us go home!
--Of course we're going home. I'm getting the tickets today.
--Aunty Cathy went home ages ago.
--She had to work, looking after the homeless people, remember? And we've been having a nice holiday. Don't try and tell me you haven't been enjoying yourself just because you're in a bad mood today.
--I love Gran and Grandad, conceded Maggie, I like it when we play Happy Families and Grandad makes up stories and does funny things, like when he asked the ice cream lady for one that twizzled round the other way. But I only like it for a while. Gran makes me do silly things, like yesterday, we had to go and see those kids I was in school with -the Fords- and it was horrible-

--Why?
--They kept copying my voice and laughing. The way I say Butter, and Howye. And they asked what I had for Christmas and they laughed at that too. They had loads and loads of stuff. And their Mum has a stupid great cake tin!
--Cake tin? What's wrong with that?
--She fills it right up every week-with shop cakes – and then she just throws out all the stuff that doesn't get eaten! She says it makes you ill. They weren't mouldy or anything! She doesn't even give them to the birds- And everyones' houses smell funny, like washing powder and plastic! And I can't go anywhere on my own, and I want to see Dad and Tessie and Molly!

There was a knock at the door. It was Granny Margot with a serious expression, wanting to talk to Maggie about a Letter Of Apology. Ciaran was awake and whimpering. Lynn lifted him up, shoving his head under her jumper as she went, too anxious to make the phone calls to the ferry and the station to sit down in a comfy chair while he had his feed.
Her father was coming back downstairs as she looked up the numbers.
--By the way, George is coming to see you tomorrow afternoon. I forgot to tell you he rang.
--I asked you to tell him I'd gone to stay with a friend! said Lynn,exasperated. Her father was so perverse. He didn't like George, but he wouldn't help her out by telling a harmless lie. Well I won't be here, because we're leaving tomorrow.
--Don't forget to let him know, then, said her father. I can't stand the fellow, he added, He uses the Children's Band.
--The what?
--That's what anyone knowledgeable calls the Citizens' Band. Thinks he knows about radios. Pah!

Chapter Thirty Two

Seamus had turned up, with Frankie and Brendan, in the van which was probably full of carcasses. Maggie was enthusiastically escorting Seamus up the track. He was laughing.
--All right, all right, we'll play a game of – What do you call -Happy Families, he agreed.
--I t'ought we were just droppin' off your man's blow and goin' for a pint, complained Frankie. Games made him nervous.
--Arrah, ye'll play just the one game so, said Seamus, taking his arm and steering him inside. Howye, Bill, Howye Lynn, tis good to see you back.
--Thank you. It's good to be here.
It was, but it had been so painful parting from her mother. After the initial hints about the playgroup, her mother had carefully held back and tried not to pressure her, but it was obvious where her hopes lay. She was quietly helpful once the decision was made and had given her money again.
--Look, it's there and I don't need it. It's not even mine anyway. Poor old Fiona would have wanted you to have it. Put it towards starting up this furniture thing and marketing your photos. If your father and I hadn't had help from MY mother we would never have got started.
Yes, but she'd been given money to Get Started on several other occasions too...

Bill had heated the home-made wine Seamus had brought and added some stuff of their own, with spices. He was asking Seamus about Guard Keane, who was always saluting him when he was working over at Patsy's.
--I think I should sign off, said Bill, I'm not being paid much because Patsy's going to help me with stuff over here later on, but it's still-
--Arrah, not at all! Why would he be bothered! 'Tisn't coming out o' his pocket anyway, said Seamus.
--I don't like being on the dole.
--Sure, don't worry about it. The guards don't care, they're not like the mean old shites over the water. There aren't enough jobs to go around anyway., he continued, Look at me, I'm doin' the rest of them a favour, because I don't need a job, I know how to live cheaply-
--That's for sure, said Bill.

Maggie was rather pointedly giving out her Happy Family cards.

--Now, how does it go again? asked Seamus, mug in hand.
--You have to collect families. You can only ask for another person in the family if you have one already, explained Maggie, And if you have the one you're asked for, you have to give it to the other person, she continued earnestly.
--You can begin, Frankie, Seamus announced generously.
Lynn wasn't playing because she was feeding Ciaran and Bill was similarly glad of an excuse to be otherwise occupied in bringing in wood and minding the brew on the range.
Brendan was quietly organising his cards but thinking about a gorgeous girl he'd recently been introduced to.
 The punch seemed to be adding to Frankie's already considerable perplexity. He frowned over his cards.
--Mishter Bung! he announced at last to the room in general.
Lynn caught Bill's eye and tried not to giggle.
--Who are ye askin'? inquired Seamus.
--Ashkin?
--You have to say who you're asking, Maggie told him.
--Oh. Frankie perused his cards again, frowning seriously. I'm askin' you then, Seamus, he decided after a long wait.
Maggie squirmed with disappointment but remembered her manners.
--Who did ye want again? asked Seamus.
--Mishter Bung.
--Not at home! Seamus told him smugly, Would ye fill up my mug there, Bill.
--Eh? said Frankie.
--NOT AT HOME. That's what ye have to say, Seamus informed him in the same lofty tone, Now it's my turn. Wait'll I see now....Frankie, have ye Mrs Grits?
--No. Not at home, said Frankie after peering at his cards for several minutes.
--It's your turn again now, Maggie told him eventually. She sighed meaningfully.
--Okay. Mishus Grits.
--Who are ye askin'? said Seamus.
--You.
--But HE just asked YOU! clamoured the highly frustrated Maggie.
--I just asked YOU, so it's no good YE askin' ME, contributed Seamus.
--Mishter Bones then, said Frankie huffily.
--Who are ye askin'?
Lynn and Bill, squashed together in the big armchair, were convulsed with mirth.

--All right? Bill asked her later, after he'd got up to refill the mugs again.
--Mmm. Just a bit sad about the chicks. To get them all this way, and they were still alive when we arrived at Limerick...
--Yea, shame about that. No doubt we'll have a full - on funeral tomorrow, he added, glancing over at Maggie, Hope you've got the sermon and flowers ready.

Lynn's father had decided that he would drive them to Pembroke. He and Margot could spend a couple of days on the way back at his favourite Bed and Breakfast.
Lynn's mother gave her a conspiratorial look. Fred thought the world of the Welsh landlady and referred to her as Old Carol, as if they were close friends. He was always doing bad imitations of the way she said, By There. Lynn doubted the wisdom of the idea, recalling all the times her father had taken shortcuts and lost his temper as well as their route on family holidays. She remembered dodging as he bashed out blindly behind him when she and Cathy annoyed him, and her mother feeding him placatory humbugs as he drove, trying to stave off the next outburst... Her mother was clearly pleased at having the extra time with them and not to be going straight back to an empty house though, and it would be a lot easier than managing the three changes of train. Well, it would have been if her father had not been so perverse and unpredictable.

It was a long drive. The three chicks were in a cardboard box with plenty of hay. Maggie had given up her attempts to make them seat belts, but she fretted about them and kept peeping into the box. Whenever someone needed a pee, and when they stopped for lunch, she put their little container of water inside.
--They're quite noisy aren't they, remarked Lynn's mother.
It was true, whenever the chicks were hungry or thirsty, they cheeped in a continuous high pitched sort of shrill.
When they got near the docks towards late afternoon, Lynn suddenly saw a sign beside the road.

FOWLPEST REGULATIONS

Shit. She had never considered there might be anything like this.
--Did you see that? she asked her mother, We're not allowed to take the chicks across!
They passed another, bigger sign.

--Oh dear, said her mother.
--You'll have to take them home again, said Lynn, glad that Maggie had fallen asleep.
--No, said her father obstinately.
--Fred, don't be silly, she can't take them over, she'll be arrested, said her mother.
--I don't care, Margot! I'm not being lumbered with a box of chicks when we're going to stay at Carol's!
Oh no. The crazy rant tone had crept into his voice.
--I'll look after them, Fred.
--No Margot. I won't have it!
--You'd rather risk your daughter being sent to prison than have a tiny bit of inconvenience. You wouldn't even have to do anything with them. I'm ashamed of you, Fred.
--That's right, the two of you always ganging up on me! I told you when we got married I didn't want children but you blackmailed me into it! Well I'm going for a nice quiet stay with Carol, God I wish I lived in digs, Lynn wouldn't get into half these messes if you didn't indulge her so much, I shouldn't have to deal with all this, she's an adult, she's made her bed-
--Fred, you're being ridiculous. She's only asking you to take a box of chicks back to their owners.
--I'm not having them in my car a minute longer!
--Gran, why's Grandad shouting so much? the worried voice of Maggie joined in.

They pulled into the car park.
--I'm getting out, Fred, said Lynn's mother firmly, I don't care if you go on to Carol's, I'll get a train home. If you want to wait, I'll meet you here in an hour.
Shakily, they all got out. Lynn put Ciaran into the pushchair her mother had helped her buy.
They hid the chicks in an old shopping bag, which would be a less obvious container for smuggled livestock than the cardboard box.
--But how will they breathe? asked Maggie anxiously.
--I've left the zip open just at the corner, see?
--Let's go for a little walk and see if we can see the boat coming in, said Lynn's mother, firmly taking Maggie's hand.

It had been a nightmare on the ferry. The chicks kept cheeping, and it was hard to stop Maggie trying to open the bag. Lynn had visions of them fluttering out and landing in the middle of someone's plate of chips. She was terrified someone would realise the criminality she was engaged in and report her. It was a relief whenever Ciaran cried and covered the tell tale noises.

Later Maggie opened the wrong bag looking for sandwiches and spilt packs of condoms everywhere. Lynn scrabbled about, desperately shovelling them back in, imagining a double prosecution and an even lengthier prison sentence than the one she currently risked, while Maggie continued pestering.

--But, Mum what are they for? Are they balloons? We could paint them better colours. I'll blow one up and see if they go as big as the ones we had at my party – OW! Why did you do that, it's not fair-

As they were coming into Rosslare early in the morning, when Ciaran and Maggie were still asleep, she took the bag into the toilets and peeped inside. The chicks looked okay. She filled their bottle top water container and pushed in some sandwich crumbs. Their bag of food had been left behind in her father's car.

Thank God, they were docking.

--Maggie, have you got your rucksack? Where's Ciaran's hat...Can you hold my coat for a minute...Where's the queue for the foot passengers, don't go that way, that's for the people with cars...We have to go along here.....

SHIT. CHRIST. JESUS MARY AND JOSEPH. FUCK IT.

A man in uniform was beckoning. She looked around. Yes, he meant her. It was the end.

--Morning, Ma'am. Let me give you a hand with that yoke. We can go down the back way here.

He lifted up the pushchair.

Seamus had just mis-read a card, handing Maggie Mrs, instead of Miss, Dose. Maggie was fluctuating between exasperation and helpless giggling at the fiasco her game had become.

Frankie might have finally grasped the rules of the game and decided that the only way he could catch up was to cheat. Or - the more likely probability - he had simply become irredeemably flustered. He began to ask for members of families that the others knew he could not have any relations of in his own hand.

--Go 'way out o' that now, Frankie, said Seamus, You haven't got any Chips at all. Because I've got three. And I'm just about to ask HER- he pointed triumphantly at the indignant Maggie-for the last one!

Maggie handed it over with a dramatic sigh.

--I've got a family, said Seamus smugly, laying down Mister, Missus, Master and Miss Chips with a flourish.
--A family? Frankie was incredulous.
--There are only four people in these families, explained Seamus in his Wise Guru tone. The shock of this information seemed to make Frankie lose track of the order of play altogether.
--Mishter Tape! he shouted randomly.
--Go way out o' that now, Frankie, Seamus was up and peering over his shoulder, Look, see, I knew ye had him already!
--Hey, it's not his turn, it's mine, complained Maggie.
--Here, what are ye doin? Ye shouldn't be lookin' at my cards! Arrah, I'm goin' for a pint! exploded Frankie, bolting for the door with Seamus hot on his heels.

Ah God, the delicious madness of occasions like these. They wrestled, laughing, in the doorway and Brendan, reveries forgotten, pretended to be a priest, brandishing an imaginary stick and threatening fearful recriminations if Frankie didn't come back.
The range blazed, shadows flickered about in the dark corners. The old chair reeked of turf and woodsmoke. Above on the beams hung washing and dried flowers.
Outside, the wildness stretched away over the black miles. The air was uncluttered except for the odd bleat of a wild goat coming on the wind. Radio Clare was on, and a lone flute playing.
Lynn was going to see Annie tomorrow, to get her list of contacts in America. She would start work again taking photos of cottages, musicians, characters. She already had a great one of Seamus, rowing a boat on the lake, taken on one of those days when he worked as a Gillie and ate oysters with tourists. She had to admit he was photogenic. He looked wise, rustic and noble..Ciaran was asleep on her lap, mouth open. In a minute she'd hand him to Bill and go outside.
In a couple of weeks, she might be raging again (maybe it was true that she had her father's unpredictable temper as her loathsome Auntie Julie had been fond of pointing out when she was a kid) - about the way Seamus had found himself another woman almost overnight, about Bill smoking too much blow again, about the Domestic Appliances still not being operational.
But now she was going to sit on the bucket toilet in the crisp night air and gaze with rapture at the stars in the vastness of the heavens.

Printed in Poland
by Amazon Fulfillment
Poland Sp. z o.o., Wrocław